By the time Martha entered the office, Major Brown's face was even redder and he was sweating excessively. She sat in the chair in front of his desk and explained about Joe, showed him the letters, and was shocked at the man's response.

'Christ Almighty, woman, don't you realize there's a war on?' He leaned forward and she could feel his spittle on her face. 'Right now, it's a case of all hands to the pump, fourteen-year-olds included. You should feel proud of your son, not come moaning to me and demanding I get him *out* of the Army. If you have any more sons, you should be going out of your way to get them *in*. Now, bugger off. I've had a hard day and . . .' His face froze in a peculiar expression, then, without further ado, he collapsed forward on to the desk and was sick.

Martha gathered up Joe's precious letters and fled the room. Arthur Hanson appeared and tried to detain her, but she pushed him away.

'Mrs Rossi,' he shouted, 'I can do something for you.'

But Martha had gone. She didn't stop crying until she got home.

Have you read them all?
Curl up with a

Maureen Lee

STEPPING STONES

Lizzie O'Brien escapes her dark
Liverpool childhood when she runs
away to London – towards freedom and
a new life. But the past is catching up
with her, threatening to destroy her
dreams . . .

LIGHTS OUT LIVERPOOL

There's a party on Pearl Street, but a
shadow hangs over the festivities:
Britain is on the brink of war. The
community must face hardship and
heartbreak with courage and humour.

PUT OUT THE FIRES

1940 – the cruellest year of war for Britain's civilians. In Pearl Street, near Liverpool's docks, families struggle to cope the best they can.

THROUGH THE STORM

War has taken a terrible toll on Pearl Street, and changed the lives of all who live there. The German bombers have left rubble in their wake and everyone pulls together to come to terms with the loss of loved ones.

LIVERPOOL ANNIE

Just as Annie Harrison settles down to marriage and motherhood, fate deals an unexpected blow. As she struggles to cope, a chance meeting leads to events she has no control over. Could this be Annie's shot at happiness?

DANCING IN THE DARK

When Millie Cameron is asked to sort through her late aunt's possessions, she finds, buried among the photographs, letters and newspaper clippings, a shocking secret . . .

THE GIRL FROM BAREFOOT HOUSE

War tears Josie Flynn from all she knows. Life takes her to Barefoot House as the companion of an elderly woman, and to New York with a new love. But she's soon back in Liverpool, and embarks upon an unlikely career . . .

LACEYS OF LIVERPOOL

Sisters-in-law Alice and Cora Lacey both give birth to boys on one chaotic night in 1940. But Cora's jealousy and resentment prompt her to commit a terrible act with devastating consequences . . .

THE HOUSE BY PRINCES PARK

Ruby O'Hagan's life is transformed when she's asked to look after a large house. It becomes a refuge – not just for Ruby and her family, but for many others, as loves, triumphs, sorrows and friendships are played out.

LIME STREET BLUES

1960s Liverpool, and three families are linked by music. The girls form a successful group, only to split up soon after: Rita to find success as a singer; Marcia to become a mother; and Jeannie to deceive her husband, with far-reaching consequences . . .

QUEEN OF THE MERSEY

Queenie Todd is evacuated to a small town on the Welsh coast with two others when the war begins. At first, the girls have a wonderful time until something happens, so terrifying that it will haunt them for the rest of their lives . . .

THE OLD HOUSE ON THE CORNER

Victoria lives in the old house on the corner. When the land is sold, she finds herself surrounded by new properties. Soon Victoria is drawn into the lives of her neighbours – their loves, lies and secrets.

THE SEPTEMBER GIRLS

Cara and Sybil are both born in the same house on one rainy September night. Years later, at the outbreak of war, they are thrown together when they enlist and are stationed in Malta. It's a time of live-changing repercussions for them both . . .

KITTY AND HER SISTERS

Kitty McCarthy wants a life less ordinary – she doesn't want to get married and raise children in Liverpool like her sisters. An impetuous decision and a chance meeting twenty years later are to have momentous repercussions that will stay with her for ever . . .

THE LEAVING OF LIVERPOOL

Escaping their abusive home in Ireland, sisters Mollie and Annemarie head to Liverpool – and a ship bound for New York. But fate deals a cruel blow and they are separated. Soon, World War II looms – with surprising consequences for the sisters.

MOTHER OF PEARL

Amy Curran was sent to prison for killing her husband. Twenty years later, she's released and reunited with her daughter, Pearl. But Amy is hiding a terrible secret – a tragedy that could tear the family apart . . .

NOTHING LASTS FOREVER

Her marriage failing, Brodie Logan returns to her childhood home, letting out the spare rooms to women with nowhere else to go. Their lives intertwine and friendships develop but then tragedy strikes and the women find that nothing lasts forever . . .

Martha's Journey

Maureen Lee

An Orion paperback

First published in Great Britain in 2010
by Orion
This paperback edition published in 2010
by Orion Books Ltd,
Orion House, 5 Upper St Martin's Lane,
London WC2H 9EA

An Hachette UK company

Typeset at The Spartan Press Limited
Lymington, Hants
Printed and bound in Great Britain by
Clays Ltd, St Ives plc

The Orion Publishing Group's policy is to use papers that
are natural, renewable and recyclable products and
made from wood grown in sustainable forests. The logging
and manufacturing processes are expected to conform to
the environmental regulations of the country of origin.

www.orionbooks.co.uk

For David, Paul and Patrick

'All for one and one for all'

Prologue

At first, Kate thought it was a dream, a dream in which the world had caught fire and the sky had turned a shocking blood-red.

She'd opened the blackout curtains on coming to bed because it felt claustrophobic without even a trace of light, as if she were at the bottom of a pit. But now she wondered if she should have left them closed.

For the red sky was a horrible, awesome sight – alien, like the landscapes on the covers of science fiction books her husband read. She wondered if he was reading one now in the Army camp in Shropshire.

Kate shoved herself to a sitting position on the bed. The alarm clock with phosphorous fingers showed nearly half past two. Her husband would be asleep by now. The sky wouldn't be red in Shropshire and he wouldn't be able to hear the muffled explosions she had imagined were making this house shake, even though she was in Ormskirk and the bombs were exploding miles away in Liverpool. It wasn't the world that had caught fire, just Liverpool. She thought about Martha in her little house close to Bootle docks. Another heavy raid had been expected tonight, but Martha had refused to leave Bootle and come to Ormskirk.

'It hardly seems fair on me neighbours, does it, girl?'

she'd said yesterday when Kate had tried to persuade her, had gone all the way to Bootle to ask. 'They've got to put up with it, so why not me an' all?'

'Then bring your neighbours if that's what's stopping you.' If it meant Martha would be safe, she could bring the whole of Bootle.

Kate's hands were shaking and her heart was thumping madly in her breast, a strong signal that she badly needed a cigarette. She deliberately hadn't brought them to bed so as to avoid being tempted. She wanted to cut down – cigarettes were notoriously difficult to get and she was sure it wasn't good for anyone to swallow mouthfuls of smoke, even if it was eventually blown out again.

After a while, the heart thumping having become worse, she knew she would never sleep feeling as she did. There was nothing else for it; she'd just have to go downstairs for a smoke and a cuppa.

On the landing, she opened Harry's door a few inches and peeked inside. His blond head was half-buried beneath the clothes and he was snoring softly, no doubt dreaming about becoming a bomber pilot or captaining a submarine, ambitions he often talked about to his mother.

'I want you to be proud of me, Ma,' he'd say.

'I'm already proud of you, son.'

He was ten, and should this awful war continue until he was old enough to take part, she thought she would go stark raving mad. Her other son, Peter, was in the Navy, and she had absolutely no idea in which part of the world he happened to be right now because it was a military secret. Lucie, her daughter, was in London training to be a nurse, and her husband was almost certainly quite safe, but nevertheless separated from her, his wife, when she badly wanted him home, wanted all her family home, particularly with Christmas almost upon them.

She closed Harry's door, leaning her forehead against the cold wood for a few seconds, hoping he would wake up and they could chat for a while. She would make tea for them both and drink hers sitting at the foot of his bed with her feet tucked under the clothes, warming them on his body. For such a treat, she would forgo the cigarette.

But Harry didn't wake. Kate sighed and continued downstairs. The Christmas tree – actually a few branches from the fir tree in the garden, bundled into a red-painted pail and draped with home-made decorations – stood in the hall. More decorations, real ones this time, bought the first Christmas she'd married, were strung across the living-room walls. The coloured lights no longer worked, as one or more of the bulbs had gone and it was impossible in war-time to buy replacements.

She put the kettle on and lit a cigarette, breathing in the smoke with an air of desperation, as if it were the first she'd had this year. There were only a few spoons of tea left, and she couldn't use the coupons in her ration book until the day after tomorrow. She poured boiling water on the leaves left in the teapot earlier and stirred like mad; it would be pathetically weak but better than nothing.

The tea made and the pot buried under a thick, knitted cosy, Kate switched off the light and went outside, to be met by a scene that could have featured in her worst nightmare.

3

The house was situated on the top of a hill – not much of a hill, but enough to see the city of Liverpool in the distance being blown to pieces. She closed her eyes and thought about Martha. In her head, she heard the howls of the victims and the screams of the fire engines and ambulances rushing to their aid. She imagined the burning and the terror, the collapsed walls, the broken bodies and shattered windows.

She was there, at the heart of the horror, when the telephone began to ring. Swiftly, quietly, she went inside, closed the door, felt her way into the hall and picked up the receiver.

'Hello?' She couldn't remember the number they'd had for nearly twenty years.

'Hello, darling.' It was her husband. 'I knew you'd be up. Someone just woke me to say Liverpool's getting another pounding, right before Christmas, too. I thought I'd give you a call from the office, though it's strictly forbidden. If Sergeant Draper finds out, I'll be cashiered.' She could tell by his voice that he was smiling. Before the war, he'd been a journalist, but in the Army he was just a corporal in the Pay Corps. At his age, forty-seven, he wouldn't be sent to fight, might not even leave the country.

Kate slid down against the wall until she was sitting on the floor. 'Oh, God! I miss you,' she said with a sob.

'I miss you, too. But I shall do my best to get home for Christmas,' he added brightly.

'Will you? Oh, will you?' The words came out in a tangle and she hoped he'd understand. 'Lucie is going to try to get home as well. It would be wonderful if you both could come.'

'Don't bank on it, Kate. Damn! Someone's just

come into the office. I'll have to sneak out the back way. Bye, darling.'

The phone went dead. 'Bye,' Kate whispered. 'Bye.'

The rest of the night, she hardly slept at all. Mostly she prayed; for her husband, her children, for Martha and everyone in Bootle, in Liverpool, and in the great, wider world. She prayed for the Germans, the innocent men, women and children who were probably receiving a similar bombardment in their own country.

It wasn't until after five that the raid came to an end, the bombs stopped falling, and everywhere was quiet again.

Kate lay there for another two hours, until forced out of bed by the need to use the lavatory, make more tea and have another ciggie.

Harry appeared while she was making the tea. She overcame the urge to give him a giant hug, which would only embarrass him. He was wearing his brother's old dressing gown that was miles too big.

Thank the Lord we had him, she thought. They'd only wanted two children, but Harry had arrived quite unexpectedly eight years after Lucie. Without him, Kate would have had to face the war alone, a horrifying idea. She would had to join something. Not just the Women's Voluntary Service – she was already a member – but become a WAAF or a WREN – that's if they would have taken her at forty-two.

'I've got something to do today,' she said, 'so I'm going to ask your grandma if she'll look after you.' He and her mother were mad about each other.

He looked pleased. 'Okay, Ma.'

★

To her surprise, when she bought the ticket from Ormskirk station to Bootle, she was informed the train was going all the way into town.

'I thought the lines might have been damaged,' she remarked to the man in the ticket office.

It seemed the lines hadn't been touched, though many other places had. The man reeled them off. 'St George's Hall caught fire, might still be alight for all I know. And the Gaiety picture house lost its roof. Some of the people inside were killed, God bless 'em.' He made the Sign of the Cross and named a number of other places that had been hit. Kate felt sick.

Globe Street, where Martha lived, was only a short walk from Marsh Lane station. Everywhere seemed remarkably active, considering there'd been an air raid lasting twelve hours the night before, though there was dust in the air and a smell of burning. Little spirals of black smoke were drifting over the rooftops – some of the fires must still be alight. As she continued on, she saw a row of houses had been reduced to a heap of rubble, which had already become a playground for children. Even so, the shops were open and there was traffic on Marsh Lane, including a milk cart drawn by a black-and-white horse, and a chimney sweep on a bike.

'Thank God!' she muttered, almost faint with relief, when she arrived at Globe Street and saw every one of the little terraced houses was still standing. More children were playing football and swinging on the lampposts. The woman who lived next door to Martha was scrubbing her front doorstep, and two other women were cleaning their windows. Kate hurried along the street to number twenty-three.

All the women waved – Kate was a familiar figure. The one scrubbing the step got painfully to her feet when Kate approached. 'Martha's not in, luv,' she said. Her hands were bright red with so much scrubbing. Her name was Ethel Daniels. 'I knocked early this morning, but there was no answer.'

'Perhaps she was still asleep.' But Kate had been unable to sleep all those miles away in Ormskirk. It would surely have been impossible for anyone in the eye of the storm, as it were. And Martha was a light sleeper.

'Well, actually, luv, I went indoors and checked, and the bed was empty. She wasn't there all last night, either. I know because she always has her wireless on during the raids and switches it off after the midnight news is finished. Then she goes to bed.' She shivered. She wasn't wearing nearly enough clothes for such a cold December day. Her cardigan sleeves were pushed up to her chafed elbows and her felt slippers were full of holes. 'I'd best get this step finished. That Hitler bloke needn't think a few bombs'll stop Liverpool women from keeping their doorsteps clean.'

'You're right.' Kate nodded approvingly, though couldn't remember if she'd ever scrubbed her own doorstep. It could well have been never.

'You'll never believe this,' Ethel continued – she was beginning to turn blue – 'but I've got me grand-daughter staying with us – Betty. She's our Eileen's girl and actually slept the whole night through. There wasn't a wink out of her.'

'That's incredible.' The nonchalance of youth, Kate supposed. She worried she would soon turn blue her-self. She put her hand through Martha's letterbox and

7

withdrew the key attached to a string. It was that easy. 'I think I'll go inside and wait for Martha to come home.' Hopefully, she wouldn't have to wait for long.

It wasn't much warmer inside the house than out, and the grate was full of ash from yesterday's fire. Everywhere was so cold these days and there was a shortage of fuel. There was no such thing any more as lighting a fire in a bedroom if someone was ill. If visitors were expected, the fire in the parlour would be lit at the very last minute.

Last Christmas, Kate had transferred the fire from her living room into the parlour using a shovel, a metal bucket, and a great deal of courage. She'd burnt her fingers badly, as well as the carpet, and had sworn never to do it again.

She threw herself into Martha's easy chair under the window, and resolved to set the fire in a minute, then make tea if there was enough of everything.

As well as being cold, Martha's little house was scrupulously clean, beautifully tidy, and highly polished. Her books stood as erect as soldiers on the shelves beside the fireplace. A brass crucifix in the centre of the mantelpiece was guarded on both sides by an assortment of religious statues. The little Christmas tree that Lily and Georgie had made years ago from green crêpe paper stood on the sideboard alongside Joe's photograph – such a handsome boy, obviously full of himself in his Army uniform. Before the war, the photo had always been accompanied by a nightlight in a glass jar, but nightlights were now as hard to get as bulbs for Christmas lights.

Kate felt a throb of anger in her throat. To think she had already lived through one major war and

8

now there was another. This time, unlike the first, you didn't have to join up or volunteer to take part in it. All you had to do was sit at home and wait to be blown to pieces in an air raid.

She was almost asleep when there was a knock on the front door and she nearly jumped out of her skin. Martha!

But Martha was unlikely to be knocking on her own front door. Kate got to her feet and lumbered down the hall, hoping it wouldn't be one of the neighbours wanting to talk about raids and Hitler and the shortage of this and that.

'Hello!' A pretty, brown-haired girl of about fourteen was standing outside bearing a cup of steaming tea with two digestive biscuits on the saucer. She guessed it must be Ethel's granddaughter, Betty.

'That looks very welcome,' Kate remarked.

'It hasn't got sugar in. Gran said you didn't take it.'

'I don't.' Kate reached for the tea. Instead, Betty stepped inside, still holding the cup, so Kate was obliged to move aside and let her pass.

'I hope you don't mind if I stay a minute,' she said cheerily. 'Gran's in one of her cleaning moods – she's always the same after a raid – and wherever I happen to be she accuses me of being underneath her feet.'

'Of course I don't mind.' Kate smiled, though she minded quite a bit, having been looking forward to a nap. 'Have you left school yet?' she asked when they were seated in front of the empty fireplace.

'No, I passed the scholarship so I'm at Seafield Convent,' the girl said proudly, and Kate felt ashamed of having taken for granted that a working-class girl attended a State school. 'I'll be there until I'm sixteen –

9

eighteen if my mum has her way. But I'd sooner leave and join the Forces.'

'You can't join the Forces until you're eighteen,' Kate informed her.

Betty made a noise similar to a raspberry. 'The war might be over by then. I'm hoping by the time I'm sixteen I can pretend to be older. I'm sure it must have been done before. By him, for instance.' She nodded at the photo of Joe on the sideboard. 'He hardly looks any older than fourteen.'

'That's what he was; fourteen.' Kate's eyes filled with tears.

'I thought as much!' Betty said triumphantly. 'I've only been here once before and I longed to ask Martha about him, but I don't really know her well enough. I don't know her surname, either. Gran only ever calls her Martha.'

'It's Rossi,' Kate told her. 'Martha Rossi. Her husband was Italian.'

'And what was *his* name?' Again she nodded at the photograph.

'That's Joe.' Kate felt the sensation of tears again as she settled back in the chair. 'I'll tell you about him, shall I?' It would be a good way of passing the time until Martha came home.

Chapter 1

Vauxhall, Liverpool
1915

Spuds! What would she do without them? Tonight, they were having spuds for tea, mashed up with cabbage and fried in a bit of dripping. Down in London they called it bubble and squeak. Her kids loved it. And you could do wonders with spuds and a bit of mouldy cheese, grated, and any sort of old vegetable, which didn't need to be fresh. Mind you, her favourite meal of all was a nice big plate of scouse smothered in brown sauce − not blind scouse that didn't have meat in, but made with proper stewing steak; she couldn't remember when she had last been able to afford that.

Martha Rossi, small, much too thin, and with a look of purpose on her once-pretty face, began to hurry along Scotland Road. Even though she had spent eight gruelling hours working in Ackerman's Sacks and Sails, the day didn't seem so bad now that she was on her way home knowing there was enough grub there for a proper meal.

The road was thick with people and heavy with traffic. Tramcars careered madly along the metal lines while tired horses pulled their mainly empty carts home for the night, no doubt looking forward to their tea every bit as much as she was.

Like Martha, the people all seemed to have a touch of a spring in their steps and the suggestion of a smile on their faces. Not only was it a grand evening, June and dead sunny, but it was also Friday and a lot of folk didn't have to work tomorrow, or at least had the afternoon off as she did. The day after was Sunday, a day of rest, not that she could ever remember having much time for a rest on Sundays.

She paused for a few seconds to admire a woman across the road who was wearing a pretty cotton frock; pink, with frills on the sleeves and a full, flared skirt. Her straw bonnet was tied with a pink satin ribbon.

Martha had once owned such a frock – had made it herself, in fact – except hers was blue and the hat was a boater she'd bought second-hand from a stall in Great Homer Street market, trimming it with blue-and-white striped ribbon.

She turned away and happened to glance at her reflection in the window of the nearest shop. 'Jaysus, Mary and Joseph!' she gasped, horrified at the sight that met her. She wore her black shawl – she never went out without it apart from Sundays or if the weather was as hot as in a jungle – over a brown, shapeless garment that purported to be a frock but bore more of a resemblance to a sack, which was quite fitting in a way, for Martha was a sack-sewer. She stitched the sides of dusty Hessian cloth together using a three-inch needle threaded with thick twine, tearing the skin off her fingers as she did so. For this, she earned two bob a day, and half that much on Saturdays.

Her spirits wilted just a little when she considered how her life had changed since Carlo's wrist had been slashed in an accident ten years ago. It meant he could

12

no longer follow his occupation as a skilled worker in mosaic, marble and terrazzo. He'd lost heart, given up, and now spent his days in bed or wandering around Liverpool city centre looking at the wonderful works of art in various public buildings that had been created by him and his Italian compatriots.

Every day before she went to work, she'd leave him four slices of bread and margarine as well as thruppence to buy a meat pie and a cup of tea because he no longer ate with his family. At night, he haunted the pubs in Little Italy, begging for drinks, returning home as drunk as that night's charity would allow. He'd stopped talking to his wife and barely acknowledged the existence of his children.

Martha shook her head. She didn't want to think about Carlo, preferring to cling to her earlier happiness. Fate, however, seemed determined to thwart her, this time in the form of five extremely smart young women coming towards her. Similarly dressed in neat white blouses and black skirts that were the very latest fashion – narrow and showing a bit of ankle instead of virtually touching the ground – they looked in the best of health and the highest of spirits. Martha's heart seemed to stop when she saw that the girl in the middle, perhaps the prettiest of the five, was her daughter, Joyce, who was eighteen and the eldest of her children. She lived with the other girls in rooms near to where the Protestant cathedral was being built, sharing the rent between them. They all worked in Frederick & Hughes, the big department store in Hanover Street.

She lowered her eyes as the girls fluttered past, all gestures and quick words. She had no idea if Joyce had seen her. If she had, she'd given no sign of it. After all, the girl had left home for a better life and because she was ashamed of her family. Martha, in her shawl and something resembling an old sack, her hair covered with a ragged scarf, her boots falling apart and no doubt smelling to high heaven, had no intention of owning up in public to being this pretty girl's mother. Poor Joyce would never live it down. Even so, she still thought enough of her family to drop in and see them from time to time.

Martha brought her thoughts back to the evening ahead. She'd par-boiled the spuds and the cabbage the night before, so they needed heating up, then mashed together and fried. Her belly quivered at the thought; she was starving. After tea was done, eaten and cleared up, she'd sit on the steps outside along with the other women in King's Court and they'd have a jangle and a sing-song. There was always the chance Jimmy Gallagher would turn up with his harmonica. After-wards, they'd see if they could scrape together a couple of pennies between them for Jimmy to buy himself a pint of ale. The poor chap had lost his sight in some war or other and couldn't get a job for love nor money, which wasn't exactly surprising given his condition.

It wouldn't be long before it was time for bed and another day would be over. She wondered if she'd manage to cling on to her feeling of happiness until then.

When she got in, Lily and Georgie were lying on the couch with their legs draped over the back. Had it been a decent piece of furniture rather than an old wreck of a thing, Martha would have given each bare leg a good slap. Instead, her heart swelled with love and she gave them an affectionate pat.

'Hello, Mam,' they said together, grinning up at her. They'd been born ten years ago in the same year; Lily in February and Georgie in December. They were a cheerful pair, as thin as sticks, though few kids in the area had more than an ounce or so of fat on them.

'Has there been any sign of your dad?' she asked.

'No, Mam,' they chorused.

'Ah, well,' Martha sighed. She lit the primus stove, put the spuds and the cabbage on to heat; the smell of paraffin filled the room. The house had a kitchen in the basement, a filthy hole mainly given over to the rats that haunted it. Instead, tenants supplied their own cooking facilities – a fire hazard, or so Martha though. She was glad the Rossis had two rooms on the ground floor – there were four floors altogether – and could easily escape if the building went up in flames. Water was fetched from a pump in the yard. There was a single lavatory, also in the yard, that stank to high heaven, used as it was by everyone in the house apart from Martha and her kids, who never went near it except when Martha emptied the chamber pot. She had rigged up a curtained alcove in the bedroom for their own private use. The smell and the filthy conditions of the communal lavvy didn't bother Carlo, and she couldn't bear to go near him after he'd used the place.

Martha sighed again. Husband or no husband, she didn't see much of Carlo nowadays. He was usually asleep when she left for work, and out when she got back, by which time she was in bed again, dead to the world.

Georgie said, 'Some man came looking for our

Frank, but we told him he'd left home, like you said we was to do.'

'What did he look like?' Martha asked.

'He was big with one of them hairy things under his nose – can't remember what they're called, Mam.'

'A moustache,' Lily put in. She was the smarter of the two. 'It's called a moustache. And, oh, Mam, it was full of snot and stuff. I didn't like him a bit.'

Georgie agreed. 'Neither did I.'

Martha made a face. 'It's Milo O'Connor. His mother is the money-lender; he's her agent.'

Her own son, Frank, was seventeen, and in and out of jobs and trouble like a yo-yo. He slept at home when he felt like it, and she had no idea where he slept when he didn't. Only occasionally did he hand over a few pennies for his keep, no matter how much she yelled at him. A cocky bugger, forever with some girl or other hanging on to his arm, he always looked as pleased as punch with himself. Until that look changed, Martha was determined not to worry about him. There was already enough to worry about, so why add to it when there was no need? At least, she hoped there'd never be a need.

'I'm starving, Mam,' Georgie said pitifully.

'You're not the only one, lad.' Martha drained the water out of the pan into another pan and began to mash the spuds and cabbage together. The door opened and her second-born son, Joe, burst in.

'That smells good.' He nodded at the food and leaned over the couch where his brother and sister lay upside down. 'Are you'se two up to munching on a nice rosy apple after you've had your tea?' He reached in his pockets and pulled out two apples.

16

Georgie fell off the couch in an effort to grab one, but Joe's hands were out of reach. '*After* tea, I said. There's one for you an' all, Mam. I got three altogether.'

'But what about yourself, lad?' Martha protested. 'You deserve an apple, too.' Joe was fourteen and for the past year had delivered fruit and veg on a bike for Johnson's the greengrocers on Scotland Road. He gave her all his wages, five shillings, every week, and she gave him back a tanner for himself.

'Mr Johnson gave us a bag of chips at dinnertime and some lady gave us a slice of cake and a cup of milk when I called at her house with the veg. She always does – I told you about her before.' His eyes shone. 'I'm fine, Mam.'

'I'm sure you are, son.' He had the biggest heart in the world. Baptised Giuseppi, after his grandfather on Carlo's side, it had straight away been shortened to Joe. Out of her three lads, he was the one who most resembled a much younger Carlo: tall, curly-haired and desperately handsome, with dark, mischievous eyes and charm a'plenty. He was just as much a cocky bugger as Frank, except he was nicer about it.

Martha pulled out the leaves of the table, margarined four slices of bread, and they ate while water was heating on the primus for tea.

The meal finished, apples eaten and greatly enjoyed, Georgie and Lily left for Downey Street playground to meet some mates from school, and Joe washed his face, changed his shirt, and went to call on Albie Lloyd, who had been his friend since they started school together. They were going to the Shakespeare Theatre where gallery seats only cost thruppence. He was on his way to becoming a young man, her Joe, no longer a boy. He liked to be clean and look neat. She could tell he had the makings of a dandy.

Joyce had been like that, forever wanting new clothes. In the old days, before Carlo had stopped working, Martha had always been on the lookout for scraps of material to make frocks for her daughter, who'd had at least two pairs of shoes: winter ones and summer ones, and sometimes party ones if Carlo was feeling flush.

It was like the Bible in a way. They'd had seven rich years, but the lean years hadn't stopped at seven; they'd gone on and on. When the lean years had started, Martha had made a secret vow that, while she was alive, not one of her children would ever walk barefoot on the streets. She would sell her body on the same streets before she would let it happen. By some stroke of luck or trick of fate, shoes had been acquired, even if they were too big – or too small and she'd had to cut off the toe tops with a sharp knife.

She washed the dishes and dried them, by which time she was overcome with a feeling of such weariness that her legs no longer wanted to support her and her eyes were threatening to close. With a sigh of relief, she sank down on to the couch and fell asleep, to be woken by the sound of the women outside singing.

'We were sailing along, on Moonlight Bay . . .'

It was one of Martha's favourites, as was the next song, 'Chinatown, My Chinatown'. She and Carlo had gone for strolls on Sundays around the Liverpool Chinatown after they'd got married but before the kids had started to arrive.

It would have been easy to cry when she thought

about the time when life had been so good and she'd felt fortunate to be married to her magnificent Italian husband with his brilliantined hair and patent leather shoes.

For the umpteenth time, she relived the night they'd met, at a church social organized by the Legion of Mary in the Holy Cross church hall. It was summer and still light outside. The sinking sun blazed through the high windows, only adding to the gaiety of the occasion. A few nuns were present, keeping an eye on things, making sure that couples didn't dance together too closely. Father MacPhee was the only priest there and looked as if he'd sooner join in than supervise. He was young, slim, blond-haired and heartbreakingly handsome.

What a waste, Martha had thought, looking at him from underneath her lashes. What a terrible waste.

She was barely eighteen, sitting on one of the chairs in rows on each side of the room, giggling with her friends. They were all pretending not to look at the men, who were clumped together by the door and regarding the women quite brazenly. At least, the Italian lads were.

Her view of the priest was suddenly blocked by a figure who was gabbling at her in a language she didn't understand, waving his hands, smiling, grabbing her own hand and kissing it passionately, then pulling her to her feet. Next minute they were waltzing together around the room. He must have been asking her to dance.

He was a prince of a man, a hero of sorts, impossibly handsome in his two-tone shoes, chalk-striped suit and little red bow-tie. His hair shone like patent leather in the evening sunshine.

'You are ver' beautiful,' he said slowly and with difficulty. 'I am Carlo Rossi.'

'And I'm Martha Farrell.'

'Ciao, Martha.' He had the nerve to kiss her on the cheek, but Martha didn't mind.

Six weeks later, they were engaged, and before the year ended they were married. Carlo carried her over the doorstep of a neat little house in Little Italy where they planned to live happily ever after.

But Fate intervened, and the course of their lives turned out to be very different.

Martha sighed, but managed to hold back the tears when the women sang 'When Irish Eyes Are Smiling'. Carlo used to sing it to her, his Irish bride. She'd told her family in Ballymena that she was going to Liverpool to find a good husband and it had turned out to be true, not that anyone in Ballymena knew – Martha had never written a letter in her life because she hadn't learned how.

'Down by the old mill stream,' the women were singing when she went out to join them, 'that's where I first met you.' Jimmy Gallagher had turned up, the sun had disappeared behind the roofs of the houses opposite and King's Court, a cul-de-sac with just six houses on each side, was in a curious sort of semi-darkness. A few little 'uns were still about, swinging on railings or kicking stones around. Martha sat on the front doorstep, too tired to do anything but hum along to the haunting strains of Jimmy's harmonica and the thin, sad voices of her neighbours, who sounded as weary as she was. The sweet songs seemed out of place in the dismal, mean little place where they were now.

She only woke up because Joe was shaking her arm.

'C'mon, Mam, it's time for bed,' he said gently. 'Look, I've brought some chocolate, a couple of squares of Cadbury's Dairy Milk. Me and Albie bought a bar between us and we saved some for our mams.'

'Oh, *son*!' She was so overwhelmed that once again she had to hold back tears. She ate the chocolate in bed and fell asleep with the taste still in her mouth.

Father Lawless of the Holy Cross had been Martha's favourite priest when they'd lived in Little Italy. He still came to see them every five or six weeks on his big three-wheeler bike early on a Sunday afternoon, usually bringing with him some sort of treat, even though the Rossis were no longer members of his flock.

This time, he came with two tins of bully beef. Martha was on her own. Carlo was still in bed, Lily and Georgie were at Sunday school, and Joe and Albie, after finishing their duties as altar boys, had gone for a walk along the Dock Road, being that it was another lovely day. Frank she hadn't seen in days.

'This was destined for our troops,' the priest told Martha as he took the tins out of his black leather satchel. He was small and round with the red nose of a drinker and the blue eyes of a saint.

'Ah then, Father, shouldn't you be sending it to them?' she exclaimed. She didn't fancy the idea of some poor soldiers going hungry on her behalf. At the same time her stomach was rumbling at the idea of spuds and bully beef for their dinner. Unfortunately, she didn't have any brown sauce. The last bottle had been finished by Lily and Georgie, who had stuffed themselves with brown sauce butties when overcome with hunger one night when she was late home from work.

'I wouldn't know how to send it,' the good Father said. 'We have a knitting and sewing circle in the parish – of course, you were a member, Martha, one of our best. We send parcels of scarves and gloves to the troops in France quite often. I don't suppose it would matter if there were a couple of tins of bully beef tucked inside as well,' he said reflectively.

Martha's heart fell a good foot. She wanted the soldiers to have the food, but she wanted it for her family just as much. It was with a sense of relief coupled with guilt that she heard Father Lawless say it was hardly worth the trouble and, as the tins had got this far, it seemed mad to give them back.

'How's Carlo?' the priest asked. 'Have you managed to get him to Mass yet?'

'I'm afraid not, Father. The only way I can see of doing it is knocking the bugger unconscious and dragging him there.'

Carlo had given up on God when he discovered he couldn't use his arm any more. He'd sooner sleep off last night's drink than go to church – she hoped the priest couldn't hear him snoring in the very next room, and wished she hadn't said 'bugger', it had just slipped out.

'I'm sure the Good Lord wouldn't expect you to go to such extremes,' the Father said dryly. 'One of these days, Carlo will see the error of his ways and come back to us. Well, I must be off now.' He made the Sign of the Cross. 'God bless you, child.'

As Martha genuflected, she heard her knees creak. 'And God bless you, Father.'

The priest hadn't been gone for long when Joyce arrived. She graced her family with a visit on Sundays at about the same rate as the priest, though it didn't often happen on the same day.

In her grey cotton frock with gloves to match and a little cocked hat with a red feather – all bought second-hand from some market or other – she looked so clean, so shiny and polished, that Martha worried she'd get dirty by just being in the room. Joyce was the spitting image of her mother at the same age, though nothing like her now – Martha always felt as if she were melting like a candle with the passage of time. Her face was too creased, her body too crumpled and her brain too muddled for a woman of thirty-six.

Joyce was an inch or two taller than her mother, with small, well-defined features, dark blue eyes and a shapely little mouth. Her almost black hair fell on to her shoulders in natural ringlets. She gingerly sat down on the edge of a chair. 'How are you, Mam?' she asked politely.

'I'm fine,' her mother replied, just as politely, feeling hurt that she hadn't been kissed. But who could blame the girl? That morning, Martha had washed her face for Mass, but she hadn't washed anywhere else. She was wearing her best frock, but it was ten years old and hadn't been near soap and water for months, mainly because she never seemed to have the time to take herself and her clothes, not to mention the bedding, to the wash house. She washed the kids' gear herself and there was a line of it strung across the bedroom right now – she daren't hang it outside for fear it would be

23

pinched. Frank managed to look after himself, and Carlo lived in filth, refusing any attention.

'You look nice, luv,' she said to Joyce, who frowned.

'I wish I could say the same for you, Mam,' she said primly. 'If the truth be known, you look a sight. And so does this place.' She sniffed and made a face. 'And it smells, too, something awful.'

'I'm sorry, luv.' Martha dipped her head in shame. 'It's just that I'm always so busy, always tired . . .'

'I know you are, Mam.' She leaned across and touched her mother's knee. 'I'm sorry, too. I shouldn't have said what I said. And I'm sorry I just ignored you in the street the other day. It's just that things are so different from how they used to be.' She shook her head and sighed. Martha hadn't realized she'd been noticed – and ignored.

'Well, you know why that is, luv. Everything changed because of your dad's accident.'

Joyce waved her little gloved hands impatiently. 'Oh, Mam, you're deluding yourself. He didn't have an accident, not a *real* accident, not an *accidental* accident. He was drunk, his mates were drunk, and they had a fight with some Irish drunks. They used knives, Mam, so it's not surprising he had his wrist slashed. He's ruined our lives, yours the most. I think,' she said grandly, throwing back her shoulders, 'that you should leave him. You'd get on better without him hanging around your neck, holding you back.'

She'd come out with all this before. 'Holding me back from what, luv?' Martha asked mildly.

'From being happy,' Joyce said indignantly. 'He's put a blight on all our lives. Why should you have to spend a penny of your hard-earned wages on him, let alone a whole thruppence a day? With that little bit extra you could get nicer digs and if you made yourself look more respectable you'd get a better job rather than sewing sacks all day long.'

There was an awful lot of truth in this, and Martha was about to quote from her marriage vows – 'through sickness and in health' and 'until death do us part' – to explain why she would always stick by Carlo, except he chose that moment to stumble out of the bedroom still wearing his grubby long johns all stained around the crotch and too tight nowadays to fit comfortably around a belly badly swollen from consuming too much ale.

'Joyce, *mio cara*.' His eyes lit up and he smiled for the first time in ages. She had always been his favourite child. He came towards her, arms held wide.

But Joyce was having none of it. She jumped to her feet, not prepared to let her father near her, let alone suffer his embrace. 'I'm going, Mam. I'm meeting someone down by the Pier Head in half an hour.'

Martha couldn't have pitied her husband more than she did now. There was such a look of hurt on his face and sheer hopelessness in the set of his shoulders.

'I'll be back in a minute, luv,' she told him, before rushing after Joyce, who was just about to leave through the front door. 'Wait a minute,' she cried.

'What, Mam?' The girl waited at the bottom of the steps. She'd calmed down a little by now.

'I didn't want you to go so soon, that's all,' Martha said breathlessly, 'and I wondered who it was you were meeting down by the Pier Head.'

'Just some chap.' Joyce tossed her head. 'His name's Edward.'

'Is he a Catholic?'

She tossed her head again and rolled her eyes at the same time. 'I've no idea, Mam. I only met him the other day. He works in Frederick and Hughes same as me, and asked if I'd like to go for a sail to New Brighton on Sunday and have our tea. I couldn't very well say, "I'll only come if you're a Catholic," could I?'

'Not really,' Martha conceded, though in fact she couldn't see why not. 'Well, tara, luv. Have a nice time.'

'Tara, Mam.' Joyce went daintily on her way.

By the time Martha got back to the house, Carlo had dressed and was ready to leave. Neither spoke.

She thought about the war while she peeled the spuds and opened one of the tins of bully beef that should have been sent to the fighting troops. She didn't know much about it, only that it was being fought in a country called France between men of different nationalities, including the English, and that it had been going on for at least a year, the enemy being the Germans.

She knew women whose husbands had died on foreign soil, making widows of them and depriving their children of a father, and other women who'd lost sons. Mr Johnson, who owned the grocery shop where Joe worked, had a grandson who'd been reported 'missing, presumed dead'.

Martha remembered when bright-eyed men had proudly gone marching off to fight, a band at their head playing 'It's a Long Way to Tipperary', and everyone cheering.

It had gone down a bit now, the fuss and the cheers

and all the talk of King and Country. Things weren't exactly going well in France. The few men she'd seen who'd come back were hollow-eyed and silent, some missing a limb, some missing two. They'd witnessed too much horror to talk about it, or so Martha deduced.

She spread a piece of oilcloth on the table, emptied the mound of spuds and bully beef on to it, then began to knead it into the shape of a cake, slapping it around quite viciously while resolving not to think about war any more. It was too depressing.

Lily and Georgie came in, delirious with excitement when they learned what was for dinner. She gave them their portions straight away because the poor little buggers were starving. According to Stegger's pawn-shop clock, which could be seen from the top right-hand pane of the front room window, it was nearly half past three, and they'd had nothing to eat but bread and marge since they'd got up that morning.

Looking back, Martha would often blame herself for what happened next. She shouldn't have accepted the bully beef. She should have insisted Father Lawless take it back and make sure it got to the troops. It was only right that she be punished for such a selfish action, so she shouldn't have been surprised when Joe came swaggering in and informed her she was looking at a soldier.

'What d'you mean, lad?' she enquired, thinking he'd joined the Boys' Brigade or something.

'I've joined up, Mam,' he announced, preening himself. 'Me and Albie joined up this avvy. They gave us a shilling each. You can have mine, Mam,' he said generously, pressing it into her hand.

Chapter 2

'Don't be daft,' Martha said calmly, though her heart was thumping like a bass drum in her chest. 'No one can be a soldier when they're only fourteen. You have to be . . .' On reflection, she had no idea how old a lad had to be, but felt confident it was more than fourteen.

As for him, he was dancing with excitement. 'I know that, Mam. But I told them I was eighteen – Albie did, too. We signed a form and they took us on. They believed us. We'll be in the West Lancashire Infantry Division, or summat.'

'Well, they can just bloody well *un*believe you.' Martha's voice rose to a shriek. 'And where did the form come from that you signed – and the shilling? Here, take it back!' She flung the coin at her son. 'I don't want it.'

But Joe was too pleased with himself to let his mother spoil his day. 'You'll be proud of me when I get a uniform, Mam. The Army will pay me, too, and I ticked the form to say it's to go to me mam.'

'I don't want nothing off the Army.' Martha was hysterical by now. 'I want you, Joe Rossi, living with us in this house.'

Lily, who never cried, surprised everyone by bursting

into tears. 'They'll shoot you, Joe,' she wept, 'like they did this girl's brother at school.'

'Me, I'd love to be a soldier,' Georgie said enviously.

'Now see what you've done!' Martha screamed at her son. 'You've got your sister in a state and a half, and your little brother wanting to join the Army, too.'

'You're not nearly tall enough, Georgie,' Joe said. 'You'd never pass for eighteen. And I won't be killed, Lil. I won't be sent to the Front until they think I'm nineteen.'

'Didn't they ask for your birth certificate?' Martha had all the family's birth certificates in a box under the bed.

'No one mentioned needing a birth certificate.' Joe was beginning to look uneasy, as if he could see his big adventure slipping away.

'Well, I'll make sure they do,' Martha said triumphantly. 'Who was it give you this form to sign, anyroad?'

'Sergeant Gilligan; he's a copper at Rose Hill police station.'

'Ernie Gilligan!' Martha spat. 'I know him; he's a nasty bugger and he knows full well you're only fourteen. Didn't he try and get you for riding your bike on the pavement 'stead o' the road?' She'd go and see him today. First, though, she'd call on Mrs Lloyd, Albie's mam; they could go together.

The Lloyds lived above a chandler's shop on the corner of Queen Anne Street. Mr Lloyd was a doorman at some posh hotel in town where he wore a royal blue uniform decorated with gold. Albie was their only child.

Martha knocked on the door and a minute or so later Gwyneth Lloyd opened it. She was a small, spare woman who looked as if she scrubbed her face daily with a pumice stone, the skin was so red and raw. She gave the caller a hard look up and down. 'Yes?' she enquired rudely, though she knew darned well who Martha was.

Martha was taken aback by her tone. 'It's about our Joe and your Albie.' Surely the woman must know why she was there. Perhaps she should have tarted herself up a bit before she came, at least taken off her pinny, and worn her hat rather than her shawl. 'They've joined up. Hasn't your Albie told you? It seems it was Ernie Gilligan, that copper from Rose Hill police station, who persuaded them to sign a form. They told him they were eighteen, but Ernie Gilligan knows it's not true, at least not where our Joe's concerned.'

Gwyneth shrugged. 'So?'

'Well, don't you care?' Martha snapped. What was wrong with the woman? 'I'm on me way to see Gilligan now and thought it best if we went together.'

'It's never too soon for a boy to become a man, Mrs Rossi.' Albie's mother shook her head disapprovingly, as if Martha were at fault for not wanting her son to join the Army. 'As far as me and Mr Lloyd are concerned, our Albie leads a feckless existence. It'll do him good to see what the world's really like, that he wasn't put on earth to enjoy himself, but to suffer in the name of the Blessed Jesus.' She bent her head at the name and Martha automatically did the same.

30

'Seems to me, Mrs Lloyd, that there's suffering enough in this world as it is, without young lads being introduced to it before their time.'

Albie's mother responded by slamming the door in Martha's face.

Martha sat on a bench outside the Gymnastic Club. Gerard Street was just across the road where she and Carlo had lived when they first got married, where all five of their children had been born, where there'd been clean running water, a lavatory of their own and a kitchen which was spotless, because that was the way she kept it. They hadn't been poor, but she'd still had to watch the pennies. Even so, the house had been warm and there'd always been enough to eat.

Joyce, Frank and Joe had known a few years of this life, but Lily had only been a year old and Georgie two months when Carlo had his so-called 'accident', Joyce was right; he'd always been too fond of the booze and had enjoyed getting involved in the occasional drunken battles between the Italian lads and the Irish.

'It's only a bit of fun, *mio cara*,' he would say when Martha would point out that she, his wife, was Irish through and through. 'It means nothing.'

However, his last fight had been one too many; instead of a few cuts and bruises to be proud of, he'd ended up with a useless right arm.

Nothing could console him. He'd given up, sunk down and down, and Martha had sunk with him. It had broken something in her, too; not her bones, but her spirit, her hope that one day things might get even better than they'd used to be.

But I'm not going to let them take my lad away from me.

31

The thought came out in a straight line, unwavering, not muddled in the least.

She got to her feet, grimly determined, and marched to Rose Hill and the police station. Sergeant Gilligan was standing behind the desk, an enormous figure, severely overweight. He had a smirk on his big slab of a face.

'Yes, Mrs Rossi?' The smirk deepened.

'What's this about you signing up our Joe to fight in the bloody war?' Martha demanded, quaking more than a bit in her broken-down boots, her newfound courage on the point of deserting her.

'You should be proud, Mrs Rossi,' the policeman sneered. Oh, how she hated him. 'Most mothers'd be proud.'

'You're wrong, Sergeant.' He towered over her, his gaze so fierce that she shrank before it and did her best to stop her voice from wobbling. 'Most mothers would find it a desperately mad idea, crazy. They'd agree with me, that it could only take a man to think it up.'

He frowned. 'You'd better be careful how you speak to a gentleman o' the law, Missus. I could have you behind bars for less.'

'You know full well our Joe's only fourteen . . .' She faltered. Perhaps he really did have the power to put her behind bars: Who'd look after her kids then? Swallowing hard, she risked a final sally. 'You're nothing but a big, fat bully, Sergeant, and most certainly no gentleman.' She held her breath and stared at him challengingly, and wasn't surprised when he lost his temper.

'And you are nothing but a filthy bitch, missus,' he

32

screamed. 'And you smell disgusting. Any lad, your Joe included, would be better off in the Army rather than living with you and your lazy eyetie husband. Out of bed yet today, is he? Had a wash? Put on his best suit? Been to church and for a nice stroll along the Docky with you on his arm?' His voice turned into a roar. 'It's folks like you that bring this country down. Get out me station before I throw you out.'

Martha could stand the copper's abuse no longer. She turned to leave, but still the sergeant screamed. 'After another shilling, is that it? Well, here's some change to be getting along with.'

She fled, coins landing at her feet. She'd sunk so low that it was all she could do not to stop and pick them up.

'Mrs Rossi! Wait a mo! It's only me, Ossie Nelson. Mrs Rossi . . .'

The words were repeated several times before they sank into Martha's frantic brain. She stopped running and turned around. It really was Ossie Nelson, the son of an old neighbour from Gerard Street. He was wearing a copper's uniform – she remembered he'd joined not long before the Rossis had moved away. He'd have been Constable Nelson for a long time.

'What do you want?' she asked, breathless from running.

'Just wanted to say I heard all that and I'm sorry, that's all.' He removed his helmet. He had a pleasant, open face, and she wondered what someone as nice as him was doing in the police force. 'Joe and Albie aren't the first under-age lads Gilligan's signed up today. He must have caught at least a dozen.'

'Caught? What do you mean, caught?'

The young man looked worried. 'I shouldn't really be opening me yapper like this, so I'd be obliged if you'd keep what I have to say about Sergeant Gilligan under your hat, Mrs Rossi.' He put his hand around her upper arm and began to lead her in the direction of King's Court. 'It's just that Gilligan's brother works as a gardener for this titled bloke, General Sir Stanley Cuthbertson his name is. He lives Rainford way, not far from the junction. Anyroad, right now, the general has a son fighting in France – an officer, a' course. He also has an ear to the ground, being ex-Army, I suppose. Seems the country's getting short of fighting men seeing as so many of the poor sods are being slaughtered over there. Anyroad,' he took a deep breath, 'the general has let it be known he'll give half a crown for every bloke the sergeant signs up to join the Army. It doesn't matter how old they are.'

Martha felt confused. 'But our Joe only got a shilling!'

'That's right. You see, luv,' he explained patiently, 'it's Sergeant Gilligan who gets the half-crowns. He's earned himself a few quid today.'

'But what can I do?' Martha wailed.

'Get your Carlo to see to it. He's the man of the house,' the young copper said sternly. 'Joe's his son every bit as much as he is yours.'

Martha went home. Fortunately for Joe, he'd gone out again, thereby avoiding the good box around the ears that his mother felt in a mind to give him. Other than that, she had no idea what to do next, where to go, or who to see. Ossie Nelson had imparted some important information, but all it had done was make her even madder than she'd been before.

Jaysus! Martha stamped her foot. The longing she'd had to box Joe's ears returned with a vengeance, along with the urge to kiss the lad until she fainted from exhaustion.

Lily and Georgie were sitting quietly at the table playing a game they'd invented with buttons, a pencil and a square of paper. Lily looked up. 'Would you like us to fetch some water, Mam, and make us a cup of tea?'

'If you wouldn't mind, luv, I'd like that.' She threw herself onto the couch and pressed her hands against her forehead. By now, her head as well as her heart was thumping crazily.

'Shall I make some bread and marge, too?'

'Please,' Martha said listlessly. Not only did she feel desperately tired after rushing around Liverpool, but she was also upset to think that she was losing her children one by one; Joyce was leading her own life, Frank may as well have left home for all she saw of him, and now Joe was about to be taken away. Soon, there'd only be the little 'uns left.

In Gerard Street, Martha and Carlo had slept in the big bedroom, the lads in the middle, and the girls in the smallest. In King's Court, the entire family slept in the same room. For privacy's sake, Martha had rigged up a curtain around the double bed – not that Carlo so much as touched her these days – while the kids slept on palliasses on the floor, Lily on one side and the lads on the other.

That night, the two youngest went to bed first,

closely followed by Joe, who looked subdued when he came in. 'Albie's mam and dad don't mind a bit about him going in the Army,' he told his mother.

'I don't care a fig what Albie's mam and dad have to say about anything,' Martha said with a sniff. '*Your* mam minds, and that's all that should concern you.'

She stayed where she was, hunched on the couch, waiting for Carlo to arrive. She would present *him* with the problem, just as Ossie Nelson had suggested. Let *him* do something about it. It was about time he remembered he had a family, and it was just as much *his* job to look after them as it was hers.

But Carlo said nothing, not even '*ciao*' when he came face to face with his wife later. Perhaps he was drunk and beyond speech, or so surprised to see her waiting for him that he was incapable of opening his mouth.

'Our Joe's only gone and joined the Army,' Martha said straight away. She had no intention of beating around the bush. 'He pretended he was eighteen, but Sergeant Gilligan, who gave him the form to sign, knows bloody well he's only fourteen. I want something done about it and I want *you* to do it. I'll take you to the baths and get your suit cleaned.' She'd be surprised if it'd still fit with the gut on him these days. 'And you're to have a shave. They'll take more notice of a man than they would a woman. And it has to be done quick, Carlo. We can't just hang about and let it happen.' She had only a hazy idea who 'they' were; men, for certain, wearing expensive clothes and having an exaggerated idea of their own importance.

But all Carlo did was droop lower and lower until he was almost bent double. He shuffled into the bedroom like an old, old man, his eyes empty of everything except his own personal misery. Martha realized it was no use depending on her husband for anything ever again.

A week later, Joe received a posh-looking letter to say he had to be outside the Rotunda Theatre in Scotland Road at ten o'clock the following Sunday, where a charabanc would be waiting to take him to an Army camp in Wigan. He was now, he was informed, a member of the West Lancashire Infantry Division with his particular section known as the Vauxhall Pals.

'They're in a hurry, aren't they?' Martha said sourly when she saw it. 'I thought you were supposed to have a medical before you could join the Forces.'

'I'll be having one when I get there,' Joe said meekly. 'And I've got to take me birth certificate.'

'Huh!' Everything was being done back to front and she'd been unable to do a single thing about it. She'd remembered Father Lawless was in a position of authority and might be willing to help, but when she'd gone round to see the good Father at the presbytery, Mrs Bailey, the housekeeper, said he was on holiday.

'In Morecambe, Mrs Rossi, with the orphans from St Bernadette's. He'll be back in a fortnight. Would you like to see another priest or wait until he gets back? Father Rafferty's at home at the moment. He's getting on a bit, poor fella, but he's very nice.'

Father Rafferty always gabbled his way through Mass and no one could understand a word. Not that anyone except the priests could speak Latin, but they recognized the order the words should be in. Father

37

Rafferty said Mass in a different language altogether, and people suspected he made it up as he went along.

But now Father Rafferty couldn't understand *her*! The poor man was clearly demented.

'What Army?' he asked tetchily, running his hands through his thatch of white hair and getting into such a tangle that he couldn't get them out again. 'Which war are we talking about? And who's Joe? And who are you, come to that?'

In vain did Martha try to explain what had happened and how she felt about it, but the priest only got in a worse muddle. He had no more sense than a newly born kitten.

Martha gave up. 'Oh, it doesn't matter, Father.' She got to her feet.

'God bless you, child.' He tried to stand, but failed.

'God bless you, Father.'

And now he was leaving; her lad, her Joe. And she'd done nothing to stop him apart from say prayers in every Catholic church in the area and light candles all over the place. In fact, she'd helped, not hindered, buying him a new pair of drawers and two pairs of socks. She'd been searching the markets frantically for a decent second-hand jacket, taking time off work, losing money, but Joe insisted she calm down.

'Don't get all moidered, Mam,' he said gently. 'I'll be getting a uniform, won't I? The Army will provide us with drawers and socks, they'll probably be the colour khaki. And I'll get a jacket an' all, 'cept it's called a tunic.'

'All right, son.' She nodded meekly, not wanting him to go away thinking his mother was in a state enough to top herself.

'And, oh, Mr Johnson said on Friday he's giving us two weeks' wages, so I'll give them both to you.'

'Oh no you won't, lad.' She insisted he keep half the wages for himself. 'You might want to buy yourself stuff now and then; a bar of toffee, like, or some liquorice allsorts.' They were his favourite sweets – she'd managed to get him a whole half pound last Christmas.

It was Sunday. Word had got around the court that Joe Rossi, only fourteen, was off to war that morning. The residents of King's Court and other places in the area came out in force to see him off. A few came bearing gifts: a knitted scarf and gloves to match, a comb, and a well-worn leather wallet that Joe proudly stuffed in his inside pocket. Douglas Houghton, an old Army man who was ninety if a day, gave him a book, *Pickwick Papers*, by someone called Charles Dickens.

'It's signed by the author, that is, son,' he told Joe. 'I bought it when I lived in London.' It was rumoured that Douglas had once had a respectable job in a bank, but had been brought down by the drink.

Through the open window of the house where Jimmy Gallagher lived came strains of the lovely song that always made Martha want to weep. She knew some of the words and sang them under her breath as she sat on the step watching through a cloud of tears as her bright-eyed, smiling lad had his hands shaken, his cheeks kissed, and his shoulders squeezed.

'There's a long, long trail a 'winding into the land of my dreams . . .'

Then it was time for him to leave. Frank had turned up a week ago, alarmed after hearing from someone what his little brother had been up to, and was walking with him as far as the Rotunda, Lily and Georgie, too, leaving their mother to cry alone. Joyce had come to say goodbye the night before.

Martha crept back into the house. She wouldn't really be alone. Carlo was still there, still snoring in bed, not bothered enough to rouse himself to say goodbye to his son.

She made the Sign of the Cross and swore she would never forgive him.

Life returned to some sort of normality, but only in the sense that Joe had gone and she no longer had to fret about his going. She thought about him ceaselessly and was surprised at how many people approached to say how shocking it was that the Government was taking lads of fourteen. Even her boss at the sack factory, a hard, brutal man that nobody liked, gave her a postal order for three and sixpence to send to Joe. Martha thanked him with tears in her eyes.

A few folks asked, 'And what's this bloody war all about, anyroad?'

Martha told them she had no idea. Nobody had any idea. Germany hadn't invaded Britain, Britain hadn't invaded Germany, so why were they slaughtering each other in their thousands in a different country altogether?

Joe had been gone a week when, for the first time since they'd come to live in King's Court, a letter addressed to Martha landed on the doormat.

She recognized her name on the envelope and Joe's name at the foot of the letter, but nothing else. It was neatly written in pencil, she could tell that much, the lines straight and the circles obviously done with a steady hand. All she wanted now was someone to read it to her and write a letter back on her behalf.

Carlo was still asleep in bed and she wouldn't have woken him had she known the world was about to end. Lily could read well, but she and Georgie had gone to school and she was anxious to know what was in the letter long before Lily came home. She wasn't prepared to ask for help from anyone outside the family and have the whole world know that Martha Rossi could neither read nor write. In her dinner hour, she'd call in at Frederick & Hughes, and ask their Joyce to do it.

Joyce was showing a customer a range of handbags that looked as if they were made out of snakes. Martha stood in front of the counter, hoping her daughter would notice her soon and thinking, no matter how much money she had, she wouldn't have fancied the idea of walking round with a poor dead snake tucked under her arm.

'Mam,' a voice hissed, 'you look a sight. Will you please go away before anyone notices you. Don't speak, don't say a word, just leave and don't ever come back here again.' Joyce had edged a few feet away from her customer. She spoke out of the corner of her mouth and didn't so much as glance at her mother.

'But I've had a letter from our Joe, luv,' Martha hissed back, 'and I'd like you to read it for me – and write one back, if you don't mind.'

'I *do* mind; at least, I mind discussing it here, while

41

I'm at work. I'll come round tomorrow night and see to it then – I'm busy tonight. Now, will you please just *go away!*'

'There's no need to come tomorrer; our Lily can do it,' Martha said stiffly. She had rarely felt so wretched. Joyce's words had hurt. She walked towards the exit, passed the leather gloves, the scent counter, the lipsticks, the powder bowls and powder puffs, the glistening jewellery. She was in a place where she didn't belong and never would.

She was about to go through the swing doors, when her arm was caught and a friendly voice said, 'Hello, did I hear you say you wanted someone to read a letter for you? I'll do it if you like.'

The young woman holding her arm was taller than her by at least half a head and as thin as a beanpole. She had lovely rosy cheeks and lips to match, clear brown eyes, and glossy hair the colour of nutmeg twisted into a thick plait and hanging halfway down her back.

'I'm Kate Kellaway,' the girl said.

'Martha Rossi,' Martha mumbled.

'About your letter, shall we go in Volanti's in Bold Street and have a coffee?'

'I don't think . . .' Martha had been sewing sacks all morning and her clothes, and no doubt her face and hair, were covered in a fine dust, something she should have thought of before entering Frederick & Hughes and embarrassing her daughter. 'I don't think I'm dressed proper enough.'

'You look fine to me, but if you like we'll go somewhere else where you'll feel more comfortable.' Unlike Joyce, Kate Kellaway didn't seem to be the least bit ashamed to be seen with her. 'How about the café on Central station? I can't stay long; I'm having my lunch break, you see, and have to be back at college at half past one. Do you mind if we hurry?'

Martha would sooner they hurried. She had a factory to get back to at the same time. 'What do you learn at college?' she asked as they crossed Bold Street into Central station.

'Typing and shorthand. I intend to be a journalist in time,' the girl answered, leaving Martha not much the wiser. 'Typing' made only partial sense, and 'shorthand' no sense at all. As for 'journalist', it was a strange word altogether.

Despite it being dinner-time, the café was almost empty. Martha supposed it was mainly used by people waiting to catch trains. It smelled pleasantly of cigars and coffee and sweet pastries. It was the sort of place where you went to the counter to order the food and the waitress brought it over.

'Would you like a cake, Martha?' Kate asked. 'If so, what sort?'

'Any sort, please.' She hoped, seeing as it was Kate who'd asked, that she wouldn't have to pay for anything. If she did, she'd be in trouble as she had exactly a penny-ha'penny in her purse. She watched the young woman as she stood by the counter waiting to order, admiring her clothes – a pretty red-and-white gingham frock with a shawl collar and three-quarter sleeves. From the rather awkward way she stood, all elbows, she looked more like a girl than a woman. Martha reckoned she was no more than seventeen or eighteen. She admired her nice, straightforward manner and her generous offer to help with Joe's letter. It didn't matter that she wasn't a member of the family.

43

Kate returned to the table, saying apologetically, 'They're bringing the things in a minute, but you know I forgot to ask if you liked coffee. I've got a thing about it, I could drink it all day long, but you might much prefer tea. It's awfully rude of me, I know, and I'm terribly sorry.'

'There's no need to be,' Martha assured her. 'I like coffee, too, though it's ages since I had any.' In the days when they could afford a choice, Carlo had always favoured coffee over tea.

'Good!' Kate smiled brilliantly. 'While we're waiting, perhaps you could read your letter to me.' She blushed. 'I'm an idiot; give *me* the letter and I'll read it to *you*.' Martha gave her the letter that had arrived that morning. 'This young man is a scholar, I can tell. What lovely writing. And he's your son and he's in the Army. Anyway, Martha, this is what he has to say.' She cleared her throat.

Dear Mam,

We only spent a single day in Wigan, then were moved to a camp just outside Lancaster where all we do is exercises, like touching our toes and stuff, learning how to march proper – it's called drill – and how to hold a rifle. I keep looking to me right when it should be me left. We are being fed well – three meals a day and a mug of cocoa with loads of sugar for supper. The uniform's a bit itchy and my boots are too big, but I suppose that's better than them being too small – I can stuff paper in the toes. Tomorrow, we're going into town to have our photos took and I'll send mine to you next time I write. And, oh, Mam, we have showers every day. The water's awful cold and I dread to think what it'll be like in the winter. Anyroad, I've never been so clean. I miss everyone at home, but not as much as I miss you, Mam.

Your loving son, Joe

The waitress had brought their order while Kate had been reading the letter out loud. 'It's lovely,' she said. 'Really lovely. You must be very proud of this Joe of yours.'

'Oh, I am,' Martha said, not far from tears. Though there was no need for her to be reminded of how much she missed him, the letter had brought home the underhand way he'd been taken from her.

'How old is he, Martha?' Kate enquired.

'Only fourteen.'

The girl's jaw dropped. 'But how can he be in the Army when he's only fourteen?'

Martha described the events that had drawn Joe into the Army while they drank their coffee and ate their cakes. She noticed people staring at her, as if wondering what such a wretched-looking woman was doing in a respectable place.

'That's disgraceful,' a shocked Kate said when she'd finished. 'Now, about the letter back to Joe: if you'd like to give me an idea of what you want to say, I could write it tonight and we could meet tomorrow at the same time in the same place and I'll show you what I've done. If you don't like it, I can always do it again. Is that all right with you, Martha?'

'Yes, oh, yes, it is. And thank you,' Martha stammered.

'Think nothing of it,' Kate said airily. 'What shall I

say to Joe?' She removed a bright red exercise book and a pencil from her capacious velvet bag.

'Tell him that we all miss him too, and to look after himself, keep warm, and go to bed early, like, not to visit any ale houses, but he can go to the pictures if he wants. Say I'm really looking forward to getting his photey in his uniform. Is that enough?'

'That's fine.' She leaped to her feet like a jack-in-a-box, nearly upsetting the table. 'I'll have to rush. Bye, Martha. See you tomorrow.'

'Something really interesting happened today,' Kate Kellaway said when she arrived at the smart modern house in Ormskirk on the furthest outskirts of Liverpool where she lived with her beloved mother and father. She threw her bag on to the settee and flung herself beside it. A delicious smell came from the kitchen – a steak and kidney pie was baking in the oven, she guessed.

'Something interesting seems to happen to you every day, dear,' her mother remarked with a smile. Margaret Kellaway was a pretty woman, as short as her daughter was tall. 'What was it this time? Did you find a lost child or somebody's wallet? I hope you didn't try to stop a fight again; one of these days you're going to get hurt. And if that nasty man has exposed himself to you for a third time, then I suggest you tell the police.'

'It was nothing like that.' Kate explained the circumstances of her meeting Martha. 'I was looking at the handbags and the girl behind the counter, Martha's daughter, told her to go away. She was obviously ashamed. Fancy being ashamed of your own mother,' she said indignantly. Kate spent a lot of her time being

46

indignant about how unfair life was for the poor and dispossessed.

'I hope you never feel that way about me, dear.'

'Oh, Mum, you always look lovely, but even if you were dressed in rags like Martha, I'd love you too much to feel ashamed.' She threw handfuls of kisses across the room. 'Anyroad, all Martha wanted was for her daughter to read this letter from her brother and reply to it – she can neither read nor write, poor thing.'

'Where is this young man now, dear?'

'Lancaster, in the Army. I have his letter in my bag. I'm going to write to him for her. He was persuaded to join up yet he's only fourteen.'

Kate's father walked into the room in the process of lighting his pipe. He was a chiropodist who worked in an extension on the side of the house. He had 'a way with women', according to his wife, and they came in their hundreds to have their feet seen to, even young women who didn't know what a bunion was, or a corn, but enjoyed having their feet massaged by a handsome, middle-aged man with warm, gentle hands.

'I heard that,' he said. 'There's been questions asked in the House about under-age soldiers. It's building up into a bit of a scandal.'

'I must tell Martha that tomorrow.'

'Are you seeing her again, dear?' Margaret Kellaway asked.

'To give her Joe's letter, yes. I'll do it after I've had dinner.'

'Mother?' she said later when dinner was over and she and her mother were washing and drying the dishes between them. 'You know those frocks our Evelyn left

47

behind? I wonder if I could give them to Martha?' Evelyn was Kate's elder sister, who lived in Nottingham with her husband and two small children. 'And she's got a daughter called Lily who's only ten – I've got loads of clothes she could have; shoes, too. And I could take her some of your lovely damson jam and bottled plums.'

'You will not take her a single thing except the letter, dear,' her mother said firmly. 'I don't know this Martha, but she could well be a very proud person. If you start treating her like your own personal charity it could upset her.'

Kate tapped her chin with the dessert spoon she was in the process of drying. 'I suppose you're right,' she conceded, planting a kiss on her mother's curly head. 'I'll offer them to her gradually over time. She's bound to want me to write more letters to Joe.'

To tell the truth, she was very much looking forward to it.

Chapter 3

Martha felt unusually cheerful when she returned home from work that night. It was all due to Kate Kellaway. Even in the old life, she had never met anyone as nice, or as posh, as Kate, who came from a completely different world. She was looking forward to seeing her again the next day.

She was in such a good mood that she decided to buy chips and fishcakes for their tea. There was still a bit of the money that Joe had left, and it wouldn't hurt to splash out a bit. Lily and Georgie were only too happy to fetch the unexpected treat from the chippy.

'Get enough for our Frank,' she reminded them. Frank had been dropping in every day around tea-time over the past few weeks, and she was expecting him any minute. Like everyone – Carlo excepted, who seemed to exist in a private, enclosed space of his own – Frank was worried about Joe. He was also contributing a small amount towards the housekeeping.

'I've got lovely kids,' Martha told herself. 'Our Frank is a bit of a rogue, but a good lad at heart.' She wondered where he slept. He usually did a bunk at around eight o'clock, but it was probably best if she didn't ask; it'd save an argument.

Joyce turned up when tea was over, as Martha had

thought she might. She didn't exactly say she was sorry about the way she'd spoken to her mother earlier at the shop, but Martha could tell that she was. She offered to write to Joe straight away, said she'd come round specially: 'I told Edward I'd see him tomorrow rather than tonight.' She'd been seeing Edward quite a lot. Martha had managed to squeeze out of her that he was a junior manager at Frederick & Hughes, not a mere shop assistant.

'That's nice of you, luv,' Martha said warmly, 'but this girl, Kate, offered to do it for me. We're meeting each other tomorrer in the dinner hour in the café in Central station.'

Joyce looked hurt. 'But I would've done it, Mam, you know I would.'

'Yes, but I didn't know you were coming tonight, did I, Joyce, luv? But when I get the letter back from Kate, you can write then, as well as Lily and Georgie – and our Frank might like to write a letter, too.' She'd suggest it when he came in. Mind you, he wasn't a letter-writing sort of chap.

'I might, Mam,' Frank said with a shrug when he turned up. He was far more interested in knowing what Kate was like.

'She's got a face like a suet pudding and she's about as wide as she's tall.' She didn't want Frank, the randy bugger, knowing just how pretty Kate was.

She thought about Joe later when Lily and Georgie were in bed, Joyce had gone home and Frank had disappeared to wherever he happened to be living at the moment. She'd almost got used to her middle son not being there. Going by his letter, he seemed happy enough in the Army, eating well, keeping warmly clothed, and nice and clean. Perhaps there'd been no need for her to have made such a fuss about him joining up. The war mightn't last much longer, and he'd come home in a position to get a better job than delivering groceries on a bike.

Kate was already in the café when Martha turned up. This time she'd managed to spruce herself up a bit, brushing the dust off herself and cleaning her face with spit and a piece of rag. To her surprise, the girl leaped to her feet and kissed her cheek, which was more than her own daughter did these days.

'I've done the letters, Martha,' she said.

'Letters? You wrote more than one?'

'I did a letter from me explaining who I was, so he'll know who it is writing to him on behalf of his mother. Do you mind?' she asked anxiously.

'Of course not. I think it's a grand idea.' They seated themselves at a round marble table.

'Would you like coffee and a custard cake again, or something different?'

'Coffee and a custard cake would be fine.' She'd been looking forward to it all morning.

After she'd ordered, Kate returned, delved into her velvet bag, and produced a leather folder, out of which she took a writing pad with mauve pages and a little bunch of purple flowers printed in the corner. She pulled off the top two sheets and waved them at Martha. The writing was big and spidery and very black without a single smudge.

'This is from you to Joe. It starts "My darling Joe" and goes on to say what we agreed yesterday.' She read the letter hesitantly, frowning slightly, as if she were

51

worried Martha would disapprove. 'Is that all right?' she asked. 'I finish with "your loving mother".'

Martha nodded. 'It's the gear, and so is the notepaper. Our Joe will be dead pleased.' None of her kids ever called her 'Mother', but Joe wouldn't mind.

'I dabbed a bit of lavender water on it.'

'Joe'll be pleased about that, too.'

Kate looked relieved. The waitress arrived with their order and Kate said she'd leave her cake until she'd read her own letter to Joe. 'I don't want to get greasy fingerprints on it.' She coughed and began to read.

> Dear Joe,
>   My name is Kate Kellaway. I met your mother, Martha, yesterday and agreed to write to you on her behalf. I am eighteen years of age and attend the Misses Barleycorns' commercial college in Hanover Street where I am being taught shorthand and typing with the intention of becoming a journalist one day. You must be terribly brave to join the Army when you're only fourteen. I told my own mother and father all about you last night and they were very impressed. They send you their best regards, as I do mine, along with my kindest thoughts and heartfelt wishes.
>   Kate Kellaway.

She beamed at Martha. 'I was going to put some kisses at the bottom, but thought it might be a bit of a cheek.'

'I think Joe would like a few kisses.' He could pretend Kate was his girlfriend. Not many lads of fourteen would have girlfriends who sent mauve letters smelling of lavender.

'In that case, I'll do the kisses now.' She very carefully wrote a row of perfect crosses in pencil at the bottom of her letter. 'I've got an envelope here, it's already stamped. Would you like to write your name at the end of your letter?'

'No, ta, luv. I'd only spoil it.' It took an age for her to write her own name and she felt too ashamed to try.

'I hope you don't mind,' Kate said, 'but like I said in my letter, I told my parents about Joe, and Daddy said questions are being asked in Parliament about the scandal of boy soldiers. Quite a few Members are all set to make a great big fuss about it.'

'Members?'

'MPs, Members of Parliament. My mother said if there were only women in Parliament, there'd never be any more wars. And if it were men's role in life to have babies, they might be a bit more careful with them when they grew up.'

Martha had a feeling she'd more or less said the same thing to Sergeant Gilligan. 'That's true,' she agreed, nodding knowingly.

She felt happy, as if she'd been lifted out the darkness in which she'd existed for so many years. The time spent with Kate, barely more than an hour, cheered her no end. She no longer felt as if she were nothing but a miserable, ignorant Irishwoman, but a person of some worth. She was determined to learn to read and write so her son would get letters written by his own mam, not from someone he'd never met, sweet though Kate was.

In the factory, as she struggled to push a needle through the thick canvas material, she imagined her

Joe emerging from the Army an officer and a gentleman and getting wed to Kate – there was only four years' difference in their ages and it would seem less as they grew older. She didn't give a damn what religion Kate was, and Carlo needn't think he could wake up and stick his oar in.

On Saturday after work, despite feeling ready to sleep till Monday, she made a bundle of the bedding and all the clothes she could lay her hands on and took them to Mary Kelly's washhouse along with Lily and Georgie. Both they and Martha emerged from their baths as fresh as daisies and with mountains of washing to take home and dry. Martha's hair felt like real hair again, not the greasy, stringy stuff it had been before. She'd had a God-awful time getting the comb through it.

In King's Court, the washing was draped all over the place. It was still damp at bed-time, so they had to sleep on the bare palliasses and use their coats for sheets. Martha and the children didn't care and Carlo didn't even notice.

'Next time I've a few bob to spare, I'll go down Great Homer Street market to buy more sheets,' she said. 'One set of bedding is no good for anyone. And you two could do with more clobber; you're getting bigger all the time.' She glared at them accusingly, as if it were their fault.

'We'll stop growing, Mam, if that's what you want,' Lily said cheekily. 'Won't we, Georgie?'

'Yes, Mam,' Georgie said with a grin.

'Oh, you two!' Martha hugged them fiercely. 'I love the bones o'yer.'

★

The letter containing Joe's photo came a few days later. Martha looked at it and caught her breath. If he wasn't the handsomest lad in the whole of Liverpool, if not in the entire country, then she'd eat her hat! She wished the sepia photograph showed the blue of his eyes and the lovely warm brown of the hair sticking out from under his cap – the Army must have cut it. He was smiling slightly at the camera, but otherwise looked quite grave.

'I'll let Kate see it, ask her to write and thank him and say what a grand photo it is.' She'd promised Joyce that she could answer this time, but there was nothing wrong with Kate sending another.

She and Kate had made an arrangement. If Martha wanted to see her for some reason, she was to wait outside the Misses Barleycorns' college at dinner time until Kate emerged.

'If it's raining, stand in the doorway of the pet shop opposite so you won't get wet.'

Given the time, Martha could have waited all day in the pet shop doorway. Given the money, she could well have gone inside and bought the entire stock. As it was, she spent an enjoyable few minutes watching the tiny puppies and kittens playing in the window. One pure white kitten tried to pat her finger through the glass.

'I wish I could buy you,' she told it.

'Hello, Martha, are you talking to yourself?' Kate was there, smiling at her, looking desperately pretty in a green silk frock with a crotcheted collar and a little hat to match.

'No, the white kitten. I was telling it I'd like to buy it one day.'

55

'We have a cat at home. His name's Horatio after Admiral Nelson because he only has one eye.' She linked Martha's arm and they began to walk along Hanover Street together. 'Your hair looks lovely,' she remarked. 'I hadn't noticed before, but it's almost the same colour as mine. Have you been to the hairdresser's?'

Martha pretended not to hear. She'd never been inside a hairdresser's in her life and didn't like to say her nice hair only came as a result of a good wash. 'Our Joe's sent a photo,' she explained. 'I'd like you to write and tell him he looks dead handsome.'

'Oh!' Kate sighed rapturously. 'I'm dying to see it – but let's wait until we're in the restaurant. I think I'll have an apple turnover today. How about you, Martha?'

'I'll have an apple turnover, too,' Martha said happily.

Kate sighed again when Martha held the photo up for her to see. 'He's beautiful,' she breathed.

Martha didn't think 'beautiful' the right word to use to describe a boy, but supposed that if Kate used it, it must be all right. 'Isn't he?' she said, agreeing with all her heart. Across the restaurant, a man was staring at the picture. Then he looked at Martha and made the thumbs-up sign. 'That's a fine lad,' he mouthed, while she trembled with pride.

'Did he only send the one photograph?' Kate asked.

'Just the one, yes.'

'Then we must get some more done. You'd like a smaller one for your purse, wouldn't you? And I'd like one, too, if you wouldn't mind. My parents would love to see what Joe looks like. And your other children might like copies.'

'How would I get more?' She felt useless beside Kate, who seemed to know everything.

'The photographer's name will be on the back of the photograph and hopefully his address. I can write to him and order extra copies.'

Martha turned the photo over and there indeed was a little square of blue print which could have been in a foreign language as far as she was concerned. She cursed herself for not having learned to read when she was a child back in Ireland. But she'd hardly gone near school. Not only was it miles and miles away, but there were always things to do on the farm or in the house, and learning came a long way behind working. Carlo had read things for her before he retired from the world, then Joyce and Joe had done the same.

Kate took the red exercise book from her bag. The photographer's address was in Lancaster, she said, as she made a note of it. 'You could go and see Joe,' she said. 'It's not all that far.'

Martha had thought about it, but it didn't seem such a good idea. 'I'd never be able to tear meself away.' And she might be the only mam to turn up and it'd embarrass Joe. 'Will the photos cost much?' she asked timidly.

'They won't cost *you* anything.' Kate waved a careless hand. 'It's all my idea, so I can hardly expect you to pay, can I?' She bit her lip and collapsed in the chair like a pricked balloon. 'Oh, Martha, I'm so sorry,' she said piteously. 'I'm a terribly interfering person. I do it all the time. My mother says I'm really bossy, that I want to run everybody's lives. She said I overwhelm people and they can't stand me. Can you stand me, Martha?'

'Of course I can.' Martha laughed. The girl was just being open and honest and helpful. 'I don't know what I would have done without you over the last few weeks. And I'm sure me kids'd think it was the gear to have a little photey of their brother in his soldier uniform.'

'That's good.' Kate looked pleased. 'But you must tell me if I'm trying to run your life and I'll stop.'

Martha wouldn't have minded someone running her life, but Kate probably only meant telling her what to do and how to do it, not actually *doing* anything. 'I will,' she promised.

'When I get the photographs, would you like me to post them to you, or shall we meet so I can give them to you personally?'

'Oh, I'd like us to meet. I really like . . . I mean . . .' She didn't know how to put it. 'It's the gear seeing you, and us having coffee . . . and a cake an' all,' she finished awkwardly. One of these days she hoped she'd be flush enough to buy Kate a coffee and a cake back.

'I'm glad about that, Martha.' Kate's eyes sparkled. 'Because I think it's the gear, too. What I'll do,' she went on enthusiastically, 'is send you a postcard with just the word "Joe" written on it. You'll know it means the photographs have come, and the next day we'll meet here at our usual time.'

With that, Kate jumped to her feet in her abrupt way – Martha wouldn't be surprised if one of these days she shot right through the ceiling. 'I have to go,' she gasped. 'I said I'd buy some toilet water for Cissie

Roberts who sits next to me at college. She's been feeling poorly all day. I think the heat has got to her.'

It was June and unnaturally hot for the time of year. More like July or August weather, people said, wiping their brows. 'It's an Indian summer,' a woman at work claimed, but another woman argued that an Indian summer came in September.

Ackerson's Sacks and Sails was situated in a little cutting off Back Seel Street, not far from the river. Mr Ackerson, had he ever existed, was nowhere to be seen, nor were the sails that had probably been made in the unused loft in the days when sailing ships were predominant on the high seas, the Atlantic in particular, where Liverpool was concerned.

The man who now ran the place was a foreigner. No one knew where he came from, or his name. He was about fifty, very tall, his skin neither light nor dark. His jet-black moustache stretched from ear to ear, and he had an abrupt manner, verging on rude. He was addressed as 'Mister', even by his wife, who supervised the women and could sew sacks as fast as any of them. She was a black woman who went by the name of Jacquetta, and told everyone that she was granddaughter of an African slave.

Martha arrived at the factory one day in the midst of the heatwave to find none of the women at work. Instead, they were standing around Jacquetta, who was seated in front of a complicated piece of equipment, moving her legs backwards and forwards, almost like riding a bike. The thing, whatever it was, was very noisy.

'What's that?' Martha asked.

'An industrial sewin' machine,' the woman beside her said, making a face.

She was about to ask 'What's that?' again, but the answer was obvious. It was a machine that sewed sacks about twenty times as fast as she and the other women ever could.

Mister stood, towering over his staff. Martha hadn't realized he'd been in the middle of the crowd, leaning over the new machine, watching his wife at work.

'You women go home, no more job here,' he barked, making shooing gestures with his hands. 'All except you.' He pointed at an astonished Martha. 'Have bought other machine for you to work. Wages will go up one shilling a day, but no more Saturdays.' For the first time ever, he actually made an affectionate gesture and patted his wife's black head. 'Jacquetta no like working Saturdays. She have other work to do.'

Martha was carrying out calculations in her head. Five extra bob a week, but less the shilling she got for working Saturdays, making a gain of four whole bob. But was she clever enough to work the new machine? Jacquetta would show her how, Mister explained after the other women had gone, giving Martha sullen glances. And who could blame them?

'How is soldier son of yours?' Mister asked.

'Our Joe? Oh, he's fine. He sent us his photo the other day. I'll bring it in tomorrer and show you.' She reckoned him knowing about Joe was the reason he'd chosen her to stay.

As far as Mister was concerned, that was enough friendliness for the day. He jerked his head at his wife. 'Jacquetta show you now. Better learn quick, or you be out on ear like other women.'

King's Court was not a good place to live when it was hot – nor when it was cold, as it happened, but in the depths of winter folks could stay within their own four walls, trying to keep warm by burning coke or orange boxes and bits of cardboard in their grates, or sheltering beneath scurvy blankets plus every piece of clothing they possessed.

In summer, they couldn't wait to get out of the houses where some of the windows wouldn't open and the smell of dry rot and other unidentifiable odours made them want to puke. In the small court, measuring no more than ten feet between the two rows of houses, small children played, men fought and women shrieked – at each other, at their husbands and at their kids.

Being at work, Martha missed most of this, but she dreaded the evenings. Fortunately, she was able to open the windows of her room and remain indoors, but the noise in the court was unbearable and the language unrepeatable. Couples argued over the most intimate details of their lives, men battered their wives and kids for no reason other than frustration that they were out of work, there was no money for even a single pint of ale. Fights were fought well into the night, and often Martha would be woken by a scream or a roar or an angry outburst.

After tea, Lily and Georgie usually went to the playground or to another street, a proper one, where tensions weren't quite so high and the residents had room to breathe. Frank and Joyce stayed away. Carlo went to the pub. Martha was glad to be alone in this powder keg where, more than once, it had been known for murder to have been committed.

She'd had a tiring day at work. Another sewing machine had been delivered and she was finding it hard to get the hang of it and sew the seams of the sacks in a straight line. The stitching wandered all over the place and Mister kept appearing, examining her work and saying irritably, 'Tch, tch.'

'Take no notice of him,' Jacquetta assured her. 'Mister likes you. He likes your Joe, although he hasn't met him. He knows you'll get it right soon. Anyroad, the sacks still sell with crooked seams.'

Martha discovered she quite liked Jacquetta, who spoke in a very refined manner and told her that after her grandmother had been released from slavery, she'd married the captain of a merchant ship and they had sailed the seven seas together. 'My mother was born in the middle of a storm when the ship was sailing around the Bay of Biscay. I myself was born in Panjam where my grandfather had gone to buy carpets. My grandfather was also my father; he married my mother on a mountain in Nepal. My grandmother was dead by then.'

'It's a good job she was,' Martha commented, not sure whether to believe her or not.

On Thursday, both the machines broke down – they were second-hand and rusty in parts. Mister oiled them, but the oil went on the sacks. This was hardly Martha or Jacquetta's fault, but it made Mister lose his temper and the atmosphere was heated by the time Martha went home. In King's Court, feelings were also at boiling point.

There'd been a fight that afternoon and the coppers had been sent for. Two men had been taken away and now their wives were gearing up to carry on the fight. Martha, watching from her window, learned later that Donal Mahon had accused Billy Quinn of making advances to his wife, Theresa, a fine-looking Irishwoman with Celtic blood, dark, glittering eyes and hair as black as soot.

Now Theresa and Billy Quinn's wife, Nellie, a fleshy, sickly-looking woman, normally Theresa's best mate, were facing each other threateningly, throwing the odd blow or the occasional kick until, as if a bell had rung for the fight to begin in earnest, they set upon each other, tearing hair and scratching eyes, snarling like wild animals and spitting in each other's faces. Their children screamed, and one mite, Tommy Mahon, who was little more than eighteen months old, tried to reach his mam and became entangled in two pairs of legs and yards of swirling skirts. Suddenly, an unintended kick sent him flying backwards and he finished up on Martha's doorstep, catching his little head on the corner of the concrete step. He lay there completely still while the blood running from his head began to form a pool.

It was now Martha's turn to scream. She ran out of the house and discovered someone had got there before her. Kate was already holding the little boy in her arms, the blood running down the front of her pretty cream flowered frock.

'We've got to get this child to hospital,' she said sternly. 'Which one of you is his mother?'

'Me, miss.' A miraculously tamed Theresa stepped forward and Kate transferred the injured child into her arms. 'Come on, I'll drive you there. Oh, hello, Martha. Are you coming with us?'

'Yes, Kate.' Stunned, Martha noticed a small black motorcar parked just inside the court, the engine still running. Everyone watched, transfixed, as Kate strode towards it. Theresa had begun to cry and her tears mingled with the blood of her child, while Martha tried to mop up both with the corner of her pinny, though not very successfully.

Two and a half hours later, they were released from hospital, Tommy with six stitches in his head, wearing a sparkling white bandage, his little, peaky face clean for once, and his much subdued mother still shaking with fright. 'I didn't mean to hurt him,' she wept still. 'It was an accident. I admit I give all me kids a crack from time to time, but never enough to hurt 'em.' She must have said this a dozen times and each time it was a lie. It was rare for a single one of her kids to be seen without cuts and bruises on some part of their bodies.

'Well, it's all over and done with now,' Kate said briskly. 'You'll have to be more careful in future, won't you?'

'Yes, miss,' Theresa said meekly.

'You'll not forget to go back to the hospital in a few days to have the bandage changed, will you?'

'No, miss.'

Kate stopped at a sweet and tobacconists and bought a dozen lollipops. She gave one to Tommy and the rest to Theresa. 'These are for the other children.'

'Thank you, miss.'

King's Court was silent when they drove in, though there were still plenty of people about. Their arrival was greeted with murmurs of relief. Nellie Quinn threw her arms around Theresa. 'Thank the good Lord the lad's all right. He is all right, isn't he, Tess?' she asked anxiously.

'It was a cut, that's all, Nell. The doctor stitched it up dead neat.'

'He suits a bandage, don't you, Tommy, luv?' Nellie chucked the little boy under the chin. He answered with a wan smile.

The women wandered off together, friends again, neither bothering to thank Kate for her kindness. Martha turned to her. 'What on earth are you doing here?' she cried. She felt deeply ashamed, having never expected Kate to see where she lived. 'Where did you get my address from?'

'From Joe's letters, of course. Was I wrong to come?' She looked contrite, but not all that much. 'It's just that I wrote and told you I'd received the photographs – you know, the way I suggested, with just the word "Joe" written on a postcard – but, although I looked out for you every day since, you didn't show up.'

Martha felt flustered. 'I didn't get any postcard. Maybe someone stole it. Oh, it's a good job it didn't have the photos in. Come on in, girl, and I'll make you some tea.' Inside the house – or the Rossis' small part of it – was an improvement on the outside.

Kate took a shopping basket out of the back of the motor car. 'I've brought some home-made jam,' she announced, 'and a fruit cake. My mother made them.' Her parents, she explained, had gone to Nottingham to see her sister. 'They've gone by train; my mother can't stand being in the car.'

'I didn't know you could drive.'

'I can't,' Kate cried gaily, as if it really didn't matter. 'At least, I couldn't until I tried earlier and found it dead simple. It just seemed a shame to leave it standing there all on its own, so I thought I'd use it to come and see you. I must leave before it gets too dark as I've no idea how to switch the lights on.'

Lily was spreading margarine thinly on two doorstep-sized slices of bread when her mother came in with an unexpected guest. She stopped with the knife hovering over the bread, and Georgie's eyes grew perfectly round as they both stared at the visitor. Martha supposed Kate must present a strange picture, her fashionable frock stained with blood.

'It seems I've come just in time.' Kate produced a jar of jam out of her basket. 'This is strawberry. I hope you like it.'

'Can we have some, Mam?' Lily asked shyly.

'Yes, luv.' Martha was feeling excessively strange and very odd. As far as she was concerned, they could use the whole jar. She prayed that Carlo wouldn't come lurching in, early for a change; that there wouldn't be another fight outside; that the coppers wouldn't be called again for some reason; that it would go dark very soon and her visitor would have to go home. On top of everything, her taste buds were fluttering at the sight of the jam that Lily was heaping on the bread. It looked as if it were made from whole strawberries. Martha worried that Lily might use the whole jar. Save some for your mam, luv, she prayed.

Kate then produced a large, square fruitcake and more jam, which she said was gooseberry. She was about to leave, but paused at the door. 'Why don't you

66

all come for a visit on Sunday?' she suggested. 'All you have to do is catch the Ormskirk train from Exchange station. It doesn't take long. I'd come and take you in the car, but Daddy might notice if I drive too many miles and he'd be cross.'

Martha was desperately trying to think of a reason to refuse. She didn't want to explain that neither she nor her children possessed a single item of respectable clothing, at least, not the sort that you would wear on a train. But Lily and Georgie's faces were squeezed into such expressions of longing that you'd think they were pleading for their lives.

'All right,' she gulped. 'What time?'

It would seem another visit to Mary Kelly's washhouse was called for. And now she was earning four whole bob a week extra, maybe it was time she treated herself and the kids to a new wardrobe.

Chapter 4

In the old days, on Sunday mornings after Mass, Carlo had sometimes taken the older children to Lime Street or Exchange stations to see the big steam trains while Martha made the dinner. They'd never gone anywhere on the trains as they were quite content to stay in Little Italy, which had seemed a big enough world to live in. She couldn't remember if Carlo had taken Joe. Had he been old enough? It was something to ask in the next letter Kate wrote on her behalf.

Lily and Georgie, only babies at the time, had never been, and today they were desperately impressed at the sight of the enormous black monsters puffing clouds of white smoke. 'Just like dragons,' Lily said. Georgie hung back, afraid, and was only willing to climb into a carriage with his mother holding one of his hands and his sister the other, making the whole operation very awkward.

At first, the view from the train window was similar to where they lived now. But after fifteen or twenty minutes, the narrow streets were replaced by bright green fields with only an occasional house in sight, or perhaps a tiny church that didn't look real from a distance.

The children stared entranced at groups of cows, so

still that at first Lily thought they were statues, little clumps of trees, gentle hills, the occasional grand mansion, tiny cottages with gardens full of flowers, fields of corn and little streams winding their way through the scenery like strips of silver ribbon.

Having lived in Ireland for the first sixteen years of her life, Martha was used to idyllic landscapes, but she regretted her two young children weren't aware that such beauty existed so close to home. She determined they would travel on the train again very soon – they would take sarnies and lemonade and have a picnic.

As promised, Kate was at the station to meet them. Dressed all in white, she was a picture, her large hat tied underneath her determined chin with an apple green chiffon scarf.

'Why, don't you three look smart!' she cried. 'Is everything new?'

'Sort of,' Martha replied.

Great Homer Street market had turned up trumps. Martha's extra four shillings had purchased a silver-grey fine woollen frock for herself as well as a natural straw hat with a red velvet band. The frock was thin under the arms, but she'd strengthened the material inside with patches of cotton fabric, which meant it would last for years. It was rather warm for what was an unpleasantly clammy June day, but at least she felt respectable for a change. Her black leather boots had felt quite comfortable when she'd tried them on and handed over the sixpence. Since leaving the house, though, they'd been rubbing her heels unmercifully. She gritted her teeth and tried not to notice.

Lily had discovered a bright pink silky frock with huge gathered sleeves and a wide sash which Martha considered a bit vulgar, both in style and colour, but had bought all the same when Lily had refused to be parted from it. Today, her daughter considered herself the most beautiful little girl in the whole world.

Georgie was dressed unobtrusively in grey in the hope that no one would look twice at him. So far, no one had. There was enough left over from the four shillings for their train fare.

'Is that material moiré?' Kate enquired of Lily's frock.

'Yes,' Lily said boldly. She looked at her mother. 'The woman on the stall said it was, Mam.'

'Did she, luv?' Martha hadn't heard.

Kate had said Ormskirk was a busy little town with a famous market, but today there was hardly anyone about and not much sign of life within the sturdy little houses. A pony and trap trotted by, the couple on board wearing their Sunday best, and the woman holding a prayer book in her lap, clearly on their way to church or on their way back.

'Come on, everyone,' Kate called. 'Jenny's made us ham salad for lunch, with apple pie and cream for afters.'

'Who's Jenny?' Martha enquired.

Kate explained that Jenny was a sort of housekeeper who didn't live on the premises. 'She does the washing and the cleaning and some of the cooking, like peeling potatoes and preparing other vegetables, while my mother makes the flans and pies and trifles and things. Normally, she only works weekdays. She's in today as a special favour.' It also turned out that Jenny's husband looked after the garden, and all Mr Kellaway did was trim things and cut the grass when he wasn't too busy.

'You probably think that I'm helpless as far as housework is concerned,' Kate said, which was exactly what Martha *was* thinking. 'Well, you'd be right. But,' she went on, 'my parents want me to have a proper career, and so do I. I want to be a person, not just a wife.'

'Don't we all?' Martha murmured, not entirely sure what she was agreeing to.

'I want to be like that when I grow up, Mam,' Lily said.

'You can be whatever you like, luv,' Martha promised.

Kate's house stood all by itself in a large garden full of trees and hedges and arches and flowers. The bricks were red and rosy with a shiny polish to them, unlike the bricks in King's Court, which were powdery and crumbling, as if they'd been afflicted with some sort of blight. Martha had always thought that the houses had been built with poor people like the Rossis in mind.

'The extension on the side is my father's surgery,' Kate told them as she unlocked the front door. The narrow building was made of even shinier bricks, and there were green blinds at the windows.

'I didn't know he was a doctor,' Martha said, surprised.

'He's not. He's a chiropodist. He looks after people's feet.' Kate entered a long room where the windows at the far end leading to the garden were wide open to the sunshine. 'Oh, look, here's Jenny. Jenny, these are my friends Martha, Lily and Georgie Rossi. That salad looks delicious. Does the ham come from one of your

Wilfred's pigs?' Jenny, an amiable-looking woman of about fifty, who was wearing an ankle-length white overall, nodded and bobbed a little curtsy in Martha's direction. 'It looks lovely and tender,' Kate went on. 'Jenny's son, Wilfred, raises pigs, Martha. I'll give you a piece of ham to take back with you.'

Jenny announced she was going home and would see to the dishes in the morning. 'And leave out any laundry that needs doing, miss. I thought I'd give the living-room curtains a wash while your mother is away. My John says it will be a good blowing day tomorrow.'

Kate uttered a little scream. 'I forgot – my cream frock has blood all down the front, I'm afraid. Do we have anything that will get it off?'

Jenny looked alarmed. 'I hope you didn't hurt yourself badly, miss?'

'It isn't my blood. It belonged to a little boy who banged his head. I took him to hospital, hence the blood.'

'Hydrogen peroxide will see to it. I think there's some in the garden shed. Well, I'll be off now, miss. It was nice to meet you, Mrs Rossi and Lily and Georgie.'

She bobbed another curtsy and went on her way, leaving Martha to wonder at the difference in people's lives. How lovely it must be to have someone wash your curtains when you were away! Even to *have* curtains was a luxury too much for at least half the tenants in King's Court. The Rossis' curtains had come from Great Homer Street market and were well worn in places. But patches in curtains looked worse than holes, so they just hung there, year after year, getting thinner and thinner.

After they'd eaten the delicious meal, Kate showed them around the garden. Georgie climbed a tree and seemed prepared to stay there, perched quietly at the top like a giant bird, and Lily found a cat with only one eye. Martha remembered Kate saying they had a cat called Horatio. Lily sat on a bench and nursed Horatio to sleep, whispering, 'There, there,' as she stroked the animal's back.

Kate said she had a little red shoulder shawl that Martha could have, which would look perfect with her hat and its red band. 'Shall we go inside and get it? My mother crocheted it for me a few months ago, but I just know I'll never wear it. It's far too old-fashioned for me.'

The shawl looked fine on Martha and she could tell it would go with her new hat. They were in Kate's bedroom, which had cream painted walls and a bed with a plain wooden headboard and a patchwork quilt that her mother had also made. It was a peaceful room, a room to pray in and think quiet thoughts. Martha made a vow that she would have the same sort of bedroom one day.

She sat on the bed and closed her eyes. All that could be heard was the sound of birds chirruping in the trees outside. Kate had gone somewhere. Presumably Georgie was still up his tree and Lily was nursing Horatio.

Kate re-entered the room, her skirt rustling like the wind, and sat on the bed beside her. 'I thought Lily and Georgie would like a little present each,' she said.

Martha had never noticed before how rich her voice was, or the way it went up and down, as if she were singing a lullaby. 'I found Lily a doll. Her name is Buttercup because her dress is yellow. I was thirteen when she was given to me, much too old for dolls in my opinion, which is why she's as good as new – I never played with her.'

'She's lovely,' Martha murmured, feeling drunk for some reason, not that she'd ever actually *been* drunk, but this must be how it felt; dazed, dreamy, dizzy.

'For Georgie, there's a metal car, the only boyish thing I have. I never played with that, either.' The car was black and about as big as the ruler Lily and Georgie had for school. 'It's a Stanley steam car. If you pour water in the engine of this one and put a nightlight underneath, it puffs smoke. Daddy played with it for a while.'

'Thank you,' Martha murmured. 'I'm sure Georgie will love it, and Lily the doll. You're being very kind.'

'I have so much.' Kate spread her arms in a helpless sort of gesture, as if having too much was a curse. 'It's nice to share it with someone.' Without warning, she threw her arms around the other woman's neck. 'Oh, I'm so glad we met, Martha. I don't quite know what I would have done without you.'

Martha felt sure she would have managed. After all, for someone like Kate Kellaway to be glad she'd met Martha Rossi was pretty hard to credit; she could only assume Kate was pretending, or perhaps she was a little bit mad.

Martha felt downright miserable on the train back. The view from the window was the reverse of the journey to Ormskirk, the green fields and little churches making way for houses and streets that became smaller and narrower as they travelled into Liverpool. The sky seemed to get darker, too, along with her spirits. Lily and Georgie were unnaturally quiet, as if the doll called Buttercup and the Stanley steam car weren't nearly as desirable as the cat with one eye or the tree.

The next morning, a letter arrived from Joe. By now, she knew what the words on the envelope meant, but she couldn't read the message inside.

In the dinner hour, she waited in the doorway of the pet shop in Hanover Street until Kate appeared out of the building across the road. She didn't say anything when she handed over the letter, and Kate didn't speak, either. Martha's spirits were still low and she had a horrid feeling the letter contained bad news.

Perhaps Kate did, too. She didn't open the envelope until they were sitting in Central station restaurant and had ordered coffee for them both.

'Joe's been transferred to Canterbury and then I'm afraid he's being sent abroad,' she said in a low voice.

'To France, where the war is?' The chatter in the restaurant melted into a dull buzz that penetrated her ears and made them tingle. The lump in her throat made her want to be sick.

'He doesn't mention France, but where else could it be if it's abroad?' Kate laid the letter on her lap. 'My parents came back last night,' she said thoughtfully. 'I'll discuss it with Daddy when I get home. He reads the *Manchester Guardian* every day from cover to cover so he knows everything there is to know about the war. Can you come tomorrow, Martha? I'll tell you then what I've found out.'

'Yes, but will you please write back to Joe straight away and tell him to stay put if he can. Say his mam's trying to keep him in England.'

Well, she would once she knew how.

'Mmm,' Mr Kellaway murmured that night, rubbing his chin. He was a striking man, tall with an impressive head of chestnut hair and a charming manner who had managed to remain modest and unassuming despite the admiration accorded to him by his clients, most of them female, whose feet he regularly serviced. 'I can't think of anywhere they'd send a young, untried boy but France, where it would appear some politicians and military bigwigs consider soldiers' lives not to be worth a fig. They're dying like flies over there — British, French, Belgian and German. Perhaps by the time Joe sends his next letter he'll know where he's going.' His lips twisted scornfully. 'By then, some idiot in authority might have bothered to tell him.'

'But what can Martha do about it?' his daughter asked.

'She could write to the War Office — or you could write for her. Or she could go and see her Member of Parliament. He might be able to get the lad home.'

'Do you know who her Member of Parliament is? She lives in Vauxhall.'

'Not offhand, but I'll look through my papers and see if I can find him.' He had files of newspaper cuttings going back for years ready for such an occasion.

'Does it concern you that our Kate is perhaps becoming a bit too involved with this Martha woman and her family?' Mrs Kellaway suggested to her husband later that night.

'It doesn't concern me in the least, my love.' Mr Kellaway waved his pipe in the air. 'She wants to be a journalist and this is ideal experience. And for Martha's sake I'd sooner Kate was involved than not.'

'You do realize she invited Martha and the two youngest children to lunch last Sunday?' She'd had no idea what to think when Kate had told her, but Jenny had said the family had appeared to be perfectly clean and respectable. So, what was she anxious about? Mrs Kellaway didn't know.

'I didn't realize, no, but I'm jolly glad that she did,' Mr Kellaway said warmly. 'We have far too much food, and Martha and her ilk have far too little.'

Sometimes, Mrs Kellaway worried that her husband's views were too liberal for his own good. 'Oh, well, as long as it doesn't bother you, darling, then it doesn't bother me.'

Once again, Martha was waiting in the pet shop doorway when Kate came out of college. The girl linked her arm. 'Your Member of Parliament is Major Norman Brown from the Labour Party,' she informed her. 'His office is in Scotland Road and it's open to constituents on Friday evenings from six o'clock on, so you can go then. Would you like me to come with you?'

'I think I should go by meself.' She was a grown woman, Joe was *her* son, and it was only right that she deal with the matter herself.

'I think you should, too.' Kate squeezed her arm in

support. 'It looks better that way, though it would be better still if your husband could go as well.'

'Carlo's not up to it.' He was drunk most of the time, dirty, and she sometimes wondered if he'd lost the ability to speak. She'd never discussed him with Kate, not once.

On Friday, she was late leaving work. Mister had a big order and sacks had to be made urgently to meet the demand. She was pleased when he gave her an extra sixpence, but had wanted to get home early so she could have a wash and change into her new grey frock and arrive at the MP's office before it became too crowded – Kate had warned her there might be a queue of people wanting to see him. Back at King's Court she gave herself a lick and a promise, changed hurriedly into the grey frock, and left Lily and Georgie to see to themselves with some bread and marge and the rest of the ham that Kate had given them.

'Help yourselves,' she said recklessly, slamming the jar of gooseberry jam on the table. 'Oh, and remember to leave some for your mam, if you don't mind. I'm bloody starving.'

The MP's office was above a confectioners in Scotland Road. There were ten people before her seated on wooden chairs around the walls of a dismal room full of red and white posters. She supposed they were Labour Party posters and studied them closely, the letters more than the words. There was an 'o' there, as in Rossi and Joe, an 'a' as in Martha and Kate, and an 'l' as in Lily, which had two. Lately, she'd been studying the way words were spelled and was beginning to get the hang of it, sort of. She grinned. In another hundred years or so she might be up to writing a letter on her own.

A man entered the room. Well, if this was Mr Norman Brown, Martha decided she liked the look of him. About forty, of medium height, with a kind face and gentle brown eyes, he had a lovely smile. He bent towards her. 'May I have your name, please?'

'Martha Rossi, Mrs,' she stammered. 'Er, Mrs Martha Rossi. Are you Major Brown?' She wondered why she was being seen before all the other people.

'No, my name is Arthur Hanson. I'm Mr Brown's assistant. Would you mind coming into my office for a minute so I can take your details, to save wasting time when Major Brown arrives? I'm afraid he isn't here yet. Some very urgent matters came up in the House this morning and he was late leaving. He's on the train at this very moment and should arrive quite soon.'

'Could the "urgent matters" 'ave anythin' to do with 'im buyin' 'is weekly supply of Napoleon Brandy?' a gruff voice enquired. 'That's 'is favourite tipple, ain't it?'

'I'm sure that's not the case, Mr Chapman,' Arthur Hanson said courteously. 'I think it was something to do with taxation – taking from the rich to give to the poor. Isn't that what you believe in?'

'I don't just believe in it, mate, it's an article of faith.' Mr Chapman was the thinnest person Martha had ever seen in her life. His face was like a skull with a thin layer of flesh stretched over it, his eyes deep in their black sockets. In fact, his entire face was black with what looked like coal dust and he wore a diseased leather waistcoat and moleskin trousers stiff with dirt. Without any warning, he stood up and addressed the room, coughing importantly. 'Four hundred quid a year, this geezer Brown gets, free travel on the railways – first class a' course – an' 'e speaks in the 'ouse about twice a year and drinks 'isself brainless the rest of the time.'

There was a sprinkling of applause and someone cried, 'Hear, hear.'

Arthur Hanson ignored this and touched Martha's arm. 'Will you come with me, please?'

She followed him into another room, as dismal as the first, but smaller. 'Is it true what that man said?' she asked.

'I'll leave you to make your own mind up about that, Mrs Rossi.' He smiled. 'Now, what is it you wish to see Mr Brown about?'

She explained about Joe, that he'd been bribed with a shilling to join the Army. 'He told them he was eighteen, though only an eejit would believe that,' she said breathlessly. 'On Monday, didn't I only get a letter saying he was being sent abroad?' She took all Joe's letters out of her pocket. 'These are his letters to his mam. He took his birth certificate away with him, but it said he was only fourteen.' She forced steel into her voice. 'I want him expelled from the Army and sent home, Mr Hanson.'

Arthur Hanson took down all the details in his desperately neat writing, asking what regiment Joe belonged to and if she knew his Army number.

'The West Lancashire Infantry, but I don't know his number. That won't stop him being sent home, will it?' Martha asked anxiously.

'I'm sure they'll be able to track him down without his number.' He smiled at her reassuringly. 'And I'm sure Mr Brown will be able to do something for you. Now, if you would kindly wait outside again.'

There was a clock on the wall that showed that Martha had been waiting for over an hour by the time Major Brown showed up. His clothes were expensive, she could tell that straight away. He was a red-faced individual of average height with a smooth, bland face and mouse-coloured hair. His age could have been anything between fifty and sixty.

'Good evening, sir.' Arthur Hanson took the MP's bowler hat and leather briefcase. 'We have quite a little crowd waiting, as you can see. Mr Chapman was the first here and he arrived two hours ago. Perhaps you will see him first?'

'If I must,' the Major growled. 'What is it now, Chapman?' He walked into his office, but instead of following, Mr Chapman, whose filthy fingers had been doing a dance on his knees the whole time Martha had been there, stood up slowly and said in a loud voice, 'You're as whiffled as a whale, you fuckin' tosspot. I could smell it while yer were still climbing the fuckin' stairs.'

'Telephone the police, Hanson,' the politician said in a bored voice, 'and ask them to come and take this . . . this . . . person away.' His face twisted in disgust. 'And should Mr Chapman ever set foot in this building again, you are to send for the police immediately. Who's next?'

A man stood up, scuttled into the office, and the door slammed.

'C'mon, Mr Chapman, sir.' Arthur Hanson put a friendly hand on the man's back and began to steer him out of the room.

Mr Chapman only began to cry. 'But who's going to take up the matter of the lease for me? I had a fifty-year lease on that buildin', and this bastard only came and knocked it down when he had no fuckin' right to.'

'I've told you before, to go and see a solicitor, sir. It's their job to know about such things, not Mr Brown's.'

'I might well do that, Mr Hanson. Thank you, sir. I might well do that tomorrer.'

For a member of the Government, an organization that Martha believed to be eminently respectable, Major Norman Brown cursed an awful lot, far more than poor Mr Chapman. His loud voice could be heard quite clearly. 'Bugger' seemed to be a favourite word. 'Bugger this', 'bugger that' and 'bugger off'.

She was beginning to dread her turn and suspected Mr Chapman had been right, that the politician had had too much to drink. There was a sweet smell in the room that could have been brandy.

Martha had been the last person to arrive and eventually she was the only person left waiting. Arthur Hanson popped his head around the door. 'You're not nervous, are you?' he enquired.

'I'm terrified,' she replied. She jerked her head towards the door of the office. 'He sounds as if he's in a bit of a temper.'

'He frequently is. Just stay calm and state your case. You can't go wrong,' he said gently. 'After all, you have right on your side, as well as the law of the land. Young men aren't allowed to join the Army until they're eighteen or be sent abroad until they're a year older.'

By the time Martha entered the office, Major

Brown's face was even redder and he was sweating excessively. She sat in the chair in front of his desk and explained about Joe, showed him the letters, and was shocked at the man's response.

'Christ Almighty, woman, don't you realize there's a war on?' He leaned forward and she could feel his spittle on her face. 'Right now, it's a case of all hands to the pump, fourteen-year-olds included. You should feel proud of your son, not come moaning to me and demanding I get him *out* of the Army. If you have any more sons, you should be going out of your way to get them *in*. Now, bugger off. I've had a hard day and . . .' His face froze in a peculiar expression, then, without further ado, he collapsed forward on to the desk and was sick.

Martha gathered up Joe's precious letters and fled the room. Arthur Hanson appeared and tried to detain her, but she pushed him away.

'Mrs Rossi,' he shouted, '*I* can do something for you.'

But Martha had gone. She didn't stop crying until she got home.

'Ah, so it's true what they say!' Kate's father remarked some days later when she told him about Martha's experience with the MP.

'What do you mean, Daddy?'

'The parliamentary sketch writers say Major Norman Brown is a piss artist, to be blunt.' He gave a wry smile. 'Excuse the language, but if you're going to be a journalist you'll have to get used to it. Do you know what a piss artist is?'

'Well, I can guess. Martha said the chap was a

drunkard. He smelled of brandy or something and was sick all over his desk. Not only that, after she'd told him about Joe, he told her to bugger off.'

Her father looked grave. 'That was a very unpleasant experience for the poor woman. I think her next move – or I should say yours, my love – is to approach the press, let the matter be given some publicity. Something might be done about it then.'

With Martha's agreement, Kate chose the *Lancashire Post* to see about Joe. After her experience with Major Brown, Martha was too upset to go with her, let alone go on her own.

'You're cleverer than me,' she said shakily a few days later when Kate proposed the idea of approaching the press. 'Me, I'd just sit there like a pill garlic and let people insult me.'

'You should have hit that revolting politician,' Kate said recklessly. '*I* would have.'

'*You* might have got away with it; *me*, I'd be sent to jail.'

Kate chose the *Lancashire Post* mainly because the local office was in Hanover Street, no distance from the Misses Barleycorns' college. She went just after four o'clock when lessons were over for the day, wearing her smartest costume – a plum-coloured linen top with short sleeves, a tightly buttoned hip-length jacket and a straight skirt of matching material that showed at least three inches of ankle. Her white shoes had high heels and a petersham bow on the toes, and her white silk hat was brimless.

She stepped into a small reception area containing a desk behind which a boy of about Joe's real age with heavily brilliantined hair was busily attaching postage stamps on to a mountain of brown envelopes.

'What's that?' she enquired, pointing to a bowl next to the young man. He was passing each stamp over it.

'It holds a wet sponge that moistens the stamps; saves having to lick the whole bleedin' lot,' the boy explained in a broad Cockney accent.

'That's a smart invention,' Kate said, impressed.

'I think so, too. I hate the taste of stamps. It makes me want to puke.'

Kate remembered why she was there. 'Can I see the editor, please? I have some really important news for him.'

'The editor don't work here; he's in the head office in Blackpool. All we've got is a reporter.'

'Can I see him, then? I take it it's a man?'

'Well, it's not likely to be a woman, is it?' the boy said contemptuously. 'Sit down a minute and I'll tell him you're here.' He disappeared through a door behind the desk and came back a minute later to ask Kate to follow him.

They went up a narrow wooden staircase into an unexpectedly large, pleasant room overlooking the shops in Paradise Street. There was a large desk in the middle of the room on which stood an exceptionally small typewriter – it must one of those portable models, Kate deduced.

'Here's the young lady, Mr Dexter, sir,' the boy said cockily.

'Thank you, Herbert.' The young man who spoke was staring out of the window. He turned and gave Kate a wintry smile before shaking her hand. 'I'm Clive Dexter. Please sit down, miss.' He indicated a comfortable chair on one side of the empty fireplace and seated himself in its companion on the other, a notebook open on his knee, a pencil poised ready to take notes. 'Firstly, what is your name and secondly – Herbert is new here and forgot to ask – what story do you have to tell?'

'You're terribly young to be a reporter,' Kate said, slightly disappointed by the man's youth. He was a lean, pale individual with a cold expression and full, sensitive lips. Some women might have found the contrast appealing, as well as the fact that his brown hair was a fraction too long and curled ever so slightly on to his slender neck. He wore pale grey trousers and waistcoat, and a rather daring, in her opinion, dark blue shirt with a floppy grey tie that only added to his attractions. Not that she was even vaguely attracted, she hurriedly told herself.

'What did you expect?' he asked in an icy voice.

'Someone middle-aged and highly experienced.'

'I'm twenty-one and moderately experienced.' He wrote something in the notebook. 'If you prefer some-one else, then either visit our head office in Blackpool or go to the *Liverpool Echo* whose office isn't very far away and will have reporters there of all different ages, some with vast experience. You can take your pick.'

'Have I just been very rude?' Her mother often accused her of speaking before she'd had time to think.

'Extremely so.'

'What did you just write in your notebook?'

He looked at the page. ' "I do not like this young lady." '

'I'm sorry.'

'You still haven't told me your name.'

'Katherine Kellaway, Miss.'

'Well, Miss Kellaway,' he said, his voice still understandably icy, 'do you intend to stay or seek a reporter better qualified to handle your story than I?'

'I'll stay,' Kate said in a small voice.

He made a pretence of looking relieved. 'Then I shall take notes.'

'It's about Joe. Joe Rossi. His mother, Martha, is a friend of mine.' She explained about Joe and his recent letter informing his mother he was about to be sent abroad. 'She wants him stopped. She went to see Norman Brown, the Member of Parliament for Vauxhall, about it but he refused to listen to her – to put it bluntly, he told her to "bugger off" – then collapsed in a pool of his own vomit.'

Clive Dexter raised his eyebrows, presumably shocked at her use of an expletive, but Kate didn't care. 'He sounds a vile creature,' he commented.

'Doesn't he? I do wish I'd gone with her, but she preferred to go by herself.'

'Is Mrs Rossi available for interview?'

'Would that be absolutely necessary?' She wasn't sure if Martha was up to it just yet.

He looked thoughtfully at his notes – his shorthand was very untidy compared to her own. 'No, not really. I think this calls for an article rather than merely an item of news, and I have quite sufficient here. Is there a photograph of Joe?'

'I've brought one with me, but I'd like it back if you don't mind.' She rooted through her bag for the photograph and handed it to him. 'Isn't he handsome?'

'Very much so.' He smiled for the first time, not at her, but at Joe's innocent face. 'No one could possibly

have taken him for eighteen.' He jumped to his feet –
he was a mere inch or so taller than she was, she noted.
'Right then, Miss Kellaway, I'll get down to work
straight away. Mr Henderson, the editor, may well use
it on Saturday when the paper has more local content
than during the week. Oh, and please may I have your
address?'

Kate stood and reeled off her address. She told him
she attended the commercial college across the road
and could call on him at almost any time if he left a
note in the school office. 'It's just inside the door. I'm
training to be a journalist like you,' she said boastfully.
'I can already do shorthand at sixty words a minute.'

'I'm sure you will make a remarkable journalist,
Miss Kellaway,' he said. She sensed a touch of mockery
in his tone. 'I wonder how you will get on when you
are younger and even less experienced than I?'

Kate didn't answer. 'Oh! You've got a telephone!'
She noticed the strange black instrument attached to
the wall. 'My father has ordered one for his business.'
Twirling round, she pointed to a photograph on his
desk of a pretty woman with dark curly hair wearing a
frock with a sailor collar. 'Who's that?' she demanded.

'What an inordinately curious person you are, Miss
Kellaway. *That* is Miss Lettice Conway, my fiancée.'

'That's an unusual name. Is it spelt the same as the
vegetable?'

'No, there is an "i" where the vegetable has "u".'

'I see. Well, goodbye, Mr Dexter.' She held out her
hand. 'It was nice meeting you.'

'Goodbye, Miss Kellaway. It was . . . an experience
meeting *you*.'

Chapter 5

Herbert left with the post at half past five, but Clive made no move. In some distant part of his brain, he was vaguely aware of the people in the shops and offices outside locking doors and shouting goodnight, while he concentrated on the article he was writing to the exclusion of everything.

Seated at his desk, scribbling away – he preferred to write in longhand rather than type in the first instance – he paused to glance at the photograph propped up against the one of Lettice; Joe Rossi, aged fourteen, possibly about to go to France and fight in the worst war of all time.

All the countries involved were civilized and immensely cultured, having produced great writers and composers, thinkers and philosophers; Voltaire, Ruskin, Nietzsche, Dickens, Wagner, Marie Curie, to name but a few. Yet it was differences between other countries altogether that had sparked off the conflict. As far as Clive could see, there'd been no reason for Great Britain, France or Belgium to become involved, yet it was in the last two countries where the battle was being fought against a vainglorious Germany.

He tried not to be too emotional in the article, not to write about wasted lives and murder of the innocents –

Joe wouldn't be the first child sent to fight, and certainly not the first to die should that happen.

Clive pulled the typewriter towards him and began to type the article from his scribbled notes, using the first finger on each hand and his thumbs on the space bar.

No doubt Miss Kellaway over the road could type like the wind, using every one of her long, white, extremely irritating fingers. Everything about the girl was irritating; her voice, her manner, what she'd said.

His neck was aching. Clive stopped typing, leaned back in the chair, hands clasped behind his head, and thought about her entrance into the room, bursting in with a rush of fresh air, her clothes rustling, her eyes everywhere, rudely inquisitive. Hopefully, they would never meet again. He returned to his article.

Half an hour later, he had finished. He slowly read the typewritten version, made several alterations and typed it again, then put it, unfolded, into a large envelope with Joe's photograph attached. Tomorrow, he would drive early to Blackpool and deliver it to Edgar Henderson, the editor, in person. He wanted to make sure there would be space available in the Saturday edition of the paper. The sooner Joe Rossi was brought home the better.

Clive walked home to Rodney Street where he lived with his family. His father, a stockbroker, boasted it was the best address in Liverpool. The Dexters also had a summer home on the Isle of Man and an apartment in London.

He was disappointed when he opened the door to find his father coming downstairs towards him – he avoided the man as much as he could.

'Had a busy day?' Jeffrey Dexter enquired.

Clive knew that the question hadn't been asked out of politeness or real interest, but as criticism of his son's days and the way in which they were spent.

'It was neither busy nor slow,' he said evenly.

'Well, I hope you enjoyed it. Your mother and I are off for drinks at the Guthries' in Princes Park. Their son has just been badly injured in the Battle of Artois in France; he's in hospital there.'

Clive removed his hat and hung it on the antler of a once proud deer who had been turned into a hat rack. It really was about time he left this house and found a place of his own. He only stayed because, with her other two children away, it would upset his mother if he left, too. 'And is that where you would like me to be, Father?' he said evenly. 'Badly injured and in hospital in France?'

'Rather than see you all dolled up like a cissie working in a cissie's job, yes, I would,' his father said scornfully. He was a short man, built like a boxer with a thick neck, wide shoulders and a barrel chest. His sons and his daughter frequently expressed their relief that they'd taken after their delicately built mother.

'Being a stockbroker is much less dangerous than being a journalist,' Clive pointed out. 'There are journalists at the Front reporting on the war, but I doubt if there are any stockbrokers. They're all safely at home counting their money.'

Jeffrey's large face turned dangerously red – Clive was convinced he had a faulty ticker or too much acid in his stomach. 'I don't see *you* at the Front, son.'

Clive didn't bother to say he'd written to every single newspaper in the land enquiring about a job as war correspondent, but had been turned down by every single one. He was too young and inexperienced, he'd been told – as Miss Kellaway had pointed out earlier. They wanted older and hardier men than him. He didn't tell his father this because he didn't care what the man thought.

His father returned upstairs, no doubt to avoid his cowardly son. Clive went into the drawing room and poured himself a large whiskey. He was pleased his brother, Guy, who was nineteen, was studying physics at Oxford University and safe from their father's odd desire to have a dead or injured son to boast about at his precious club. On leaving public school, Clive had preferred to train as a journalist rather than waste his time at university. Veronica, his sister, who was only fourteen and at boarding school, was of the same mind and was determined to become an actress on the London stage. She would no doubt fight her own battles with their father when the time came.

His mother, Berenice, came into the room and kissed him softly on the cheek. She was ready to meet the Guthries in pale grey chiffon and elaborate jet earrings. 'Hello, darling. Had a good day?'

He told her about Joe and the article he'd written. 'I'm taking it in person to Edgar Henderson in Blackpool first thing in the morning.'

'Poor little boy. Only fourteen! I bet his mother's really cross with him.'

'Not as much as she is with the chap who enrolled him in the Army – a police sergeant, if you'll believe it.'

She shuddered. 'Nasty man! Oh, by the way, Clive, I had tea with Hester Gainsborough today and she said there might be conscription brought in soon. What will you do then, if you *have* to fight in this frightful war?'

'I shall refuse and come out as a conscientious objector.' Clive had made up his mind about that ever since the word 'conscription' had been mentioned. He would willingly go down the mines or drive an ambulance in a war zone as conscientious objectors were required to do. 'Would you mind?'

His mother laughed. 'I don't give a hoot, darling. I like the idea of having three maverick children; a journalist, a budding actress and a physicist – whatever that is.' She laughed again. 'Your poor father, though. Still, he can always blame me for having such disappointing offspring.'

Around eight o'clock, not long after Clive Dexter's conversation with his mother in their splendid residence, on the other side of Liverpool, Martha Rossi was sitting in the window of the house in King's Court. Her two younger children were asleep in the other room and she was listening to Theresa Mahon's little boy sobbing his heart out, and Theresa responding with a screech of, 'Shurrup, you little sod.'

There were other sounds, too. Drunks were sprawled on some of the doorsteps, men were playing cards on another, half a dozen boys kicked a football, which was almost split in half, against the wall. But whatever songs they sang and words they spoke, were drowned out by the cries of the child and the answering shrieks of his mother.

Within twenty-four hours of his visit to the hospital, the bandage on Tommy Mahon's head had disappeared. Fortunately, the stitches had stayed firm, the bandage had been found and wrapped back around his head. Since then, the child had hardly stopped crying – during the day as well, Martha had been told. She hoped the wound hadn't turned septic. She wanted to help, but Theresa was a touchy, violent woman likely to tell her to go to hell. She'd only let Kate order her about because she was awed by her clothes, her motor car, her manner, and because she was genuinely worried about her son. She regularly battered the hell out of the little boy, but she didn't want him to die.

'Keep care of your little 'uns while you can, Tess,' Martha wanted to say. 'It won't be long before they're big 'uns, and who knows what terrors might come their way.'

She couldn't get Joe out of her mind. It seemed ages since she'd got the letter saying he was being sent abroad, yet it was only the other day.

Well, she wasn't going out for a sing-song tonight, Martha thought when the men playing cards began a fist-fight. There were times, often in midsummer for some reason, when King's Court could be dangerous, attracting vagrants looking for somewhere to lay their heads, as well as drunks, criminals and gamblers. They knew they were safe from the bobbies, who never bothered to enter the court except when called upon to do so. The bobbies reckoned the people living there weren't worth protecting and while the villains were safely out of harm's way, they weren't bothering respectable folk who lived in the streets nearby.

Martha jumped when the front door of the house opened. 'Frank!' she gasped, relieved, when her eldest son appeared.

There was a bolt on the door that was fastened while

the family slept. Frank slid the bolt across and put a finger to his lips. 'If anyone comes for me, Mam, you don't know where I am.'

'Why, what have you done?' she demanded angrily. 'Is that money lender chap after you again, Milo O'Connor? He came here weeks ago.'

'I owe his mam a few bob,' Frank admitted. He attempted a grin that failed, and looked frightened instead.

'How much do you owe him . . . her?' Maggie O'Connor was a tough old bitch. Martha would sooner starve than borrow a penny from her.

Frank made a face. 'Only about five quid.'

'*Only* five pounds?' Martha gasped. 'Jaysus, Frank, where are we supposed to get that sort of money from?'

'*You* don't have to get it from anywhere, Mam.' He puffed his chest out. 'I'll get it meself. Anyroad, money's not the reason I'm here.'

'Then what is the reason?'

'It's nothing important. I'll sort it out.'

'Will you now?' Martha got up to light the Primus and put the kettle on. She needed a cup of tea to calm her nerves. Worrying about Joe was bad enough, but now there was Frank as well. 'Any minute now our Georgie will go on the rob or summat,' she grumbled. 'Me sons seemed determined to drive their poor mam into an early grave. What was the money spent on, if you don't mind me asking?' she said sarcastically.

He stuffed his hands in his pockets and stared shiftily at his shoes; good shoes, she noted, well-polished. 'The gee-gees, Mam. I had a bet or two. They were supposed to be sure-fire winners, but they turned out to be losers

95

instead.' He looked straight at her. 'I'm sorry, Mam. Can I stay here for a few days?'

'You can stay here for as long as you like, lad, you know that.' She would never turn away one of her kids. 'But you need to pay Maggie O'Connor back quick. If her Milo gets his hands on you, he'll have your guts for garters.'

'I know. I'll just have to think of something.'

'And you'll have to think of it soon,' Martha advised him.

It was the most beautiful morning. Clive had arrived in Blackpool early, and only a few members of staff were in the office of the *Lancashire Post*. He left Joe's article on Edgar Henderson's desk and went for a walk along the sea front.

It was still early enough for a fresh, invigorating wind. The sun shone palely in the milky blue sky and the Irish Sea twinkled like silver. Clive leaned on the railings and took several deep breaths of salty-smelling air. On a morning like this it was good to be alive.

He noticed a little wooden shack on the sands was already selling drinks and a few fishermen had taken advantage of the fact. He went down and joined them, ordering tea that came in a tin mug heavily sugared, though he hadn't asked for sugar. It was delicious to drink, though. He listened to the men comparing yesterday's catches, discussing the weather and a fishing competition on Sunday in Fleetwood. No one mentioned the war, for which he was grateful.

He strolled back to the *Lancashire Post*'s office and found the office now frantically busy. Edgar Henderson was a forward-thinking chap and at least half the staff were female, even one of the news reporters, though her remit covered only women's issues. Clive thought of Miss Katherine Kellaway and couldn't resist a sardonic smile.

Mr Henderson was in his office reading Joe's article and smoking a vile-smelling pipe. He was a small, portly man in his fifties with prematurely white hair. When he saw Clive, he pointed to a chair, but didn't speak. Five minutes later, he pushed his own chair back, removed the pipe, and looked at the younger man over his wire-rimmed glasses.

'Good,' he said. 'More than good. It's excellent, tugs at the heart strings, makes you want go outside and scream, "What's wrong with this bloody world?" But I'm not going to publish it, Clive.'

Clive gaped. 'Why ever not, sir, if it's so good?'

'Because it's the truth and our readers don't want to know the truth. I wonder how many young men from Lancashire are presently fighting in this damned war? Thousands, probably, and hundreds, if not more, will have already lost their lives or been injured. Do our readers really want to be told their sons, husbands or brothers died in vain or were sacrificed for a lie?' He shook his head. 'I doubt it. Would you, Clive, if your brother was a soldier in France at this moment in time? I know *I* wouldn't.'

'If Guy were killed I'd want to know the truth. I'd want to know why,' Clive said hotly.

'Then all I can say is you must be an exception.'

'And all I can say is that you under-estimate people.' To think he'd considered the man to be forward-looking! Clive picked up the article. 'If you don't mind, sir, I think I'll go home now.'

'But I thought you might like to have lunch while you're up here.'

'No, thanks.' He preferred to be alone.

'Have I upset you, Clive?' Edgar looked slightly amused at the idea. He may well think the war a bloody crime, but it obviously didn't stop him from sleeping, as it did Clive.

'No, sir,' Clive lied.

He made his farewells and drove slowly back to Liverpool, his mood bleak. The delightful weather didn't help, merely reminding him what a beautiful world it could be if only countries would bring themselves to stop picking fights with one another.

Back in his own office, Herbert reminded him that he was due at the town hall in half an hour to interview Councillor Cedric Kershaw-Jones about his objection to the building of a picture house in the Woolton area.

Clive said he hadn't forgotten, though he had. It was just that he considered Herbert an objectionable little squirt and didn't want him thinking his boss had nearly let the paper down. He was glad he hadn't stayed in Blackpool and had lunch with Edgar Henderson.

He hadn't met Councillor Cedric Kershaw-Jones, but he didn't like the sound of him. As far as Clive was concerned, every city in the country would benefit from having a picture house on every corner rather than a pub.

That afternoon, he was due at a hundredth birthday party of a woman from Ormskirk who had more than one hundred and fifty living descendants. He would need to take his camera to both events.

Councillor Cedric Kershaw-Jones turned out to be a total bore, as Clive had more or less expected, but the one-hundred-year-old lady was an absolute delight, full of quite provocative memories of what she got up to as a girl. She had been born under the reign of King George IV, then Prince Regent, and christened Caroline after his wife. She wore a black silk dress and a white organdie bonnet that fastened with a huge bow underneath her wrinkled chin. She had been a widow for more than fifty years and her wedding ring had worn away to the thinness of gold wire.

Quite a large proportion of the one hundred and fifty descendants had come to her party, though only a few could fit into the tiny cottage with its stone floors and mullioned windows. Most were in the gardens, back and front, or standing outside The Toadstool, a nearby public house.

Clive had only intended staying long enough to have a chat with Caroline, take her photograph, then return to the office, but found it difficult to tear himself away from the agricultural workers, real sons of the soil, who talked in their broad Lancashire accents about the land as if it were alive and had moods and sulked if it didn't have enough rain or there was too much sun. 'Her not pleased if she get dry as dust, like,' one said.

Their wives, whatever their ages, were mainly stout, comfortable women with rosy cheeks. They talked about the state of the apple crop this year – it would be poor, Clive understood. There'd been strawberries a'plenty, but not enough folk to pick them, due to the war needing so many men for soldiers. Hopefully, women would come forward to help.

The war was a popular topic, though the women spoke about it bitterly. They all appeared to know someone who had lost a relative, even two, or had been hurt. One woman, slightly better dressed than the others, was quite outspoken. 'How dare they take away our babies,' she demanded of no one in particular. 'Just who do they think they are, these grand old men full of cold piss and hot air and without a sensible brain between them?'

Caroline seemed to know everyone by name. She nursed the babies and chucked their chins with her bent, ancient fingers. Clive photographed her with her youngest descendant, her two-month-old great-great-great-grandson Wilfred.

He left finally at about five o'clock, only because nature called and he couldn't bring himself to use the outside latrine, which had tattered canvas walls and was merely a hole in the ground. The smell made his stomach heave.

He remembered passing a station on his way into Ormskirk and reckoned there'd be a gentlemen's lavatory there. He stopped the car outside, used the convenience, and was about to get back into the car, when people began to pour out of the station. It would seem a train had just arrived.

'Why, Mr Dexter! What on earth are you doing here?' exclaimed a voice he recognized immediately. 'Have you come to see me?'

'Miss Kellaway.' Clive removed his hat and bowed courteously. Did she really think he'd driven all the way to Ormskirk to meet her getting off a train when his office and her college were a mere few yards away from each other in Liverpool? 'I have been to a party,' he explained coldly. 'A wonderful Ormskirk lady celebrated her one hundredth birthday today and it was my job to interview her.'

'That can only be Caroline Winterbotham. Everyone knows her. My mother took her flowers this morning. Did you write the article about Joe?' she asked eagerly.

'Yes. If you would like to call into my office some time tomorrow, I will explain to you what happened.'

'Can't you tell me now?' Instead of pouting, as other woman might have done, she frowned at him sternly.

'I'd sooner not.' The news he had was upsetting, and he'd sensed yesterday that she felt very strongly about the fate of young Joe Rossi. 'Tomorrow would be better.'

'Oh, don't be so stupidly silly!' she snorted in a most unladylike fashion. 'Do you expect the news will cause me to faint or something? If you think that, then tell me in the car so I won't have far to fall.' She flung the car door open and threw herself inside.

Clive gritted his teeth, retained his temper, got into the driver's side of the car, and told her what had happened when he'd taken Joe's article to Blackpool that morning and given it to the editor to read. 'He turned it down flat. I'm not sure what to do now — apart from take you home. Whereabouts do you live?'

She described the way to her house, finishing with a gritty, 'I could kill that editor of yours.'

'You're not the only one,' Clive said.

They didn't speak again until Clive drew up outside her house. In the drive, a middle-aged man was cleaning the windscreen of a car identical to his own Ford Model T. Miss Kellaway thanked him for the lift and went indoors. And that, Clive assumed, was that.

★

'You're early,' her mother remarked when she went in.

'I got a lift from the station.' Kate fell into a chair and tried to sort out her thoughts. What were she and Martha supposed to do now?

'I am trying to think,' her mother said, 'of who we know in Ormskirk who could have given you a lift. The vicar is on holiday this week, so it can't have been him. And Doctor Draper is usually busy in his surgery at this time.'

'It was Clive Dexter,' Kate said. 'You don't know him. He's a reporter on the *Lancashire Post*.' Her mother was looking at her expectantly, waiting for further information. She was getting on Kate's nerves. Wasn't her daughter entitled to any privacy? 'I went to see him yesterday about Joe Rossi,' she explained. 'Joe wrote to Martha to say he was being sent abroad.'

'To where?' her mother asked.

'He didn't say where. I don't suppose he knows.'

'And what is Clive Dexter doing in Ormskirk?'

Kate ground her teeth. 'It's nothing to do with me. He came to interview Caroline Winterbotham.'

'I saw her this morning.' Her mother smiled as if this was a really remarkable coincidence. 'She's a grand old girl. She was looking forward to today. Did this reporter friend of yours take her photograph?'

'I've no idea, Mother.' Kate hoped, if she should reach a hundred, no one would refer to her as a 'grand old girl'. It sounded terribly patronizing.

'Am I getting on your nerves?' her mother asked.

'Whatever makes you think that?' She didn't wait for a reply, but went upstairs to wash her hands and face, and think what a useless, ineffectual individual Clive Dexter was. His article about Joe had almost certainly been completely hopeless. She wished she hadn't bothered to approach him in the first place. He was probably a dreadful journalist and didn't know a thing about the war.

She lay on the bed glaring at the ceiling until her mother shouted that dinner was ready. To her horror, when she went downstairs her father was only showing Clive Dexter into the dining room and introducing him to his wife.

'He just dropped Kate off,' Daddy was saying, 'and I saw he had a Ford Model T, same as mine. We've been comparing notes.' He looked at Kate. 'Apparently, you and he are acquainted. Why didn't you introduce him, love?'

'I didn't think,' Kate said weakly. She glowered at Clive Dexter and he glowered back. She hadn't expected to set eyes on him again after today.

'Our Kate saw him yesterday about Joe Rossi.' Her mother seemed anxious to take part in the conversation.

'Yes, Clive said.' Mr Kellaway rubbed his hands together noisily. 'I've invited him to dinner, Margaret. I take it there's enough in the pot for four of us?'

'Yes, Gilbert. It's lamb stew and there's plenty.'

'That's extremely kind of you.' Clive bowed and Kate wanted to be sick.

Halfway through the meal, Kate kicked their dinner guest accidentally on the shin. She considered not apologizing, but her good manners got the better of her.

'I'm sorry,' she said aggressively.

'There's no need,' he assured her. 'I hardly felt it.'

He and her father were getting on like a house on fire. Between them, they decided it would be a good idea if Kate arranged for Clive to meet Martha Rossi. 'The three of you should be able to get something done about Joe,' her father said.

Inwardly, Kate fumed. Martha was *her* friend and Joe was *her* cause. She stuck out the meal until the pudding had been eaten, then excused herself, saying she had a headache and wanted to lie down.

'Don't fall asleep with that heavy meal on your stomach,' her mother advised. 'You'll wake up with indigestion in the morning.'

Mrs Kellaway came upstairs and sat on Kate's bed after Clive Dexter had gone. It would appear she was completely charmed.

'He's a handsome young man with an interesting pallor,' she exclaimed enthusiastically. 'He thinks deep thoughts and is very knowledgeable about the war. Your father was very impressed. Oh, and *his* father is a stockbroker. They live in Rodney Street so must have pots of money.' She actually winked. 'He'd be a good catch, Kate.'

'Oh, Mother, don't be daft.' Kate pretended to yawn. 'I only met him yesterday.' As for the interesting pallor, she thought he looked grossly unhealthy.

Chapter 6

It was going to be another blindingly hot day. Martha was already sweating cobs by the time she reached work. Mister didn't smile when she went in, nor did he reply when she said 'good morning'. But she was used to his up and down moods and they no longer bothered her. He disappeared into a room in the corner that he referred to as his office.

'What does he do in there?' Martha had asked Jacquetta, who merely shrugged. There could hardly be much paperwork required for a company with two employees making sacks.

Jacquetta complained she was coming down with something.

'What sort of something?' Martha asked.

'Something oriental,' Jacquetta sniffed.

Martha didn't know what she meant, but hoped she wouldn't catch it. She set to work on the sewing machine, pedalling away while she ran the lengths of sacking under the needle twice on each side to make French seams, then stitching a hem around the top.

In the summer, the door to the factory in Back Seel Street was left wide open to whatever fresh air could reach the building in the dark, narrow passage. Martha was treadling away when a voice said, 'Hello, Mam.'

'Joe!' She screamed and leaped to her feet, hugging him with all her strength until the poor lad must have felt he was being squeezed to death. 'Oh, Joe, lad.' She stroked his face and showered it with kisses.

'All right, Mam,' he said self-consciously. He wriggled out of her embrace. 'There's no need to go overboard.'

She released him and his cap fell off, so she picked it up and kissed that, too. 'Oh, but, lad, it's lovely to see you.' In his Army uniform, too. 'How long are you home for?' Her heart leaped with hope. 'Is it for good?'

'I'm afraid not, Mam. We're off to . . .'

Before he could finish, Mister came out of his office, a smile stretching from ear to ear on his strangely coloured face. 'Is this Joe?' he almost shouted. 'Is this Joe Rossi?'

Martha pushed her son forward. She was quivering with excitement because she'd got him back, at least for now. 'It's our Joe, Mister. He's come home to see his family.' She turned to Joe, 'Remember it was Mister who sent the postal order for three and a tanner.'

'Thank you, sir,' Joe said politely. Martha had never heard him call anybody 'sir' before. It must be what he'd been taught in the Army.

'You very heroic boy,' Mister said, thumping Joe's shoulders with both hands. 'We all very proud of you at Ackerman's Sacks and Sails.'

'I thought when it was dinner-time I could go out with me mam for a cup of tea,' Joe said.

'It dinner-time now. Go for ten cups of tea, go for meal.' Mister plunged his big hand into his trouser pocket and it came out clutching a pile of copper and silver coins. 'Have tea on me, Joe Rossi, have meal.' He pressed the money on Joe and began to push him and Martha towards the slice of sunlight by the open door.

'He's a funny bloke,' Joe said when they were outside and Martha had been told not to come back until that afternoon. He shoved the coins into his pocket and jangled them. 'And a pretty decent sort of bloke, too.' He winked at his mother. 'Where shall we go now, Mam?'

Martha linked his arm. 'I'd like to go home and change me frock, lad. I've a nice, new one. And I know where we can go for our cup of tea, an' all – Central station. It's dead posh there.'

The Queen of England herself couldn't have felt grander than Martha did as she sat in Central station café, Joe having ordered coffee for his mam, a pot of tea for himself, and a plate of assorted cakes between them. What's more, she was wearing her grey frock, the straw hat with the red band and the little red shawl that Kate had given her. She felt delirious having Joe at the same table; her beaming like a lighthouse, him the target of admiring glances from all around.

A well-dressed man approached. 'Are you home on leave, son?' he asked Joe.

'Just for forty-eight hours,' Joe told him.

'Have you been fighting in France?'

'I haven't been to France yet, but we're being posted there next week.'

He'd already told Martha that, but for the second time she pretended not to hear. She didn't want to think about it until he'd gone. She didn't want him seeing his mam sobbing her heart out, but to leave Liverpool with the memory of her laughing face. She hoped Carlo would manage to perk up while his son was there. His dad had already gone out, Joe said, when he'd got home earlier.

'Well, good luck, son.' The man shook Joe's hand and managed to give him a ten bob note at the same time.

'Jaysus!' Martha commented. 'I think I'll get meself an Army uniform.' She would never forget this day. It was the grandest of her life.

They came out of the café and strolled arm in arm along Bold Street. She was aware that Joe had grown a mite since going away and she had to raise her head to peer up at him. She commented on the clothes and shoes in the windows of the dead posh shops and pointed out the things she would like to buy one day when the Rossis were better off. 'After all,' she said, 'we can't be poor for ever.'

Joe wanted to buy her something gold with the ten bob the bloke in the café had given him, earrings or a ring, but Martha flatly refused. 'You can buy it for me when this bloody war is over and you're back home safe and sound.'

After they'd walked up one side of Bold Street and down the other, she said it was time she got back to work, and Joe said he'd go and see Joyce in the big shop where she worked.

'She'll be thrilled to bits,' Martha said. He'd get a much better reception than his mam had received the day she'd gone in with his letter for Joyce to read. 'I bet she'll want to show you off to all her mates.'

★

Mister let her go home early and she found Joe sprawled on the couch and Lily and Georgie more or less sitting on top of him while he told them about life in the Army.

'Mam, our Joe has a shower every single day,' Georgie told her. 'I wish we could have showers here.'

'An' he has three big meals – three!' Lily squeaked.

'I wish we could have them too,' Georgie said longingly.

'An' he has puddings every time, too, except with breakfast,' George said enviously. 'Us, we only have puddings on a Sunday.'

'Then I reckon all the Rossis should join the Army,' Martha joked.

Lily bounced on her brother's belly. 'I wish you weren't going to France, Joe. It's on the other side of the world.'

'No, it's not, daft girl. It's only on the other side of the English Channel,' he assured her. 'And *I* wish *you* weren't crushing the life out of me with your bony bum.'

Lily bounced again and he gasped for breath. Martha ordered her to get off straight away or she'd make him sick. 'And you, too, Georgie. Sit on a chair or something.'

Joyce arrived, terribly smart in her shop uniform of white blouse with a black skirt. Martha wondered why she smelled of steak and kidney until she produced two large pies she'd bought in Kroner's butchers on the way home.

'They're still warm, Mam. Have you got some spuds ready?'

Martha said she had. 'But I was going to have them

with carrots and turnips and a bit of grated cheese.'
Everything was ready in the pan.

'Well, you can have them with steak and kidney pie
as well.'

'Yum, yum.' Georgie rubbed his tummy.

'I must keep some for our Frank – oh, here he is
now.' Frank was going out again, worrying her stiff
because he couldn't possibly have paid Maggie O'Connor back the five quid he owed. And he'd come all
done up like a dog's dinner in a chalk-striped suit that
was too big for him. What on earth did he do with
himself all day dressed like that? she wondered. His eyes
lit up when he saw his brother. They hugged and
pretended to fight each other for a good five minutes.

Martha felt a lump come to her throat. Joyce may
well be a bit stuck up these days, and she had no idea
what their Frank was up to, but all in all she had a
lovely family. They stayed together till it was time for
Joyce to go home, talking about old times and having a
little sing-song now 'n' again.

Before she left, Joyce said her boyfriend, Edward,
would like to take the whole family to the theatre
tomorrow night if that was all right. 'It's a Victorian
music hall and it's on at the Rotunda in Scotland
Road,' she announced. 'He thought it was about time
he met everyone, and with our Joe being home it
seems the ideal opportunity.'

They all agreed it was even more than all right and
Joyce took her mother to one side. 'Mam,' she said
sternly, 'please see to it that you have a bath tomorrer –
wash your hair an' all – and wear that grey frock of
yours. I don't want you making a show of me in front
of Edward. Don't forget he's a *junior manager*. And oh,'

she said as an afterthought, 'try 'n' bring Dad an' all, or Edward'll be wondering what's up with us.'

Martha wondered, too, how was she supposed to do all those things as well as go to work. She wanted to see Kate, tell her Joe was home. If only she'd thought earlier to wait with Joe by Kate's college and they could have met. But she'd been so excited to see him.

'What's wrong?' she asked when Joyce said, 'Damn!' for no apparent reason.

'I wish I'd told Edward now that me dad was dead.'

'Oh, Joyce, luv, you don't mean that.' Martha was horrified.

'Yes, I do, Mam.' With that, she was gone. Joyce nearly always contrived to leave her mother in a state of shock or something equally unpleasant.

Lily and Georgie had gone to bed when their dad came home, but Martha and Joe were still up. Carlo swayed, as if he were about to fall, and blinked at the flickering gas light, a look of confusion on his face, as if he didn't recognize them and thought he might be in the wrong house. He was badly in need of a shave, and smelled like a midden.

'Hello, Dad,' Joe said, and got up and went towards him, squeezing his arm.

'Joe!' His voice was so tired and wretched that Martha flinched. She should have done something about Carlo; she shouldn't have let things get so bad. But she'd tried, she remembered. She'd tried and Carlo just wasn't interested.

Joe was impressing upon his dad that the whole family were going to the theatre tomorrow and he had to clean himself up. 'Go to the baths, Dad, get a shave and a haircut, and give your suit a good going-over.'

'Yes, Joe,' his father said helplessly.

'I'll be off early in the morning looking up some old mates, but I'll leave a few bob on the table to pay for the shave and stuff. All right, Dad?'

'All right, Joe.' Carlo nodded dutifully.

For Martha, it felt like one of her biggest achievements to have done all the things Joyce had demanded, *and* have the entire family ready to go to the theatre by half past six. Mind you, she wouldn't have managed had Mister not said she could go home early – without her having to ask.

Carlo looked desperately bewildered in the suit that he'd actually taken somewhere to have sponged clean and pressed. Lily, in her dazzling pink frock, and Georgie, dressed for Sunday Mass, had managed to sort themselves out and she was really proud of them. Frank looked like one of them models in the window of a gentlemen's clothes shop, and Joe wore his Army uniform.

They were catching a tram on Scotland Road which would take them to the Rotunda, where they were meeting Joyce and Edward. All day, Martha had been so excited that she'd hardly thought about Edward, yet he was the first of her daughter's boyfriends that the family had been allowed to meet. Did this mean it was serious between him and Joyce? She supposed she'd be told soon enough.

She felt overwhelmed by the theatre, with its dark red walls and elaborate plasterwork painted black and gold. And how much, she wondered, had the crimson velvet curtains lined with cream satin that hung in such neat, even folds in front of the stage cost? Imagine having to make *them* on a sewing machine!

The Rossis had the best seats, Joyce said, the third row from the front. Edward's uncle was a friend of the manager and he'd got the seats cheap.

'It's all due to our Joe,' Joyce said. 'Everyone loves our soldiers; there's even a song about it.'

Edward seemed quite a nice young man, but there was nothing remarkable about him. Martha reckoned she was just being awkward thinking he was *too* nice, a bit oily, a touch too respectful. Mind you, the other way around and she'd think him rude. Maybe he was shy. And he wasn't nearly as handsome as Frank and Joe or as Georgie would be when he grew a bit older. Still, he was Joyce's choice. It wasn't Martha he was courting.

They had barely settled in their seats when the lights went out, the curtain rose, and two young men tumbled on to the stage, over and over, their bodies curled like balls. They were followed by another two men, then another, until the stage was full of tumbling men. Then they stopped tumbling and began to climb on top of one another, forming a tower that waved about all over the place. Martha shrieked and hid behind the seat in front in case they collapsed on top of her. She tried to pull Georgie down with her, but he pushed her away.

'Mam, they're only *pretending*,' he said in what was supposed to be a whisper, but the whole theatre must have heard.

Martha sat up. How did he know that? The people sitting behind were laughing and she felt dead embarrassed.

The next act was a man with a dancing dog. Martha

felt dead sorry for the dog. The poor little thing looked so anxious to please that she'd like to bet the man was cruel to it. When the act finished, she positively refused to clap, but sat with her arms firmly folded. Afterwards, she hoped that the man hadn't noticed; he might take it out on the dog.

After that, a woman came on, a good eighty if a day, Martha thought, and sang some dead horrible songs in a dead horrible voice. Georgie, who had a programme, said they were operatic arias. Martha resolved never to go and see an opera in her life.

She would never tell Joyce, but she didn't like the theatre. It was too noisy and they were sitting too near the front; she felt as if the Rossis were part of the performance. She'd sooner be right at the back, hidden beneath the balcony.

A man came on next who played the violin and sang and danced at the same time. Martha felt convinced that he was grinning right at her. The magician who followed wore a top hat and a black cape lined with scarlet. He didn't fool *her* by pretending to cut his pretty little assistant in half. Yet, although she knew it wasn't real, she still kept expecting blood to come pouring out of the wooden box in which he'd put the poor girl. Anyroad, real or not, it was an awful thing to do.

It wasn't much better after the interval, except for a man and woman in evening clothes dancing gracefully together. It brought back memories of the time before the children had arrived and she and Carlo had gone dancing on Saturday afternoons at the Rainbow Rooms on Scotland Road. She glanced along the row of seats to where he was sitting and, to her horror, saw there were tears in his eyes.

The final act, a tightly corseted woman in emerald green velvet with bright red hair down to her waist, was introduced as, 'The toast of London, the biggest star of them all, the one and only Maudie McCrea!'

She must have been very popular because the audience cheered wildly as the woman swayed on to the stage, blowing kisses with both hands.

'Darlings,' she said in a curiously harsh voice, 'how lovely to see you.'

'Lovely to see you, too, Maudie,' a man shouted back.

Maudie acknowledged him with a shower of kisses, then posed, one arm raised, the other extended towards the audience, and began to sing, 'If you were the only boy in the world . . .' Immediately, the audience joined in, including Joyce and Edward, who apparently knew the words.

She then sang 'Down at the Old Bull and Bush' and 'It's a Long Way to Tipperary'.

Martha had to concede she was indeed a star, taking the audience with her, making them hang on her every word. When she held up her hands, everyone fell completely silent.

'Ladies and gentlemen, we have a special guest with us tonight, a young man who is about to join our brave soldiers fighting on our behalf in France. I would like you to meet' – there was a long pause – '*Joe Rossi!*'

And there was Joe in the spotlight, being pushed to his feet by the people behind, blinking shyly, smiling nervously, looking as if he'd like the floor to open up and swallow him.

'And Joe's off to France . . .' Maudie McCrea shouted, 'when is it, Joe?'

'The day after tomorrer,' Joe replied. 'Sunday.'

'Sunday. Well, we don't want to lose you, Joe,' she began to sing, 'but we think you ought to go.' It was a famous song; Martha had heard it before.

Joe, *her* Joe, was beckoned on to the stage, while Maudie sang, 'The Boys in Khaki Get the Nice Girls'.

'Ladies and gentlemen,' she said when she'd finished and Joe was standing at her side, 'there's a recruiting sergeant in the foyer of this theatre. If there are more young lads present like this fine young chap here, then the sergeant will take your names and before you know it you'll be off to France fighting for your country.' She put her arm around Joe's shoulder and began to sing 'Keep the Home Fires Burning', and the audience sang with her, all except Martha, who didn't want her son used to sell the war to other young men. Maudie hadn't bothered to say that Joe was only fourteen and she wanted to scream the truth, but she'd make the family feel uncomfortable, Joe most of all.

At last the show was coming to a close. Maudie was cheered offstage and returned to louder applause. The audience demanded another song and she sang, 'Come into the Garden, Maud' in a highly suggestive manner and then – Martha would never forget how absolutely sickened she was – she removed her red hair and revealed herself to be a man.

While the Rossis were strolling home from the theatre, someone else was approaching King's Court from a different direction. Arthur Hanson, personal assistant to Norman Brown, Member of Parliament for Liverpool Central, had realized his employer would never become involved in anything so controversial as underage soldiers, and had approached a politician he knew who would.

Sir Arthur Markham, member for the Mansfield division of Nottingham, had taken up the cause of boy soldiers in Parliament. Arthur Hanson had approached him about young Joe Rossi, and the MP had offered to take up Joe's case, but needed written approval from one of the boy's parents before naming him in the chamber of the House of Commons.

Arthur Hanson never ceased to be shocked at the conditions under which many of his employer's constituents lived. He was aghast when he saw the state of King's Court and the pitiful people in it, including the small children still playing out at this late hour. One child, little more than a baby, with a filthy bandage covering his head, looked so miserably sick that he should surely have been in hospital.

He identified the Rossis' house and knocked on the door. When no one came, he tapped on the window. There was still no reply, so he quickly scribbled a note and pushed it through the letterbox where it landed amid the scraps of paper, bits of string, dustballs, feathers, even a couple of sea shells that had ended up in the hallway of King's Court.

When the Rossis came in, the note was blown towards the back of the house by the draught from the front door. By the next morning, it was in the back yard and had been trodden on by all the people who'd used the lavatory, and no one could have read the message had they picked it up and tried.

As for Joe Rossi, the following day he was taken by lorry to the other side of the country, and on Sunday he sailed for France.

Chapter 7

Joe had finally gone, Frank had left home again for the umpteenth time, and Joyce arrived with a message to say that Edward had liked Martha very much and he wanted to introduce her to his own mam and dad – Lily and Georgie, too. They were invited to high tea on Sunday at four o'clock at his parents' house in Spellow Lane. And, Joyce went on in a bossy tone, would Martha please buy another frock from Great Homer Street market; *she* would give her the money. The grey one looked as if the previous owner had used it to wash floors with. The hat with the red band was all right, but Lily's pink frock needed a sash, something white with pink spots or stripes. And please, on no account was she to call Edward 'Eddie'. He hated it.

'And does Edward have a surname?' Martha asked frostily. With so many instructions, it was like being invited to tea with royalty.

'Of course he has a surname. It's MacDonald.'

Martha couldn't be bothered to ask if the MacDonalds were Catholics. To tell the truth, right now she didn't care, though she might one of these days if Joyce and Edward decided to get married.

According to Joyce, Frank still owed Maggie O'Connor a few quid, having paid back more than half. Where did he get it from? Martha fretted. The reason he'd come home in a fright that day was nothing to do with money, in fact. He'd been living with a woman whose husband, a sheet music salesman, had returned home unexpectedly and found Frank upstairs in bed with his wife. It was the husband, not the money-lender, Frank had been hiding from.

Martha asked how old the woman was. 'About twenty-five,' Joyce said. 'She's very pretty, or so he told Edward.'

Frank had thought Edward would be impressed by his conquest, but instead Edward had been shocked and had told Joyce, who'd told her mother. Martha was more than shocked – scandalized would have been a better word – but Frank was her son and it was her opinion that Edward was being very old-womanish about it – and a clat-tale to boot.

Father Lawless had shown up on Sunday, but Joe had left the day before so missed a special blessing. Martha, normally the most loyal of Catholics, felt annoyed when the priest remarked that Joe would make a good soldier.

'He's not old enough to make any sort of soldier, Father,' she said sharply.

The Father had then come out with all sorts of rubbish about pride and sacrifice and it being a privilege to fight for your country. She'd almost lost her temper and had a terrible job holding it in. She felt angry most of the time, mainly with Sergeant Gilligan and the Government and with Carlo.

After the visit to the theatre, her husband had returned to being a shadow, and was in bed snoring when she left for work on Monday morning feeling very low. By now, Carlo was badly in need of a shave and she'd noticed that Joyce hadn't included him in the visit to Edward's mother on Sunday. It was a relief in a way because Martha didn't think she could be bothered polishing him up again. It was Joe who'd seen to him on Friday, but Joe had gone and all Martha wanted to do was weep. At least Lily and Georgie were there to remind her she was still needed as a mother, if not as a wife.

At dinner-time on Monday, she waited for Kate in the doorway of the pet shop, longing to see her friend again and tell her that Joe had been home. The white kitten had gone out of the window, but there was a litter of tabbies, six miniature tigers playing with each other, and she wished she could buy them all.

'But, Martha, imagine what it would be like when they're all grown up,' Kate said when she arrived and Martha expressed her yearning for the kittens. 'Six big cats wandering all over the house! You'd be forever falling over them.'

'I expect I would.' Martha sighed. And imagine having to feed them! She told Kate about Joe. 'I wish you could have met him.'

'I do, too,' Kate said earnestly. 'But never mind. There'll be another time.'

'The thing is,' Martha said tearfully, 'yesterday he sailed for France. He'll be there by now.' She hadn't the faintest idea what a foreign country would look like – she didn't count Ireland as foreign. Were the houses built the same? Did they have roads and horses and carts and motor cars like they did in England?

'Oh, Martha.' Kate threw her arms around the other woman's neck. 'I'm so sorry. But it's all a mistake, isn't it? They won't keep him there for long. I reckon he'll be back in no time.'

They strolled along towards Central station. The table they'd come to regard as their own, just inside the door, was vacant. This time, Martha insisted Kate sit down and she'd pay for the coffee and cake for a change. At the theatre, Joe had been given quite a few bob and had left most of it behind with his mother. Martha still burned with resentment at the idea of him being used to persuade other young men to join up. She described their visit to the theatre to Kate, who said it sounded really awful.

'I think the worst thing of all was this man singer pretending to be a woman. I mean, I don't see the point of it.' Martha still hadn't got over her astonishment and dismay. She considered it far worse than what their Frank had been up to. 'Anyroad,' she said, making a face, 'all that matters is our Joe's gone and I didn't manage to stop him, did I?'

'But Martha, you tried,' Kate insisted. 'You went to see that detestable police sergeant and that even more detestable politician, didn't you? And that chap from the *Lancashire Post* wrote an article, but the newspaper wouldn't publish it.'

'I'd like to read it,' Martha said, before remembering she couldn't read. Kate would have to read it for her. 'I ought to thank him. What's his name?'

'Clive Dexter. I'll see if I can bring him with me tomorrow.' He'd left a note in the college office saying he would like to see her, but Kate hadn't bothered to go. As far as she was concerned, he was a hopeless reporter who had let her and Martha down.

★

121

Kate called in the office of the *Lancashire Post* on her way back to college. The boy downstairs said his boss was in his office and to go on up.

'Shouldn't you announce me first?' Kate said sternly.

'It's not a dinner party, miss. It's a newspaper office. The boss can't refuse to see anyone in case he misses a big scoop or something.'

Kate bounded upstairs and knocked on Clive Dexter's door. He responded with a shout of 'Enter'.

'Enter?' she said scornfully when she went inside. 'Isn't it customary to say, "come in"?'

He was seated behind his desk reading a copy of his own paper. He wore a pale fawn suit with a matching waistcoat and a cream shirt. His jacket was draped over the back of a chair. She supposed he was good-looking in an insipid way. 'I think people can say whatever they like, Miss Kellaway,' he said lightly. He got to his feet and gave a little bow, and she thought, a touch reluctantly, how elegant and slim he was. 'How nice to meet you again.' He smiled sardonically. 'You are being your usual courteous self, I see. And how are your parents?' he went on. 'I liked them very much indeed.'

'Oh, they liked you, too.' Kate chuckled. 'My mother thinks you have an "interesting pallor".'

He raised his eyebrows. 'Really? I thought a pallor would be regarded as an indication of ill health; anaemia, say.'

'So did I,' Kate said, nodding cheerfully.

'Yet I feel perfectly well.'

'It just shows that appearances can be deceptive.'

'It does indeed, Miss Kellaway. Now, do sit down if you intend to stay so that I might take the load off my

122

own feet in case my pallor gets even more interesting – or maybe less. I'm not sure which I would prefer.'

Kate flopped into the chair in front of his desk, ignoring his comments. 'You left a message for me at the college,' she reminded him.

'I did indeed, and here you are – *at last*,' he finished, putting emphasis on the final two words. 'It's a good job it wasn't something frightfully important.'

'What was it, then?' she demanded in a peremptory fashion.

'I thought you would want Joe's photograph back. I didn't like to leave it in the college office in case it went astray. It's here.' He picked up a sheaf of papers with Joe's photo attached out of a filing basket on the desk. 'Would you like an envelope for it?'

'Yes, please. Is that the article you wrote? Can I read it?'

'If you wish.' He handed her the papers. 'I would like it back one day for my files. You never know, feelings might change in the country. It might be published in a different climate.'

'Would you mind if I read it here? I'm a very quick reader.' It would save having to come back at a later time.

'If you wish,' he said again, shrugging slightly. 'I'm sure you must be very quick at most things.' He returned to reading the *Lancashire Post*, while Kate started the article.

Minutes later, she raised her head and said in a small voice, 'It's marvellous. You've written it not just with your mind, but with your heart, too. I never realized it was so good. I thought, with the editor having turned it down, that it was hopeless. Is this how you really feel about the war?'

'Of course,' he snapped. 'It would be sheer hypocrisy to write like that if I didn't mean it. My editor was of the opinion it would either scare the population out of their wits or offend them.'

'I'm sorry,' she said humbly. 'I really like this bit: "Do the generals with all their medals know their war is being fought for them by children? And if they did know, would they care?" Do you think they know?'

His face darkened and his eyes burned. 'I think they know and I don't think they care. People who fight wars, the ones at the top who organize it, are all mad. What sane person would seriously sit down and make plans for men to slaughter each other? It's not as if this country had been attacked or invaded. Then there'd be an excuse and I'd be one of the first to volunteer. But *this* war!' He spread his hands in a gesture of sheer helplessness.

Kate didn't answer, just sat and stared at his enraged face while her feelings for him turned a complete somersault. He was incredibly handsome. He clearly thought deep thoughts, just as her mother had predicted, and was very knowledgeable about the war. She wondered if he'd like to come to dinner again – she'd persuade her parents to invite him. In fact, she'd like to marry him – she *wanted* to marry him.

It was only then, noticing the back of the silver-framed photograph on his desk, that she remembered he had a fiancée called Lettice.

Oh, *buttons*! She almost said the words aloud. Then she remembered something else. She hadn't told him the latest news about Joe. She coughed to gain his attention – he was clearly miles away thinking deep thoughts.

He looked at her with his dark eyes and she said, 'I've just met Martha – Joe was sent to France only yesterday.'

'That's atrocious,' he murmured. 'A boy that age.' He drummed his fingers on the desk. 'This Martha, can I meet her?'

'One of the reasons I came was to suggest it,' Kate said. 'She wants to thank you in person for the article.'

'Much good did it do.' He stared gloomily at his desk. 'It wasn't even published.'

'But even so, you tried. You tried so hard, and she did, too. You both tried.' Kate clasped her hands together, as if she were praying, in an effort to express how greatly his article had impressed her. 'Look, if you come to the café on Central station tomorrow at about quarter to one, Martha and I will be there.'

Clive Dexter said, 'Then I'll be there, too.'

After Kate had gone, Clive stood up and kicked the desk. He walked over to the window and kicked the wall, which was a stupid and painful way of getting rid of his frustration, but the best way he could think of under the circumstances.

Kate still hadn't taken the photo of Joe. He returned to his desk and picked it up. The boy looked such an innocent, probably never been kissed except by his mother. Damn and blast the people running the bloody country and this heinous war.

'What do you think about this, Letty?' He sat down and addressed the photograph of his fiancée. 'You're really enjoying this damn war, aren't you?' She worked for the Admiralty in London, sharing a flat in Mayfair with some of the other female clerks. 'All those handsome young officers to flirt with,' he said to her laughing face. She probably slept with a different one every night.

Lettice Conway was a distant cousin whom Clive had known his entire life. They'd always been the best of friends, but Clive wouldn't have married her had she come with a thousand-pound dowry, nor would she have married him. He was too dull for her, too introverted, a terrible dancer, hopeless at socializing, while he found her too loud, too much of an extrovert, totally ignorant of current affairs, and too risqué for words.

Being engaged to one another was highly convenient. It meant Clive's mother could stop keeping an eye out for an appropriate bride for her eldest son, and Letty's parents need no longer keep hoping for a suitable husband to turn up — should one exist. It also meant they didn't mind her living in London for, as her mother had said to him, 'If it doesn't worry you, Clive, dear, then why should it worry us?'

Why indeed? Though actually, Clive did worry just a bit. He admired Letty for throwing her inhibitions to the wind, but she was travelling down a dangerous path and he was concerned she would be hurt. At the same time, he was extremely glad she wasn't really his fiancée.

Clive liked Martha Rossi instantly when they met next day in the Central station café. She apologized for the state she was in. 'These are me work clothes,' she said regretfully, smoothing her soiled skirt with red, chapped hands. The skin on her fingers was sore from handling hard, rough material for several hours a day. She carried with her the strong smell of dust and sacking.

Once, she must have been very pretty, but time had taken its toll and now her skin looked tired and there were deep worry lines around her eyes and a pinched look to her mouth, though the prettiness returned when she smiled, which she did every time she talked about Joe or her other children. Her hair, what he could see of it, was dark and mostly hidden underneath a ragged scarf covering her ears and tied at the back of her head. Her eyes were a nice brown, quite large.

He presented her with a posy of pink roses mixed with scraps of fern after Miss Kellaway had introduced them. He would have brought a large bouquet, but was concerned she might not possess a vase, whereas the roses would fit in a jam jar.

She was so impressed, so grateful, gasping and marvelling, stammering her thanks. It made him wonder if she'd ever been given flowers before, but surely there'd been some at her wedding. She insisted that he call her Martha, and he said in that case she must call him Clive.

'I don't know why, but I already think of you as Martha rather than as Mrs Rossi,' he said.

'Thank you for writing the article about Joe,' she murmured. 'Kate's going to read it to me one of these days.'

'Perhaps,' he suggested, 'you could come to my office tomorrow and I could read it to you myself.' He was aware of the young woman's head jerking angrily, and hid a smile. 'Maybe you would like to come, too, Miss Kellaway?'

'Thank you, Mr Dexter. I would be pleased to,' she said in her supercilious way.

He said to Martha, 'Miss Kellaway told me you went to see the Member of Parliament for Liverpool Central, Major Norman Brown, and that he was no help.'

'No help at all,' Martha admitted with a grimace. 'He seemed to think I should be pleased Joe might end up in France where the fighting is. The truth is, he was pissed out of his brain.'

'He has the reputation of being a drinker,' Clive told her. 'If you agree, then I think the next thing to do is for me to write to the War Office on your behalf, remind them that the law is being broken and demand that Joe is sent home immediately.'

'I do agree.' Martha nodded solemnly.

'Then I shall write this afternoon,' he promised.

The next morning, Clive sent Herbert round to the The Cups in Paradise Street for beef sandwiches and a bottle of wine. 'Sweet white wine,' he said. 'It's for a lady. And while she's here, will you kindly hang around in case she asks for tea instead?' There was a stove and things to make tea and coffee in the lavatory downstairs. 'And make sure we have fresh milk.'

'Yes, boss,' Herbert said smartly. 'Is this in connection with a story you're writing?'

'If it's any of your business, Herbert, then yes, it is.' Clive said haughtily. 'It's what's called journalism. How old are you, by the way?' He guessed the lad was about Joe's age. His father, a Londoner, had come to work for the printers of the *Lancashire Post*. It was through sheer nepotism that Herbert had landed the job of Clive's assistant.

'Fourteen, boss; fifteen at Christmas.' He looked terribly pleased with himself, as if he were one of the few people ever to reach the age of fifteen.

'And how would you feel about being sent to fight in France. I mean now, straightaway?'

The boy made a ferocious face. 'I'd hate it, boss. This chap next door to us, he was sent to France and wasn't there five minutes before he was as dead as a bleedin' doornail. Shot in the head he was, poor sod.'

The boy had a colourful way of putting things. Clive was left with the impression that there was no chance of Herbert being persuaded to join the Army for any amount of shillings.

The two women arrived together. One of the few things he found likeable about the outspoken Miss Kellaway was how gentle she was with her friend, always making sure she was seated first, putting sugar in her tea, linking her arm as they walked. At least snobbery wasn't among her numerous faults.

'If you and Martha intend calling each other by your first names, then I think you and I should do the same,' Miss Kellaway said challengingly, as if she thought he was likely to object.

'That's fine with me – Kate,' Clive said affably.

He made sure they were both seated comfortably in front of his desk where the sandwiches and wine had been placed.

Martha accepted half a glass of wine. 'No more, or it'll go to me head,' she predicted. 'I've got to work this avvy. It's a pity, that all this,' she waved her hand around the office, the gesture including the sandwiches and wine, 'and meeting Kate here, had to happen because our Joe was prevailed upon to join the Army.'

'I would have much preferred we had met under different circumstances,' Clive concurred.

'Me, too,' echoed Miss Kellaway – Kate – who seemed anxious not to be left out. She also asked for only half a glass of wine as she had to go back to college.

First, Clive read aloud the letter he had written to the War Office, followed by the article that the *Lancashire Post* had turned down. Hearing it now, Clive supposed it was a bit too intemperate, too angry for a family paper to print, but he wasn't prepared to tone it down, make it less angry, just so it would be published.

As he read, Martha kept nodding, seeming close to tears. He hoped she wouldn't cry as he wouldn't know what to say. He was glad when she began to sip her wine.

Clive experienced a strange sensation as he read his own words, as if the whole world had stopped what it was doing to listen to his tirade, that traffic had ground to a halt, machines everywhere had been switched off, people had ceased talking, that his voice and his alone was the only one telling the world what a terrible mistake it was making. When he had finished reading, he almost felt that soldiers on both sides would lay down their arms, the fighting would stop and there would be peace forevermore.

But when he came to the end of the article, the sound of a horse and cart could be heard passing over the cobbled street outside, making a fine old clatter, a man shouted, a girl laughed, and downstairs Herbert was whistling as loud as a train.

Then the telephone rang, making Clive and Kate jump, but Martha almost leaped out of her seat, having never heard a similar noise before. As she explained, she hadn't even known that such a thing as a telephone existed.

But at least no one was crying. A relief, because Clive suspected he would have cried most of all.

'You never got that from a market!' Joyce exclaimed when she arrived at King's Court on Sunday afternoon and came face to face with Martha wearing a moss green silk frock with a deep V-neck, dolman sleeves, and a darker green satin cummerbund. 'It looks dead expensive.'

'It was a present,' Martha informed her.

'She got it off Kate.' Lily gave the shiny material of her mother's frock a tweak, as if just touching it gave her pleasure. 'It belonged to Evelyn, Kate's sister, who's gone to live in Nottingham. Kate said it's a bit out of date because it doesn't show enough ankle, but Mam doesn't mind.'

'Not a bit,' Martha confirmed. She'd never had such a posh dress before, not even in the old days. She was scared to move in it. The red velvet band on her straw hat had been exchanged for a green one, and she was wearing the second-hand boots with curved heels that pinched.

Joyce scowled. 'Was it Kate that gave you the sash?' she enquired of Lily, who was wearing her garish pink frock. Everyone was dressed ready to visit Edward's family in Spellow Lane.

Martha guessed Joyce didn't like Kate, though they'd never met. It was just that she resented Kate writing letters to Joe on her mother's behalf when it should have been her.

'It isn't a sash, it's a scarf.' Lily undid the band around her waist and unfolded it. Large and square, the myriad colours included bright pink. She put it on like a shawl and twirled around. 'See, it can be worn all sorts of ways.'

'Oh, very clever.' Joyce sniffed. All of a sudden, her sour look disappeared as if by magic, and she gave her sister a warm hug and a kiss. 'It looks lovely on you, Lil.' She turned to Martha. 'And that frock does on you, Mam, You really suit green.'

'Thank you, luv. Is everyone ready to leave?' she enquired. She felt dead uncomfortable about stepping out into the court all done up like a dog's dinner. People would start thinking the Rossis had come into money or something.

Mrs MacDonald had the loudest voice in the world, or so it seemed to Martha. She also possessed a shrill scream that she was apt to release for no apparent reason.

At first, Georgie was quite frightened when he was introduced and she screamed, apparently surprised at his teeth, which she insisted were extremely large for a boy of ten.

'No one's ever said that before,' Martha said, annoyed. Georgie was sheltering behind her, still shaking. She felt buoyed up by Evelyn's frock. It had given her confidence.

'They look very strong teeth,' Mr MacDonald said,

as if in excuse for his wife. He was a jovial little man with twinkling eyes and a heavily waxed moustache twirled to a point at each end. He said very little, mainly because Mrs MacDonald dominated the conversation. She was a long, thin woman with drooping eyes, a funereal expression and an overbearing manner.

The house in Spellow Lane was a large terrace with spacious rooms, though the parlour in which they were seated was packed with so much gloomy furniture that it was difficult to move. The curtains were brown velour and drawn so close together there was little space left for the sunlight to shine through. There were several pictures on the darkly papered walls of rather sinister wooded scenes in which animals of one sort or another stood around looking intensely miserable or on the verge of death.

Martha would sooner have been in King's Court where there was at least daylight. What's more, there was an unsanitary smell, as if the drains were blocked, and Mrs MacDonald's screams were giving her a headache.

'Joyce tells me your husband is an inspector on the trams,' the woman hooted, 'and that is why he was unable to come today, because he has to work most Sundays.'

'That's right.' Martha glared at her daughter. She could have at least been warned that Edward's family had been lied to.

Mrs MacDonald screamed. 'How dreadful! Oh, how I'd loathe it if my poor Reginald was forced to work on Sundays.' She looked smug. 'It is, after all, a day of rest.'

'Not for everyone,' Martha answered smartly.

'Some people have to work in hospitals or hotels or . . .' Her brain came to a halt.

'On the ferries,' Lily helped her out, 'and on trains and in restaurants.'

'Coppers work on Sundays and have to catch trams.' Georgie spoke while trying to hide his teeth.

'And some people have to catch trams to church services, dear,' Mr MacDonald pointed out in his genial manner, only to be greeted by a look of contempt from his wife, who clearly didn't enjoy losing an argument.

It was turning out to be a rather disagreeable visit. Martha resolved that from now on she would agree with everything Mrs MacDonald said, no matter what, and prayed the rest of the afternoon would pass more smoothly.

This, however, was not to be. Mrs MacDonald announced that tea would soon be ready. 'I trust everyone likes tripe and onions.'

A sort of numbness spread over the room and Georgie began to scream, the sound far exceeding the screams of their hostess in both their strength and length. His face turned red and he clung to Martha, yelling that he wanted to go home.

'All right, luv,' Martha soothed. 'All right, we'll go straight away. He's having a fit,' she explained to their hosts.

'Would the little lad like to lie down upstairs for a minute?' Mr MacDonald suggested kindly.

'No, ta. He'd be better off at home. Come along, son.' Martha tried to pick Georgie up, but he was too heavy. He began to drag her towards the door. 'I want to go, Mam.'

'Does he often have fits like this?' Mrs MacDonald enquired.

'Not very often.' She apologized profusely for the upset and left, with Lily helping to support Georgie.

As soon as they'd rounded a corner and the Mac-Donalds' house was out of sight, Georgie stopped screaming. 'I couldn't have eaten tripe, Mam,' he gasped, 'not for love nor money.'

'Neither could I.' Lily laid her hand on her heart. 'I'd sooner die than eat tripe. That was clever of you, Georgie, to pretend to have a fit.'

No matter how poor they might be, no matter how hungry, not a single member of the Rossi family was able to eat tripe.

'That's an odd thing to serve up for afternoon tea, anyroad,' Martha said crossly, 'tripe and onions. In the old days when people were invited to tea, I'd serve ham sarnies and buttered scones.'

'You were invited to *high* tea,' Joyce raged when she came round later that night, claiming her family had made a show of her, even after Martha had explained why they'd made a quick exit. '*High* tea's different altogether from afternoon tea. It includes meat or fish.'

'I'm sorry, luv, but I never knew the difference,' Martha said calmly. 'Anyroad, since when have you been able to eat tripe? And what's all this about your dad working on the trams?' The calm was deserting her and she was getting worked up. 'And where does that woman think we live? I mean, is she likely to turn up one day expecting King's Court to be like Bucking-ham Palace?'

'She thinks we live in Gerard Street.' Joyce threw herself on to the couch.

'You're going to get yourself in a proper tuck with all your lies, Joyce.'

'I know, Mam.' Joyce sighed. 'But I can't very well tell the truth, can I? I'm beginning to wish I'd told Edward I was an orphan.'

'So, you'd deny you had a mam an' all, would you? Joyce, luv,' Martha said gently, 'if you can't tell the lad the truth about yourself, it'd be best if you stopped seeing him.'

Joyce began to cry. 'I can't, Mam. I love him.'

Martha stroked her daughter's curly head. 'In that case, he'll just have to get used to your dad the way he is, and you to his mam. She's not exactly a nice woman, luv. Quite frankly, I don't like being compared to her and coming off the worse.'

'Oh, Mam, you're never worse than Mrs Mac-Donald; she's a right old cow.' Joyce sniffed and wiped her nose. 'The things people do for love, Mam.' She sighed.

'You don't know the half of it, girl.'

Chapter 8

Jacquetta had managed to talk Mister into going on holiday to the Isle of Man. 'He's a much nicer person these days,' she said to Martha. 'I think it's because of your Joe. He always wanted a son, but we never had children.'

Martha was thrilled to bits when Mister said that while he and Jacquetta were away she could have the week off – and he would still pay her wages.

'You take it easy and be brave for Joe,' he commanded, patting the top of her head. He gave her a giant key and asked if she would mind looking in on the factory a few times to make sure everything was all right. 'If not, tell bobbies and they come and fix it.'

'What are you going to do with yourself all week?' Kate asked.

'I'm going to learn to read and write,' Martha told her, sounding more confident than she felt.

Kate looked distressed. 'But if I don't have to write to Joe any more, there'd be no more need for us to be friends.'

'Don't be daft, girl,' Martha snorted. 'We're already friends and we won't stop just because I can write me own letters to me own son, will we?'

It was the final week of Lily and Georgie's school holiday. The previous weeks had been spent wandering around Liverpool, either by themselves or with their mates. They left the house early with a bottle of water and a couple of rounds of bread and marge, spending hours down by the Pier Head, playing on the steps of St George's Hall or in Lime Street station, where they watched the great trains thunder in and out. When Martha could spare them a few coppers, they caught the ferry across the river to Birkenhead, Seacombe or New Brighton, and wandered around there instead before sailing back home.

As Carlo rarely left the house before midday, the ideal place for Martha to learn to read and write was Ackerman's Sacks and Sails where she would be left entirely alone and undisturbed.

Apart from Kate, she told no one that Mister and Jacquetta had gone away. On Monday, she left the house at the normal time, taking with her *Miss Flower's ABC Book* that had been bought for Joyce when she started school and now belonged to Lily. Unlike the girls, not one of her lads had ever shown any real interest in learning, though Joe and Frank could read and write well enough. As for Georgie, he was hopeless. Martha had also brought Joe's letters, a halfpenny exercise book, a pencil, and a kitchen knife to sharpen it with. She set everything out at the end of the long table with the sewing machines at the other end and began work.

Joe always started his letters 'Dear Mam' and signed them 'Your loving son, Joe'.

Martha opened the exercise book and printed 'Dear

Joe' very carefully at the top of the first page and 'Your loving Mam' at the bottom. Now all she had to do was fill in the middle. She felt as if she were already halfway there.

After a great deal of deliberation, she concluded that if she removed the first letter from 'dear' she would be left with 'ear'. She felt exhilarated by this discovery, though it didn't help with writing the letter.

Turning to another page of the notebook, she wrote her own, her husband's and her children's names, along with Rossi. After more deliberation and saying the names out loud, stressing the sounds, she returned to the letter and wrote, 'Miss yu Joe', after which she came to a halt. If the last letter was removed from Frank and replaced with two out of 'Rossi', it would make Franss. She wanted to ask Joe if he liked being in France, but didn't know how. She wrote 'Franss' anyroad, just to see what it looked like.

Leaning back in the chair, she studied the rough wooden planks above. Like a giant shelf, taking up half the area of the building, it was where the sails used to be made. The only sound was that of seagulls squawking angrily on the roof. Noises seemed to echo now that the place was empty except for her. She coughed and the sound repeated itself until eventually it faded. It was scary, yet she was revelling in the strangeness of being there, light-headed at the idea of having absolutely nothing to do except please herself. Not a soul in the world was expecting anything from her.

She went into Mister's office, tiptoeing for some reason. It was a small area without a door or window, and lined with dusty metal shelves full of old newspapers, books and cardboard boxes. She walked around the room, examining everything, but it mostly meant nothing to her. A heap of white paper had Ackerman's Sacks and Sails printed at the top — she knew what the words meant because the same ones were on the street door.

Half a dozen pencils of various lengths lay haphazardly on the desk, as well as a book with a colourful cover, a tin of tobacco and a box of matches, a packet of snuff, a very old shrivelled apple and a rusty tray holding bottles of alcohol. There was a clock on the wall big enough for a railway station. It chimed the half-hour.

Martha sat on a padded chair full of loose springs in front of the desk and tried to pull the cork out of one of the bottles to taste it, but the cork was too tight to be moved and she wouldn't have dreamed of forcing it. She sniffed it instead and it made her sneeze. Like the cough earlier, the sound wavered in the air until it became nothing.

She took a piece of the white paper over to the table where she'd been sitting and copied Ackerman's Sacks and Sails into the notebook. She noticed if you put the first letter from Sacks in front of Ackerman it became Sackerman. Now she knew how to spell 'and', so she wrote it on the page of her letter to Joe. It now read: 'Dear Joe mis yu Franss and your loving Mam.'

Martha smiled. It didn't make sense, but before the week was out she was determined to write a whole letter. Then she'd have to wait for a letter to come from Joe before she would know where in France to send it.

The ABC book had a flower for each letter. In the afternoon, Martha copied the letters into the notebook, giving each one a page to itself, and a new word instead of a flower. 'And' went under A, but she didn't know a word beginning with B. She put Carlo under C, Frank under F, Georgie under G, Joe and Joyce under J, Lily under L, and herself under M. She wrote Sacks and Sails under S and, as an afterthought, wrote Kate under K, and Edward on the E page.

When she'd finished, the book was looking impressively full. She flicked through it several times; it gave her a feeling of satisfaction that she'd actually written it herself.

For the rest of the day she just stared into space until it was time to leave. She felt as light as a feather, as if the slightest puff of wind would blow her away.

On her way home, she bought half a dozen faggots to have with the spuds she'd already prepared. After they'd eaten, she asked Lily to write words in the notebook by the empty letters.

'Empty letters, Mam,' Lily laughed. 'There's no such thing as an empty letter.'

'Empty page then, Little Miss Know All.' Martha wanted to laugh, too. 'I mean, what's this letter called?'

'That's a B, Mam. B is for bat, like you play bat and ball with. I'll draw one, shall I? Then you'll always know how it sounds.'

'Let me draw the bat,' Georgie demanded. His delicate little face lit up. 'Our Lily can write it. I like drawing, Mam.'

The next empty page was D, and Georgie drew a dog and Lily wrote the word underneath in big letters.

The three of them went through the entire alphabet together. When they came to Z for zoo, Georgie drew a collection of little animals behind bars. He was turning out to be a clever little drawer.

Lily offered to write the letter for Joe, but Martha insisted she would do it herself. 'I'm thirty-six years old, girl. It's about time I learned to write a letter on me own.'

'I'll treasure this for ever,' she said afterwards when they'd finished, clutching the cheap little notebook to her breast. Even if she knew all the words in the world, there still wouldn't be enough to describe how much she loved her kids.

The next day Martha wrote a few more words of her letter to Joe. Then, aware of how free she was to do anything she chose, she left the factory, locked it, and walked down to the Pier Head where she sat on a bench and stared at the sparkling water with its occasional frill of white. The sky was just as sparkling, though there was a touch of a chill in the air and she wished she'd brought her shawl.

It was September. Lily and Georgie were due back at school on Monday. She wondered where Joe was in France. Not that she'd recognize the name of the place if she was told. Then she wondered what would happen when Joe came back.

Just how much longer was she prepared to put up with Carlo's behaviour? Until he died? Or she died? Lily and Georgie deserved more than spuds and a couple of faggots for their tea. They deserved a better home, too, with proper bedrooms, a lavatory of their own, a place to play, somewhere nice to invite their friends.

Martha closed her eyes, clenched her fists, and took

a silent oath. She had no idea how she would manage it, but she was determined that one day soon things would be better for her children.

Joe's letter now read:

> My dear Joe,
> how are yu too day in Franss.
> Mister send lov.
> Lily and Georgie send lov too.
> Miss yu Joe.
>   Your loving Mam.

On Thursday, she walked as far as William Brown Street and entered the dead posh library where she sat in a grand room surrounded by shelves and shelves of books that must contain millions of words altogether. She breathed in their smell and sensed their magic. As soon as she had learned to read, she would join the library and borrow a book every single week.

Friday was her last free day. Having a whole half-crown saved for this very purpose, she took Lily and Georgie to New Brighton. They went early on the ferry while a mist still hung over the river and the sun shone through a veil of cloud. The excited children ran from one side of the boat to the other, the cries as shrill and sharp as those of the gulls that hovered over the water in search of food.

On their arrival in New Brighton, Martha bought three cups of tea from a stall at the end of the landing stage. They drank it, staring back across the dark silver river and at the enormous tower with its magnificent gardens, which they were about to explore. Her stomach wriggled with pleasure at the thought of the day ahead.

'I wish our Joe could have come with us,' Georgie said with a sigh.

'If Joe was home, he'd be at work delivering groceries for Mr Johnson,' Lily reminded him.

'Well, at least we'd be able to tell him tonight where we'd been,' her brother argued.

Martha hadn't been to New Brighton Tower since the old days. She remembered seeing a Wild West exhibition with real cowboys and Indians, and she and Carlo had foxtrotted in the great ballroom.

Now, it was nearing the end of the holiday season and everywhere was quiet. Not many people were in the gardens, which meant Lily and Georgie had plenty of room to skip along the paths, asking their mother the names of the exotic plants; she didn't know a single one apart from something that might possibly have been a palm tree.

'I'm dead ignorant, I am,' she moaned, and suggested they went up the lift to the top of the tower to see the Isle of Man in the distance. It cost sixpence, but children went for free.

But when they arrived at the entrance to the tower, Lily read a notice to say visitors were banned from entering for 'military reasons'.

'What do they think we'd do up there, Mam?' she asked, but Martha didn't know the answer to that, either.

At midday, by which time the sky had become bluer, the sun appeared to be larger and the air warmer, a band began to play somewhere, so they tracked down the red and gold-suited musicians to a little bandstand in an area surrounded by trees and wooden seats. They sat for a long time, listening to the band play stiff marching music.

In one of the pauses between tunes, Martha heard Georgie's belly rumbling, and reckoned it was about time she bought him and Lily something to eat. There were restaurants within the tower grounds, but they looked expensive. They'd best go somewhere more ordinary for a meal.

'I think a plate of fish and chips would go down very nicely,' she said. For herself, she was dying for a cup of tea and some bread and marg – no, not marg, butter, *real* butter. Her own belly growled powerfully at the thought.

After the meal, they went for a gentle walk on the sands to allow the food to settle. The children took off their shoes and socks, and paddled in the frothy water – Lily complained it was 'as cold as snow'. Martha began to fill her pockets with seashells and pretty-coloured pebbles to take home and put in a glass jar on the window sill as a memento of their day in New Brighton.

Her pockets full, the children with their shoes and socks back on, they returned to the tower, this time to the fairground where she had just enough money left for Lily and Georgie to have a ride on the switchback railway, buy three ice-cream cornets, and pay for the return ferry.

Martha sailed home, a child tucked on either side – Georgie's head laid on her knee and Lily's resting on her shoulder – their bodies warm and precious against her own. Close to sleep herself, she lazily watched the sun, poised like a flaming ball in the dusky sky, as it slowly dipped towards the horizon, its blurred reflection dancing in the darkening waters of the river.

They arrived at King's Court to find a letter from Joe. Lily read it aloud.

Dear Mam,

    It's funny in France, only because its hardly any different to England. We landed in a place called Calais and went in lorries to a camp no distance away in the countryside. When they see us, the people shout, 'Vive les Anglais', which means 'Long live the English'. Everywhere is flat and green with cattle grazing in the fields, just like in England. The cows and sheep are just the same as in England, too.

    The camp doesn't have any proper buildings, only tents. Me and the other lads sleep in a tent and there's a really big one for eating and going to Mass and leckchers. Even the lavvies are in a tent . . .

'What's a lekcher, Mam?' Georgie enquired.

'I've no idea, luv.'

Lily said she didn't know, either. She continued reading.

Anyroad, all of us in the camp are youngsters and there's talk of us being sent home because we're underage and shouldn't be here in the first place.

    So, you never know, I might be seeing everyone a lot sooner than you think.

    Your loving Joe.

When Lily finished, Georgie cheered. 'Sooner than we think, he said. 'We might be seeing our Joe sooner than we think.'

Martha could have sworn she could feel her heart grow bigger with happiness. Other than the arrival of Joe himself, his letter was the best possible way of ending what had been an absolutely perfect day.

On Monday, she waited for Kate in the doorway of the pet shop and waved the letter in her face. 'It's from our Joe in France,' she chortled.

Kate clapped her hands. 'I can't wait to read it!' She grabbed Martha's hand. 'But let's get our coffee first.'

Five minutes later in the Central station café she raised her eyes from the letter. 'He might be coming home soon,' she said, face glowing. 'Oh, Martha, that would be wonderful.'

'I can hardly believe it,' Martha sang. 'Last night, I couldn't sleep. All I could think of was Joe. As soon as he comes, I'll have that sodding uniform off him before you can say "Jack Robinson", and into his old clothes. And if the war's still on when he's eighteen, I'm going to tie him to the furniture so there's no chance of him getting out the door.'

'But what about your Frank?' Kate reminded her. 'He's seventeen, isn't he? Wouldn't you mind if he joined up?'

'Of course I'd mind, but our Frank's the sort who knows what side his bread is buttered.' She didn't want to explain exactly what Frank was up to at the moment. 'He's not the type to go joining armies for a measly shilling a day and take the risk of being injured – even killed.' She shivered at the idea that either of those things might have happened to Joe. But not now that he was coming home.

★

Martha had hardly been gone a minute when someone slid into the seat she had vacated. 'You look pleased about something, Miss Kellaway,' Clive Dexter remarked. He looked incredibly smart in a donkey-brown tweed suit and a Paisley cravat.

'That's because Joe is coming home, Mr Dexter,' Kate said, stifling her feelings of pleasure and surprise at his unexpected arrival.

'That's good news.' He smiled, but she suspected his heart wasn't in it. He was just pretending to be nice. Oh, but she loved him! Her stomach was turning cartwheels at the nearness of his pale, handsome face, his quirky lips, the fine nose that was neither too long nor too short, just absolutely perfect. She called in the office at college so many times a day to see if he'd perhaps left her a message that it had become embarrassing. There hadn't been a single message, either.

'Were you looking for me?' she asked.

His reply wasn't exactly flattering. 'Sort of. I was really looking for Martha. Has she gone, or are you expecting her?'

'She's gone.'

'I just wondered if my letter to the War Office has produced a result.'

'If it had, I'm sure Martha would have mentioned it to me. She has, though, had a letter from Joe in France.'

'And he told her he's coming home?'

She nodded and wished he was interested in her as he was in Joe and Martha. And weren't they now supposed to be on first name terms? She certainly had no intention of calling him Clive while he continued to address her as Miss Kellaway.

He rubbed his hands together joyfully. 'When he does – come home, that is – I shall arrange a party for him.' He looked at her kindly. 'You are, of course, invited, Miss Kellaway.'

'Thank you, Mr Dexter.' Throw a party for Joe and invite *her*. How terribly kind of him! If it hadn't been for *her*, he wouldn't have known Joe existed. What an irritating person to fall in love with, she thought tragically.

'Which reminds me,' he continued, 'I must write to your parents and invite them to dinner soon. Or perhaps Sunday lunch would be preferable. Ormskirk is a long way to drive in the dark. And it is already getting darker earlier and earlier. Had you noticed?'

Kate nodded numbly. Across the café, a row of little gas lamps had been lit at the back of the counter, the flames burning steadily and reflected like stars in the mirror behind. They looked pretty, but reminded her of winter and Christmas not being too far away. Soon, she would have to start buying presents, something she normally enjoyed, but not this year. In fact, she enjoyed every part of the year; winter giving way to spring; spring heralding in the beautiful summer; summer leading to autumn; and, suddenly, winter again with the air crisp and clean. She adored snow, putting up Christmas decorations and wearing her mother's grey astrakhan jacket and matching hat, which made her feel like foreign royalty.

Now everything had been spoiled – all because she'd fallen in love with this hateful individual sitting opposite.

'When I invite your parents for a meal, would you like to come, too, Miss Kellaway?' he enquired. 'If I remember rightly, when I had dinner at your house, you didn't seem very pleased at my presence.' He gave her a forgiving smile. 'But I am not one to bear a grudge. You are welcome to feel included in my invitation should you wish.'

'Thank you, Mr Dexter, but on Sundays I usually visit my friends in . . . in . . . all over the place. Thank you, though, for your invitation; it is appreciated.'

Sometimes she was her own worst enemy.

Chapter 9

When Martha returned to the factory after seeing Kate, Mister and Jacquetta were in the throes of an apparently good-natured argument. Jacquetta was speaking quickly in a high-pitched voice in a language Martha didn't understand, while Mister replied more slowly in English.

'Stop worrying,' Martha heard him say when she went into the building. From Jacquetta's gabbled reply, accompanied by a dramatic shrug, Martha guessed she'd muttered something like, 'On your own head be it!' a phrase she often used herself, usually when talking to Frank.

The pair had enjoyed themselves on the Isle of Man. Mister had bought himself a walking stick with a handle in the shape of a bird, Jacquetta said, and a frilly parasol for her. 'We went for a stroll each morning along the front in Douglas,' she boasted, 'Mister with his walking stick, and me wearing my best bonnet and carrying my new parasol. We felt very grand.'

'And so you should,' Martha agreed. She visualized the striking couple walking along arm in arm, turning many heads. She recalled that it had always been Carlo's intention that they visit the Isle of Man where one of his cousins, Freddy, had an ice-cream parlour, but after 'the accident' he had lost contact, not just with the cousin, but with his relatives in Italy, including his mother.

She had shown Joe's letter to Mister and he had read it three times, his smile getting wider with each reading. He seemed to care more about Joe than Joe's own father. Yesterday, she'd left the letter on the table for Carlo to read, but he hadn't mentioned it, so she had no idea if he'd read it or not.

That evening, when she arrived in King's Court, Martha discovered she had a visitor. Arthur Hanson, who worked for Major Norman Brown, Member of Parliament for Liverpool Central, was being entertained by Lily and Georgie.

He got to his feet when she went in and bowed formally from the waist down. She felt doubly embarrassed; to appear before him in her old working clothes was bad enough, but for him to see the disgusting place that had been her home for ten long years was even worse.

'You have two very charming children, Mrs Rossi,' he remarked before Martha had had a chance to apologize for any aspect of her life. 'Lily has made me a cup of tea and Georgie has been drawing pictures that shall go on the walls of my office tomorrow.' He slipped a few sheets torn out of Georgie's drawing pad into his leather bag.

Martha smiled weakly. He seemed so nice, so sincere, and the children appeared to be quite enamoured with him. She wondered what on earth he was doing there. She indicated he should sit down again and seated herself on a stool.

'Did you get the note I left . . . when was it?' He

frowned. 'Oh, several weeks ago now. I knocked, but there was no one in so I put it through the letterbox.'

'It probably got lost.' She felt guilty for not keeping the hallway clean, but it was the responsibility of everyone in the house, not just her. The other tenants just waded through the rubbish until Martha attacked the place with a broom about once a month. She recalled Kate had sent a postcard that must have gone the way of Arthur Hanson's note.

'I thought something like that might have happened. In the note, I asked for your written approval for Sir Arthur Markham MP to raise Joe's case on the floor of the House. He has expressed his willingness to do so, having taken the scandal of boy soldiers to his heart.'

'I would have approved, except there's no need now. You see, I've actually had a letter from Joe himself; he's coming home.' Martha could feel the blood coursing more quickly and warmly through her veins at the thought. She took the letter out of her pocket. 'Would you like to read it?'

'I would indeed. Thank you.'

She handed him the letter and watched as he scanned Joe's words. He had such a nice, friendly face and obviously cared about her son. She remembered how impressed she'd been when they'd first met.

'I've heard of the camp for youngsters near Calais,' he said. 'Well, let's hope Joe is back in England soon.'

'We can't wait,' Lily said with a happy sigh.

'None of us can,' Martha said.

'He is a lucky young man,' the visitor said cordially, 'having such a loving family to come home to. Money, fine houses and good food are of great importance to some people, but nothing matters more than a home full of love, and that is what you have here, Mrs Rossi.' He stood once again. 'I shall leave you now to get on with your evening meal. But if I can ever be of any assistance in the future, please do not hesitate to come and see me.' He walked towards the door, where he paused, 'Good-bye, children. Thank you for the tea and drawings.'

'Tara, Mister Hanson,' Lily and Georgie chorused.

Martha went with him to the front door and showed him out.

'I'm glad Joe is coming back,' he said on the step. 'The situation in France, already bad, is looking worse than ever. The feeling is that another big battle is looming.' He reached for her hand and shook it. 'Joe will be much better off here.'

With that, he was gone. For a little while, Martha watched the children playing in the court. No account had been taken by their mothers of the coldness of the day. Little Tommy Mahon, his bandage long gone, wore nothing but a grubby vest much too big for him. She quickly closed the door, her own happiness too precious to be ruined by such a sight. Instead, she crossed herself and thanked God for sending her son back to the family that loved him.

By Christ, it went dark much earlier than was natural in this godforsaken country. Sergeant Reggie Moules shivered as he extended his hands towards the pathetic fire in the kitchen of the otherwise deserted farm-house. There was too much fuel and not enough grate – no, it was the other way around – too much grate and not enough fuel to fill it. The little firewood that was left would be gone in a couple of hours and it was too dark to go searching for more. Tomorrow, he'd get up early . . .

He sighed. He'd been dropped off at the farmhouse a few days before with a field radio, and told the farm was now a communications centre. A bloody joke if ever there was one. There was no telephone in the damn place and the radio signal was piss poor. No one had bothered to leave him a vehicle of any sort. Mind you, he'd never learned to drive, but was willing to have a go. What was he supposed to do with any message that might come through once someone remembered a communications centre had been set up close to a village called St Omer between Calais and Loos?

There were a couple of old bikes in a barn outside, but if he took off on a bike with a message, who would look after the wireless? Anyway, he'd never been good at riding bikes, not even as a kid. Turn the pedals more than a couple of times and he was exhausted. And what would happen if there were *two* messages meant to go in different directions? There was fighting taking place in the direction of Loos, and a camp full of kids in Calais waiting to be sent back to Blighty. He was seriously in need of staff, not only to help run the place, but for company, too, along with more food, fuel, clean clothes, books, brown ale, a pack of cards, and a black-haired woman with breasts like footballs who was partial to forty-year-old bald men with pot bellies.

He went over to the window and looked out. Flat, flat, everywhere as flat as a bloody pancake; the sky a mottled grey blanket. Not a hill to be seen, just the odd skeletal tree, the occasional farmhouse. No lamp posts, no lights in windows, no people, no moon. As soon as the grey sky turned black he would start worrying he'd gone blind, as nothing at all could be seen from the windows. The view was just about as different from the one back home in Bolton as a view could be.

'Bloody hell!' He groaned out loud, but the groan ended in a grin. Back in Bolton he had a wife, Emily, and he'd sooner be living in this dark, deserted, barely furnished, extremely cold farmhouse, even if he never saw a human being again, than be with Emily. After all, it was to escape his wife that he'd joined the Army in the first place.

'Joe Rossi? Is Private Joseph Rossi present at this time?' a voice yelled. 'Rossi? Private Joe Rossi?'

'Here, Corpy.' The voice continued to yell and Jo to reply until he and its owner, Corporal Horace Miller, came face to face in the mess where the midday meal was almost over.

'Oh, there you are, Rossi,' the corporal said, clearly irritated, as if Joe had been trying to avoid him. He was a short, slight individual with a bushy moustache and a permanent frown. 'Is it true you used to deliver groceries on a bike for a living?'

'Well, not exactly for a living, Corpy.' It wouldn't have been much of a living, existing on a few bob a week. 'It just happened to be me job.'

'Isn't that the same thing?'

Joe wasn't prepared to argue the point. 'I suppose so,' he conceded.

'In that case, follow me.'

'Where are we going, Corpy?'

'If you follow me, lad, you'll know.'

'This is him, Sergeant Moules,' the corporal said a good five minutes later after they'd shoved themselves through the slowly emptying marquee. 'This is Private Joe Rossi. He's an intelligent lad, he reads books, and knows a bit about the footy – what team is it you support, lad?'

'Everton,' Joe said proudly.

'Are you a scouser, Joe?' The sergeant enquired.

'Yes, Sarge,' Joe replied, even more proudly.

'What books have you read?'

'Some of the Sherlock Holmes ones and I'm halfway through *Pickwick Papers*.' Mr Houghton from King's Court had given it him. He didn't tell the sergeant that it was a bit of a struggle. Unlike the Sherlock Holmes books, in *Pickwick Papers* nothing much happened. So far, no one had been murdered.

'Good lad,' Sergeant Moules said approvingly. 'I've read them meself, but not when I was your age. How old are you, by the way?'

'Eighteen, Sarge,' Joe lied promptly.

'Pull the other one, lad, it's got bells on. You wouldn't be in this 'ere camp if you was eighteen.'

'Fourteen then, sarge.'

'When is 'is lot being sent home?' Sergeant Moules asked the corporal.

'No idea, I'm afraid, Sergeant. We're waiting for notification from HQ.'

'It could well be arriving at the communications centre right now,' the sergeant remarked drily. 'If I could borrow Joe for a few days until I get someone permanent, would that be all right? There's a couple of bikes on the farm and he could take messages for me.'

'I'd like that, Sarge,' Joe said eagerly. The camp was boring, with nothing to do most of the day except listen to lectures, usually on some aspect of religion or hygiene. There'd been one about keeping away from scarlet women that had been dead funny. 'But what about me mate, Albert Lloyd? I can't go and leave Albie behind.'

'You'll do as you're told, Rossi,' the corporal snapped, but Sergeant Moules said easily, 'Let Albie come if he wants, Corporal. He can keep the farmhouse clean, help with the cooking, like. To tell the truth, I'm a lazy bugger; not used to looking after meself. Now if you can get both the lads' papers ready within the next couple of hours, I'd appreciate it. I got a lift here this morning on a supply lorry and it's going back around half past three.' The sergeant turned his humorous gaze on Joe. 'And as for you, young fellow, you and your mate Albie can go and pack your kit.'

Joe loved being a messenger. He loved the emptiness of the countryside as he sped through it. It gave him a feeling of freedom that he'd never had before, as if he were the only person in the world. His favourite time of day was early morning with the sun wet on the horizon – he could actually *see* the horizon, which he never could in Liverpool – and the trees and hedges dripping dew, everywhere smelling fresh and earthy and natural, the way he imagined the world had smelled right at the beginning of time before factories had been built and pumped smoke into the sky.

His destination was usually a place called Loos where the war was being fought, or the camp in which he'd lived with Albie. He only rarely came across another vehicle, and it was usually a military one, British or French. The passengers and Joe would be as excited at the sight of each other, and there'd be a great deal of cheering and hooting of the horn. Joe would get off his bike and wave until the vehicle was out of sight and his arm felt ready to drop off.

Occasionally, he would meet a horse with a single rider, or a couple of animals pulling a trailer of agricultural machinery, like ploughs and other stuff. These belonged to the French, most of whom had vacated the farmhouses and cottages that he passed, not surprising as the German Army wasn't too far away. A few French had stubbornly stayed to look after their land so it wouldn't become overgrown.

He couldn't wait to tell his mam about his adventures as a messenger. He kept meaning to write her a letter, but his nights were taken up with playing cards with Sergeant Moules and Albie, swapping stories of their lives back in good old Liverpool and Bolton, and discussing the footy. Sarge had a fiend of a wife called Emily, who had 'nagged the flesh off his bones' back in Bolton.

Whenever he reached his destination, he was always warmly welcomed by the staff. There was a camaraderie between the soldiers, a warmth, the feeling that they were all in this together, and it was taken for granted that they'd be the best of friends. Joe was usually taken under someone's wing and provided with a mug of tea and a meal – whatever the men were about to eat or had just eaten – then sent back to the communications centre in St Omer.

One morning, a fortnight after he'd been transferred – the days he and Albie had been borrowed for having stretched into weeks – he was on his way back, when he was overtaken by a nagging thirst and resolved that the next farmhouse he came to he would stop and ask for a drink, if there was anyone living there. It was more likely that it would be empty, in which case he would help himself to water from the tap in the yard.

The next place was a tumbledown house with a few buildings at the back. There were curtains on the window, but no one appeared to answer Joe's knock. As expected, there was a tap round the back. He was helping himself to mouthfuls of cold water when he heard a noise, a sort of pathetic hiccup.

Having quenched his thirst, he looked for the source of the sound and, to his horror, found the owners of the house had not only left their dog behind, but had left it tied to a post outside a small barn. It was a collie, but at first it appeared to be merely a heap of white and golden brown hair thrown on the stony ground.

Joe knelt beside it. 'Hello, old chap,' he whispered.

The dog opened its bloodshot eyes with an effort and made the same hiccupping sound as before.

'Well, I can't leave you here, can I?' He picked the animal up — it felt as light as a feather. It rolled over in his arms until it was lying there like a baby, and rewarded him with a nuzzle on his chin. 'But how am I going to get you back?' He couldn't very well ride his bike while carrying a dog.

He took the creature over to the tap and let a trickle of water run into its mouth. It swallowed until exhausted.

'Now let's see what's in the barn,' he said.

The barn had only three walls and half a roof. It contained a collection of rusty implements like spades and hoes and rakes — and a roughly made wheelbarrow with a single wooden wheel. Ideal!

Obviously, the dog would have to be tied to the wheelbarrow, otherwise it would fall out, which meant he'd need rope, including enough to tie it to the bike so that he could pull it. He noticed a clothes-line strung across the yard that would do nicely.

He decided to go inside the house and see what else he might find. He laid the dog in the wheelbarrow and informed it he was going to look for some blankets to make it more comfortable. 'And I'll bring you a piller if there is one.'

Not surprisingly, the back door of the house turned out to be locked when he tried it, but Joe, angrier than he had ever been before at the idea of leaving an animal behind to die alone of starvation, just gave the door an outraged kick. It opened immediately.

It was a miserable place, dark and dirty, not that it bothered him. He searched the kitchen for anything that might do for the communications centre, but the drawers and cupboards were empty. Upstairs was the same, apart from a couple of tatty blankets and a pile of old shoes and dirty clothes.

'This is all I could find,' he told the dog as he wrapped it in one of the blankets. The other he folded and put in the wheelbarrow for the animal to lie on. He took down the clothes-line and wound it around the wheelbarrow, the dog and the blanket, then tied everything to the saddle support on the bike.

'Ready?' he asked.

The dog hiccupped and they set off.

Sarge and Albie were waiting by the farmhouse gate when Joe and his passenger arrived after a long, slow and bumpy journey.

'Where the hell have you been, lad?' Sergeant

Moules demanded tetchily. 'We've been dead worried about you. Haven't we, Albie?'

But Albie was too interested in the dog to hear. 'I think he's dead,' he announced after a brief examination.

'He'd better not be.' Joe hoped the ride hadn't done for the poor creature. He undid the ropes and carried the animal into the house. 'Put some water in a bowl on the floor,' he told Albie. 'Let's see if he can drink it.'

The dog managed a few noisy laps of water before collapsing back on to the blanket. 'What should I do now?' he asked Sergeant Moules. 'We never had a dog in our house.'

'I think we should put it by the fire with the blanket over it,' the sergeant advised, 'not too near, though, and leave the water within reach so it can drink whenever it feels like it. We'll put some food there, too, some bits of bread. In fact, it might be a good idea to put the bread in the water to soak. Tomorrow, it might be feeling better and can have a proper meal.'

'We'll have to give him a name, too,' Joe said. 'We can't just keep calling it "it".' Albie was sitting on the floor beside the dog saying a Hail Mary for its safe recovery.

The sergeant regarded the animal thoughtfully. 'It's not a he, it's a she, and I suggest we call her Emily after me wife. I really fancy pissing an Emily about for a change, even if she isn't human. Oh, all right, I won't piss her around,' he said when he saw Joe's alarmed face. 'But I can at least give her orders. That'd be enough.'

The next few weeks were the best of Joe's life. The three of them – four if you counted Emily, who became as fit as a fiddle in no time – got on really well with one another. Albie, who'd always been a bit unsure of himself and had often needed Joe to stand up for him at school as well as a few times since they'd joined the Army, became more outgoing and confident. Sergeant Moules was a self-confessed lazy bugger, so it was Albie who did all the cooking and cleaning and took Emily for a run around the fields. Occasionally, he accompanied Joe on the other bike. At first, Joe had had to leave him behind about halfway and catch up with him on the way back, but Albie, like Joe, was fitter than he'd ever been and soon acquired enough energy to ride almost as far and as fast as his friend.

Joe started to write a letter to his mam; she'd hardly be able to believe the sort of life her son was living, but he never seemed to have the time to finish it.

Sergeant Moules liked throwing sticks for Emily. 'Fetch,' he would cry. 'There's a good girl. Bring the stick back to your master.'

The sergeant was also having the time of his life, but he knew it wouldn't last. There was a war on, a pretty bad one, and it weren't right that he or anyone should be enjoying it. He didn't know if the lads had noticed, but if you went upstairs as far as the attic when it was dark and looked through the window in the direction of Loos, the sky was a horrible, malevolent shade of red, mixed with black smoke and bursts of orange when something exploded. And if you opened the window and listened hard, the rumble of gunfire could be heard and – the sergeant was convinced – the screams of the dying.

It was another typical September day, a Sunday, slightly colder than the one before, with a bleary sun and the air fresh and fizzy enough to take your breath away. Appropriately, a telephone had been installed in the communications centre, and, before Joe and Albie set off for Loos with pages of battle orders, Sergeant Moules did what he did every day and contacted the camp in Calais on the field telephone to make sure it wouldn't be the day the lads would be going back to England.

'They said it'll probably be next weekend when you pair will be sent home,' he informed them that particular morning. A small downstairs room had been turned into an office. An armchair had been moved in and a log fire burned in the grate. Emily lay in front of it, her long nose resting on her paws, thinking deep thoughts.

Joe and Albie looked at each other and shrugged. They were enjoying themselves too much to think about home.

They left after breakfast with a wad of messages for three different locations in Loos. 'Things are going badly over there,' Sarge said grimly.

Joe often heard the sounds of battle when he was in the area, but had decided not to think about that, either.

Sarge came to the door of the farmhouse to wave them off. He didn't have kids of his own and it was like having a family.

'Tara,' he shouted as the lads rode away. Both raised an arm and waved without turning around. 'Tara,' he shouted again, but they could no longer hear. He watched until he could hardly see them any more, then returned indoors. He wasn't an imaginative man, more a down-to-earth, quite dull individual, so he had no idea why he should have the feeling that he would never see his lads again.

Chapter 10

At around the time Joe and Albie were on their way to Loos, Kate Kellaway woke up with a feeling that something unpleasant was going to happen that day. She squeezed her eyes and tried to remember what it was. It came to her after a few seconds: her parents were going to lunch with Clive Dexter in Southport.

But, due entirely to her own utter foolishness, she wasn't going with them.

'I wonder why he hasn't asked you, too, dear?' her mother had said one morning last week when the post, including Clive's invitation, had arrived while they were having breakfast. 'I think that's rather rude. I've a good mind to turn ours down. Let's see what your father has to say.'

'He invited me,' Kate felt obliged to tell her, 'but I told him I would be busy.' Idiot that she was.

Her mother frowned as she sliced the top off her boiled egg. 'What exactly will you be busy doing at lunch-time a week on Sunday?'

'Dress-making,' Kate improvised. She'd completely gone off her own egg. 'I've decided to make myself a winter coat. Bright red with brass buttons.'

Her mother looked vaguely horrified. 'It sounds hideous, dear. It'll look ghastly on you – on anybody.'

'Thanks for the encouragement, Mother.' Kate had no intention of making a red coat, yet at the same time felt stung by the criticism.

'What a strange girl you are, Kate Kellaway,' her mother observed affectionately. 'When I write to accept his invitation, shall I say you've changed your mind?'

'*No!*' She shoved her spoon into the egg with such force that it broke through the bottom and all the yolk ran out. 'Don't you dare. I have no wish to go to lunch with Clive Dexter.'

Her mother must have decided to lay all her cards on the table. 'Actually, Kate, I quite fancy him for a son-in-law,' she confessed, quite openly. 'He's ever such a nice young man who clearly comes from a good family.'

Kate abandoned the egg and stuffed a piece of bread and butter in her mouth. She knew she was behaving disgracefully. 'Well, you'll just have to go on fancying, Mother. He's got a fiancée; I've told you so before. Her photograph is on the desk in his office.'

'He never mentioned a fiancée while he was here, so he can't think all that much of her. And as far as I'm concerned, a man is still single until he returns down the aisle with his bride on his arm.'

Since then, her mother had continued to try to persuade her to come to lunch. The more she tried, the more stubbornly Kate refused, yet the more she wanted to go.

On the Sunday morning of the lunch, she thought how blissful it would be to be in his company for two whole hours.

Her mother came into the bedroom and asked if she was bothering to get up that morning.

Kate leaped out of bed and opened the door of her wardrobe. 'I'm tidying my room.' She rattled the wooden hangers.

'For how long? And what about the red coat you were planning to make?'

Kate had forgotten about the coat. 'I couldn't see any material I liked,' she lied. 'Anyway, this afternoon, I have homework to do.' That much was true. She had shorthand to practise as well as an exercise in writing business letters to do. It would all be hideously dull.

'I think this is one of those mornings it would do you good to go to church,' her mother observed irrationally.

'We *never* go to church,' Kate said scornfully. They weren't that sort of family. Daddy was an atheist, her mother agnostic, and she had no idea what she was herself. Neither she nor her sister had been baptized.

Her mother took ages getting ready, changing her outfit twice before being satisfied with how she looked. What a pity *she* couldn't marry Clive Dexter, Kate thought with a sniff, then felt terrible because that could only happen if her father, who she loved with all her heart, were dead.

When her parents were leaving, she clung to her father, wishing she could apologize for having had such an awful thought. 'Drive safely,' she implored him. Say if he was killed in an accident. It would be all her fault. And her mother might die with him and that would be her fault as well.

'Are you sure you're all right, dear? You're behaving very oddly.' Her mother placed a hand on her forehead. 'You feel awfully hot.'

'How can you possibly tell, Margaret?' Mr Kellaway observed. 'You're wearing gloves.'

'I don't like leaving her alone in this sort of mood,' her mother said worriedly.

'I'm perfectly all right,' Kate said bravely. 'I'm not in any sort of mood.'

Her parents gone, she threw herself in a chair and cried her eyes out. After a while, she sat up, dried her eyes, and thought what a trivial person she was, entirely devoid of character. Half the population of the world was male. It was silly to become preoccupied with just one of these creatures when there were millions more around, some nicer and far better-looking than Clive Dexter. He just happened to be the first interesting one she'd met, and was unlikely to be the last. At least, she hoped not.

For some reason, she badly wanted to talk to Martha, but couldn't very well visit on a Sunday when she might have all her family there, apart from Joe, of course.

Kate's parents arrived home later that afternoon having had a lovely time, according to her mother. Daddy said he'd had 'a remarkably interesting conversation with that young man of yours'. She didn't like to ask if Clive had mentioned her and went to bed as cross with herself as she'd been that morning when she'd woken up.

On that particular Sunday, Martha had four of her children with her in King's Court. Just before dinner, Joyce had knocked and asked if her father was there.

'He's gone to the pub,' Georgie, who answered the door, informed her.

'In that case, we'll come in. I've got Edward with me. He knows about the problem with our dad, but I don't want them coming face to face. At least at the

168

theatre he looked vaguely respectable for a change, as well as being sober.'

Georgie had no idea what his sister was talking about. What problem with their dad? He knew loads of kids whose dads stayed in bed half the day, spent the other half in the pub, and went round with a permanently miserable gob. Some got far drunker than his own dad and knocked their wives and kids about until they were black and blue, whereas his dad had never laid a finger on anyone. 'Our Frank's here,' he announced.

Joyce wrinkled her nose. Georgie didn't know what that was for, either. He was dead proud of their Frank, though he liked their Joe better. Frank always had loads of girls after him. Often, he and Lily would be stopped in the street and some girl would ask, 'Eh, kid, what's your Frank up to nowadays?'

As he and Lily hadn't the faintest idea what Frank was up to, they would make the answers up. Frank was a pirate, a doctor, he was learning to gallop horses, he'd gone to France and become a Frenchman – that had been Lily's idea – he owned that big shop in Hanover Street where their Joyce worked, or walked a tightrope in a circus. The girls were usually mightily impressed.

Today, Frank was wearing a camel overcoat with a fur collar; it had been bought in Paddy's market for half a crown, he told Mam.

Georgie sat stroking the coat's arm when Frank took it off. Poor camel, he thought.

Joyce had come to suggest they have a celebration for Joe when he came home. 'A party, say, though it doesn't have to be a *party* sort of party,' she said in her rather strained ladylike voice – she was doing her best to get rid of her Liverpool accent. 'I mean,' she looked witheringly around the room, 'we couldn't very well invite people to a party *here*.'

Martha wouldn't have fancied a party there, either. 'Our Joe really enjoyed that fish and chip supper,' she remarked.

'So did I,' Joyce said thoughtfully. 'We could go to the theatre again and then to supper, just like last time.'

'Who's going to pay for everything, luv?' Martha asked. 'I'm not exactly made of money.' She hadn't told anyone, but she'd been saving up for a treat for Joe when he came home, and had so far accumulated twelve shillings and a tanner, not nearly enough for the evening Joyce had planned.

'Edward will, just like he did last time,' Joyce said grandly. Edward modestly studied his feet and didn't say anything. 'Edward really liked our Joe,' Joyce went on, 'and he wants to do something nice for him.'

Frank, who loathed Edward, said sarcastically that he was willing to put two quid into a kitty, whereupon Edward offered to put in five.

Martha said angrily that it wasn't an auction. Joe would be perfectly happy with Joyce's suggestion, and Frank and Edward could put in half each. She hoped that this time there would be no more men at the theatre dressed as women. Just thinking about it made her feel sick.

She asked Joyce if she and Edward were staying for their dinner, at which Joyce made a face and said, 'No, thank you, Mam,' in the tone of voice that inferred there was dead cat on the menu. Frank excused himself and said he'd be back later.

'Someone's making me a dinner somewhere else,' he said vaguely.

'I'm glad it's just us,' Martha said when the older children had gone. 'Them two have become too particular with their food by a mile.'

'What have we got for dinner, Mam?' Lily asked.

'Meat stew with dumplings,' Martha informed her.

'Dumplings are me favourite food,' Georgie said, rubbing his tummy hungrily. 'They were our Joe's favourite, too. I wonder if they give you dumplings in the Army?'

'We'll ask Joe that when he comes home,' Martha said comfortably.

That morning, before leaving St Omer, Albie had prepared a vegetable stew and left it to cook slowly in the oven. It meant the fire had to be lit so, by now, the room would be warm and the stew ready to eat. They were having it with bully beef.

Now Joe and Albie were on their way back from Loos, riding soberly side by side, neither speaking. The sights they'd seen that morning had struck them dumb and they could think of nothing to say to each other.

Of course Joe had heard the explosions before, the crack of rifles, the rat-tat-tat of machine-gun fire, but he'd never seriously thought about the consequences of these horrible noises, that as a result men would have died or been fearfully injured. Perhaps he hadn't *wanted* to think about it; he'd heard the sounds and *deliberately* let his mind go blank.

This morning, there'd been no avoiding it. On the way there, they could hear the battle was getting closer, though there was a bit of a lull when they arrived.

Dozens of injured men were lying on the ground waiting for ambulances to take them to hospital behind the lines. Some were already wearing bloody bandages, indicating that they'd been attended to by the stretcher-bearers who'd collected them from wherever they had fallen. Others were covered, head to toe, with blankets, no longer real men, but bodies of men whose souls had flown to heaven. Joe hoped that God had welcomed them with a smile, a blessing and wide-open arms.

And today, there'd been a different sound, a new one that Joe had never heard before. It was of men groaning, sighing, crying, talking to themselves. They called out names: Jean, Pauline, Esther, Minnie . . .

'Is that you, ducky?'

'Where are you, Mam?'

'Me leg don't half hurt, our Marie.'

'Are you there, Pa?'

After the messages had been delivered, Joe had wanted to stay and help the injured men, answer their questions as best he could, stroke their foreheads, give them the drinks they were pleading for. He'd actually said to the officer who seemed to be in charge, 'Can I give a hand here, sir?'

But the chap had turned his offer down. 'You get back to St Omer, son. You shouldn't have been sent here in the first place. Didn't I hear you young 'uns were going back to Blighty some time this week?'

'That's right, sir. I'm not sure what day.'

'Well, off you go, the pair of you. Shoo!'

It had seemed unfitting, the way he'd said 'shoo', not quite the right word to use on such a solemn occasion. Nevertheless, the lads had left, were pleased to have left, and wished they hadn't had to go there in the first place.

'We could have gone to Mass this morning at the Holy Cross and be strolling along the Docky now if we hadn't joined the bloody Army,' Albie said, breaking the long silence on the ride back.

Joe continued with the fantasy. 'And met Pete and Bertie Slater by the Pier Head.'

'And mebbe gone for a ride on the ferry.'

'Or walked as far as Lyon's Corner House for a pot of tea. Those girls might have been there from the Adelphi.' The girls were chambermaids, mostly from Ireland, having their only afternoon off. All they did was flirt a bit.

Albie said thoughtfully, 'Are you sorry we joined up, Joe?'

Joe nodded. 'I didn't like upsetting me mam so much. But if I didn't have a mam or dad or any brothers and sisters, I don't think I'd mind being a Tommy and fighting for me country. In fact, I wouldn't even mind dying all that much, not if there was no one to miss me.'

'I'd miss you, Joe,' Albie said.

'And I'd miss you, mate.'

They came to the only dip in the otherwise boringly flat road, a long slope downwards, then up again. Joe's ambition had always been to freewheel down the hill so fast that he would reach the top of the upward slope without having to pedal once. So far, he hadn't managed it. He grabbed the handlebars tightly, spread his legs, and yelled, 'Whee!' as he hurtled downwards, nearly falling off the bike when a car overtook them at speed and sounded its horn.

'Jaysus!' Albie swore, close behind. 'I almost came a cropper there.'

The car, an Army one painted khaki, had stopped at the crest of the hill. When the lads reached it, the driver got out and stood beside the door, arms folded. They got off their bikes, but the soldier didn't speak.

From the back of the car, a curt voice snapped, 'Open the door, Corporal.' The soldier obeyed.

The first thing Joe was aware of was a pair of boots polished so highly that he could actually see his reflection in them. He saw his blurred image drop the bike and salute; behind him Albie did the same.

The owner of the boots leaned forward. His uniform had been beautifully pressed; there wasn't a crease anywhere. The brass buttons on his jacket gleamed, as did the buckle on his belt. That morning, his batman must have worked hard to present such an immaculate image to the world, an image that Joe thought quite unnecessary when you considered the state of the men they'd not long left behind.

The officer was a handsome bloke with features so lacking in expression they might have been carved out of wood. Even when he spoke, his lips scarcely moved. There was something about his stillness that frightened Joe to death, far more so than had he been angry.

'Who are you, soldiers?' he demanded in a cold, dead posh voice, as if Joe and Albie were of a type he'd never seen before.

'Private Joseph Rossi, sir.' Joe saluted a second time.

'Private Albert Lloyd, sir.' Albie's voice shook.

'And where are you going in such an outrageous manner? You are both a disgrace to the Army.'

'I'm sorry, sir,' Joe said smartly. Until the officer's

car had appeared, there hadn't been a soul in sight to see how they were behaving. 'Having just delivered some messages to Chalk Pit HQ, sir, me mate and I are on our way back to the communications centre in St Omer for our dinner.' He thought longingly of the stew that Albie had made.

The officer leaned back in his seat until only his boots could be seen and once again Joe was left to study his own smudged reflection and wonder just how much elbow grease had gone into obtaining such an intense shine. He felt sorry for the batman who'd been given such a useless task to do in the middle of a murderous war.

The voice came again, so cold it made Joe shiver. 'Not any longer, soldiers. You will return immediately to Chalk Pit HQ and present yourselves to Lieutenant Clifton. Tell him that Captain Whitley-Neville sent you. They are short of fighting men in that division and you will be of far more use to the Army there than playing around on bicycles in what is virtually a war zone.'

'But, sir,' Albie protested. 'We're being sent back to—'

'Be quiet, man.' The captain banged his stick against the door.

To argue would be demeaning, Joe thought; he didn't speak. He noticed Albie's chin wobble as if he were about to cry.

'What about their kits, sir?' asked the corporal.

'Arrange to have them collected from communications HQ and delivered to Chalk Pit, Corporal. Now, will you kindly close the door, and proceed.'

The rear door was closed. The corporal looked at

the lads and gave a little shrug, as if to say, 'Sorry, but there's nothing I can do about it.' He climbed into the car and drove away.

'Bugger!' groaned Joe.

'Soddin' hell,' Albie sighed.

They turned their bikes around and rode back the way they'd come.

A beaming Martha was waiting for Kate in the pet shop doorway next day.

'Is there some news?' Kate asked eagerly. 'Have you heard from Joe?'

'No, but we're arranging something for when he comes home – not exactly a party. We thought we might go to the Rotunda again, then to supper.' Martha's eyes shone so brightly Kate half expected her to explode. 'I wondered if you and Clive Dexter would like to come?'

'Well, *I* certainly would. I don't know about Mr Dexter,' Kate said casually. She'd been thinking about Clive over the entire weekend and her homework had suffered.

'Would you mind asking him for me?'

'If you wish.' She'd call in at his office on her way back to college – or should she wait until tomorrow when she could wear something nicer than her old navy-blue skirt and jacket? She linked Martha's arm. 'Shall we have coffee and a cake?'

'What's on at the Rotunda?' she asked when they were seated at their usual table in the Central station café.

'Something called *Charley's Aunt*. It's a play. It's on

for the next fortnight. Joe is bound to be home before it's finished.'

'I should hope so. I've always wanted to see *Charley's Aunt*.' She'd do her best to sit next to Clive in the theatre. Hopefully, she'd have time to make a new frock before then.

'I'm dead excited,' Martha confessed. 'It's awful funny, but since our Joe joined the Army, all sorts of exciting things have been happening. This'll be the second time I've been to the theatre, and I've met some really nice people, you in particular, Kate.' She squeezed Kate's hand. 'I don't know what I'd've done without you, girl.'

'Oh, Martha,' Kate said emotionally, 'meeting you is one of the best things that's happened in my life.'

'I'd very much like to go to the theatre,' Clive Dexter said later. Kate couldn't bring herself to wait until the next day just so she could wear something nicer. When they met, he looked so extraordinarily handsome that she almost fainted. 'I'd like to meet the rest of Martha's family. We can accompany each other, can't we?' He grinned. 'Or does that idea offend you? I'd forgotten what a prickly person you can be.'

Kate pretended outrage and claimed never to have been offended. She wished she hadn't made such a terrible first impression on him. 'I think we ought to be nice to each other for Martha's sake,' she said.

'I agree. But does Martha have to be present, or can we be nice when she's not around?'

'Are you making fun of me, Mr Dexter?

'Of course not, Miss Kellaway,' he said smoothly with a patronizing smile. 'I am rather wary of your sharp tongue, that's all, I don't want to be nice to you and have it thrown back in my face, as it were.'

'I wouldn't dream of doing such a thing,' she assured him.

'That is indeed a relief, Miss Kellaway. In that case, may I say how pretty you look today. Also, as we are now being nice to each other, do you think it is time I called you Kate and you called me Clive? After all, I know your parents by their first names, so why not their daughter? I do believe I suggested that before.'

'Why not indeed, Mr Dext . . . *Clive*,' she said demurely. 'And, yes, you did indeed suggest it before.'

She still had a strong feeling that he was making fun of her.

Charley's Aunt appeared on the Rotunda and finished its run two weeks later without there being any sign of Joe. Martha fretted, but knew there was nothing she could do except pray he would come soon.

One Saturday afternoon, she took Lily and Georgie to Central station café for coffee and a cake, just for the experience, like. Lily loved the coffee, but Georgie couldn't stand it and swore he'd never drink it again. Afterwards, they went to St John's market where Martha bought Georgie a magic painting book, a girl's manicure set for Lily, who wanted pretty nails like Joyce, and a dictionary for herself.

Joyce said she and Edward were thinking of getting engaged at Christmas, and Frank slept at home for a whole week. He didn't explain the reason to his mother and she didn't ask.

★

It had never happened before. She hadn't known that Carlo knew the whereabouts of Ackerman's Sacks and Sails. But he must have, because he appeared one morning at the beginning of October, quietly opening the door and just as quietly closing it behind him. She had no idea how long he'd been there before Jacquetta looked up and noticed him.

'Yes?' she enquired in her peremptory fashion, thinking he was a stranger.

Martha turned and saw it was Carlo. He was holding something in his good hand, an orange envelope. She knew what orange envelopes meant. Dazed, she got up, went towards him, and he roughly pushed the envelope at her as if he wanted rid of it, couldn't bear to touch it any longer. She took it, pulled a piece of paper out and stared at it. But the printing was strange and made no sense.

'What is it?' she asked, knowing full well what it was, but wanting her husband to confirm it. 'What does it say?'

Oh, his eyes, his eyes! Once so lively and full of fun, now his eyes were like those of a corpse. They were directed, not at her, but at some point behind her. And there was nothing in them, no feeling. Nothing.

'It says our Joe is dead.' His arms hung loosely at his sides as if he hadn't the strength to lift them, and his Italian accent took her by surprise. 'It says our Joe is "missing presumed dead".'

Martha didn't sleep at all during that long, dark night. She didn't tell Lily and Georgie about their brother because she couldn't bring herself to say those four simple words: Our Joe is dead. She didn't believe the 'missing'. Nobody did. Everyone knew that a man who was missing was already dead.

Our Joe is dead. She wrote the words in her head in big, heavy letters. *Our Joe is dead.* She imagined them written in gold on a white marble gravestone or engraved on her heart with blood.

Our Joe is dead.

Her two younger children slept peacefully on the floor, one each side of her, unaware their mam was in such overwhelming, all-consuming pain that she had to stuff her knuckles in her mouth to stop herself from screaming.

At some time during the night, Carlo came in, climbed into bed and began to cry inconsolably.

Despite the coldness and indifference of the last ten years, Martha took her husband in her arms and comforted him with a quiet 'Shush, now' and 'There, there', as if he were a child who'd fallen and grazed his knee.

To her astonishment and dismay, he made love to her in a strange, detached way, as if it could have been any woman at all he was taking, without a trace of passion, even affection. When it was over, he turned round and went asleep, leaving Martha feeling even more pain than she'd done before.

But Carlo wasn't asleep. He was still crying, but only inside. He heard Martha give a sigh of wretched-ness and despair, but couldn't bring himself to offer comfort. He felt personally responsible for his son's death. He should have done more, not left everything to Martha. He knew for certain that the guilt would stay with him for the rest of his life. There was no escape.

It was turning light, just a glimmer could be seen through the thin curtains, when Martha got out of bed, put on her shawl, and crept out of the house into the court. There, she dropped to her knees, lifted her arms towards the sky and began to howl at the Lord for taking her son away from her.

Her screams woke people from their well-deserved sleep: they disturbed dreams, turning them into nightmares; they aroused children who thought the bogie man was after them, as their mams and dads had always threatened if they were naughty; they awoke the women in the court, who recognized the howls of a sister who had lost something precious.

The women rose from their beds, reached for their shawls, and went outside to join their grief-stricken friend, kneeling around her, spreading themselves until Martha was buried beneath a blanket of tender arms.

There wasn't a woman there who hadn't suffered some sort of tragedy. It was the way of the world, it happened, it was life. It was why they were there – to lose babies, to lose husbands and to lose hope.

Chapter 11

Martha was angry, so angry that days later she still couldn't sleep. So angry that her head, her whole body throbbed with rage. She was tormented by images of her beloved son at the point of death. At work, she didn't speak, just treadled furiously away on the sewing machine while Jacquetta and Mister maintained a respectful silence.

On her way home on the Monday after learning about Joe, she went into Rose Hill police station where Sergeant Gilligan lorded it over the innocent and the guilty alike from behind his high desk. He was there now, shuffling papers around and trying to look important.

'Murderer!' Martha spat.

A flush came to the man's broad face. 'Now, look here, missus,' he began, but Martha wasn't prepared to listen to a word that came out of his ugly mouth. She reckoned the reason for the flush was because he knew about Joe – and what he could expect from the lad's incensed mam.

'No, *you* look here, you bloody fat pig,' she shouted. 'It's your fault my lad's dead, my Joe. He was only fourteen and he wouldn't have gone near the Army if it hadn't been for you.' She stretched out her arm

182

until it was so tight and so taut that it hurt. 'Murderer!' she spat again. 'Fine policeman you are, going round murdering kids.'

The sergeant's temper must have been on a very short leash because he lost it immediately. 'Arrest her! Arrest that woman' he yelled at the two constables who happened to be about. Neither man moved. The sergeant's face turned bright red and he began to cough, turning redder all the time as he fought for the breath that rattled hoarsely in his throat.

'I hope you choke to death,' Martha snarled, turning on her heel.

Lily and Georgie were in tears when she got home. Since she'd told them about their brother, they'd cried themselves sick, unlike their mother, who felt mad enough to dismantle the world brick by brick.

She swept the children up in her arms, raining kisses on their sad little faces. 'I wonder if our Frank and Joyce will come tonight?' she muttered.

'Joyce promised to fetch us fish and chips, Mam,' Lily reminded her.

'Of course, luv. I'd forgotten.'

The whole family was devastated over Joe. Carlo had stayed in the whole weekend, actually sitting in the room with them, his eyes red-rimmed and tragic. He didn't speak much and Martha didn't speak to him. She felt that, as Joe's dad, he should have done something to stop his son from going away instead of leaving it to her, a mere woman. She felt guilty for not having done more, like sending Joe across to Ireland, for instance, where she had relatives he could have lived with until the war was over. She'd given in too easily when she should have made a desperate fuss.

Soon, she'd go and see Arthur Hanson and ask if he could find out exactly how Joe had died, and where. She *had* to know; it just couldn't be left. She imagined a hundred different ways in which her son had come to the end of his too-short life. Anyroad, until she knew the truth, she would never honestly believe it.

Joyce came with the fish and chips and Frank arrived later with a bagful of humbugs. Martha was surprised that she was hungry enough to eat, though she didn't enjoy the food a bit. Carlo had gone out.

'There was something about conscription in yesterday's paper,' Joyce said when they'd finished eating. 'That means the Government calling up men to fight, rather than waiting for them to volunteer,' she explained when her mother looked at her blankly.

'Why do they only call up men?' Lily enquired.

'Because women can't fight,' Frank told her. 'Not like men can.'

'*I'd* fight,' Lily said boldly. 'I'd get me own back on the German soldier that killed our Joe.'

'I don't *think* . . .' Martha paused as she tried to put her woolly, unruly thoughts into order. 'I don't *think* it was the German soldier's fault, Lil. He might have been just another young lad who hadn't wanted to be there – maybe he was tricked into it like our Joe. He might be dead himself by now. No, it was the fault of the men who started the war; the ones that probably don't go anywhere near the fighting. And I bet they're not just Germans, either.'

'Well, I'd like to kill *somebody*,' Lily said grittily.

Frank spoke. 'Does conscription mean I'd be called up, sis?'

'It means every man eighteen and over,' Joyce told

him. 'Once you pass your next birthday, you'll get your calling-up papers. The reason I know so much about it is Edward is twenty-one and he'll be called up, too. We were talking about it last night. As you can imagine, he's not exactly looking forward to it. Actually, Mam,' she glanced at her mother, 'if he does go, me and him are thinking of getting married beforehand.'

Martha was still trying to get her head around the fact that, before she knew it, she'd have another son in the Army. She could actually lose Frank as well as Joe. Then her daughter's words sank in. Joyce was talking about getting married – and Edward was likely to join up, too, so he could be lost an' all. What on earth was the world coming to? Had it gone completely mad? Pretty soon, there'd only be women left.

'What are we going to do about it?' Kate asked.

'What *can* we do?' Clive said fiercely a few days before. Kate had just met Martha and had called in at his office to tell him the shocking news. 'You know I wrote to the War Office. I got an acknowledgment, but never a proper reply. Why the hell didn't I follow it up, be more persistent?' He slammed the arm of the chair with his fist. 'I'll never stop blaming myself.'

'It's not your fault,' Kate said softly. She was perched perilously on the edge of her own chair and wanted to leap to her feet and press his head against her breast and gently stroke it, then for him to do the same to her. She'd never met Joe, but his photograph had left her feeling as if she'd known him personally, that he was a friend. What's more, Martha's grief was catching. There was a lump of sadness in her throat.

185

'Martha's all for blaming herself as well,' she said. 'I feel awful about it, too, yet I can't think of a single thing I could have done. My father says the armed services and all the Government institutions are just like steam engines travelling at full speed; absolutely nothing can stop them unless the drivers themselves care to put on the brakes.'

'That's just the sort of thing your father would say,' Clive said with a strained smile. 'He's a very wise man.'

'I suppose everyone thinks their father is wise.'

'Oh, I don't know,' Clive said, a touch dryly. 'Wise is not a word I would apply to my own father.'

'I'm sorry.' His words came as a jolt. He was such a confident person that she hadn't imagined his family life being anything other than perfect. She tried to think of something that might make them both feel a little better. 'I've just remembered my parents planned to invite you to lunch on Sunday, should you be free, that is.' Her parents planned no such thing, but she was sure they would jump at the chance – well, her mother would when Kate made the suggestion.

He looked at her distantly. 'I'm afraid I shall be in London on Sunday, Miss Kellaway . . . Kate, visiting my fiancée.'

'Miss Lettice Conway.' Kate sighed, and immediately wished that she hadn't.

'Indeed, Miss Lettice Conway. I am impressed that you remember her name.'

'It's such an unusual name.' Kate recovered some of her aplomb. 'It's the only woman's name I know that is also a vegetable. Oh!' She stamped her foot in vexation. 'Why are we talking like this when Joe is dead?'

'I wasn't aware I was talking in any other way than

normal,' he snapped. 'It is you who are being rude and offensive about the name of a woman whom you have never met and are never likely to meet.'

Kate leaped to her feet and began to walk around her chair, taking long steps. 'I'm so upset. I don't know what I'm doing or saying. I think I would like to have a fight with you, scream and shout at you, pull your hair and kick your shins and stamp on your toes.' Only minutes ago she'd wanted to comfort him.

'Why me?' He looked more hurt than annoyed.

'Because you're a man and it's men who start wars.'

'And it's men who have to fight them,' he pointed out.

'Then they should refuse.' She came close to jumping up and down with rage. 'The generals wouldn't get very far if they couldn't get men to fight their loathsome battles for them.'

He looked at her tiredly. 'You are talking about some sort of Utopia that is never likely to exist.'

'Then women should refuse to have children so there'd be no soldiers to fight.'

'If women didn't have children the world would end.'

She stopped walking and faced him, spreading her arms. He rubbed his eyes as if she'd been making him dizzy. 'Then what can be done?' she asked.

He shrugged helplessly. 'I don't know if you are talking about Joe in particular or wars in general, but as far as I know, nothing can be done about either, nothing at all.'

'I understand,' Jeffrey Dexter said to his son that night, 'that there's a good chance conscription will be introduced in this country in the very near future.'

'I know, Father,' Clive said lightly. 'I read it myself in *The Times*.'

'And what will you do then, my brave son?' the older man sneered. 'You'll *have* to fight. You'll be given no choice.'

'No, Father, you are wrong. I will still have a choice and I will choose to become a conscientious objector – a conchie, your type of person would call them, for there are a great many around. I could well be sent to work down the mines or to the front line to work in a military hospital or as a stretcher-bearer. I might actually end up dying for my country; I am just not willing to fight for it.'

Still Martha couldn't sleep. She blamed herself for what had happened, and also Carlo and Sergeant Gilligan, but there were others, far more powerful, who had given him the gun and the uniform, put him on a train, then on a boat, and transported him to France. Someone else had ordered him to the place where men were killing each other, and Joe was duly killed.

In her mind, she pored over the events of the last few months, of Joe coming in one Sunday afternoon to say he'd joined the Army. 'I'm a soldier now, Mam,' he'd said, or something like that.

Later that day, she'd gone to see Sergeant Gilligan and given him the rough edge of her tongue. She'd just left the police station when Ossie Nelson from Gerard Street, who'd become a copper himself, had caught up with her and said the sergeant was enrolling kids on behalf of some titled bloke, a Sir . . . she racked her brains, Sir Stanley Cuthbertson, she remembered with a feeling of triumph. The sergeant's brother worked for him as a gardener. Sir Stanley was a general an' all, she recalled, and lived in Rainford. She had a feeling Rainford was only a train ride away.

'He has a son fighting in France, the general,' Ossie had said. 'An officer, a'course.'

On Saturday, she resolved, she'd visit Rainford, track down General Sir Stanley Cuthbertson, and have it out with him.

A woman on the train told her where the general lived. 'You can't miss it, luv. There's a flagpole in the front garden flying the Union Jack. You can see it from the junction. Just walk in that direction and you'll come to the house in minutes.'

It was a sizeable house set in large grounds in a road full of similar, but otherwise assorted styles of properties. There were statues in the gardens, as well as some of the most beautiful flowers she'd ever seen, trees of different shades of green, some turning gold with the advent of autumn, and here and there men were digging the soil, cutting the grass, and cleaning the windows.

The Cuthbertsons' house had a turret on each corner, a motor car in the drive, and the flag she'd been told about flying briskly at the front. Inside, a middle-aged maid could be seen wielding a feather duster. Martha marched up the path and pulled the rope beside the arched front door. She heard a bell ring and a maid in a black-and-white uniform, who looked like the one who'd been using the feather duster, opened the door and gave her a hard look up and down.

'The servants' entrance is round the side,' she said with a curl of her lip.

'I am not a servant,' Martha said haughtily. She was wearing her grey dress, her hat with the red band, and the respectable if painful boots, and didn't see why she should automatically be taken for a servant. 'I am here to see General Sir Stanley Cuthbertson.'

'Do you have an appointment?' the maid asked, just as haughtily.

'No, I do not.'

'Well, in that case you can't see him.'

The door was about to close, when Martha put her foot inside. 'If you don't let me see him now, I'll stand outside and pull the bell until you do.'

'I'll call the coppers,' the other woman threatened.

Before Martha could think of an answer, a voice sounding like that of a child intervened. 'Who is it, Polly? What's going on?'

'It's a woman wanting to see the master, Miss Rowena. I told her to go round the side.'

'Father's visitors aren't normally sent round the side, Polly. Kindly let the lady in.'

The door opened and Martha stepped into a large, gloomy hallway, throwing a dark glance at the discomfited maid, who went away, sullen-faced. The speaker turned out to be a girl of no more than fourteen or fifteen wearing a plain black dress and a black ribbon in her pretty blonde hair. Martha wondered if she was in mourning, particularly when she noticed a mirror in the hall was obscured by a black veil.

'Hello.' The girl held out her hand. 'My name is Rowena Cuthbertson. I'm afraid my father isn't very well at the moment and can't see anybody. Is it something I can help you with?'

'I'm Mrs Rossi, Martha Rossi.' She shook hands with the girl. 'No, I don't think you can help, not at all. It was something personal I wanted to see him about.' It was entirely inappropriate that she say to the general's daughter what she had intended saying to the general himself.

The girl narrowed her eyes. 'Did you help in the nursery when I was little? I feel as if I remember you from then.' Her face split into a tearful smile. 'I suppose you've come to tell Father how sorry you are to hear the awful news about Gideon. That's terribly nice of you, but you can tell me, his daughter, instead. Gideon wasn't just my brother, but my very best friend. I'll never stop missing him for the rest of my life.'

'I'm sorry,' Martha stammered. From Rowena's words, she gathered that Gideon, the general's son, was dead. She wondered if he'd had more than one son. Had Gideon been in the Army?

'Gideon's memorial service is being held on the first Sunday in December in St Luke's church not far from Rainford Junction. We've been told never to expect his body back – it was a shell that got him, you see, and he was blown to pieces – so there won't be a funeral. That's what upset Father the most, the fact that we won't ever see Gideon again, not even when he's dead.' Rowena was doing her best not to cry. 'Did you come on the train?' Martha nodded numbly. 'Then you'll easily find the church.'

Martha nodded again. 'Thank you.' Rowena hadn't appeared to notice that she'd hardly said a word.

'Thank *you* so much for coming,' Rowena said sadly. 'I would have offered you tea, but the doctor is expected any minute to see Father. Poor old thing, he's had this horrible lung disease for years and the news about Gideon has really laid him low.' She opened the door, then closed it again. 'I've just remembered, you won't have seen Gideon since he was a little boy. Would you like to see what he looked like now – or at least before he was blown to pieces by a German shell?' Without waiting for an answer, she disappeared into a nearby room and returned with a silver-framed photograph of a young man in Army uniform who looked so much like an older Joe that now it was Martha who wanted to cry.

'This is him at twenty in his uniform,' Rowena said, beaming proudly. 'Isn't he just the handsomest young man? My mother would have been so proud. She died just after I was born – but of course, you'll know that, won't you?'

'I'm really sorry for your loss,' Martha murmured, touched and impressed with how well Rowena was coping with the tragedy. 'I hope your father is better soon.' She really meant it.

'Oh, so do I! If Daddy died, I would be left with no one in the world to call my own.'

Martha almost ran as far as Rainford Junction where she caught the train back to Liverpool. In no way did General Cuthbertson losing his own son make him any less to blame for Martha losing hers, but she couldn't very well have faced him with the fact, not while he was ill and in mourning.

Her own loss still didn't quite feel real. Had Joe been blown to pieces like the general's son? Or had he been shot? Would she ever see him again or would he be buried in a French grave? And what was he doing fighting when he'd said he was expecting to be sent home any minute? Would anybody ever tell her? Albie Lloyd hadn't come home, either; no one knew whether he was dead or alive. She needed to know what had happened to Joe or she would go mad.

'This is strange,' Mrs Kellaway said one morning when she was opening the post. 'There is a letter here from Clive Dexter apologizing for being unable to lunch with us on Sunday. Yet, for the life of me, I can't remember inviting him. Surely your father wouldn't have asked him without telling me?' Mr Kellaway was outside polishing the car.

'I invited him,' Kate confessed. 'Like me, he was terribly upset over Joe, so I asked him to lunch to cheer him up a bit, as it were.' And cheer herself up at the same time. 'But he couldn't come because he's going to London to see his fiancée.'

'Oh, dear.' Mrs Kellaway looked despondent. 'I so wanted him for you. Is it serious with this London girl?'

'How on earth would I know, Mother? He's not likely to discuss his fiancée with me, is he? All I know is that she has this awful name – Lettice.'

'I think Lettice is a nice, fresh name.'

'Perhaps that's why he's marrying her, because he likes her name better than mine.'

Her mother took the remark seriously. 'That's most unlikely, dear.' She continued reading Clive's letter. 'Anyway,' she said when she'd finished, 'it appears he is free the following Sunday and can come to lunch then. I'll write and tell him he is more than welcome.'

Once again, Clive had driven to Blackpool to confront the editor of the *Lancashire Post*.

'I'm sorry, Clive, but no.' Edgar Henderson pushed away the obituary Clive had written for Joe Rossi. 'It's too emotional. *And* too hot-headed; the sort of thing that starts revolutions.' He paused to draw on his noxious pipe. 'No,' he repeated. 'This week, like every week, we've received dozens of obituaries for men in our area who've been killed in France. They're short and to the point, not a great rant on how unfair it is that a particular person has died.'

'I understand, sir, but *this* particular person happened to be a child.' Clive tightened his fists in an effort to contain his anger, the nails pressing painfully into the flesh of his palms. 'It's against the law, for one thing, and sending children off to fight our battles isn't exactly something the country should be proud of.'

'I agree, but nor is it something that our readers should be ashamed of.' Edgar had begun to look as if he were tired of being reasonable. 'It's not them doing the sending off. Putting aside their own relatives being slaughtered, they've got enough to worry about without reading about this kid of yours. Tell you what,' he leaned back in his chair and blew smoke at the ceiling, 'I'll put in his photo – same size as all the other photos – and his details underneath, just like the other details. Will that do?'

'You couldn't very well have refused to do that much.' Clive tried not to sound as bitter as he felt. 'You can't pick and choose which obituaries you publish. Will you deign to put Joe's age? Or are you worried *that* will upset the readership?'

'Of course I'll put his age. And if some reader is provoked into writing a letter to the paper expressing outrage about it, then I shall publish it.'

'Oh, thank you, sir,' Clive said mockingly. 'Thank you very much.'

He still felt in a bad mood days later when he went to London to see Lettice Conway, his supposed fiancée. He travelled by train and bought a first-class ticket so he could think in peace. At six o'clock, he met Lettice in the Ritz where they were to have dinner. An orchestra was playing 'Peg o' My Heart'.

'You're looking well,' he said admiringly. He was in London at her request. Lettice was wildly beautiful with jet-black wavy hair and bright red lips. Her gown was emerald green satin held up by two narrow straps. Virtually every other man in the restaurant was staring at her.

'Darling Clive,' she said, licking the red lips suggestively. He wasn't even faintly moved.

'What do you want, Letty?' he asked. He was familiar with her tricks.

'A husband,' she cooed. 'Champagne!' she breathed huskily at the wine waiter when he approached.

'A husband?' Clive queried. She had always sworn she wouldn't get married until she was at least forty, as she said, 'When I'll be too old and ugly to have a good time.'

'I'm preggers, darling,' she said with mock tragedy. 'Up the stick, got a bun in the oven, in the family way.'

'Who's the father?' Usually he found Lettice amusing, but today she was getting on his nerves.

'Lord something or other; he's a chinless wonder, as boring as hell and old enough to be my father.' She waved a long white hand with nails the same red as her lips. 'Goes huntin', shootin' and fishin' and all that sort of tripe.'

'If he's such a bore, then why did you associate with him?' Clive asked. 'Let alone go to bed.'

'That, my darling Clive, is something that I will never cease to wonder myself. It could be that I was dazzled by his enormous bank balance.' She smiled at him dryly. 'He bought me a mink wrap for my birthday.'

'Oh, Letty, you are outrageously irresponsible.' He was genuinely shocked. This was no way to bring a child into the world. 'Can't you have an abortion?' he asked baldly.

She sighed and stopped acting like a vamp. 'Can't, darling. It's too late. I'm more than four months gone and it would be dangerous.' She shuddered. 'Anyway, the idea of abortion terrifies me. I'm going to have to have it, I'm afraid.'

'And you want me to find you a husband?'

'No, Clive, my love. I want you to *be* my husband.'

He couldn't help it. Clive laughed out loud. Lettice, bless her, took it with good grace and began to laugh with him.

'Am I being rejected?' she asked with a giggle.

'I'm afraid you are, Letty. I will always be your friend, but never your husband, though am flattered to be asked. What about the boring lord, will he marry you?'

'Like a shot,' she said despondently. 'He doesn't know about the baby, but proposes at least once a week. I visited his estate once, it's somewhere like Dorset or Durham; I can't remember which.'

'Is it definitely his baby?' Clive asked. He didn't bother to point out that Dorset and Durham were hundreds of miles apart.

She pursed her red lips and looked vague. 'I'm more or less certain.'

'But not a hundred percent?'

'Not entirely, darling.'

'Oh, Letty!' He looked at her beautiful painted face and, for some reason, thought about Kate Kellaway, pretty and unpowdered, with natural pink lips and guile-less eyes. The girl was so downright honest and straight-forward, entirely devoid of Letty's winks and wiles and swooning sighs. He surprised himself by wishing he was with Kate, having a healthy argument about something that really mattered, like this damn, stupid war, rather than with Letty, who only thought and talked about herself.

It wasn't until December that Martha learned Albie Lloyd was home, by which time she was in a very strange mood indeed, having realized that she was expecting a baby. To think that God was sending her another child after those brief and loveless few minutes with Carlo seemed little short of a miracle. It could only be another boy to replace the one she'd lost. All that worried her was that she had vowed to make Lily and Georgie's lives better, but how could she do that with a new baby to look after?

She'd mentioned it to no one. Soon she would tell

Kate, who would be as pleased as punch, but Martha couldn't begin to guess how Carlo would feel. All she could imagine was his gloom deepening. 'Another mouth to feed,' he might well think, not that he fed any now, not even his own.

She called on the Lloyds on her way home from work. A bone-chilling wind blew and there was ice on the pavements. Some of the shop windows were decorated with holly and paper chains – Christmas was only a week away.

Mrs Lloyd opened the door. To Martha's astonishment, she was warmly embraced and pulled inside. She recalled the last time they'd met, when the woman had been dead rude. She'd been left standing on the step outside with the door slammed in her face.

'Mrs Rossi! I'm awful pleased you've come. What a wicked night it is out there!' She rubbed her hands together. 'Would you like a cup of tea? Our Albie's in the parlour by a nice warm fire. I'm sure he'd like to talk to you. Me and Idris, we can't get a peep out of him. He hasn't uttered a word, poor lad, since he came home.'

'Is he home for good, like, Mrs Lloyd?' Martha enquired on being led into the living room where a small fire burned. There were two comfortable easy chairs on either side and a smart embroidered cloth on the table that was set for tea.

'Not yet, Mrs Rossi. The Army are taking him back after Christmas to fix his face a bit more. They said he ran right into an explosion, but the doctor thought a few weeks with his mam and dad would do him the world of good.' Her eyes filled with tears. 'Trouble is, he won't talk to us.'

'I'd like to ask him about our Joe,' Martha ventured.

'Ask him all you like, Mrs Rossi. I just hope you get a response. I'll fetch that tea and you can take it with you into the parlour.'

It appeared Martha was being allowed in the parlour on her own, which meant she'd be able to talk to the lad more freely without his mother present.

A bigger, warmer fire had been lit in the parlour and Albie was half sitting, half lying on a leatherette sofa with his eyes closed. Martha removed her shawl and sat on a tapestry-covered stool on the other side of the fireplace.

'Hello Albie,' she said clearly. She winced at the sight of the lad's face. It was covered with cuts and bruises. Part of his nose had disappeared and one of his eyebrows had been split in two. His entire head was covered with bandages that wound around his neck and underneath his chin. 'It's Mrs Rossi, Joe's mam.'

For a while, perhaps an entire minute, the boy didn't stir. Then, as if the words had taken all that time to sink in, his eyes slowly opened and he blinked and tried to focus on her face.

'Mrs Rossi,' he whispered. 'Joe's mam.'

'That's right, son.' She reached across and patted his knee. 'Your mam said you're going to get better soon.'

'Joe's dead,' he said hopelessly.

'I know.' She couldn't bring herself to ask a single question. It would have felt like she was pestering the poor lad. The last thing he might want to talk about was how his friend had died.

'We should have come home, me and Joe,' he said after another long pause. She noticed the backs of his

199

hands were badly cut and bruised, too, though free of bandages.

'Why didn't you, Albie?' she whispered.

'This chap, this officer, a captain, he stopped us.'

There was another long pause, until Martha said, very gently, 'Why, luv?'

'We were playing about on our bikes, racing down this hill, like. We'd been delivering messages. The captain, he sent us back to Loos. He had this funny name. Afterwards, Joe kept laughing about it.'

'What name was that?'

The boy's damaged lips actually twisted in a smile. 'I can't remember, only that Joe called him Neville the devil.'

'Neville the devil,' Martha repeated.

'You sound just like Joe, Mrs Rossi.' He tried to sit up and Martha went over and tucked a cushion beside him to lean on. He seemed to be rousing himself a bit.

What had the pair been doing on bikes? she wondered. And where had they been delivering messages?

'Joe, he shouted for you for ages, Mrs Rossi. "I want me mam. Where's me Mam?" he'd cry. Then, "Albie, Albie." ' The lad began to sob. 'But I couldn't go to him, I couldn't see proper, like. I'd been hurt bad and Joe had saved me, but then the devil made him go out again and wouldn't let him back. But he'd broken his leg and he had to drag it along with him. And then he was stuck there, in the mud, and the fighting was still on; men were shooting at each other. The dead were everywhere, on the ground and in the trenches, everywhere. Joe didn't stop crying until a clock somewhere struck midnight. I remember counting the numbers. They seemed to go on for ever and I thought they'd never stop. It must've been about then that Joe died. I prayed and prayed, Mrs Rossi, but I never heard any more from him after that.'

His voice was rising and he was beginning to gabble. Martha patted his knee again. 'Shush, son,' she said. 'Shush, now. Don't distress yourself.'

She left her hand on his knee until the boy began to doze. Then she picked up the tea, she hadn't so much as supped it, and took it into the other room where Mrs Lloyd leaped to her feet.

'Did you get anything out of him?' she asked anxiously.

'Mainly about Joe. But don't worry, Mrs Lloyd, I'm pretty certain he's going to be all right. It's the memories that are hurting more than the cuts and bruises. Will you do us a favour, please? Once he's feeling a bit more like himself, ask him to write everything down, all that happened on the night he was hurt and Joe was killed. You never know, it might do him the world of good, get it out of his system, as it were.'

'I'll do that, Mrs Rossi. I'll try and get him to do it before Christmas, before the Army takes him back again.'

'Well, I'll be off now, Mrs Lloyd. I'm glad you got your lad back.'

'Tara, Mrs Rossi. I'm sorry you didn't get yours.'

Chapter 12

'And where will you be spending the holiday, Clive, dear?' Kate's mother asked.

It being Clive's turn to invite them for a meal, they were in the Adelphi, the most exclusive hotel in Liverpool, having Christmas lunch, though Christmas itself was several days away. Even with the Kellaways' middle-class income, they could never have afforded such a treat. Although her husband and daughter seemed indifferent to their surroundings, Mrs Kellaway was extremely conscious of the snow-white Irish linen cloths, the silver tableware, and the waiters who seemed to glide rather than walk. She sighed contentedly as she listened to music from Gilbert and Sullivan's *The Mikado* played by a string quartet, a show that she had been to see with her husband at the Empire Theatre the year before last.

'I shall be staying here in Liverpool,' Clive replied. 'My family are going down to London – we have an apartment there and they have parties to go to – but I would sooner stay at home.'

Kate gasped. 'By yourself! Oh, but that's awful. If we weren't going to Nottingham to stay with my sister, you could have spent Christmas with us.'

Clive looked at her reproachfully. 'Remarkable though it might seem, I do have one or two friends. I won't be completely by myself. Also, I have work to do. I might well take the typewriter from the office and work at home.' He turned to Mr Kellaway in whom he found it easy to confide. 'I feel as if I should be doing something for this damned war. I will not fight in it, but I am considering going over to France and offering to drive an ambulance. I shall definitely write some letters over Christmas.'

'Why not indeed, young man.' Mr Kellaway nodded his approval. Had he and Margaret had a son, Clive was just the sort he would have wanted.

'I feel so frustrated,' Clive continued, his voice rising slightly. 'In France and Belgium, men are dying like flies, while over here men like me sit comfortably at home and enjoy life.' He glanced around his luxurious surroundings in disgust. 'It doesn't seem right.' He banged the table with the handle of his knife and the couple at the next table looked up and frowned. 'It *isn't* right. How can anyone have a happy Christmas knowing that a few short miles away across the English Channel young men are being slaughtered in their thousands?'

'Oh, but if you go you might be killed!' Kate cried. 'I should hate it if you were killed.'

'Kate, dear, don't be so emotional,' her mother urged. 'We'd all hate it if Clive were killed.'

'What on earth is wrong with being emotional, Mother?' By now the couple on the next table were staring. 'I don't want Clive to die.'

'Neither do I, Kate,' Mrs Kellaway said quietly, 'and neither does your father, nor Clive's family nor Clive himself, but let's not shout about it all over the restaurant.' She turned to their host. 'Tell me, does your fiancée share your thoughts about the war? Would she mind if you went to France?' Mrs Kellaway had long been looking for the chance to question Clive about Lettice Conway and was thrilled to have been offered the opportunity.

'Really, Margaret,' her husband said reprovingly. 'It's none of our business.'

'I am afraid that a few weeks ago Lettice and I broke off the engagement,' Clive said shortly.

'Oh, Clive, my dear boy, I am so sorry.' Mrs Kellaway, who had rarely been so pleased about anything in her life, actually managed to introduce a throb into her voice. 'I do hope you're not too upset.'

'Margaret!' her husband expostulated.

'I am perfectly well, thank you,' Clive said with a gracious smile. 'Now, what would you like for dessert?' he asked when the waiter arrived like a ghost at the table to clear the dinner plates.

'Christmas pudding,' Kate said quickly. 'I love Christmas pudding and Christmas cake and mince pies – anything to do with Christmas.'

Clive ordered the pudding for himself, though not with any enthusiasm. He felt he should be eating nothing but bully beef, like the troops across the Channel. But if he did, who would know and who would care? Only him, and what good would that do anybody?

'Martha! Is that you?'

The woman in the shop doorway turned at the sound of Clive's surprised voice. 'I'm waiting for Kate. I've got something I want her to read for me.'

It was raining slightly and she looked so wretched

under her black shawl that Clive's heart went out to her.

'But Kate's college has closed for the Christmas holiday,' he explained. 'It won't open again until January. Kate isn't even in Liverpool; she's gone with her parents to stay with her sister in Nottingham.'

'O'course.' She ran her fingers distractedly through her damp hair. 'She already told me and I forgot.'

'Can I read whatever it is for you?'

'Would you?' Her face lit up. 'I've been teaching meself to read and I thought I'd learned enough to read Albie's letter – well, it's not exactly a letter – but his writing's nothing but scribble and I can't make head nor tail of it. And it's not as if I can ask one of me other kids to do it, not when I know what it's about, like.'

He took her arm. 'Shall we go to my office? It's quiet there and I'll get Herbie to make us some tea.' Herbert was supposed to look after the place when Clive wasn't there. If he'd gone out, which he was inclined to do, he'd be in receipt of a severe dressing-down when he deigned to return.

'Will the man come in and feed these poor little things over Christmas?' Martha asked.

'What things?' He had no idea what she was talking about.

'The puppy and the kittens in the winder.' She pointed to a cage full of kittens who were rolling about joyfully, and a tiny black puppy that looked sad and miserable all on its own.

'He's bound to feed them,' Clive said with conviction. 'They're his stock in trade, aren't they? He'll want to sell them eventually.'

'I suppose so.' His answer made her look a tiny bit happier.

'What exactly is this?' he enquired when they were in his office. Downstairs, Herbie was making tea. Martha had given Clive two sheets of paper torn from an exercise book covered with childish, barely legible writing. The spelling had to be seen to be believed.

'Albie wrote it, our Joe's best mate. He was with Joe when he died, but he wasn't able to talk proper when I spoke to him a week or so back. His mam agreed to get him to write it down when he was feeling a bit more up to things.'

'Do you know, roughly, what it says, Martha?' Skimming through, Clive had noted the odd word and phrase that he found quite horrifying.

She nodded, her face deathly pale. 'I haven't been able to get it out me mind. I'd wanted to know how Joe died, thinking it might set me mind at rest sort of thing, but once I knew it only made me feel worse. I haven't told anybody what Albie said – not me husband, not Kate.'

Clive studied the first of the scribbled pages. 'It says here that Albie and Joe were charging the enemy when there was an explosion and Albie was thrown back-wards and after that he couldn't see. He must have been temporarily blinded.'

'His face was all cut and black and blue,' Martha interjected, 'what you could see of it.'

It was at this point that Herbert came in with tea on a tray and a slice of currant cake. 'Me ma made that,' he said. 'It ain't for you, boss, but for the missus here.'

'Thank you, son.' Martha smiled plaintively at Herbert as he left.

Clive was doing his best to make sense of Albie's rambling statement. 'It would seem Joe dragged him back to the trench and they both fell in. Joe's leg was badly hurt, either as a result of the explosion or falling into the trench.' He looked at Martha and hoped the truth wouldn't distress her. 'Albie says Joe managed to lean him against the side of the trench, but then the "devil" came and ordered him out again.' He frowned. 'I think he means Joe not himself.'

Martha nodded. 'That's right – and the devil is an officer, that's what the lads called him. His real name is Neville something.'

'I see.' Clive continued to read. 'Somehow, Joe managed to climb up the ladder despite his hurt leg. Everywhere was "dead muddy", according to Albie.' He'd heard before that the battlefields had been turned into a sea of mud, resembling a sort of hell on earth, and that the troops ate and slept in it, their clothes never dry. It sounded like a place unfit for any human beings to be, let alone two lads of fourteen.

He looked at Martha to see how she was taking it. Her face was still pale and as sad as a face could be. He wished Kate were there to hold her hand and give her arm a squeeze now and then.

The rest of the statement was pretty bloody shocking, but it wouldn't do to censor it. 'Apparently,' he said with a little dry cough, 'Joe must have collapsed not far from the trench and he started to cry for you. "He was shouting for his mam," Albie says. "Sometimes, he called for me, too, but I couldn't move. I shouted back, but I don't know if he heard me."'

At this, Martha began to weep. 'Ever since Albie told me, I can hear Joe calling all the time: in the house, at work, even in me sleep. I wake up, but he's nowhere to be seen.' She pressed her hands against her breast. 'Me heart aches when I think about the way he died, wanting his mam, like.' Her head drooped and she whispered, 'It'll never go away, the ache. It'll be with me till the day I die.' She raised her head and looked at him beseechingly. 'Why haven't I heard from the Army to say they've found his body and he's been buried? I mean, I'm entitled to know what happened to him, aren't I?'

'Albie reckons Joe's body was collected the next morning. "Two men came and took him away." They said, "He's a young 'un."' Clive sighed as he laid Albie's statement on the desk. 'I reckon you'll hear from the Army soon, Martha. I doubt if it's all that organized over there.' Clive didn't know what else to say. He wondered, had he been there, at the Front – a stretcher-bearer, say – would he have been able to help Joe, or perhaps help another Joe at another time?

Martha struggled tiredly to her feet. 'I'll have to be getting back to work,' she said. 'Mister's been in a terrible mood all morning and I'd sooner not be late.'

'You'd better take this back with you.' Clive began to fold Albie's statement, but Martha held up her hand.

'Thank you for reading it, but would you mind keeping it for me? I don't want any of me kids finding it. I'd sooner they didn't know how their brother died.' She shuffled towards the door and Clive hurried ahead to open it for her.

'I hope you . . .' Have a Happy Christmas, he was about to say. 'Try not to worry too much,' he said instead. Impulsively, he bent and kissed her cheek.

'God bless you, Martha.' Many years had passed since he'd stopped believing in God.

'God bless you, too, son.'

He watched her pass by the office window. When she disappeared, he returned to his chair behind the desk and noticed she'd left the cake that Herbie's mother had made. Without warning, tears began to pour down his cheeks. If his father were there now, he'd disown him!

Early on Christmas Eve, two deliveries were made to the Rossis in King's Court. First, a private car delivered a turkey from Kate, already roasted, as well as a big basket full of other food – a cake, two Christmas puddings, two dozen mince pies, a packet of gravy powder, and a box of assorted Bournville chocolates.

Not long after midday, a pale green van, with Frederick & Hughes written in gold on the sides, rattled into the court, and a white cardboard box was delivered. It was from Clive Dexter and contained a cream shawl as fine as a cobweb, a life-sized baby doll, a train set that puffed smoke, and a bottle of Irish whiskey.

'This must be for you.' Martha handed the whiskey to a bemused Carlo, who opened it and drank a mouthful there and then.

Martha looked at the delicious food and the other gifts, thinking she would much rather have still had Joe and worn rags and eaten gruel for the rest of her life. She knew without doubt that the rest of the family would feel the same.

On Christmas Day, Martha, Carlo and their two youngest children sat down to dinner. Carlo had made no move to go out. He'd even shaved, put on a clean shirt, and contributed a little to the conversation, remarking that the turkey was remarkably tender and the whiskey was as smooth as cream. '*Bella*!' he muttered, holding the bottle up to the light; the liquid inside shimmered like molten gold.

Early that morning, he'd lit a fire in the grate, using a small sack of nutty slack bought especially for the occasion, and a couple of old orange boxes that Lily and Georgie had found by the docks.

The dinner was eaten in a sombre atmosphere that lightened a little afterwards when Joyce turned up with Edward and an engagement ring to show off.

'It's a diamond solitaire,' Joyce boasted, twiddling the fingers on her left hand so the tiny jewel sparkled brilliantly.

'Congratulations to the pair o' yis,' Martha said warmly. Good news was welcome for a change.

Frank arrived later. He'd eaten elsewhere and seemed determined to raise the spirits of his family with an assortment of jokes to tell and a box of games to play, as well as a pack of cards. He entertained Lily and Georgie for hours, until sidetracked by Georgie's train set, whereupon he lay on the floor in his best suit and, like a child, happily watched the little engine and carriages chuff around the circular track. Even in the old days when Carlo was in work, they couldn't have afforded such an expensive toy.

'Our Joe would've loved this,' he said. He was still playing with the trains when he realized the pubs were open and took his father away for a drink.

'I might be back later,' he shouted as he left. 'If not, I'll see youse lot on New Year's Eve.'

Joyce dressed and undressed Lily's doll, Buttercup, until it was time for her and Edward to go back to the rooms, where the girls were throwing a party.

Martha was standing on the step waving them tara, when she noticed Tommy Mahon, quite unsuitably dressed for December, sitting on the step of the house across the road, where the Mahon family lived in the basement.

Outraged, Martha picked her way over icy cobbles and banged on the basement window. 'Is anyone there?' she screamed. There was no answer.

'Where's your mam and dad?' she asked the shivering child. He wore shorts, a tattered jersey and a pair of wellies that were different sizes.

'Out,' the child said vaguely.

'Did they forget to take you with them or something?'

'I dunno.'

'Pigs!' she snorted. The child didn't protest when she scooped him up in her arms and carried him back to her own place.

She sat nursing him for most of the evening, feeding him pieces of turkey and the odd chocolate, worried he might be sick if he ate too much, while Lily and Georgie played with the games and sang carols, vying with each other to sing the loudest.

Theresa and Donal Mahon returned hours later, as drunk as David's sow and screaming insults at each other, their other kids trailing behind. An angry Martha marched across with Tommy, who, it turned out, must have walked all the way home by himself from Theresa's sister's house in Everton where the family had spent the day.

211

'I'll give this little bugger what for when we get inside,' she swore, roughly dragging her son out of Martha's arms. The child began to cry.

'Not when it's Christmas, Theresa,' Martha pleaded.

'Mind your own sodding business.' She stumbled down the steps to the basement.

Martha made her way home. She felt too sad for words as she helped Lily and Georgie get ready for bed.

The world was quiet and the fire was nothing but a few fading embers when Carlo came home alone – Frank had gone to see a friend, he said. Carlo was still relatively sober. Seeing this, Martha took the opportunity to tell him about the baby she was expecting.

At first, he was too stunned to speak. She thought dispassionately how handsome he still was when he'd shaved and wore decent clothes. 'When's it due?' he asked after he'd recovered.

'End of June or early July.' Her belly was just starting to swell.

'Maybe God's sending us a replacement for our Joe,' he said in an awed voice.

'I'll be glad to have five kids again, but there'll never be a replacement for Joe.' There'd been an emptiness to the day, a space in it that would never be filled, no matter how many more children she had.

'I must write to Mama,' Carlo said. 'I'd always write and tell her whenever we were expecting a baby, and send a photo afterwards. In return, Mama would send a present like a shawl or a blanket that she'd knitted herself.'

'I remember,' Martha murmured, secretly thrilled. She hadn't expected Carlo ever to mention his mother again, let alone write to her. 'We planned to go and see

212

her one day,' she reminded him, 'as well as sail to the Isle of Man to visit your cousin Freddy.'

The fire in the grate was slowly disappearing, little mountains and bridges of red ash collapsing in showers of sparks. The room was getting noticeably colder and the last of the fuel had been used.

'I miss Italy,' Carlo said. 'I miss the hills and the vines and the smells. It was peaceful there.' Martha didn't remind him it had been peaceful in Liverpool until he'd decided to get into a fight with the Irish lads. He shivered. 'And in the south it's always warm at Christmas.' He was full of moans all of a sudden. 'I'm not sure if I'm up to writing in my old language any more.'

'You can try,' Martha said encouragingly. It was a bit late, more than twenty years, for him to start feeling nostalgic about his homeland. But perhaps it was a good sign; he was beginning to feel like a real human being again, rather than moving through life like a sleepwalker.

'I can't remember when I last wrote a letter to anyone, in English or Italian.'

'It was when we had Georgie. Not long afterwards you hurt your arm.'

Carlo made a face at his right arm, grumbled good-night, and went to bed, leaving Martha to sit in front of the grate watching the red ash turn to grey, feeling aware of the room getting colder and colder.

There was the sound of shouts and singing in the far distance. She listened harder, conscious of a closer noise coming from right outside the house; thumping sounds, muffled groans, a threatening voice. She peered through the window and saw her Frank being knocked silly by a monster of a man, who was nearly twice his size.

Martha screamed, seized the poker, and rushed outside. The big man had pulled her son upright by the lapels of his camel coat and looked as if he were about to throw him across the court. She hit him hard on the back of his legs with the poker, and he roared and fell to his knees. Frank managed to scramble to his feet.

'Get inside,' Martha snarled. 'Leave this bugger to me.'

'Don't be daft, Mam. He'll make mincemeat out of you. Here, give us that poker.'

'I'll do no such thing, lad. You'll only kill him and Sergeant Gilligan will make sure you're hung by the neck until you're dead, me an' all if he can manage it.' She swung the poker around her head as her son's attacker got slowly to his feet. 'Come closer, and I'll break your bloody head this time,' she threatened.

Keeping his head low and his face hidden, the man stumbled out of the court.

It turned out that Frank had long ago settled his debts. He had no idea why anyone should want to attack him. Earlier that day, he'd been innocently visiting a friend when her husband had arrived unexpectedly, got hold of the wrong end of the stick, and Frank had felt obliged to leave. He thought the man outside was the husband's neighbour, a retired boxer.

'One of these days you'll get yourself into *real* trouble,' Martha chided, dabbing his lip with iodine. His eye was swollen and he had red marks on his neck where the neighbour had attempted to strangle him. 'If I hadn't gone out there when I did, that bugger might well have killed you.'

The enormity of what she'd said, the idea that she could have easily lost another son, was so terrifying that she burst into tears, closely followed by Frank, who promised faithfully to behave like a saint for the rest of his life.

'I'm not kidding, Mam. Honest.'

Clive Dexter had begun to make enquiries about serving in a non-military way at the Front. A few days after Christmas, he was driving down to London, intending to present himself personally at the War Office, when, just outside Oxford, he turned a bend and came face to face with a horse and cart travelling on the wrong side of the road. To avoid a collision, he turned his car into a ditch, banging his head and breaking his arm in two places.

Kate visited him in his office a week later. He was in a foul temper.

'What do you want?' he snapped when she burst in. The bump on his forehead had turned yellow and his right arm was encased in plaster. He was finding it enormously difficult to write or type with his left hand.

'Martha's having a baby,' she announced. 'She's just told me.'

'Good for her,' he said grumpily.

Her eyes sparkled. 'Oh, but isn't it marvellous news?'

'It's wonderful.' He could see nothing good or wonderful about it.

'Herbert said you'd had an accident. You look awful,' she said sympathetically. 'How are you feeling?'

'Wonderful,' he repeated. 'I feel wonderful.'

She sat at the other side of his desk and beamed at

him. 'I don't suppose you'd appreciate being wished a Happy New Year.'

'You're right; I wouldn't.' He indicated the sling on his arm.

'It *is* good about Martha, though, isn't it? It'll take her mind off Joe a bit.'

'I doubt if it will,' he said. 'A birth doesn't cancel out a death. How is she?' He was genuinely interested in anything to do with Martha. 'Have you just seen her?'

'Today's my first day back at college so it's the first time we've met since before Christmas. How about you? Did you have a nice holiday, putting aside the accident, that is?'

'Wonderful.'

'Everything's wonderful with you today, isn't it, Clive?' she said animatedly. She was looking extraordinarily pretty in a rose pink costume and a fluffy pink hat, her cheeks just as pink from the cold.

'Were you just a tiny bit more perceptive, Miss Kellaway, you might have noticed that my tone of voice when I uttered the word indicated that I meant the opposite.'

'I thought we were on first-name terms, Mr Dexter. And I had noticed that the tone in which you said "wonderful" was at odds with the word itself, but I was too polite to say so.'

She giggled and he half-expected her to stick her tongue out. Oh, but he did feel better for her being there. He sat and glared at her for a full half-minute while she held back another giggle. After a while, the glare changed into a look of admiration. Clive wasn't aware of this, though Kate was and felt exhilarated.

According to Kate, it was a boring winter. There was hardly any snow and she loved snow. She loved shuffling through it in her rubber boots, and building snowmen. It wasn't even all that cold, though that was a good thing for people like Martha, who couldn't afford to light fires for most of the year and had only that silly little stove to keep warm.

Martha seemed to have recovered from the initial shock of Joe's death. Kate was surprised but pleased. A letter had come from the War Office addressed to Mr and Mrs C. Rossi to say that Private Giuseppi Antonio Rossi was to be buried in France. When shown the letter, at first Kate thought a mistake had been made when she saw Joe's name in its original Italian. Maybe it was this confirmation of her son's death that had helped his mother to accept his loss. She hardly mentioned him nowadays. Her mind was probably taken up with the new baby.

Kate plied her friend with oranges, having read in *Patty's Paper*, a magazine concerned with women's health and beauty, that eating plenty of oranges protected against loads of different diseases as well as being essential for pregnant women.

'If this baby turns out to be coloured orange, I'll have a few words to say to you, young lady,' Martha said good-naturedly when another bag of the fruit was pressed upon her.

The days became warmer and longer – something called British Summer Time had been introduced with the war, but hardly anyone understood it. The journey to work on the train from Ormskirk to Liverpool was enhanced by the grassy banks of snowdrops, bluebells or crocuses on both sides.

One fine, sunny day early in April, Kate came out of school at lunch-time in the hope of finding Martha waiting for her. Instead, she found two of Martha's children, Lily and Georgie, seated on the steps of the college. They leaped to their feet when they saw her, two thin little waifs, though better dressed than most of the other kids Kate remembered seeing in King's Court.

'Mam's gone away,' Lily informed her.

'She's gone to London,' Georgie added.

Kate was puzzled. 'On the train?' she enquired.

'No, she's walking,' Lily replied. 'She caught the ferry to Birkenhead this morning and she's walking to Chester first.'

'*Walking!*' Kate could scarcely believe her ears. 'But what about the baby?' Martha was now six months pregnant.

'Our dad asked her that. She said if she waited until after the baby's born, then she'd never get away.'

'And who's looking after you two?'

'Our dad is,' Lily said affably. 'Mam said if he didn't look after us proper, she'd bloody batter him.'

'*Walking,*' Kate said again. 'To *London*? It'll take for ever. Did she ask you to come and tell me?'

'No, she said we weren't to tell anyone, but me and Georgie thought you ought to know.'

'Oh!' Kate felt pleased that they had such confidence in her, and wondered what they expected her to do. Catch up with Martha and give her the money for the train, for instance? 'Would you like an ice cream?' she asked. She could think while they ate.

'*Please*,' they chorused.

She took them to Woolworth's in Church Street where there was a counter selling ice creams and soft drinks. She bought cornets for the children and lemonade for herself.

'Exactly why is your mother walking to London?' she asked, wondering why she hadn't asked before.

'For our Joe,' Lily explained. 'She's walking to London to see the Prime Minister about our Joe.'

Chapter 13

After disembarking from the ferry, Martha walked quickly through Birkenhead, with its busy shops and little streets of terraced houses that mainly housed workers from Cammell Laird, the ship builders.

She was pleased to reach the countryside where the air no longer smelled of soot and smoke, where birds sang and there wasn't a single roof or chimney pot to be seen. The pale yellow April sun was almost directly overhead, bringing back memories of when she was a girl living in Ireland.

The narrow road she took was bordered by thinly leaved hedges through which she glimpsed the occasional bird's nest. She wished she could peer in and see the young birds, or perhaps a clutch of tiny eggs. What time was it? she wondered. Either very late in the morning or early in the afternoon, she guessed.

As she walked, she hummed a little song. Today, she didn't feel a bit like herself, Martha Rossi, but some other woman altogether on her way to London to see the Prime Minister whose name was Herbert Asquith. She wanted to tell him about Joe and ask if lads of his age were still being sent to France to die. Arthur Hanson had told her the matter had been raised in Parliament more than once.

Eventually, she came to her first milestone, a little hump of granite on the corner of a path just wide enough for a horse and cart or a small motor car, with 'Little Bebington 3 miles' etched on the side. According to Mister, Little Bebington was one of the villages off the main road to Chester, about fifteen miles from Birkenhead. Mister had booked and paid for her lodgings in Chester that night, though from then on she would find her own lodgings and pay for them herself. She'd been saving the money ever since Christmas — a penny here, a penny there — and had pawned the lovely green frock that had belonged to Kate's sister, as well as, for the umpteenth time, her wedding ring. With what she'd already saved for Joe's coming home party, she had nearly twenty-five shillings.

There was a list in her shopping bag of the places where she would stop, as well as a map of England on which Mister had joined the places together with a line of purple ink. She would pass many, many more milestones on her way to London, he had advised her.

'Are you sure fifteen miles isn't too far to walk in a single day?' he'd asked.

'When I was a young girl back in Ireland, I used to walk nearly three miles to school every day,' she said boastfully, forgetting there were long periods when she never went near school. 'And another three miles back.' Fifteen miles to Chester was nothing when she had an entire day to do it in.

'But you're in a condition,' he said, his big brown eyes sliding down to her swollen belly, apparently too embarrassed to mention what the condition was. 'And you're not a young girl any more.'

'But I'm not an old one, either.'

She wondered now how far she'd already walked. The milestone made no mention of Birkenhead or Chester.

'Are you watching me, Joe?' she said out loud. 'I'm doing this for you, lad. I'm sorry I wasn't there when you died and went to heaven, but I'm making up for it now.' She suppressed a sob and wiped her nose on her sleeve – she'd forgotten to bring a bit of rag for a hanky.

A horse approached, pulling a ramshackle cart that carried a wire cage packed with angry, squawking hens. The driver, a big man with a chin full of warts, tipped his cap and bade Martha a curt 'Afternoon'.

'Good afternoon,' Martha said, just as curtly. In her opinion, it was downright cruel to pack the creatures so tightly in the cage that they could hardly breathe. No wonder they were angry. She was concerned that not all would survive the journey.

She strode along, breathing in deeply and letting the breath out again with a loud 'Haaah!' After a while, she removed her shawl, folded it and put it in her string shopping bag – she'd lengthened the handle so she could carry it over her shoulder. It contained a towel, a face flannel, soap, a comb and a pair of knickers, as well as the list from Mister, which he'd written in large capital letters, and one or two other bits and pieces. Her purse was safely in the pocket of her grey frock.

Another cart passed, this one carrying a small plough. The driver was talking to himself and ignored her. She felt faintly hurt and at the same time slowed her pace. It would be silly to tire herself out needlessly.

Was it nearly time for Lily and Georgie to come home from school? she wondered some time later.

Carlo had promised to make their tea. They'd been getting along much better, she and Carlo, since Christmas when she'd told him about the baby. They had the occasional conversation and he'd stopped wandering the streets staring at the beautiful mosaics he'd once made, though still spent too much of his time cadging drinks in the pubs.

'You'd better be finding yourself a job of work before this baby comes,' she'd warned him. 'I can't take a baby to work with me; Mister would never stand for it, and you're not fit to look after it on your own, are you?'

'No, Martha,' he'd admitted. 'I'll find a job of some sort. Don't worry.'

'If you don't, we'll all end up in the workhouse.' This was an empty threat; there was no way she would allow her kids anywhere near a workhouse.

According to the next milestone she came to, she was eleven miles from Chester.

Eleven! That meant she'd only walked four miles and it felt more like eight, ten even.

'Bugger,' she muttered. Her boots had begun to rub her heels, even though she had lined them with brown paper, and the baby felt exceptionally heavy in her belly. 'Bugger.' She kicked a stone, put both her arms around her belly and hoisted it upwards.

She was walking more slowly now and dragging her feet. She felt much too hot, but, having removed her shawl, she had nothing else to take off apart from her straw hat. She removed it and put it in the bag; it might help.

'I'm doing this for Joe,' she reminded herself, throwing back her shoulders and doing her best to keep up a decent speed just in case he was watching from on high and noticed she'd begun to lag. She'd get to Chester today if she had to crawl there on her hands and knees and didn't arrive until midnight.

She sat down on the next milestone, wishing she'd thought to bring a bottle of water and something to eat. Despite her recent vow, it wasn't *absolutely* necessary that she walk all the way to Chester today. The first village she came to she could look for a bed and breakfast place, stay the night, and make for Chester tomorrow. Mind you, she hadn't actually passed through a village so far. There'd just been the occasional big house set well back from the road, which was no help.

She was preparing herself to stand up and start walking again, when she heard the clip-clop of hooves, and a small horse pulling a smart trap with navy livery and polished wheels came trotting towards her. The driver, a stern-looking woman wearing a tweed skirt, brown velvet jacket, and a suede hat sporting a green feather, shouted, 'Whoah, Noble,' and the vehicle stopped.

'Are you all right?' the woman enquired of Martha, who was desperately trying to separate herself from the milestone.

'Yes, thank you. I'd just stopped for a rest.'

'Would you like a lift? Where are you off to?'

'Chester.' Chester required less explanation than London.

'Well, I'm going to Thornton Heath. It's along this road, then I turn off about three miles hence, but I can take you that far to Chester. Hop on if you're interested.'

It didn't seem right. She'd sworn to walk to London, not be given lifts part of the way. But perhaps she'd bitten off more than she could chew. Anyroad, Joe wouldn't mind. He'd understand that she felt all in.

'Thank you.' It required an almost superhuman effort to get to her feet and another to climb on to the trap. She could see over the hedges to where villages nestled at the foot of little hills, and cows grazed in the fields.

The woman didn't introduce herself or ask Martha's name, but was nevertheless very talkative. She was on her way to see her daughter-in-law, a lazy, good-for-nothing girl who came from Manchester, of all places. She pronounced Manchester in a disgusted voice, as if if she were saying 'Sodom and Gomorrah'.

'Some afternoons, she has *friends* around from *Manchester* and they *smoke cigarettes* and drink *sherry*. They are young married women like herself who come in a *motor car*. Now she is demanding that my son buy a *motor car* for herself, and I have a horrible feeling that he is *weakening*.'

Martha wished she could spend her own afternoons drinking sherry, but thought it wise not to say so.

'When she married my son, she couldn't even bake a *loaf of bread*,' she continued wrathfully. 'As for jam, she thought it was born in a jar, not made in a pan.'

'Does she have children?' Martha asked. She felt intimidated by the woman's intensity of feeling.

'Not yet,' the woman said grimly. 'When she does, I think I shall have to move in with her and my son. The stupid girl won't have the faintest idea how to look after the poor little mite.'

'I think it's something that comes to a woman

225

naturally,' Martha said timidly, and was taken aback by the answering snort.

'*Nothing* comes naturally to Victoria. She is possibly the most useless person on *earth*.'

From then on, Martha didn't say another word, worried she'd be thrown off the cart if she expressed an opinion ever so slightly in favour of Victoria.

Eventually, though, they came to a signpost pointing to Thornton Heath. The woman tugged at the reins and shouted, 'Whoah, Noble,' again, and Martha was forced to dismount, after expressing her grateful thanks for the lift and saying a silent prayer for Victoria.

The break from walking had done her feet no good at all. To her horror, she found she could no longer walk at all, only hobble. Every step felt more painful than the one before. She began to hope and pray for another lift, but there was little traffic on the road. A motor car passed, going in the opposite direction, followed shortly afterwards by a man on a horse who cheerfully wished her 'Good afternoon'.

'Good afternoon,' she almost sobbed, by which time horse and rider were out of earshot.

What a dead stupid person she was! And why hadn't Mister tried harder to convince her that fifteen miles was too much for someone like her to walk in a day? Her feet felt too tender and sore to take another step.

How was she to spend the night? she wondered. Sleeping in a field, she supposed, hoping it wouldn't rain. In fact, she wouldn't mind doing that right now; she'd lie down and use the shopping bag as a pillow.

Limping onwards, she kept her eye out for gaps in the hedge that she could shove through, but, although the trees were bare, they were tightly woven together and there was no sign of a break anywhere.

'Holy Mary, Mother of God, help me,' she muttered loudly.

As if by magic, the Holy Mother responded immediately, bless her. A car approached from behind, roaring past and stopping a few yards in front with a screech of brakes.

A man leaped out. 'Martha!' he cried, flinging his arms around her as if she were a long-lost relative. 'I thought I'd never find you. How on earth did you manage to get this far?'

'I got a lift.' Martha burst into tears. She had only met Clive Dexter a couple of times and considered him a very nice young man. The fact that he'd come looking for her, actually appeared extremely relieved to have found her, only made her cry more. 'Me feet hurt,' she wept, 'and the baby weighs a bloody ton.'

'Would you like me to take you home?' Clive asked tenderly, leading her to the car.

She violently shook her head. 'Of *course* not. I'm walking to London, aren't I? Tonight I'm sleeping in Chester.'

'Oh, Martha!' He shook his head as if to say she was beyond his understanding, opened the rear door of the car, and helped her inside. 'Take your boots off,' he commanded. 'Where are you staying in Chester?'

'Somewhere called The Fleece; Mister booked it for me.'

'This Mister chap has a lot to answer for. I doubt if *I* could walk all the way to Chester in a single day – and *I'm* not expecting a baby!'

★

227

The Fleece turned out to be a white-washed building criss-crossed with black beams, and set in the corner of a cobbled square. Clive stopped the car in front of it and helped his passenger out.

'There's no need to put your boots on,' he said. 'We'll do something about your feet in a minute.' He marched into the building and Martha followed. At the end of a long, dark, corridor, a middle-aged woman in a black dress was seated behind a desk.

She looked up at their approach and her face expressed grim astonishment when she saw Martha, who was shoeless, hatless, limping badly, her hair wild and her belly swollen, and carrying her belongings in a string bag instead of a smart leather case like most guests. Martha was sure she would have been turned away, despite Mister having made a reservation, had not Clive arrived at the desk before her and demanded the key to Mrs Rossi's room.

'Mrs Rossi is booked into room three on the second floor which is a single,' the woman protested, as if she were concerned it was Clive's intention to share the room with her. The thought made Martha blush.

'And a single room is what she expects,' Clive confirmed haughtily. 'Will you kindly send up a bowl of warm water, a towel, and a pot of tea for two immediately.'

'The tea is an extra and will have to be paid for separately,' he was informed in a voice that barely avoided being rude.

'I shall do that on my way out, madam. Come along, Martha.'

The woman virtually raised her hands in horror.

'Sir! Unless you are Mr Rossi, which I doubt, I cannot possibly allow you in this lady's room.'

Clive bestowed upon her a look of contempt. 'Madam, I am Mrs Rossi's doctor, and it is my intention to attend to her injuries in her room. However, if there is a guests' lounge available, I shall do it there, in public, if you prefer.'

The key was handed over without another word. Clive put his hand under Martha's elbow and led her upstairs.

'I shall look out of the window while you take your stockings off,' he said when they were in the small but comfortable room overlooking the square, and she was sitting on the edge of the narrow bed.

'What are you going to do, then?' Martha asked.

'Nothing. The water is for you to soak your feet in. Oh, I shall pour us both tea, then sit and listen while you explain to me exactly what you are up to.'

There was a knock on the door and two women entered, one very old and the other young. The old one carried a tin basin and had a towel draped over her arm; the younger one a silver tray containing the tea things. The tray was placed on a little bureau in front of the window and the basin on a wash-stand that already held a muggin bowl and chamber pot to match. Each woman bobbed a curtsy and left the room.

By now, Martha had released her stockings from their tatty garters and her feet were bare – not just bare, but bloody, too. She pulled a face. The skin on every single toe had been broken and her heels were red raw.

'Look at that!' Clive said, throwing a stern glance at her injured feet. He brought over the water, knelt down and gently placed her left foot in the bowl, then the right. 'Does that feel better?'

Martha breathed, 'Oh, *yes*,' as both feet instantly began to throb the tiredness away. 'Why are you doing this?' she asked. 'Being so nice, like. I mean, you hardly know me.'

He looked at her, still kneeling at her feet. 'Because I admire you tremendously, Martha. You are brave and tenacious. You shout at policemen and bearded a particularly unpleasant politician in his den. You learned to read, just so you could write to Joe and read his letters. You work to support your other children and an apparently useless husband. You are braver and tougher than any man I know.'

Martha lowered her head, embarrassed. 'How did you know where to find me?'

'Kate told me – your children told her.'

'I said they weren't to tell anybody.'

'They told Kate that as well.' He got to his feet. 'Would you like some tea now, while your feet are soaking?'

'I'd love some, ta.'

Dishes rattled behind her. 'Do you take sugar?' he asked. 'They've sent lumps.'

'Seven lumps, please.'

'Seven!'

'We hardly ever have sugar at home, 'cept at Christmas, like. Seven lumps would be a treat – as long as there's enough left for you, luv,' she added hastily.

'There's plenty – I only take one, anyway. Here you are.' He handed her the tea in a fine China cup and saucer. 'Tea with seven lumps of sugar. It'll probably taste vile.'

She supped it noisily. 'It tastes the gear,' she said happily.

'When you've finished, we'll discuss exactly how you intend getting to London on those bloody feet,' he said.

Before leaving, while paying for the tea, Clive ordered Martha's evening meal to be served in her room. He left the hotel, threw himself into the car, and sped back to Birkenhead where he drove on to the ferry, tapping his fingers impatiently on the steering wheel, until he drove off again in Liverpool.

Back in his office, he rolled a sheet of foolscap paper into his typewriter and began to type furiously, only vaguely aware of Herbert popping his head round the door to say goodnight and people leaving the shops and offices outside to make their way home.

About half an hour later, he tore the paper out of the machine and read it through. It was typed in double spacing on two sheets.

MARTHA'S JOURNEY

Today, a woman called Martha began a journey. Martha is a very ordinary woman who works in a small factory sewing sacks. Until not long ago, she had five children, the middle child a son, Joe, aged fourteen.

One day in June, Joe informed his mother that he'd joined the Army. He'd been tempted into doing so with a shilling offered by a local police-man, a sergeant, who was well aware of the boy's age. Martha immediately went to the police station and protested to the sergeant, but to no avail. She also visited Major Norman Brown, her Member of Parliament, who insensitively told her that she should feel proud her young son was about to fight in the war to end all wars, as it has been called.

Soon Joe's papers arrived from the Army. He was to join the West Lancashire Infantry Division, and Martha felt she had no alternative but to let him go, an action that she has come to deeply regret.

Four months later Joe was killed, just one of the thousands of victims of the Battle of Loos. It turns out that this brave young lad dragged his childhood friend, Albie (also fourteen), who'd been temporarily blinded by an exploding shell, back to the trenches, his own leg being severely damaged on the way. Having saved Albie and despite his injury, Joe obeyed, though in great pain, orders from an officer to return to the scene of battle. Sometime afterwards, he incurred an injury that eventually proved fatal. During that dreadful period, Albie was forced to listen to the sound of his dying friend crying for his mother and for Albie himself, until the time came when Joe cried no more.

Although Martha wasn't there to hear her son's last words, she cannot forget them, which is why yesterday, six months pregnant with her sixth child, she started on her journey to London. There she will call upon the Prime Minister, Herbert Asquith, and plead with him to make sure no more youngsters like Joe die before their time.

Today, this reporter came upon Martha several miles away from her first destination, Chester. Her feet were bloodied, she was exhausted, but she is determined, somehow, to finish her journey.

It is my intention to accompany Martha on her journey, take her a few miles in my car when she can walk no more. My reports will be published daily until Martha arrives in London, her journey complete.

There are thousands more women like Martha in this country today; women who have lost sons or husbands in this terrible war, a war that has no real purpose, that is being fought over a few feet of mud in a country that is not our own. It is a war to do with vanity and the love of power, and nothing to do with justice or freedom, a war in which children are being coaxed with a shilling to fight, a war that should never have started and a war that should quickly end.

It must be stressed that these views are those of the writer of this article and not those of the newspaper in which they appear.

Clive ran from the office and jumped into his car for the third time that day. This time his destination was Blackpool, and he drove with the same recklessness as he'd driven earlier.

The *Lancashire Post* in rough form didn't usually reach the print shop until going on for ten o'clock. Clive found Edgar Henderson virtually tearing his hair out when he burst into his office and threw Martha's article on to his desk.

'Read that,' he demanded. 'If you refuse to publish it, then I'm handing in my notice here and now and taking it to another paper. I've decided I only want to work for a newspaper that's got something serious to say about serious matters.'

'You've got a bloody cheek,' the editor spluttered.

'I've also got a damned good article telling a story that can be continued for a week, perhaps, or even longer.' He pushed the article forward until it was underneath the man's nose. 'Are you going to read it or not?'

'I'll read it,' Edgar Henderson said grudgingly. 'In return, you can read this. It's the minutes of last night's Blackpool council meeting, and the spelling and grammar are atrocious. They don't teach either at school with the thoroughness they did in my young day.'

Clive grabbed a pencil and seated himself on the other side of the desk. The reporter had actually left the 'u' out of building and used the incorrect spelling of 'their'. His own article was being read in complete silence.

Eventually, Clive's manuscript was thrown on to the desk. 'OK, I'll use it,' the editor said as grudgingly as he'd offered to read it.

'It's going to be a sort of diary,' Clive explained. 'Do you agree to publish every day until Martha reaches London?'

'I suppose we'll be obliged to finish what we've started. Let's hope this Martha does the same.'

'Martha would never let anyone down,' Clive promised.

'And how exactly is this "journey" of hers going to be covered when she nears London?' Edgar Henderson asked sourly. 'Who's going to cover it and send the details back to me? If I remember rightly, *you* are the *Post*'s Liverpool reporter. How much reporting from that city did you do today?'

Clive nodded at his article. '*That* much,' he said,

'People who aren't normally readers of the *Post* might start buying it to keep up with Martha's story. Circulation could increase enormously.'

'Or it could decrease by even more,' the man grumbled. 'I'll send someone to Liverpool to cover for you over the next few days or whatever. I don't think you realize, son, the fervour with which people in the country support this war.'

Clive managed to suppress the anger that wanted to choke him. 'Once, perhaps, but too many young men have died needlessly for the support to be as strong as it was. Are you not aware of the number of people *against* the war? Have you never heard of the Women's International League, the Independent Labour Party, the No-Conscription Fellowship, the Fellowship of Reconciliation, the Union of Democratic Control? There are more if you would like their names.'

He paused for a reply, but none came. Considering his point made, Clive went home.

Chapter 14

'She's gone,' the woman behind the desk at The Fleece said churlishly the next morning when Clive asked for Mrs Rossi. It was the same woman who'd been so rude the day before.

'Gone!' He'd told her to wait for him – well, *suggested* that she wait, so they could work out a strategy together, check Mister's list of the places she would pass through, and count the number of miles in between.

'How was she?' he asked.

'I didn't consider it my business to ask.' The woman turned away with a dismissive shrug.

'Well, I don't consider it my business to ask why you are so unpleasant because quite frankly I don't care.' He gave her another look of utter contempt. 'One day, you will be proud to say that Mrs Martha Rossi slept underneath the roof of this hotel.' He'd bought a copy of the *Lancashire Post* that morning and his piece on Martha had appeared prominently on page three, the next best thing to being on the front. He put his cap back on with a flourish. 'Good day to you, madam. Here's hoping we never meet again.'

He left her with her mouth hanging open, and was about to step outside the hotel when an older woman –

the one who'd brought the water to Martha's room yesterday – caught his arm.

'I heard you asking about the lady on the second floor with the bad feet,' she said. 'Earlier, she enquired how far it was to Waverton. I said it were about five or six miles, and she set off that way.'

Clive thanked her profusely and set off that way himself.

Just outside Chester he drove on to a grass verge and braked, leaving the engine running. He was worried that Martha didn't understand the enormity of her decision to walk to London. At this rate, it was going to take her at least a week to get through Cheshire, then there was Shropshire to cross, Worcestershire, a bit of Gloucestershire, Oxfordshire, Buckinghamshire, Middlesex and finally London. She could be walking for the next few months. Yet he didn't want to dissuade her – it was none of his business; if Martha's husband and children were willing to see her go, then who was he to put her off?

What was he supposed to do now? Keep driving until he caught up with her and took her to Waverton in the car? He could take her all the way to London. They would arrive well before the day was out. But he knew that this wasn't what she wanted. She was making a gesture, walking for Joe and all the other young men who'd become soldiers well before their time.

Loosening the brake, he steered the car back on to the road. He would drive slowly and as soon as he saw Martha ahead he would follow at a discreet distance while trying to judge how she was feeling, to see if she was limping, hobbling or creeping. Or perhaps walking briskly, though he doubted it considering the state of her feet yesterday.

He was still driving slowly when he reached Waverton. There'd been no sign of Martha. Stopping, he studied the map for the next village she would come to. Halton Heath. He set off again, faster now, reaching Halton Heath without a glimpse of Martha on the way.

'Damn and blast!' he swore, worried that she'd collapsed in a ditch and he'd passed without noticing or, worse still, that someone unsuitable had offered her a lift and she'd been taken who knows where.

He had stopped beside a small inn of russet brick with a moss-covered roof. There were tables outside where people were being served by a waitress of some sixty years, who was wearing a sparkling white bonnet and apron. A hanging sign informed him this was The Goat and Boot, an unusual name for an attractive place. His watch also informed him that it was nearly one o'clock. He felt both hungry and thirsty. He parked at the side of the building and made his way to an empty table where he sat and waited to be served.

The waitress approached. Close up her face was heavily wrinkled, but she had a lovely smile. Clive requested a brown ale and asked if they served refreshments.

'We do indeed, sir; crusty rolls or baps with cheese and pickle, ham and mustard, or beef with horseradish sauce.'

'A ham bap, please.' The waitress had turned to go when Clive said, 'Oh, by the way, have you seen a woman pass by today? She's wearing a grey dress with a black shawl and she's . . .' He didn't like to say quite baldly that she was pregnant, but there was a French word. 'She's *enceinte*,' he said eventually.

'Well, sir, if by that last word you meant to say she's in the family way, well there's a woman of that description resting upstairs at this very minute. She arrived on the cart with the ale delivery about half an hour ago, dead on her feet, poor lamb. I had her lie down immediately.'

'Can I see her?' Clive asked eagerly.

'Course you can, sir,' the woman said heartily. 'It's the door directly at the top of the stairs. I'll have your bap and the ale ready for when you come down again.'

'Thank you.'

Clive entered the distinctly left-leaning corridor of the inn, and climbed the stairs that lurched to the right. He knocked on the ill-fitting door at the top and Martha called dully, 'Yes?'

He opened the door. 'It's me,' he said. 'I thought I'd lost you. The woman outside said you arrived in a quite a state.'

'At this rate,' Martha said, sniffing despondently, 'I'll not get to London by Christmas.'

Clive nodded. 'You're right, Martha. So what are we going to do about it?'

'I don't know.' She appeared close to tears. 'Joe apart, what will Lily and Georgie think if I go back after I'd hardly been gone a minute? They'll say their mam's a failure, just like their dad. I'd be letting them down as well as Joe.'

'But you've set yourself an impossible target,' Clive protested. 'As for Lily and Georgie, I reckon they'd be thrilled to see their mother back home. I'll take you there right now,' he offered, 'if that's want you want.'

Should she agree, he would have made a complete fool of himself in front of Edgar Henderson, who hadn't been all that enthusiastic about publishing the series of articles. He'd be understandably cross if the whole business were over within forty-eight hours.

Martha frowned and pursed her lips angrily. 'It's not what I want. I'm not going home, not for anything.'

Clive felt relieved as well as ashamed. For as long as Martha was on the road, he had a story. 'How are your feet today?' he asked.

'Bloody awful, if the truth be known.'

'Would you like me to bathe them again?'

'Who d'you think you are – Mary Magdalene?'

Clive hid a grin and ignored the comment. 'You need new boots. Let me take you somewhere and I'll buy new ones,' he offered.

'Where?' she asked suspiciously. 'I'm not going back to Liverpool for any reason.'

'Nantwich; it's about ten or twelve miles away.'

'We wouldn't be going backwards?'

'No, Martha, forwards,' he said patiently.

She agreed grudgingly, but on the strict condition that one day she would pay him back every single penny for the boots and anything else he might buy. 'I wouldn't want anyone thinking I was a cadger.'

'I'm sure no one would think any such thing,' he assured her.

It was gone four o'clock by the time he got back to his office in Liverpool and there was no sign of the reporter Edgar had promised to send in his place.

'He's out on a story,' Herbert said in his jaunty way.

'He's an old geezer, at least forty, not a patch on you, boss.'

'Where is he now?' Clive asked.

'At the cop shop.'

Clive raised his eyebrows. 'The cop shop?'

'The police station, boss.' Herbert smirked. 'The old geezer didn't know what it meant, either. Some idiot tried to hold up a bank with a toy gun.'

Clive wished he didn't always have such a strong urge to cause Herbert physical harm. 'Has anything else much happened?'

The boy began to read from a list he had made of unimportant events, most of which he'd passed on to the *Post*'s Blackpool office or dealt with himself by making a few phone calls. 'Oh, and that tasty wench Kate Kellaway came looking for you. I told her I didn't know when you'd be back.'

'Thank you, Herbert.' He slapped the lad on the shoulder. 'You've done very well.' He wondered what Kate would think about being referred to as a 'tasty wench', though it was an apt description. He dialled the number of the *Lancashire Post* and asked for the editor.

'How was Martha today?' Edgar Henderson enquired immediately. Clive was surprised by his friendly tone.

'Not so bad, sir,' he said cautiously.

'The thing is, son, I had a phone call from the *Manchester Guardian* this morning.' He was pretending to sound casual, as if it were every day that he was contacted by one of the most highly regarded newspapers in the land. 'They'd read "Martha's Journey" and would like to cover it with us. They'll publish tomorrow along with what happened yesterday and today, so both papers will have reached the same point in the story. That'll be a fine feather in your cap, Clive; an article by your good self in the *Guardian* when you're only twenty-one.' He paused for breath. 'Another thing – can you get us a photo of Martha by tonight to go in tomorrow's paper? I can wire it to the *Guardian*.'

'I'll do my utmost, sir,' Clive promised. As soon as he'd written today's article, he'd go to King's Court and ask for one. There was bound to be a photo there of Martha's wedding.

'How far did our heroine get today, by the way?'

'Nantwich. Tomorrow, she's off to a place called Drayton in Shropshire.'

'Good work, Clive old chap; keep it up.' There was a sound like the ticking of a clock that could only be the editor tapping his teeth with a pencil, something he only did when excited. 'That reminds me, from now on there's no need to come back to the office of a night. You and the *Guardian* chappy, his name's Alex Scott, can write the reports between you. He'll get it back to Manchester and they'll wire it to us here. Is that all right with you?'

'Yes, sir. Thank you.' Clive resented things being taken out of his hands, though couldn't very well argue. The further away he got from the *Lancashire Post*'s offices, the more difficult it would be getting his articles back to them. Unlike the *Guardian*, they had no contacts in other counties.

Edgar Henderson rang off. Clive pulled his typewriter towards him and typed 'Martha's Journey, Day Two' at the top of the page. Hands poised over the keys, he was wondering how to begin describing Martha's progress today when, with a feeling of horror, he realized he had no idea what to write. Nothing much had happened. He hadn't even caught up with Martha until lunch-time and then all he'd done was drive her as far as Nantwich and buy her a pair of expensive leather boots, which she assured him were comfortable, a roll of bandage, a bottle of iodine, some cotton wool, and nail scissors to cut the bandage with.

He'd wanted to book her into a decent hotel, but she'd insisted on looking for somewhere 'dead cheap', as she described it, that she could pay for herself, assuring him that she had enough money. He'd dropped her outside a rundown lodging house, which didn't look all that clean.

He went cold and the hands poised over the keys began to tremble. Don't be such a sap, he told himself. You're a reporter. If you don't know what to write then make it up.

The spring sun shone vividly out of a pale blue sky yesterday morning when Martha left Chester with a gay wave and a prayer on her lips. She had slept soundlessly and dreamlessly and felt refreshed. As she walked towards the pretty village of Waverton, her next port of call, she thought about her dead son, Joe, and the young children she had left at home who were being looked after by her invalid husband.

Eventually, though, her pace grew sluggish, for she is, after all, a woman of thirty-seven, a woman carrying her sixth child, a woman of great courage, and although her heart is willing, her flesh is weak. When eventually a cart stopped and offered to take her further, she had no option but to accept.

This reporter met up with her in Halton Heath and it was there I discovered her feet were covered with fresh blisters along with yesterday's sores. I took her to Nantwich where she was provided with more suitable footwear to take her on tomorrow's journey to Drayton.

I left her in the depressing lodging house where she insisted on staying.

'Goodnight, Martha,' I whispered as I walked away. 'Pleasant dreams.'

Martha's story will be continued tomorrow.

Clive read and re-read the finished article. To his ears, it sounded far too sentimental, the sort of sweet, sugary journalism that he loathed. Edgar would like it, but he hoped, when they read it, that the *Guardian* wouldn't regret having committed the paper to publish 'Martha's Journey' to its end. He remembered that his own next port of call was King's Court where he hoped to get Martha's photo.

To his astonishment, he found Kate playing cards with Martha's children, whose names turned out to be Lily and Georgie. They both looked pale and a touch undernourished, though their clothes were warm, if not exactly clean. They shook hands nicely when they were introduced. The room they were in was depressingly shabby.

'Hello, Clive.' Kate seemed terribly pleased to see him, and he was just as pleased to see her. 'I came round to make certain the children had a decent meal. Carlo, that's Martha's husband, is doing terribly well. He's just gone for a quick drink. When he comes back, then I'll go home. Have you seen Martha?' she asked. Lily and Georgie stared at him anxiously as they waited for him to reply.

'Yes, and she's doing fine,' he said, unsure whether that was the truth or a lie. 'Actually, your mother's in two newspapers; the *Lancashire Post* and the *Manchester Guardian*. The reason I'm here,' he said, 'is to ask if you have a photograph of your mother – the day she and your dad were married, for instance.'

'There's a wedding photo and Mam looks beautiful in it,' Lily said solemnly. 'Dad looks the gear, too. It's in the sideboard drawer.' She jumped to her feet. 'I'll get it for you.'

She'd been so pretty in those days! Clive held the photograph up to the fading light. And what a beautiful smile; it completely transformed her face so that it was barely recognizable. It wasn't so much that she looked older now, inevitably older, it was more a case of her looking unhappy and worn down with disappointment and loss, not just of Joe, but of the hopes and dreams she was bound to have had on her wedding day. Yet nothing had happened to lessen her will to live and fight for her family.

'Your dad was incredibly handsome in those days,' Kate remarked.

'He still looks handsome when he wears his best suit,' Lily assured her.

'And has a shave,' Georgie added. 'And after he's had his hair cut, and cleaned his teeth.'

Clive wondered if Carlo still had the same head

of thick black curls as he did in the photograph. He smoothed back his own dead straight hair, always worried that one day he'd go bald like his father.

He turned down the offer of tea, saying he had to drive to Blackpool with the photograph.

Kate came with him to the door. 'Can I come with you to Blackpool one day?' she asked nicely. 'I'd love to see what it's like in a newspaper office. After all,' she said importantly, 'I'll be a reporter myself one of these days.'

'You'd be very welcome.' Clive wished she could come with him now. He quite fancied having some cheerful company to and from Blackpool. Once back in Liverpool, he could have taken her to a late dinner somewhere like the Adelphi.

But it was not to be. 'Bye, kids,' he shouted.

'Tara, Mr Dexter,' they shouted back.

Martha trudged towards a place called Drayton in a county she'd never heard of – she hadn't even known England was divided into things called counties until Mister had explained it to her. Anyroad, this county she was making for was Shropshire and the one she was about to leave was Cheshire.

*Any*road, she was fed up to her bloody teeth. Her feet were giving her gyp, despite the new boots, and she was finding it hard to remember a time when her feet had been ordinary, painless parts of her body. She was hungry, too; the lodging house where she'd stayed had produced a bowl of something for breakfast that vaguely resembled porridge but had tasted horrible.

She'd already refused a lift on a coal cart because the poor, sad horse was over-laden with two dozen or more sacks of coal or nutty slack piled on the back. She didn't want to add to the poor creature's load.

What time would Clive appear? she wondered. Should she just plop herself down on a milestone like a jelly and wait for him? But that didn't seem right. She wasn't making any real effort to get to London, just relying on Clive. And quite why such a nice young chap like him was bothering to help, indeed getting so worked up about it, she had no idea.

A car was coming towards her, bigger than Clive's. As it got nearer she saw it was being driven by a woman. She was stunned when it stopped, the woman opened the door and yelled, 'Are you Martha?'

'Yes,' she stammered.

'In that case, hop in, darling, and I'll take you to Drayton.' She patted the seat beside her encouragingly. She was extremely old with skin like crumpled yellow paper and a bird's nest of silver hair.

'But how do you know who I am and where I'm going?'

'I read about you in the paper, darling. It was in the *Manchester Guardian* this morning with your picture. Are you coming or not? If you don't, my sisters will be extremely disappointed. Oh, by the way, I'm Imogen Cunningham.'

'How do you do?' Nervously, Martha climbed into the car. 'We're going the wrong way,' she pointed out.

Imogen laughed. 'This car is actually capable of turning round and going in the opposite direction.' She did just that, violently twisting the steering wheel so that the car shrieked and nearly toppled over.

Minutes later, they were driving at a rapid rate to

Drayton. Martha asked, 'How many sisters do you have?'

'Three related sisters and hundreds of unrelated ones with whom I do not share blood but ideas and ideals,' Imogen said dramatically. 'I belong to the Women's International League, Shropshire branch, and we are all sisters. Have you heard of us?'

'No,' Martha whispered. She felt desperately ignorant. 'What do you do?'

'Well, we're against the war for one thing,' Imogen said in her deafening voice. 'We believe in votes for women, we support trade unions, some of us are in the Labour Party, some are Communists, we've a couple of Anarchists, and Mrs Beulah Whittaker is a Buddhist. And what are you, Martha?

'I'm a Catholic,' Martha replied timidly. Was being a Catholic posh enough to belong to the Women's International League? 'Will that do?'

'It'll do nicely, darling,' Imogen shouted. 'Now, hold on tightly and I'll get you to Drayton in a jiffy.' She sounded the horn, though the road was completely clear, and began to drive even faster.

Terrified, Martha clung to her seat and closed her eyes. She didn't open them again until they reached Drayton.

They stopped outside a small yellow-brick house standing all by itself in a field full of trees. Martha was later to discover that it was called an orchard. She was introduced first to Imogen's real sisters: Abigail, who was even older than Imogen and walked with crutches; Priscilla, cooking in the kitchen; and Josephine, the youngest of the family at around sixty, who was wearing the frilliest, laciest, most embroidered frock Martha had ever seen on an adult. Josephine fanned herself frequently and posed prettily, allowing her sisters to treat her as the baby.

There were other women present in the tiny parlour; Mrs Something-Or-Other from Manchester; Mrs Something-Else from Madeley Market where Martha was due to go later in the day. She was so confused that when even more women arrived, she just stopped taking things in to save her sanity.

She was given tea in a pretty china cup along with a plate of tiny crustless sarnies in the shape of triangles, but as soon as she took a bite of one she'd be asked a question and have to eat it without having chewed it properly and it would stick in her throat until she'd drunk more tea. She never managed to discover what was in them.

It would be the gear to have a little lie-down somewhere, she thought. Last night's palliasse had been dead lumpy and she'd hardly slept a wink.

Then Imogen got to her feet, banged her teacup with a spoon, and announced that Martha was about to say a few words. 'She is going to tell us just why she is walking to London. What motivated you, darling?'

What did motivated mean? Holy Mary, Mother of God, what the hell was she expected to say? Imogen was looking at her encouragingly. With terror in her heart, Martha rose to her feet. Every single bit of her was shaking horribly. Oh, dear God, now she had an urgent need to wee.

'Our Joe was only fourteen when this fat copper gave him a shilling to join the Army and it didn't seem fair. Then they sent him to France and that didn't seem fair, either. You see,' she coughed slightly, 'normally lads aren't allowed in the Army till they're eighteen and then they're not allowed to be sent abroad until a year later.' She swallowed hard. 'They promised they would send Joe home, but he never came and that seemed the unfairest thing of all, to let him be killed when he was no more than a lad who'd only left school a year before. His voice hadn't broken yet and his chin was almost as soft and smooth as when he was a baby. There wasn't a single hair on it. He weren't old enough to go in pubs, so why was it all right for another soldier to kill him? Not that I blame the soldier,' she said reasonably. 'He might have been no more than a lad himself and he could be dead an' all by now. And he almost certainly had a mam and a dad like me and my Carlo. And sisters and brothers, too, who'll only remember him as being young while they grow old. The time might come when they forget they ever had a brother, when he's not even a memory any more.' Of course, that would never happen to Joe.

Thinking about it, saying it out loud, was beginning to make her angry. 'Well, it's not right, is it?' she asked the women, as if they could come up with an answer. 'None of it's right,' she snorted. 'War isn't right. Why should us women have babies and let some . . . some bloody drunken bigwig' – she was thinking of Major Norman Brown MP – 'or some fat slob of a copper take them away and be killed for no reason at all that I can see.' She groaned. 'Can someone please show me where the lavvy is?' If she didn't go soon, she'd wet her knickers in front of the entire Shropshire branch of the Women's International League.

★

Although he wasn't a drinker, right now Clive badly needed something alcoholic underneath his belt. Whiskey or brandy. Neat. And he also badly needed to get to a telephone and contact Edgar Henderson.

He was in Chester and remembered The Fleece where he could avail himself of both drink and telephone. He arrived there perspiring profusely and with his heart hammering in his chest, as it had been for the best part of the day.

His least favourite woman wasn't behind the desk of The Fleece, he was pleased to note when he arrived. He went straight to the bar, and ordered a double whiskey, then carried it into the lobby where there was a telephone cubicle. He took a handful of change out of his pocket, dialled o, and asked the operator to connect him to the *Lancashire Post* in Blackpool.

'Can I speak to Mr Henderson, please?' he asked when he was put through. 'Tell him it's Clive Dexter.'

Telephones were a minor miracle, he thought, as he listened to the voices and the clatter of typewriters at the other end of the line all those miles away.

'Hello, Clive,' the editor said.

'I did my best,' Clive panted into the receiver. 'I've been driving around Shropshire for the entire day, but I'm sorry, sir, I couldn't find Martha anywhere. I've been to Nantwich and I've been to Drayton, but there was no sign of her. Now I'm back in Chester and I don't know what to do.' He wiped his still wet brow and waited for the man to explode.

'There's no need to get upset, son,' Edgar Henderson said easily. 'The chap from the *Manchester Guardian* organized her day. She spent the morning in Drayton with the Women's International League and the afternoon at a place called Madeley with a group of conscientious objectors who'd been sent to work down the mines. Alex said she made one or two really decent speeches.'

Martha had made *speeches*? The reporter from the *Guardian* had organized her day? What the hell was going on? 'Someone might have told me,' Clive complained bitterly. 'I've spent at least eight hours driving round the countryside looking for her.' He made a face at the receiver. 'Does this mean Alex Scott is taking over "Martha's Journey" from now on?'

Mr Henderson laughed. 'Of course not, Clive, though he's written a nice little piece about Martha for tomorrow's paper. By the way, she's spending the night at a vicarage in Coalthorpe. Apparently, it's next to the church so you should be able to find it easily. Alex is expecting you,' he added, as if Alex Scott were doing Clive a terrific favour.

'Thanks,' Clive said shortly. He rang off in a huff.

He may as well stay where he was, he thought, spend the night at The Fleece, and arrive in Coalthorpe first thing in the morning, hopefully catching Martha before she left, possibly with Alex Scott in tow.

Having reserved a room, he asked for his shirt to be laundered and his suit pressed. He returned to the bar, feeling angry. Did *Coal*thorpe mean there were coal mines in Shropshire? If so, *he'd* known nothing about it. And if asked, he would have said the place was somewhere up north.

As well as feeling sidelined, he felt ignorant as well.

Chapter 15

It was barely daylight when the baby gave Martha a kick that jolted her awake. She rubbed her belly to calm the child, and thought how much she'd love a cup of tea. At home, the first thing she did each morning, after getting out of bed, was make a cuppa. Even if there was little but dust in the tea caddy, with hot water added it was enough to get her going.

Then she remembered where she was, groaned, and buried her head in the soft feather pillow.

A *vicarage*! A house belonging to a Protestant vicar, Paul Hughes and his wife, Flo. She felt as if she were committing a tremendously big sin, actually *sleeping* under the roof, saying her *prayers* there. She'd bring it up next time she went to Confession, be on the safe side, like, in case it was a sin, possibly mortal. They, the vicar and his wife, were desperately nice, had asked to be called by their first names, which she'd found awful hard. After all, a vicar was the same as a priest, and just imagine being on first name terms with Father Lawless, calling him 'Bill' or 'Jack' or something. As for the good Father having a wife . . . well!

She crept out of bed and pulled up the dark green blind. There was a suggestion of watery light on the horizon and she wondered what time it would be before Paul and Flo got up.

Ages, she supposed gloomily. She got dressed and sat on the edge of the bed, prepared to be bored stiff for the next few hours, but was cheered by the sound of a tap running. She went downstairs, and found Flo in the kitchen about to put the kettle on.

'Good morning, Martha,' she said cheerfully. 'Paul's gone to milk the cow and see to the hens.' She was about Martha's age, trim and neat, her dark hair held back with a tortoiseshell slide. She spooned tea into a pretty willow-patterned teapot. 'Couldn't you sleep, either? I'm usually up at the crack of dawn. Mind you, you had an awfully busy day yesterday. You could probably have done with a lie-in.'

'Yes, but I didn't do much walking,' Martha said indignantly. 'I know I can't walk as much as I'd like, what with me being pregnant, like, but that Alex person must've driven us hundreds of miles.' Actually, she quite liked the Alex person, though not as much as she liked Clive.

'From Drayton to Madeley Market is only about twenty-five miles, dear.'

'It felt like hundreds.'

Flo must have decided not to argue. 'Would you like some tea?' she asked.

'I'm dying for a cuppa, I always am.' Martha sat at the big wooden table and glanced around the room. What must it be like to work in a kitchen such as this, with its warm tiled floor, a row of polished copper pans hanging on the wall and a pine dresser stacked with pretty plates, not all of them matching? A fire was just starting to take off in the black-leaded grate, which had a copper bed-warmer hanging on one side, bellows to match on the other, and a scuttle full of logs on the hearth. A vase of bluebells stood on the window sill.

Yet Paul and Flo didn't have kids and Martha would sooner have kids any day than the best kitchen in the world. In fact, she couldn't imagine life without them.

'Do you take sugar, Martha?' Flo asked.

'Just one spoonful, please.' She didn't like to ask for more.

'And what about something to eat?'

'Oh, a bit of toast'll do.'

'No guest in this house is allowed to leave without having a proper breakfast,' Flo said sternly. 'As soon as Paul milks Clara – that's the cow – and collects the eggs, I'll make you an omelette with some bread and butter.'

'Fancy collecting your own eggs,' Martha marvelled, 'and having milk off your very own cow.'

'Don't you have a garden in Liverpool?'

'No, just a yard.'

'I'll give you a bottle of fresh milk to take with you,' Flo promised. 'It'll do you and the baby good. Are you going to wait for that nice Mr Scott to take you to . . . where is it you're going next?'

'Wolverhampton.' Martha had never heard of the place before.

'Oh, that's right. It's the Independent Labour Party today, isn't it?' Paul and Flo were part of a peace movement, and because of it Paul was in trouble with the Church.

'I think so,' Martha said vaguely. Yesterday it had been Imogen Cunningham and the Women's Inter-national League, and in Madeley Market she'd met a group of really lovely young men who were conscientious objectors and had been sent to work down the mines.

It took great courage, she learned, to be a conscientious objector. People spat on you and the coppers gave you a crack on the sly. Women handed you white feathers, though she couldn't see much harm in that. She was amazed that any of these immensely brave and clever people were interested in what someone like her had to say.

'I'd sooner not wait for Mr Scott,' she said. 'I'd like to leave straight after breakfast and get a little bit of walking done, if you don't mind.'

'Of course I don't mind, Martha,' Flo said gently. 'After all, you're walking for God.'

Martha contradicted her. 'No, I'm not, luv. I'm walking for our Joe.'

Paul had to study a map to decide the best road to take her in the direction of Wolverhampton. 'The one to Boningdale,' he decided after a while. 'But I'd much sooner you waited for that reporter, Martha. He'll know exactly which way to go.'

But Martha's mind was absolutely made up. She thanked them for letting her sleep in their house, and they kissed her and told her to go in peace.

It was barely eight o'clock and the sun was shining brightly. She wondered if she'd get as far as London without it raining. It was still a bit nippy and she adjusted her shawl so it was around her neck as well as her shoulders. The road to Boningdale was more a wide path than a proper road, and the hedges each side glistened with dew that made plopping sounds when the drops fell into the ditch below.

Perhaps it was the nourishing breakfast that made her feel so full of energy, enabling her to walk briskly, even though she knew it wouldn't be long before her legs would get tired, there'd be a pain in her back, and the baby would weigh a ton.

She hoped Clive would arrive before Alex. Alex was desperately handsome, tall with blond hair and blue eyes and a dead charming manner. Clive was just as handsome, though in a different, quieter way. And he was sensitive and loyal and she'd trust him with her life.

A horse and cart could be heard behind. She turned and saw it was being driven by a stout, well-dressed man wearing a round felt hat.

The cart began to slow down and a voice called, 'Are you Mrs Rossi?'

'I am indeed.' It felt awful peculiar being in the newspaper. Yesterday, there'd been a photo of her and Carlo's wedding. There was a copy of the paper with the photo in her bag to show Carlo and the children when she got home.

'Well, missus, this is what I think about you suffragette bitches.' The man picked up a bucket from beside his feet and threw the contents over Martha who ducked, but not nearly enough to prevent the liquid from soaking her from head to foot. She screamed as the driver of the cart cracked his whip and the horse trotted speedily away.

It was only water! It was also freezing, but although freezing water was bad enough on such a chilly morning, at first she'd thought it might be something really disgusting, and was a little relieved.

She shook herself, removed her shawl and shook that, and picked up her hat, which had fallen off. She began to stomp along the road in the vain hope that it would help her get dry more quickly.

'Please, God, don't let me catch a cold,' she prayed. It wouldn't do the baby much good if she fell ill, and it wouldn't do her trip to London much good, either. She visualized being carried into Downing Street on a stretcher.

'Martha! What on earth has happened? You're soaking wet.'

'Clive!' She'd been so busy stomping that she hadn't heard his car. 'Oh, am I pleased to see you! Some horrible old bugger threw a bucket of water over me. He called me a suffragette or something.'

Clive was pushing her into the passenger seat. 'I think the best thing is to get you back to the vicarage and they'll look after you there,' he said, slamming the door. He turned the car around and drove back the way they'd come.

About twenty minutes later, she was sitting in front of the fire in the vicarage kitchen wrapped in Flo's woollen dressing gown and drinking a mug of warm milk while her clothes were drying on the rack above. Flo had gone to visit a young woman who was expecting a baby in a few days, and Paul was seeing to things in the church.

'You're not safe out on your own,' Clive said fondly. He was seated at the table behind her. 'You should have a bodyguard with you all the time.'

Martha laughed, though it wouldn't have taken

much to make her cry. Say if Clive hadn't come along when he did, or the man had thrown something worse than water . . . And what a wicked thing to do to a pregnant woman! She could easily have fainted from the shock – well, some women might.

'How are you feeling?' Clive asked.

'As if I'd like to kill that bloody man,' she said. She didn't feel the least bit charitable or forgiving. 'Did you know that women can't vote in elections?' she asked Clive.

'Yes, Martha, I did. Who told you that?'

'Flo did just now. When I said that the man who flung the water had called me a suffragette bitch, she told me what a suffragette was. It seems that until the war started, they used to set things on fire, break winders and stuff, all so women'd be given the right to vote. There was even one woman called Emily something who deliberately got herself run down and killed by a horse on Derby Day.' She paused, stared into the fire, and supped more of the milk. 'That seems a bit daft to me,' she said thoughtfully. 'I mean, votes are important, but not as important as life. Anyroad,' she continued, 'most suffragettes have given up demonstrating until the war's over, though not Flo. I don't blame her,' she finished with a sigh.

There was a knock on the front door and Clive went to answer it. The young man outside looked as if he had just stepped out of a romantic novel, the dashing hero who swept the heroine off her feet in the final chapter. He wore fashionable tweeds, a leather cap and driving gloves.

'Good morning,' he said courteously, touching the cap. 'I've come for Martha.'

'You must be Alex Scott,' Clive replied, just as courteously. Although he resented the fellow, there was no point in making an enemy of him. 'I'm Clive Dexter from the *Lancashire Post*. How d'you do?' He hadn't expected the *Guardian* reporter to be so fashionably dressed or hardly any older than himself.

Furthermore, Alex Scott was either a very good actor or was genuinely pleased to meet him. He shook Clive's hand with almost painful enthusiasm. 'So, all this is due to you! That was a marvellous idea of yours, to make a big feature of Martha and her trek to London. I hope you don't mind my paper butting in, as it were.'

Clive muttered something to imply he didn't mind a bit, while actually minding rather a lot, though it could only be a good thing. 'The more publicity she gets, the better,' he mumbled.

'Where is she, by the way?' Alex looked over Clive's shoulder, as if he expected Martha to be standing somewhere behind.

'Something happened earlier.' Clive stepped outside so Martha wouldn't hear. 'Some bastard only threw a bucket of water over her and soaked her to the skin. She's inside getting dry.'

Alex's handsome face expressed shock. 'Is there any chance of catching up with the bastard and breaking both his legs?' he enquired. It appeared to be a serious suggestion.

'I didn't witness the event, I'm afraid.' Clive was shocked for an entirely different reason. He reckoned Martha's attacker deserved to have more than his legs broken, but wouldn't have dreamed of carrying out the act – that was the way wars started, people wanting to get even. 'Would you like to come in? As I said, Martha's drying herself in front of the fire.'

'Is she decent?'

'Perfectly so.'

Alex greeted Martha as if they were the best of friends. Clive couldn't help feeling slightly jealous. The chap was the sort of person who made a close chum out of virtually everyone he met. Martha was subjected to a monster hug and a kiss on both cheeks, though she didn't look exactly comfortable about it.

Flo, the vicar's wife, returned and blushed when her hand was shaken with a gusto that verged on the passionate. 'It's really nice of you to have looked after Martha so well,' Alex said warmly.

'It's been a privilege,' Flo claimed.

Another hour passed before Flo judged that Martha's clothes were dry enough to be worn again. The men went outside to wait.

'Which car shall we take her in – yours or mine?' Alex asked.

'Mine, if you don't mind, and you can follow behind.' Clive wanted to catch up with Martha's news, find out exactly what she'd been up to the day before. 'Do you have your paper?' he asked. He'd left Chester too early to buy one.

Alex handed him a copy of the *Manchester Guardian*, and Clive began to read while they waited for Martha. Alex's prose was even more flowery than his own the day before. Martha was 'extraordinarily courageous', a 'modern-day Joan of Arc', a 'working-class Sylvia Pankhurst' who possessed 'the same ability to set hearts on fire with her inspiring speeches'.

'Very good,' he said when he'd finished.

'I should tell you,' Alex said, 'that I've arranged for Martha to have a reception when she reaches Wolver-hampton. One of our photographers will be there.'

'A reception?' Clive queried.

'Anti-war protestors, members of the Independent Labour Party and other groups. They'll be waiting for her outside the town hall. It'll be in the paper to-morrow.' He chewed his lip. 'I've just had an idea.'

On her way to Boningdale for a second time, Martha looked for the spot where the water had been thrown, but the ground was dry by now and she couldn't re-cognize it.

Clive drove the car at a steady pace, not hurrying, and at some point they left Shropshire and entered Staffordshire where he stopped in a hamlet so they could have lunch. About a dozen houses were situated at a crossroads, one of them being an old building called The Slipper Inn.

He and Martha had hardly been seated a minute when they were joined by Alex, who'd been follow-ing. They ordered steak and kidney pie with mashed potatoes, followed by Spotted Dick and custard. After-wards, Martha had a pot of tea and the men a jug of brown ale.

She'd barely sipped the tea, when she put the cup on the table and said in a quiet voice, 'This is all wrong. I'm eating better than me husband and kids I left at home. I'm *enjoying* meself. But that's not why I came, to *enjoy* meself. I came for Joe, and it's only right that me feet should hurt and me back ache. I should be suffering, like he did, poor lad, not sitting here like

Lady Muck stuffing meself with food.' She sniffed back the tears. 'From now on, all I'm going to eat is sarnies.'

'That won't do the baby much good, Martha,' Clive pointed out. 'And what would Joe say if he knew you were starving yourself when you're carrying his little brother or sister?'

'Brother,' she corrected. 'I'm carrying a boy.' She sniffed again. 'Oh, I don't know what to do. I'm dead confused.'

Alex put his arm around her shoulders and Clive wished he'd thought to do it first. 'Cheer up, old girl,' he said consolingly. 'Every cloud has a silver lining, or so they say.'

Martha dug him sharply in the ribs with her elbow. 'Don't "old girl" me,' she said acidly. 'I'm not even old enough to be your mother. And as for silver linings, you're talking bloody rubbish. Some days all that can be seen is black clouds without a lining of any sort.'

'Well, I can't argue with that, Martha,' Alex conceded. He removed his arm, rubbed his ribs, told her she was an extremely wise woman and promised not to patronize her again.

'What does "patronize" mean?' Martha asked Clive when they were even further on their way towards Wolverhampton. The weather was lovely, fresh and tingly. It had been fine since she'd set off from Birkenhead, which felt like months ago, not days.

'Er, talk down to someone.' He knew what the word meant, but found it hard to explain. 'Speak to them as if they were a child.'

'Well, I won't let him do it again. Alex, that is,' she said firmly. 'Have you ever patronized me?'

263

'I hope not. If I have, then I'm very sorry.'

'In future, I'm going to keep an eye out for people patronizing me.'

With that, she lapsed into silence and hardly spoke another word until they passed a milestone with 'Wolverhampton 3 miles' etched on it. The car began to slow down.

'Why are we stopping?' Martha asked.

'I'm afraid I'm out of petrol,' Clive announced glumly. 'I noticed earlier the tank was getting low, but we haven't passed a garage since we left the vicarage at Coalthorpe. I should have filled up earlier.'

'We'll just have to wait until his lordship catches up with us.'

'But Alex left the inn before we did and will be in Wolverhampton by now. I've arranged to meet him by the town hall.' Why had she called him 'his lordship'? Clive wondered.

'So, what shall we do now?' She didn't seem in the least concerned.

'We could be stuck here for ages.' He turned his head. 'There's someone coming. I'll ask for you to be given a lift.'

'There's no need,' Martha protested. But Clive had already leaped out of the car and was waving both arms at the approaching pony and trap, which was being driven by a grandly dressed woman in a wine velvet cloak and matching hat.

'Can I help?' she enquired when she'd reined the pony to a halt.

'I've run out of petrol,' Clive explained, 'and my passenger needs to get to Wolverhampton town hall. She'd appreciate a lift, if you would be so kind.'

'I don't want a bloody lift,' came a voice from inside the car, but Clive took no notice.

'I'm not going quite as far as the town hall,' the woman explained, 'but I could take your passenger quite close.'

Clive opened the car door and helped Martha out. She scowled at him and climbed on to the trap. 'I suppose I'd better tell Alex you're in a predicament and he'll sort you out,' she grumbled.

'I'd appreciate that, Martha. Thank you.'

'The town hall is first right, first left, then second on the left,' the woman said about half an hour later, as she tugged the reins to stop the trap in a little side street. They'd hardly spoken to each other during the short time they'd travelled together.

Martha politely thanked her and set off on foot. She was still feeling annoyed with Clive, though wasn't sure why. She followed the directions she'd been given and eventually arrived at the front of a magnificent building with a pillared entrance in front of which a small crowd had collected. The crowd began to clap as she approached, and she realized that they were applauding *her*. People pushed forward and shook her hand, patted her shoulders, squeezed her arms, and said how pleased they were to see her and what a grand job she was doing with her walk.

'So *thrilled*,' said a woman, who flung her arms around her and kissed her on both cheeks.

Someone thrust a bunch of daffodils into her hands, and she suddenly found herself halfway up the steps of the fancy entrance with the crowd in front. Silence fell and they looked at her expectantly. To her horror, it dawned on her that they were expecting her to speak.

What the hell was she supposed to say? This was worse than yesterday when there were just a few women to talk to, not half the population of Wolver-hampton.

She coughed, swallowed, coughed again, and said, 'Thank you for coming to meet me.'

'Thank you for coming to *us*,' someone shouted.

Martha took the opportunity to clear her throat. 'I'm against the war,' she continued, and these few words were greeted with a tremendous cheer. 'And I'm against boys like my Joe being made to fight in it.' More cheers, and she realized that the crowd would cheer every word she said because they were good people who felt the same as she did about the evil war that was taking away so many young lives. It could be that some of these people were relatives – wives, mothers and fathers, brother and sisters – of the men who were fighting or the men already lost.

Somehow, she managed to finish the speech, her voice hoarse from having to shout. Once more, she thanked people for coming to meet her, and the crowd began to break up. People shook her hand again, as if they felt the need to touch her. Eventually, there was only one person left.

'Jolly good show, Martha,' said Alex Scott.

She came to, having forgotten all about Clive being stranded somewhere in the countryside without petrol.

'It's all right,' Alex said when she told him. 'He turned up a few minutes ago and has gone to book us into a hotel.'

'Where did he get the petrol from?'

266

'He didn't explain.' He held out his arm and she linked it. When did she ever think she'd be escorted across the country by two such attractive young men? There must be hundreds of young women who'd give their eye teeth to be in her place. 'The hotel's along this way,' Alex said.

It was a big hotel, really posh, the entrance almost as grand as the town hall. Clive was in the lounge. It had gold papered walls and a beautifully patterned carpet, probably Indian or Persian. She remembered having a Persian rug in the Gerard Street parlour. She'd bought it from a second-hand shop for ten whole bob. It had seemed a monstrous extravagance at the time.

Clive jumped to his feet when he saw them. 'I've ordered tea,' he said. 'And I've got the dinner menu here too.'

'I'm dying for a cuppa.' Was there ever a time when she wasn't? Martha sank into a grey plush arm-chair. The afternoon and its unexpected conclusion had left her feeling dizzy with excitement. Her head was whirling.

'You did really well out there, Martha.' Alex looked as pleased as punch. 'You deserve more than a cuppa. How about some champagne?'

'Champagne!' Not only had Martha never been within spitting distance of champagne, she'd never so much as spoken the word before. 'Oh, I don't know,' she said cautiously.

'I think Martha would prefer tea,' Clive murmured.

'Yes, I would.' Martha remembered what she'd said earlier in the day, that she wasn't there to enjoy herself, but had come with a purpose. 'Just tea, please,' she said. And they needn't think, the pair of them, that she was about to order a big posh dinner; soup would do. It had some goodness in it and would be better for the baby she sometimes forgot that she was carrying unless she walked too far or too fast.

She noticed a fashionably dressed woman across the lounge who looked vaguely familiar. 'Who's that?' she asked, nodding in the woman's direction.

Alex answered. 'Oh, that's Mrs Kavanagh. She's a member of the Women's International League in this area.'

Martha stared and wondered where she'd seen the woman before. Yesterday, perhaps, at Imogen Cunningham's. No, it was more recent than that. She noticed, then, that Clive was looking distinctly uncomfortable. The penny dropped.

'She's the woman who brought me here in a pony and trap!' She stared at Clive. 'Does that mean you hadn't run out of petrol?' For some reason, he'd arranged for the woman to give her a lift.

Clive turned to Alex and said, 'You blithering idiot. Now look what you've done.'

'What have I done?' Alex appeared mystified. Then, 'Oh, God!' he said. He winced and dipped his head. 'Sorry, I forgot.'

What had he forgotten? What was going on? The tea came, but Martha ignored it. Why had Clive pretended to run out of petrol and arrange for a strange woman to give her a lift, not directly to the town hall, but a short distance away? It was a while before a second penny dropped.

'You wanted me to *walk* to the Town Hall, didn't

you?' she said accusingly. 'You wanted everyone to think I'd walked all the way from Coaltown?'

'Coal*thorpe*,' Alex reminded her.

'That's cheating. That's downright bloody cheating.' She'd been . . . she couldn't think of the word . . . *somethinged*. 'You're a pair of bloody cheats – and you made me look like one, too.' She jumped to her feet, forgetting about the baby once again, and nearly swooning from the effort. 'I'm going to look for lodgings. I'm not staying here like some posh git.'

'Martha!' Clive caught her arm. 'It'll be dark outside soon. Stay for tonight, please. You must be tired and it's Alex's paper that's paying for everything.'

'It doesn't matter a fig who's paying. But I'll stay,' she conceded grudgingly, too tired to wander around looking for cheap lodgings. Tomorrow she'd take over her life again, however, and Clive and Alex could go back to whatever they were doing before she decided to walk to London.

A uniformed porter showed her to her room on the first floor. He carried her string bag as carefully as if it were a desperately expensive item of luggage. She tipped him a ha'penny for his trouble.

Once inside the luxurious room, she lay on the bed, brooding over what had happened, feeling baleful and wanting to knock the two young men's heads together. After about an hour, a waiter came with a plate of thinly sliced cold beef, some pickled onions, and bread and butter. There was also trifle and a pot of tea. She ate everything except the trifle, and drained the tea. Then she took Mister's list out of her bag to check where she would be tomorrow. A place called Birmingham, she discovered, though with Clive and Alex in charge, she could well end up somewhere entirely different like the North bloody Pole.

She was about to go outside and look for a lavatory, when she noticed a door in the corner of the room that had been left slightly ajar. Pushing it, she discovered that she had her very own bathroom, boasting black tiled walls and an enormous bath with gleaming silver taps.

After using the lavatory, she washed her hands in the sink and wiped them on one of the fluffy white towels supplied, then examined her reflection in the mirror.

'Holy Mary, Mother of God!' she muttered. This must be what people meant when they spoke about someone looking like death warmed up. Her face hadn't a scrap of colour in it, her eyes drooped, her mouth drooped, and her hair looked as if she'd been dragged through a hedge backwards.

She eyed the bowl of bath crystals on the shelf beneath the mirror and thought what a treat it'd be to empty the lot in a bath of hot water and soak herself for half an hour or so. But it wouldn't be right. She wasn't there to enjoy herself.

Later on, though, after she'd had a little rest, she'd kneel in the bath and have a good wash. Just now, she suspected she smelled a bit like a dead rabbit.

But Martha was denied her 'little rest'. In fact, that night she didn't sleep a wink, for she'd hardly been lying down a minute when there was a knock on the door, a real thump, and a coarse voice shouted, 'Open the door, Mrs Rossi. Come on now, open up.'

'Who is it?' she quavered, sitting up.

'It's the police, missus, Open up.' A different voice, just as coarse.

She felt she had no alternative. She opened the door and the coppers pounced, manhandling her out of the room and then the hotel, two big geezers with dingy moustaches and vile-smelling breath.

Outside, she was bundled into a horse-drawn van. One copper stayed in the van with her, and the other drove.

'What've I done?' she asked the copper who'd stayed.

'Only broken the law, missus,' he sneered. Oh, how she loathed bloody coppers. 'Only offended against the Defence of the Realm Act, as it's called. By your recent actions you could well be guilty of Causing Alarm. Furthermore, during wartime, aliens are forbidden to travel further than five miles from their home.'

'Aliens! I'm Irish and Ireland's part of the British Empire.' She may well be ignorant, but she knew that much. She'd been taught it at school.

'We'll have to see about that,' the man said threateningly, as if he would move Ireland somewhere else altogether if he felt like it.

When they reached the station, she was helped out of the van none too gently, considering her condition, and pushed into a small room furnished with only a table and a bench on either side. There, she was ordered to sit and explain her reason for travelling through the country making treasonable speeches at every stop.

Martha didn't answer. She wasn't willing to speak her dear son's name in front of these two beasts, which she would have to do if she tried to explain. Perhaps it was foolish, but she had no fear of coppers; she'd done nothing wrong. This pair of ugly buggers didn't frighten her; they just made her angry.

After a good hour of bullying, they went away, returning later to tell her she was being held overnight.

'And tomorrow,' she was told, 'we're bringing in a doctor to give you a gynaecological examination to see if you've got VD.'

'VD?' Martha queried.

'Venereal disease, missus.'

'*What*?' she screamed. 'Are you suggesting I've got the bloody clap?'

Both men grinned and, seizing an arm each, they carried her along to a cold room with a couple of planks for a bed and a flock pillow that felt as hard as iron.

'Sleep well,' one of them chortled.

Chapter 16

'If you've come to examine me, you've got another think coming,' Martha said to the doctor when he arrived next morning. She tossed her head and swung her legs off the so-called bed, which she'd been sitting on all night, having not slept a wink. The doctor was a tall, thin, clean-shaven man wearing a pinstriped suit, which had been pressed to perfection, and a polka-dotted bow tie. She guessed he was the doctor because he was carrying a black leather bag.

He removed his hat and smiled at her coldly. 'I wouldn't dream of examining a heavily pregnant woman for venereal disease; it could be harmful for the baby. I shall wait here a few minutes and report to the sergeant that you are free from infection. They will then release you and you can continue with whatever you were doing before.'

'Ta very much.' Martha was taken aback. She couldn't work out whether he was on her side or not. She was appreciative of his words, but not his un-friendly expression.

He threw her a look of contempt that told her there was no chance he was on her side. 'I don't want your thanks, Mrs Rossi. I am not doing you a favour. Were I an ordinary member of the public, I would be all for taking you down a peg or two, though not in the way the police intended.'

Martha was hurt by the look. 'Why do I need to be taken down a peg or two?' she asked curiously.

'This country is at war,' he said, as if she didn't know. 'It does not need the likes of you trumpeting how evil it is and criticizing the way things are being run. I have a son in France risking his life for his country and you, Mrs Rossi, are no use to him or anybody else.'

'How old is your son, doctor?'

'Twenty-two.' His face softened and there was a tremor in his voice.

She immediately felt sorry for him. 'Well, my son, the one that was killed, was only fourteen.'

'I'm sorry about that. It was a dreadful thing to have happened, but there is no need to make such a public fuss about it. You could have taken the matter up quietly.'

'What makes you think I didn't?' she said angrily. 'First, I took it up with the coppers, then I went to see this dead stupid politician who was stewed to his bloody eyeballs and told me I should feel lucky our Joe had gone off to fight. Then this chap from the paper wrote to the War Office, but they didn't take any notice. Nobody cared,' she said flatly. 'Nobody gave a damn. He was only a poor, working-class lad that nobody gave two hoots for.' She stared at the doctor, conscious of her eyes burning into his.

The man turned away and left the cell without saying another word. Barely seconds later, one of the fat coppers appeared and told her she could go. With the cell door open, she could hear someone yelling outside – no, two people, both yelling at the top of their voices and banging things.

It turned out to be Clive and Alex in the station lobby, shouting and thumping the counter with their fists.

'Where is she?' Clive screamed, giving the counter a kick.

'What have you done with Mrs Rossi?' Alex was every bit as cross.

A third young man was standing silently behind them.

'I'm here,' Martha said quietly, and was nearly bowled over when Clive and Alex virtually fought with other to give her a hug.

The third young man turned out to be a local solicitor who was there to find out exactly what Martha had been arrested for and if she was being kept in custody for much longer.

A different policeman was behind the desk from the night before, a nice young constable who produced a ledger and requested that she sign out. Martha refused. 'I didn't sign in, so I'm not signing out,' she said spiritedly.

'I don't blame you, Missus,' the constable said. 'If I were you, I wouldn't sign out, either.'

Back at the hotel in the comfortable lounge, Clive explained he'd gone to her room that morning to wake her, but couldn't get any answer. He'd asked a maid to open the door and she'd found no one there. 'It was then I began to panic,' he said. When questioned, the night porter informed him that two policemen had taken her away not long before midnight.

275

'He said they were very rough with you. Were they?'

'Well, they weren't exactly gentle,' Martha conceded. There'd been no need to pull and push her around the way they had.

'Did they use undue force?' the solicitor asked.

Martha winced, thinking about it. 'I reckon so. I wasn't exactly resisting arrest, not in my condition.' She yawned, feeling desperately tired. 'What day is it?' she asked. 'Where are we? I can't remember.' If told they were in Timbuctoo she wouldn't have been surprised.

'It's Saturday and we're in Wolverhampton,' Clive informed her. 'That's in Staffordshire,' he added, knowing that she was interested in such things. 'This afternoon we're going to Birmingham, and tomorrow, Sunday, we're going to have a day of rest, just as the Bible tells us to. Our next stop will be Warwick.'

'I could do with a day of rest right now. I didn't get any sleep last night in the police station.' Martha stretched and yawned again, and Clive suggested she went to bed there and then to catch up on her sleep.

'I'll see the manager and make sure your room's still available.'

Martha gazed fondly at his retreating form, recalling that last night she'd been really cross with him – and with Alex. But she was both touched and impressed by the extent of the anger they had displayed on her behalf in the police station that morning. They were lovely young men. She sighed. When conscription came in, both were likely to be called up. She hoped and prayed they'd come through the horrible business alive.

Once in bed, she felt strangely comforted by the muffled bumps coming from the neighbouring rooms. She visualized the furniture being dusted and polished, the carpets swept and the linen changed.

She quickly fell asleep, and woke with no idea of how long she'd slept. She felt desperately depressed. The events of the previous night were only now catching up with her, and she wanted to weep when she remembered how rough the policemen had been and that they hadn't cared a bit about hurting her baby. And it was stupid to feel frightened now about being locked in such a suffocatingly small, cold room with bars on the window. Just thinking about it made her want to scream with terror.

What a horrible world it was. She didn't want any part of it. And she was fed up these days, never knowing where she was or where she was going or where she'd been. Time had lost all meaning and the days were merging together until they were a worrying jumble in her head. She wondered if her life would ever be calm again, calm and organized and plain ordinary.

She was concerned about Lily and Georgie. Was Carlo looking after them properly? She even missed Carlo, who had little impact on her life now but was still her husband. Oh, and she really missed Kate. Thinking about Kate made her think about clothes, and she wished she had another frock to wear and another pair of knickers.

If she thought she'd be left alone for long enough, she'd have had a good old cry, bury her head in the pillow and sob her heart out. It was a good job she didn't give in to the feeling because the next minute there was a tap on the door and Clive said in a low voice, 'Are you awake, Martha?'

'Yes,' she sighed.

'We're just about to have something to eat, then make our way to Birmingham,' he said. 'Are you hungry?'

She realized she was starving. 'I'll be out in a minute,' she promised.

MARTHA'S JOURNEY

Until recently, as pointed out before, Martha Rossi was just an ordinary housewife, but these are extraordinary times and Martha has become an extraordinary woman.

Our country is at war for reasons that are hard to put into words. While seeking for an explanation why her fourteen-year-old son, Joe, was killed in action on foreign soil, Martha is making her way to London, sometimes on foot and sometimes not – she is six months pregnant with her sixth child and not capable of walking far – in the hope that our Prime Minister will answer her question.

The reader of this article, like the writer, has no doubt always considered this country – *our* country – to be free; that we have certain liberties that have been acquired slowly over centuries as man has learned to judge what is fair and just, and what is unacceptable in a civilized society.

Last night, Martha discovered how disgracefully the so-called guardians of our society can behave, when she was roughly removed from the hotel in Wolverhampton where she was staying and taken to a police station, where the forces of the law informed her that her noble walk to London infringed the Defence of the Realm Act. She was locked in a cell overnight, without bedding and without a warm drink, and told that in the morning she would be examined by a doctor for a disease that this newspaper would prefer not to mention because it is a foul and unconscionable slur on the character of an upright and virtuous woman.

Clive read the article aloud. Alex nodded approvingly from time to time. They'd written the piece between them.

'Sounds good,' said the young solicitor, whose name was Samuel Rootes. For him, it had turned out to be a far more interesting day than he'd expected when he'd been called to the police station that morning. 'Is it finished yet?'

'Almost,' Alex said. 'As soon as it is, I'll telephone it through to the office.'

'I must buy tomorrow's paper. Did you say it was the *Manchester Guardian*?'

'That's right, but you can't get it tomorrow because it's Sunday when neither of our papers are published. The next edition is on Monday, and it will include a photograph of Martha on the steps of Wolverhampton town hall.'

'Why are you stopping at Birmingham?' Samuel asked, 'when you could make it as far as London by late tonight?'

'Well, our dear Martha is spreading the word, isn't she?' Alex replied. 'And the more places we stop, the more people she can spread it to.'

★

She must be dreaming. It was the next morning and Martha burrowed her head beneath the pillow, as if this would shut out the dream, even though it was such a pleasant one. She could hear Lily and Georgie calling her, knocking on the door, which couldn't possibly be happening. She was too tired to be woken up. Today was Sunday, she blearily remembered, she was in Birmingham, and this was supposed to be a day of rest, so that's what she wanted to do – rest.

The shouting and the knocking continued. 'Mam,' Lily shouted. 'Wake up, wake up.'

Martha obediently woke up and rubbed her eyes. She heard Georgie say, 'If she doesn't get up soon we'll miss breakfast.'

'Jaysus, Mary and Joseph!' She leaped out of bed and opened the door. Lily, in her bright pink frock, and Georgie were dancing up and down outside.

'Mammy!' They threw themselves at her and she came close to crushing them to death in her arms.

'What are you doing here? How did you get here? Has your dad come, too? Who brought you?' She showered them with questions as well as kisses. It wasn't even a week since she'd left Liverpool, but it felt like months since she'd seen her kids. Lily actually appeared to have grown taller.

'Dad's here. He's downstairs talking to Clive. And Kate's outside.'

'Outside where?' She was halfway to the window when Lily said, 'She's in the corridor, Mam.'

'Kate!'

She went outside and there was Kate. 'I thought I should let the children in to see you first,' she said.

'Oh,' Martha gasped. 'Well, if this isn't a big

surprise, then I don't know what is. Did you come in your car?'

'Yes. My father brought us. He's spending the day with an old friend.' She smiled her lovely ear-to-ear smile. The two women embraced and she held up a small suitcase. 'I've brought you some things.'

She came into the room and opened the suitcase on the bed. 'Lily and I thought you'd like another frock. We bought it in Great Homer Street market, didn't we, darling?'

'I picked it, Mam. I picked it.' Lily grabbed a rose-sprigged brown frock out of the case and showed it to her mother.

'It's the gear, luv.' Martha held the frock against herself in front of the wardrobe mirror. It had a high frilled neck, frilled cuffs and was made from heavy cotton material warm enough to wear in spring and autumn. The skirt looked full enough to allow for the baby. She took a few seconds studying the label on the back, reading it letter by letter. Viyella! Six months ago she wouldn't have been able to make sense of it. 'Thank you, everybody.' It was an excuse to kiss everyone again.

'You'll have to kiss our Frank when you get home,' Lily told her. 'He bought you some scent in a dead pretty bottle.'

'Our Joyce sent a pink hat,' Georgie was saying, 'though it looks more like a pudding basin to me.'

'There's a few other things in the case,' Kate said, 'as well as the scent, underwear and the hat. You can unpack it later. And you can keep the case; I got that in the market, too. Now you're travelling mainly by car, it doesn't matter how much luggage you have.'

'How d'you know I've been travelling by car?' Martha asked.

'I read Clive and Alex's articles, don't I?' Kate said. 'Unless you're like Tarzan and are able to swing from tree to tree, you couldn't possibly walk the distances you travel every day. My mother and father read the articles, too, and loads of other people I know.' She linked Martha's arm. 'You're very famous in Liverpool, Martha. I'm really proud to call you my friend.'

'Mam.' Georgie was bouncing on the bed, reaching dizzying heights. 'Clive said if we don't come down before ten o'clock they won't give us any breakfast. And after breakfast, we can go to Mass.'

'You all go downstairs while I get dressed, and I'll see you in a minute.'

Martha hummed under her breath while she put on the lovely clean underwear, the lisle stockings that were brand new and the flowered frock that hadn't a break in it. She washed her face, combed her hair, dabbed Frank's scent behind her ears and felt like a new woman.

Carlo looked like a different man from the one she'd got used to over the years. Someone, perhaps himself, had seen to his suit, ironed his shirt, pressed his tie and polished his shoes. She actually felt quite proud of him. He even had an immaculate white hanky tucked in his breast pocket. It later turned out that Joyce had seen to the laundry side of things, and Carlo had polished the shoes and had actually bought the hanky new.

Martha kissed him shyly on the cheek. 'It's nice to see you, luv,' she said quietly.

'And you too, *cara*.' His brown eyes smiled into hers.

Martha felt that, in that instant, they had regained some of the warm intimacy they'd once had, though it would take more than a smile to mend their marriage.

Alex rubbed his hands together. 'If we don't have breakfast soon,' he said, 'I shall faint from hunger.'

'Me, too,' Georgie said fervently.

The whole family went to Mass in the breathtaking building that was St Chad's Roman Catholic cathedral. Kate had asked to come 'for the experience', and promised not to move an inch without genuflecting first.

'I feel cleansed,' she announced when they emerged to find Clive and Alex, two grown men, playing football with a piece of wood in a street outside.

Clive proposed they went to Cannon Hill Park where there was a boating lake and a band that often played on Sundays.

The children jumped at the idea. Martha would have preferred to return to the cathedral, kneel quietly at the back and have a word with God, but it would be unfair to desert the people who'd come all this way to see her. She watched from a bench as they played tick and pig-in-the-middle and football again with the same wooden stick.

After about half an hour, everyone departed for the boating lake except for Carlo, who came and sat beside her. They talked about the past and the future. 'I will turn over a new leaf,' he promised – his English was fine, but he still had a touch of an Italian accent, despite all the years spent in England. 'As soon as you're home, tell Mister you don't want to work for him any more and I'll find a job.'

'What sort of job?' Martha asked.

'They're looking for people, men and women, to work in a munitions factory over the water,' he told her. 'It's said the wages are unbelievably high.'

'But what about your arm, luv?' The veins and tendons in his wrist had been badly slashed in the knife fight all those years ago. The doctor in the hospital had said he'd lost so much blood he was lucky to be alive. His hand and the lower part of his arm had felt dead ever since. She picked up his hand and stroked the damaged wrist. She knew from her own experience that two hands were essential for working in a factory.

'They'll find me something to do.' She looked at his face and he was smiling at her wistfully. 'I'm sorry,' he said in a low voice, and she understood he was apologizing for all the years that he'd been such a useless husband.

Martha put his hand carefully back on his knee. She was glad he was sorry, but it still wasn't enough. What's more, she didn't fancy her husband working in a munitions factory, making guns and bullets for use on young soldiers on the other side of the war. But, as the old saying went, 'beggars can't be choosers'.

After a while, the children came back with Alex. Kate and Clive had disappeared. He looked particularly handsome today, Alex, in a grey and white striped blazer and summer-weight grey trousers. Martha had been amazed to learn that he had been rejected for military service as a result of having had asthma as a child. He asked if it was all right to give the children money to buy ice creams. Lily and Georgie were frowning, as if daring her to refuse.

Martha wouldn't have dreamed of saying no. Alex gave them a threepenny bit each and, after they'd run off, he flopped on the bench next to her, declaring himself completely exhausted. After a brief silence, he asked if Kate was Clive's girlfriend.

'No,' she answered. 'And he's not her boyfriend, either.'

'They've been gone for ages,' he said a trifle sulkily. He shuffled his feet on the grass. 'She's awfully pretty – Kate, that is.'

'She's a lovely girl,' Martha agreed.

'I wouldn't mind having a chat with her myself before she goes back.'

'I'm sure there'll be plenty of time for that,' she soothed, thinking how agreeable it must be to have two fine-looking young men like Alex and Clive after you! Mind you, she'd turned a few heads in her day, but the only man she'd ever truly loved was sitting beside her now and that was agreeable, too.

Mr Kellaway returned, having spent an enjoyable day with his friend. It almost broke Martha's heart to say goodbye to Carlo and the children and, of course, her friend Kate. She waved at the departing car until her arm felt ready to drop off, and Lily and Georgie waved back through the rear window.

Chapter 17

Kate dropped Carlo and the children off at King's Court, thinking what a dismal place it was. Martha deserved to live somewhere much nicer. When he was sober, Carlo seemed a really nice person and turned out to be quite attractive once he'd been cleaned up. From the rather smudged wedding photo in the *Lancashire Post* the other day, you could tell that he and Martha had made a handsome couple.

As for Alex Scott, he was exceptionally good-looking. Kate, though, didn't fancy him as much as she did Clive, who was serious and clever and could be terribly charming when he felt like it. Earlier, when they were in the park in Birmingham, he'd asked if he could take her to dinner once Martha's journey was over and he was back in Liverpool. She'd agreed, naturally. But later, Alex had also invited her to dinner when he was home in Manchester. She hadn't really meant to, but she'd agreed to that, too, and now she felt like a siren.

In the hotel in Birmingham, Clive and Alex were sharing a room. They sat up in their beds, discussing the week ahead. Tomorrow, Monday, not only would the photograph of Martha on the steps of Wolverhampton town hall appear in their respective papers, but the article would describe her treatment at the hands of the police. There would be plenty of time for them to buy both papers in the morning before they left for Warwick.

'We really should have showed Martha that article,' Clive said, making a face. 'It's very personal. She should have been asked for her opinion before we sent it. Trouble is, say if she hadn't wanted it published? What would we have done then?'

'I thought about that, too.' Alex wrinkled his nose as a sign that he too felt uncomfortable. 'We're manipulating her and it's not fair.'

'She knows that. She said as much a few days ago when we stopped at that inn in the middle of nowhere. Where was that place? D'you know? I'm not sure where we are most of the time.'

'It wasn't long after we'd left Coalthorpe,' Alex declared after some thought, 'but it was because she was upset about eating decent food for a change and then she was mad at me for calling her "old girl". That night she was *really* mad for being tricked into walking on her own to the town hall because it made everyone think she'd been walking for miles.'

'That's true,' Clive said, nodding. 'I seem to remember it was your idea, not mine,' he added dryly.

'You're right,' Alex conceded. 'But not long afterwards, those beastly coppers got their hands on her. She's been subdued ever since.'

The two young men were silent for a while. 'We're being beastly, too,' Alex concluded. 'Maybe it's because we're reporters and, to us, the only thing that matters is the story.'

Clive raised the mug of cocoa he'd ordered from room service. 'The story!' he said by the way of a toast.

'The story!' Alex mock-saluted in return. There was another silence, then he said, 'I think we should make an exception for Martha. Shall we stop manipulating her?'

'Hear, hear.' Clive raised his mug. 'I also think it's time we stopped padding out the journey. I suggest we give Warwick a miss.'

'Sorry, old chap, but we can't. Tomorrow, a welcoming party will be waiting to meet her. Tell you what, though . . .' He got out of bed and studied the map. 'After the reception, let's go straight to Oxford where Martha can have a good rest, then make our way to London the next day. She's worn out, and I think she's had enough of travelling and giving speeches.' He got back beneath the bedclothes. 'What do you say?'

'I'm all for it.' The articles were becoming repetitive and so were the speeches. And it was true that Martha was exhausted. 'Yes, that's what we'll do.'

'Kate's all in favour.'

Clive glowered. He hadn't realized Kate and Alex had had a conversation. 'Is she now?'

Alex nodded. 'Is it all right if I turn this lamp off?'

'Fine.'

'Goodnight, old chap,' Alex said jovially.

'Goodnight,' Clive said, rather less so.

Five minutes later, Clive had finished his milk and both young men were sleeping like babies.

As soon as Berenice Dexter went downstairs, she asked the housekeeper to send somebody out to buy the *Manchester Guardian*.

'But the lad'll be round with *The Times* any minute,' the woman reminded her.

'I know, Mrs . . . er . . . but it's the *Manchester Guardian* I want, you see,' Berenice explained earnestly. She was unfailingly polite to the servants and never lost her temper, but couldn't remember their names, no matter how long they'd worked for her.

She floated into the breakfast room in her coral-pink negligee and fluffy slippers, poured a tiny cup of coffee, and sat at the table waiting for the newspaper to arrive.

When it did, she opened it eagerly on page three and there it was, 'Martha's Journey', in big black letters and underneath, in smaller letters, 'from Clive Dexter and Alex Scott'.

She clasped her hands together underneath her chin and gave a happy sigh, though felt quite sick when she read the article that her son and the other reporter had written, describing how poor Martha had suffered at the hands of the police. Even so, it was wonderful to see Clive's name in one of the most respected newspapers in the land. Her two other children were presently at home for the Easter holiday. She'd show it to Guy as soon as he woke and Veronica when she returned from her overnight stay with friends in North Wales. They'd be so pleased.

Jeffrey, her husband, came into the room, grunted something, and helped himself to a large breakfast from the side table. He tucked his napkin into his collar like a baby's bib – an awful working-class habit, she thought – and attacked the food as if it were an enemy he felt obliged to overcome.

'What's that you're reading?' he remarked after a while.

'A newspaper, dear.'

'That makes a change. You usually have your head stuck in that silly fashion magazine of yours.'

'*Vogue*? It's not silly, Jeffrey,' she assured him. 'There are many quite sensible and sober articles in it that you would enjoy.' She also loved reading *Punch*. It was full of acerbic wit and the most delicious political cartoons. Jeffrey didn't know she read it. Berenice had found him easier to live with if he thought her stupid. 'Today, though,' she went on, 'I am reading a newspaper that has our darling Clive's name in.' She knew that would annoy him. He thought that she, being his wife, should feel obliged to follow his lead and virtually disown their eldest son.

'The *Lancashire Post*!' he sneered. 'It confines itself to local affairs so trite and unimportant that it's not worth reading. What exciting news does it have for its readers this morning? Which poor soul has had a chimney fire or a wheel stolen from his bicycle?'

'It isn't the *Post* I'm reading, but the *Manchester Guardian*,' Berenice informed him. 'Clive and another young man are the authors of a major series that has attracted great interest throughout the country.' She had made the last bit up, though it might actually be true.

Jeffrey frowned. The yolk of the egg he was about to eat dripped onto his napkin – good job he was wearing it as a bib. 'How did you know it would be in today's paper?' he spluttered.

'You won't have noticed, but Clive has been away for almost a week. He's very slowly making his way to London with a lady called Martha Rossi, a heroine of our time, and telephones every night to inform me of his progress.' She stood, leaving the newspaper open on page three. 'You can read it for yourself, but don't throw the paper away. I want Guy and Veronica to see it. I know they'll be as proud of their brother as I am.'

She left the room. Jeffrey finished shovelling down his food before picking up the paper and reading 'Martha's Journey' for himself.

Clever idea, he thought after a while, to turn the article into a sort of diary. And much as he supported the war, it was rather a cheek to rope in kids to do the fighting. He quite admired this Martha woman for what she was doing. As for the police, they needed a jolly good hiding.

Outside, a car hooted three times. It was Thomas, his 'man', who did all the heavy work in the house, as well as the chauffering. Jeffrey put on his hat, picked up his briefcase, tucked *The Times* underneath his arm and went outside.

As he climbed into the Daimler, he requested Thomas stop at the nearest newsagent and purchase a copy of the *Manchester Guardian*. He could show it at his club tonight. At last Clive had given him something to boast about.

It was at about this time that Clive and Martha set off for Warwick. The sky that morning was grey and the temperature had fallen a few degrees since yesterday. Martha was almost invisible inside her black shawl.

Alex had gone ahead to book the small party into a hotel that had been recommended. The latest episode of 'Martha's Journey' had announced where she would be today and, by some miraculous means, he'd arranged for some members of anti-war societies to meet her when she arrived in Warwick.

Her photograph on the steps of Wolverhampton town hall, arm raised in a gesture of defiance, looked very dramatic, and her sojourn in the police station had been spiced up so that it gave the impression she'd been on the point of being executed for treason. Clive hoped people would feel angry about the way she'd been treated. *He* did! He had slipped the newspapers into a pocket on the side of his suitcase, then put the suitcase in the boot. He wouldn't show them to Martha unless she asked.

She didn't speak at all for the first few miles. He suspected she was upset after spending yesterday with her family who'd all gone home, while she was travelling further and further away.

In order to break the ice, he asked about her husband and what sort of job he had, though he knew darn well Carlo hadn't done a stroke of work in almost a decade. Kate had told him. She said he was a lazy slob who spent most of his time in a drunken stupor, leaving Martha to support herself and the children.

But Martha provided him with an entirely sympathetic version of Carlo's accident and his inability to work ever since. It gave Clive yet another reason for liking her, the fact that she stood by her useless husband – Kate's description again – to the hilt. Loyalty was an admirable quality.

'He's going to find work soon in one of them munition factory places,' Martha told him. 'He ses the wages are out of this world. Wouldn't it be grand if we could have a little house to ourselves again?' She looked at him sideways. 'We used to have a house once, you know. We didn't always live in King's Court. We used to have cups and saucers that matched and spare sheets for the beds.'

'Let's hope those days come again soon, Martha.' He meant it with all his heart.

'I hope so, too.' But she didn't sound all that confident. 'Hello, what's this?'

They were in the heart of the countryside and had just passed through a pretty, ancient village called Knowle. Just ahead, outside the gates of some establishment yet unseen, stood a grey-haired man holding a piece of cardboard on which was painted in very large letters 'Martha Rossi, Please Stop'.

Clive duly stopped, got out of the car, and said, 'Hello?'

'Mrs Martha Rossi?' the man enquired. He looked as ancient as the village itself and was acutely knock-kneed. His face was a mask of wrinkles.

'Well, that's Mrs Rossi in the car,' Clive acknowledged.

'We were hoping you would travel this way, sir.' The man's voice was surprisingly youthful. 'Her ladyship would very much like a word with Mrs Rossi.'

'What for?' Clive asked suspiciously. 'And who is her ladyship?' He didn't want Martha suffering any more physical assaults.

'Her ladyship, Lady Kerry, is a descendant of the Earl of Warwick, and she would like to thank Mrs Rossi for making her journey and to commiserate with her over her treatment by the police and the person with the water.' He bowed slightly from the waist down and appeared to have difficulty straightening up again. 'My name is Walter Butler, sir, so perhaps it's not surprising that I eventually became butler to Lord Kerry when I was a young 'un.'

'Will her ladyship come out to see Martha, or are we to go to her?' Clive asked quickly, worried that if Walter Butler wasn't stopped he would relate his entire life story.

'Her ladyship is approaching her century and hasn't walked in many a year. If you would kindly turn your vehicle into the drive, sir, I will take you to see her.'

The drive was short and led to a splendid house with narrow gardens on each side that had been reduced by time and neglect to strips of overgrown grass and weeds. A once elegant gazebo was gradually falling to pieces and a fountain almost black with age leaked water by the drop instead of in a sparkling rush as it must have done in years gone by.

Walter said the Kerrys had once owned almost fifty acres of land, but 'the solicitors keep selling off little bits to keep the rest going. Now there's no more land left to sell and only heaven knows what will happen to her ladyship when the house has to go as well.'

Lady Gabrielle Kerry stared into Martha's face. Her blue eyes were faded with age and her gaze was unsteady, as if she could scarcely see. Unlike her servant, there wasn't a single wrinkle in her face. Her skin was pale and waxy and stretched over her fragile bones like the thinnest silk. 'You are so brave, my dear,' she whispered, 'walking all the way to London just to make your point.'

'Brave?' Martha felt obliged to whisper back. 'No, I'm not. I'm a daft 'a'peth, if the truth be known, and I'm probably making a grand exhibition of meself. I'm anything but brave. I'm not walking much, either; I'm being driven most of the way.'

'Oh, you *are* brave, my dear. I admire you so much.' The woman lay on a sofa draped with something that Martha supposed was a bedspread made of dark green velvet with a thick gold fringe. The material looked old and worn and the fringe was badly frayed. The room was the same; full of ancient furniture, with threadbare curtains at the windows, and mirrors that badly needed re-silvering. There were bits missing from the chandelier, which was shrouded in cobwebs, and the pattern on the carpet had almost disappeared. Everything looked even older than the woman herself.

'When is your child due?' she asked. 'It said in the paper that you were expecting. In my day, no woman would dream of advertising her condition in the newspaper. And we mainly stayed confined to the home once the child began to show.'

'About the end of June,' Martha told her.

'Before you leave, Walter will give you a gift for your baby.' Her eyes wavered towards the butler. 'Fetch me the silver baptismal spoon out of the bureau in his lordship's study,' she ordered. 'And one of those tartan rugs that his lordship and I brought back from Edinburgh after our Silver Wedding. Mrs Rossi looks as if she could do with one in the car.' Walter left and she reached for Martha's hand; her grip had no strength at all. 'Walter read the paper to me earlier. Did you give those frightful policemen what for?'

Martha looked at Clive. He said, 'She told them a thing or two.' He was clearly impatient to be off, but Martha had no intention of leaving until the old lady had said all she wanted to say.

But her ladyship had fallen asleep. The delicate blue skin of her eyelids was deeper than the blue of her eyes. Her breath had the strength of a butterfly's wings.

'Should I wake her up and say tara?' Martha asked Walter who had returned.

'It would be best to leave her, Mrs Rossi,' the butler advised. 'She sleeps very little and every bit of rest is welcome.'

'I hope she won't think me awful rude if I go.'

'By the time she wakes, she could well have forgotten you've been here. She might remember later in the day or even the week, but she won't have noticed that you didn't say . . . tara.'

They left the house through the hall. White marble statues of partially clothed women stood on either side of the giant front door.

'Did her ladyship want to talk to me about anything in particular?' Martha asked Walter. Her voice seemed to float eerily upwards towards the faraway ceiling.

'About the Ladies' Progressive Party,' Walter replied.

Clive looked curiously at the man. 'I've never heard of it,' he said.

'Her Ladyship started the Party with friends and managed to keep it going for forty years,' Walter said proudly. 'She had hundreds of members at one time, but then her health began to fail, by which time the suffragettes had set themselves up, but it was Lady Kerry who promoted votes for women long before they did.'

'Very interesting.' Clive steered Martha out of the front door by her elbow towards the car where Walter handed her a tartan blanket and a small velvet box.

Martha thanked him profusely, kissed him goodbye, and they drove away.

As soon as they were outside the gates, she demanded that Clive stop the car.

'Have you forgotten something?' he asked irritably.

'No, but I want to put this blanket thing in the cupboard at the back.'

'What cupboard at the back of where?' He was even more irritable.

'At the back of the car, daft lad, where the cases are put.' She shook her head at his stupidity.

'You mean the boot?'

'Do I?

'Yes, you do,' he said through gritted teeth. 'But why do I have to stop, Martha?'

'So I can put this blanket there. It's full of moths. You can see the eggs all over it. We don't want moths in the car, do we?'

'Then just throw it out the window.'

'And have Walter find it later! That'd be awful rude, Clive,' she said reasonably.

He braked and waited till she'd put the blanket in the boot. 'What happens if I get moths back there?' he asked when she'd climbed back in.

'We can get some mothballs in Warwick.'

'Phew!' He wiped his forehead. 'That is indeed a relief.'

Alex was waiting for them where he'd promised – in the lounge of the Swan Hotel right in the heart of Warwick, another lovely old town with a plethora of attractive buildings.

Clive had hardly ushered Martha into the hotel,

when a beaming Alex ushered them out again. 'You'll never guess,' he said excitedly, 'but *The Times*, the *Mail*, the *London Evening Standard* and some of the regionals have got hold of "Martha's Journey".' He kissed Martha jubilantly on both cheeks. 'There's reporters waiting to speak to you in the Silversmith's Hall just around the corner, along with quite a few other people.'

A cheer went up and there was clapping when Martha entered the building. For the first time in her life she was aware of herself blushing as she was surrounded by people who just seemed to want to touch her, who waved or blew kisses if they were unable to get near. She was propelled towards a small stage at the end of the room and, without warning, the small crowd fell silent as they waited for her to speak.

She cleared her throat. 'I hope you don't think I've been walking all the way,' she eventually began. 'I don't like the idea of fooling people. When I started off, I really did mean to walk to London, but I never realized it was so far. I'd hardly walked more than a couple of miles when me feet started killing me. I was sitting on a milestone not all that far from Liverpool, when Clive turned up in his motor car and gave me a lift to Chester. Clive's been turning up ever since . . .'

Unusually for Clive, who usually kept in the background, he jumped on to the stage and embraced her.

Everyone laughed and cheered. 'You're one in a million, Martha,' someone shouted. Martha could sense the atmosphere becoming a touch overwrought.

'I've got a son fighting in France,' a woman shouted angrily. 'I thank you from the bottom of my heart, Mrs Rossi, for what you're doing by bringing the government's attention to the slaughter that's going on over there.'

'Do you think the government don't already know?' another woman called. 'What Martha's doing is letting *them* know that *we*, the general public, know what's going on; that we're not the stupid idiots they think we are. That we've got brains like they have.'

'*Better* brains than they have,' called a man.

'What was it like, Martha, spending the night in prison in Wolverhampton?'

'Bloody awful!' Martha shuddered.

'What are you going to say to the Prime Minister when you get to London?'

'I don't know yet,' she confessed. 'I haven't really thought about it. I'll just have to wait and see how I feel when the time comes.'

She was enjoying herself, enjoying the attention and the admiration and the bright flashes that indicated her photo was being taken. She was pleased at her just-discovered ability to hold her own in front of a crowd. Then, suddenly, she realized, she'd forgotten all about her dear, sorely missed son. In fact, she'd hardly thought about Joe all day. Instead, she'd just sat in Clive's car admiring houses, calling on an old woman who was referred to as 'her ladyship'. And now here she was showing off, thrusting herself into the lime-light.

It wouldn't do, it really wouldn't do. Martha did no more than fall to her knees and burst into tears. Lights flashed as more photographs were taken. The crowd sighed, 'Aaah!' and some people began to cry with her.

Chapter 18

The next morning, before it was light, Martha left the hotel in Warwick and began to trudge in the direction of Oxford. The sky was dramatically red and, in her present hazy state of mind, she couldn't remember whether this was a good or a bad sign of the weather to come.

On reflection, she thought it must be a bad one, for the red was more than a bit threatening. For a while, she kept her eyes on the ground and when she looked up the sky was dark grey all over, apart from a little glow near the horizon where the sun was beginning to rise, though she doubted it would be visible through the grey when it did. Birds sang, but only limply, as if they were as fed up as she was.

She doubted if it was possible to feel more miserable than she did now. Tomorrow, she would be in London and was dreading it more than anything on earth. Why had she come? If granted her dearest wish, she would want to be back in King's Court where Lily and Georgie would shortly be getting ready for school, she would soon be off to work at Ackerman's Sacks and Sails, Carlo would be in bed, and London a place she'd heard of but had never planned to visit.

But she didn't want *that* Carlo back, did she? If he

hadn't been left to look after the children, he'd still be spending his days wandering around Liverpool and drinking himself stupid night after night. Or would he? Of late, he really had seemed to have turned over a new leaf.

The baby, cross at being woken so early, was playing a brutal game of football in her belly, and the suitcase felt dead heavy, the handle digging painfully into her palm. The string bag she'd brought had been easier to carry – she'd been able to sling it over her shoulder if it became a nuisance. But now she had more than twice as many clothes than she'd started off with and they wouldn't all fit in the bag. Her feet hurt, too, and she'd barely slept a wink the night before.

'Bugger!' she shouted at the hedges and the trees and the tired birds – the houses at the start had trickled away without her noticing.

A car passed and stopped a few feet ahead. Clive got out, his face expressionless, walked around the car and opened the passenger door. When Martha arrived, he took the suitcase, stowed it in the cupboard at the back, while she climbed in the passenger side. Neither said a word.

They'd driven quite a few miles before Clive spoke. 'Are you feeling all right now?' He could tell she was in a bit of a state.

'What makes you think I've *not* been all right?' Martha growled.

'I expect it's because you must have risen before dawn, ignored breakfast, and set off by yourself without telling a soul. Me, I thought perhaps you'd spent another night in the police station.'

'That's not funny,' she said.

'I wasn't joking. I genuinely thought something bad had happened. By the way, I was told someone threw a brick through the window of Wolverhampton police station the other night.' He chuckled. 'It had a message chalked on it. "That's For Martha".'

'*That's* not funny, either,' she snorted. 'And as for *last* night, it was desperately awful, me falling on me knees in that hall place, making a terrible show of meself. I made other people cry and I never set out to make anyone cry or break winders.'

'Martha,' Clive said soberly, 'when I saw Joe's photo, *I* wanted to cry. You're not going to London just for yourself, but for all the men and women who hate this awful war but haven't got the time or the courage or the capability or the willpower to make the journey themselves. You may not consider you're doing it on their behalf, but that's what they think.' His voice became unintentionally tender. 'Everyone admires you – including me.' She would be embarrassed if he told her just how much.

She thought about this for a while, must have recognized the truth in what he said, because her response was merely to ask where Alex was.

'Still at the hotel eating all our breakfasts; greedy so-and-so.'

'Haven't you had anything to eat yet this morning?'

'Not a sausage,' he said mournfully.

'I'm sorry for leaving so early.' She shook her head distractedly. 'I just felt I had to do something on me own accord. I was fed up being managed.'

'Have you got over it by now?'

She snorted and made a face. 'No, but I don't

suppose it matters. I'll be glad to be home again.' With that, she fell into a trance.

Clive didn't mention that she would discover one big change once she was home. This 'Mister' had been exposed in one of the newspapers as Dariush Baig, who was wanted for a list of ugly crimes in Persia where he'd been born. It wasn't Clive who'd given the chap's details to the press, but some bright spark had gone on to investigate his background, and the information was being used by a few of the newspapers to discredit Martha. Not all the press approved of what she was doing. A number of journalists were using the fact that her employer was a criminal as a stick with which to beat her. So far, Martha knew nothing about it. From what she'd said, the chap had been a good friend. Now he was likely to be deported. Although justice had been done, it was still a shame.

He looked at her dejected face and the way she was hunched up in her seat. 'Would you like me to turn around and take you back to Liverpool here and now?' he offered, knowing darn well she would refuse.

She straightened up immediately and thrust her shoulders back. 'Don't be so bloody daft,' she said derisively. 'As if I'd go back now! We'll be in London tomorrer, won't we?'

Clive agreed. 'By the end of the week it'll all be over.'

'What's Oxford like?' she asked.

Clive said he had no idea. 'I've never been to any of the places we've visited, apart from Chester – and London. Most of this is as new to me as it is to you.' He thought he'd quite like to travel once the war was over, and wondered if Kate would be willing to come with him. His thoughts began to run away with him. Would Kate marry him, have his children, agree to live with him for the rest of their lives?

'Shall we stop and get some food?' he asked when he saw a hotel, an old coaching inn, ahead.

'Yes, please, Clive. Me stomach thinks me throat's been cut and I'm aching for a cuppa.'

Alex turned up while they were halfway through breakfast, having seen Clive's car parked outside. He ordered a plate of muffins and sang 'Some of These Days' while he waited.

'Sing before breakfast, cry before tea,' Martha reminded him.

'I've already eaten three breakfasts,' he boasted.

'Then you'll be sick before tea instead.'

They spent a quiet day in Oxford. That morning's article hadn't mentioned where Martha would be, just that she would be enjoying 'a day of rest' before arriving at her goal – London.

The hotel wasn't as grand as other places they'd stayed. Martha expressed total disinterest in sightseeing, but said she might do another time. 'Though I probably won't. When the war's over, I'd like to go to France and see where our Joe's buried. I'll take him the biggest bunch of flowers anyone's ever seen. After that, I never want to leave Liverpool again.'

Dinner over, they went into the empty lounge where Alex bought Martha a port and lemon.

'What's going to happen tomorrer?' she asked Clive.

'I'm going to drive you to Downing Street where you'll get out and knock at the door of number ten,' he told her again.

'It's as simple as that?' She was terrified, her face deathly pale.

'Yes.' He didn't tell her that her destination and time of arrival, Downing Street at twelve thirty, had been in the 'Martha's Journey' column that he and Alex had written that afternoon. Alex had already telephoned the information to the *Guardian*'s office in Manchester and from there it had been passed to Edgar Henderson at the *Lancashire Post*. Instead of a single photograph, there would be a montage of photos covering the entire journey.

'And what will I say if someone answers the door of number ten?' Martha was urgently chewing her thumb. It probably hadn't been her intention to drink half the port and lemon in a single gulp, but she had and was suddenly seized by a fit of coughing.

'Tell them why you're there.' Clive reached out and took her hand. He could feel her trembling. 'That you've come to see the Prime Minister.'

'I've forgotten his name.'

Alex squeezed her other hand. 'Herbert Asquith. Apparently he's a really nice bloke.'

'A really nice bloke,' she echoed. 'But what if he tells me to sod off?'

The young men looked at each other and grinned. Clive shrugged and said, 'I suppose there's a chance he won't have time to see you – in fact, he might not be there at all – but you can always leave a message, tell him about Joe and that he must make sure no more young boys are allowed to join the Army, let alone be called upon to fight.'

She nodded tremulously. 'All right, I'll learn the words off by heart before I go asleep tonight. In fact, I think I'll go to bed now.' She stood, releasing their hands and leaning down to stroke Alex's cheek, then Clive's.

'God bless you, lads,' she said gently. 'I'll never forget what you've done for me over the last week.'

With that, she was gone. The door closed behind her and Clive was forced to sniff away a tear.

'Damn you, Clive Dexter,' Alex said in a choked voice. 'You've got me at it now.'

The two young men might well have indulged in a brief, embarrassing shedding of tears had the lounge door not been noisily flung open and a voice cried, 'I couldn't bring myself to miss Martha's day in London. Daddy found out on the telephone where you were staying and booked a room for me at the same time. I came on the train. Where is Martha?'

'Kate!' Clive fell backwards into the chair in which he'd been sitting. 'What on earth are you doing here?'

'I've just told you.' Kate giggled at his fall. 'I didn't want to miss Martha's great day. Where is she?'

'Gone to bed,' Clive choked.

'I'll just pop up and say goodnight.'

'You can't.' Alex leaped from his seat and blocked her way. 'She really needs her sleep in preparation for tomorrow.'

Kate seemed taken aback. 'But I won't be a minute,' she protested.

Clive said, 'She might already be asleep.'

'Oh, all right.' Kate shrugged. She sat down. 'I came by train and on the way I scribbled a few notes. I thought all three of us could write the last instalment of "Martha's Journey" between us.'

'*No!*' Clive and Alex said together.

'Why ever not?' Her voice squeaked with rage.

'Because it's *our* job; we're being paid.' She must be the most irritating woman on earth, Clive thought.

'That's right.' Alex nodded his agreement.

She glared at them both, took a red-backed notebook out of her bag and began to scribble in it.

The men stared at her suspiciously for a while, until Alex gave an amateurish yawn and said, 'I think I'll turn in.'

'I will, too. I'll just order a cup of cocoa first. Would you like a drink of some sort, Kate?'

'Yes, please, Clive.' She was scribbling away and didn't look up. 'I'd like a cup of hot milk.'

'I'll ask for it to be brought to you.'

'Thank you very much. Goodnight.'

'Women,' Clive said when he and Alex were on their way upstairs. 'I'll never understand them.'

'Neither will I, old chap. Neither will I.'

The next morning, Kate was persuaded, albeit unwillingly, to let Alex take her to London. Clive wanted Martha left to experience the day herself without Kate's loudly expressed opinions on anything and everything before she'd had time to form her own.

After the long drive to London, during which she hardly spoke, Martha suddenly burst into life when they reached the capital, grey and magnificent, pulsating with life, smoke and traffic that was a mixture of the old and the new: handcarts, horse-drawn lorries, open-topped motor buses and the very latest motor cars. It seemed like the hub of the world.

'What's that?' Martha would cry, pointing at a tower or some magnificent building. Clive had no idea. His chief experience of London was within the area of South Kensington, where the Dexters' apartment was, and the West End, where they went shopping and ate at his parents' favourite restaurants. He knew Buckingham Palace, the Tower of London and Trafalgar Square, that was all.

It didn't matter, though, that he didn't have the answers, because Martha didn't wait for a reply, just pointed at something else. 'What's that?' 'Who's that statue of?' 'Who lives there?'

'There's some superb buildings in Liverpool down by the Pier Head,' he reminded her after a while, hurt that she was lavishing such praise on London when she already lived in a truly splendid city. 'And St George's Hall is one of the most admired buildings in the whole of Europe.'

'Is it?' She looked surprised. 'I'll have a proper gander at it when I get home.'

She actually looked quite pretty today, Clive thought, in the brown flowered frock that Kate had brought, pink gloves, and a little pink hat with a veil. That morning in Oxford, she'd fought a fierce battle with Alex, who'd wanted her to wear her old grey frock and shawl.

'I'm not meeting the Prime Minister dressed like a tramp,' she said heatedly.

'But that's what you wear at home.' Alex was trying to be utterly reasonable.

'Well, I'm not at home, am I? I'm about to go to London. D'you think I've got no shame, that I wouldn't wear me bessy clothes for something so important as meeting the Prime bloody Minister? Anyroad, this frock only cost a couple of bob in Great Homer Street market.'

'But I want him to think you're poor and working class,' Alex cried. His face had fallen once he realized he was embroiled in an argument he was certain to lose.

'I *am* poor and working class,' Martha said proudly, 'but all I want off Mr Asquith is for him to stop fourteen-year-old lads from joining the bloody Army. He won't care two hoots if I wear a shawl or a nice pink hat.'

There were so many people, hundreds, a good proportion of them policemen, in the area around Downing Street, that Clive was unable to find a space to park. He left the car in Parliament Square and he and Martha got out.

'There must be something going on in Downing Street,' he said. 'A demonstration of some sort. We'll just have to walk the last bit.' He took her arm and tucked it in his own. 'Nervous?'

'I'm scared stiff.'

'Come on, then.' He pressed her arm against his side.

As they got closer to the demonstration, he could sense the atmosphere was sombre. Few people smiled. Some men were present, several carrying cameras. The rest were women displaying placards with names written on, men's names, he saw when he and Martha got closer: Cyril, Mikey, Hubert, Charlie, Francis . . .

Close by them, a woman gasped, '*Martha!*'

'She's here!' another woman shouted.

Clive cursed himself for being a fool and not realizing that the women were there for Martha. He'd never dreamed there'd be so many. Somehow, she was separated from him and quickly disappeared inside a thick circle of black-clad females. Occasionally, he glimpsed the top of her pink hat. He was pleased to note she appeared to be the only woman there not wearing black.

'Martha's here.' He heard the words over and over.

'Come along, gal.'

'This way, darlin'.'

She hadn't got a placard! The names must be those of men, the sons, brothers and fathers, the loved ones who'd been killed or injured in this heinous war – and Martha didn't have a placard with Joe's name on to take to Downing Street.

By now, he had no idea where she was, and there was no sign of Alex or Kate. He felt terribly alone, despite being in the midst of so many people – though gradually he was being pushed towards the edge – despite it being *his* idea to record Martha's journey to London. None of this would be happening if it hadn't been for him.

'Ah, there you are, old man. I've lost Kate.' It was Alex, looking so happy and full of beans that Clive felt even more miserable in comparison. Why couldn't he look like that?

Right now, he didn't give a damn about Kate. 'Martha hasn't got a placard with Joe's name on.' He was almost crying with frustration and inexplicable rage.

'She has now; I had one ready. Oh, you should see her, Clive, at the head of the procession. Any minute now they'll turn into Downing Street.'

'Is the Prime Minister there? Do you know?'

'He's on his way. Should be here in an hour or so, but whether he'll speak to Martha, I couldn't say.'

In Downing Street, Martha was standing on the pavement directly opposite number ten, with women lined up in rows behind her; hundreds more had been left in the street outside, as the police had refused to allow them in for safety reasons. On the pavement opposite, photographers were lined up shouting, 'Look this way, Martha.' 'Turn around a bit, love.'

The women began to sing 'Onward Christian Soldiers', a Protestant hymn that she didn't know the words to, then 'Keep the Home Fires Burning', a war song, and this was no place for songs of war.

Yet perhaps Joe might have heard it sung on his last night at war, the night he lay sobbing for her, his mam, the night he died. Alex had made her a flag on a stick. It read: '**Joe Rossi, hero, killed in France, aged 14**'.

By now, the women were singing something else, but Martha didn't hear. She was thinking about Joe and it felt so real that she managed to conjure him up until he was standing in front of her, grinning, only half visible, so that she could see right through him. She reached out and touched his shadowy face, his lips, his chin, his hair. She could smell him, feel his breath on her skin. She would have embraced him, had he not vanished into thin air, though she could still sense his presence.

The door to number ten opened and a man came out. He was greeted by a small cheer, although he was nothing like the Prime Minister, Herbert Asquith, whom Clive and Alex had described to her the night before. This man was modestly handsome with light brown hair and a pleasing smile.

Yet she knew him! She wasn't surprised when the man approached and seized both her hands in both of his and kissed them warmly.

'Martha,' he said, 'how brave you are – and what commitment you have shown. I'm so proud to think of you as a friend.' It was Arthur Hanson, assistant to Norman Brown, Member of Parliament for Liverpool Central. 'When the Prime Minister was told we two were acquainted, I was granted special permission to welcome you to Downing Street.'

'Hello, luv.' She was too full up to say any more, what with Joe being around and so many people able to hear her every word.

His hands tightened on hers. 'The Prime Minister is on his way back from Chequers. Would you like to come inside? When he arrives he will speak to you in private.'

Martha was about to do his bidding, but had second thoughts. 'No,' she said firmly. 'I'll not go inside, if you don't mind. I'm not the only person here who's lost a dear one in this God-awful war; most of the women here have. I don't want no special treatment. If the Prime Minister wants to speak to me, he'll have to do it in front of everyone.'

Arthur Hanson smiled. 'I should have expected you to say that, Martha.' He gave a little bow. 'I'll see what I can do.'

'Good on yer, Mam,' said Joe, who was still around.

Neither Clive nor Alex had any idea what happened outside Downing Street. They were too far away, but according to the *Evening Standard*, published the same afternoon, the Prime Minister's car swept into the street, the Prime Minister alighted and went to shake hands with Martha. They conversed for roughly two and a half minutes, then other hands were shaken, the politician made his way towards the door of number ten, waving all the time. He disappeared inside and the crowd began to sing 'Jerusalem'.

Clive and Alex heard them singing as they leaned on railings in Parliament Square, close to where Clive's car was parked. They wondered aloud how long they would have to wait for Martha. There was no suggestion of the crowd beginning to thin.

'I'll go and look for her,' Alex offered. 'And just in case we miss each other, let's meet up somewhere later to write the final step of "Martha's Journey" between us. Where shall it be?'

'Birmingham?' Clive was thinking how odd the song sounded when it was sung solely by women. 'It's about halfway between Liverpool and Manchester. Let's meet at the hotel where we stayed.'

'Good idea, old chap.' Clive winced when his shoulder was treated to a vigorous slap. 'Tell you what, if Martha comes, you take her home. If I come and you've gone, then I'll realize that you found her. If I find her first, I'll bring her to you, so as not to cause any confusion. Oh, and the same goes for Kate.'

'I understand,' Clive lied, totally confused.

He stayed where he was for about half an hour, feeling more and more isolated, more and more alone, and was heartily relieved when he saw a dishevelled Martha come limping towards him.

'People have stood on every single one of me toes,'

she complained. 'And once I've had the baby, people want me to make speeches all over the bloody place. Can I get in the back and lie down?' she pleaded.

'Of course, Martha.' He opened the door. 'What did you say to the Prime Minister?'

'What I'd planned on saying, but I can't remember what he said back.' She got into the car. 'He was ever so nice, but Joe kept interrupting.'

'Joe!' Clive's spine tingled.

'Cheeky little sod,' she said affectionately. 'He kept making really rude remarks. Y'know what, Clive? I very nearly curtsied to Mr Asquith. If I had, I'd've hated meself for the rest of me life.'

He turned around and looked at her face. Her cheeks were flushed and her eyes feverishly bright. 'How do you feel?' he asked worriedly. He wished Kate were there to look after her.

'Buggered, if you must know.' She laughed a touch hysterically. 'Me head feels as if someone's wound it up with a key. If it goes whizzing off somewhere, then you'll know the reason why.' She sank sideways on to the seat and her hat fell off. Clive picked it up and threw it on the shelf behind. He was worried about her. He didn't know much about pregnant women, but had a feeling they were supposed to rest. He'd only been seven when his mother gave birth to Veronica and, from what he remembered, she'd rested every day for hours on end. Mind you, Martha was made of sterner stuff.

He got out of the car and wound up the engine. Back inside, he set off for Birmingham.

MARTHA'S JOURNEY – THE FINAL DAY

A remarkable thing happened yesterday. A very ordinary woman spoke to the most important politician in the land. They spoke as equals, which is how it should be, for it is often the very ordinary people who show their so-called 'betters' how to behave. Readers who have followed 'Martha's Journey' will know that her husband is an invalid and she raised five children while working full-time in a factory sewing sacks. But then her son, Joe, aged only fourteen, was wrongly persuaded to join the Army by someone who should have known better, and tragically killed in the heat of battle.

Martha did not take his death lying down. She tried to complain, but no one listened. Determined to make herself heard, Martha, six months with child, set off on foot to present her case in person to the powers-that-be, to insist that children under the age of eighteen should not be allowed to fight in a war.

We do believe that she would indeed have walked all the way to London if people hadn't helped her on her way. She had been told that as her son lay dying on a muddy field in a foreign land, he had cried for her, his mother, and this was her way of seeking justice for him.

It is said that there would be no more wars if the world was run by women. We think that is probably not quite true. There are women who are every bit as cruel and ruthless as men. Most women, though, are like Martha; they do not see their children as tools to make war, to be cannon fodder, to lay down their lives for a country that has not fed them properly or educated them well, will not find them employment as they grow older, or provide decent medical care should they fall ill.

We would like you to salute the bravest woman we have ever known, a heroine of her time – Martha Rossi.

WELCOME HOME.

Alex laughed when he read Clive's neatly written article. 'Have you become a supper of women's suffrage, old chap?'

'I might have done,' Clive admitted.

'It's good, it's brilliant, I love it. I admire it enormously.'

'Would you like me to make any changes?' After all, it was going out under both their names.

'No, I'm quite happy with the way it is,' Alex assured him, 'except it would be fairer if you changed all those "we's" to "I's". You deserve the credit for the article. I didn't contribute a word.'

Clive was indignant. 'I wouldn't dream of doing such a thing. We shared this experience together.'

'You're a decent old stick, Dexter.' He slapped Clive's shoulder as vigorously as he slapped the other one earlier in the day, and followed this by noisily rubbing his hands together. 'Is there any grub available in this establishment? What is it Martha says? Me stomach thinks me throat's been cut.'

'I'll go and fetch some menus.' Clive hurried away.

They were in the lounge of the hotel in Birmingham where they'd stayed before. He and Martha hadn't been there long when Alex had arrived with Kate. Martha announced she intended nodding off for

316

half an hour, and Clive and Alex spent that time being as nice as they could possibly be to Kate to make up for them being not nice at all the night before. By the time they were ready to leave, she had forgiven them.

Kate transferred to Clive's car for the drive back to Liverpool; Alex had to go in the direction of Manchester where the final piece of 'Martha's Journey' would be taken to the print room and made ready for the paper the following day.

With Kate still present, Clive took Martha to King's Court where Carlo and her four children were anxiously waiting for her to arrive. They kissed her tenderly and led her inside.

'Well, *that's* over,' Clive said with a satisfied sigh. 'It's time for us to celebrate. What say we have dinner at the Adelphi?'

'It's just gone eleven o'clock,' Kate reminded him.

'Has it really?' He hadn't realized it was so late. The day was over, but he wasn't ready for it to end.

Kate must have sensed how he felt – or perhaps she felt the same. 'You can take me home,' she offered, 'and we'll have something to eat there – a midnight feast. You can stay the night in the spare room. My mother will be dead pleased.'

Clive began to back the car out of King's Court. What a good idea!

317

Chapter 19

Her journey over, Martha had barely any strength left. It was all she could do to rise from her bed and get Lily and Georgie ready for school. She couldn't have gone to work in Ackerman's Sacks and Sails to save her life. Frank went to Back Seel Street on his mother's behalf to explain the situation, but came back to report the door to the factory was padlocked and no one had answered when he knocked.

Kate insisted on calling the doctor, who pronounced the patient to be desperately run down and in urgent need of bed rest for at least a couple of weeks. 'You need a tonic,' he added. 'Iron's the best. I suggest you take it in liquid form rather than tablets.'

'Yes, doctor.' Martha rather liked the idea of staying in bed for a fortnight, but how was the family supposed to live without her wages?

'You are *not*,' Kate's mother said sternly to her daughter, 'to offer money. I know we can afford it, but now is the time for Carlo to show what sort of mettle he's made of. Buy Martha's medicine by all means, and make sure she and the children don't go hungry, but that's all.'

It was Frank who showed his mettle first. He came back to live at home and got a job on a fish stall in St

John's market. He called in the public baths on his way home for a good scrub, but still arrived home carrying a faint, fishy aroma. Now that conscription had been introduced, Frank, who would soon be eighteen, was expecting to be called up and he wasn't looking forward to it. He didn't possess his younger brother's enthusiasm to be a soldier.

Joyce's fiancé, Edward, twenty-one, was also anticipating his call-up papers any minute, and the young couple were planning to get married as soon as Martha had her baby. 'So you can wear a nice frock at the wedding, Mam,' Joyce said. 'But if Edward's called up sooner, we'll get married with an emergency licence, or whatever it's called.'

By now, Carlo was desperate for work. He could read well and was feeling cringingly ashamed of seeing himself described in the newspapers as an 'invalid', and being reminded again and again that it was his wife who had supported the family for so many years. But what could a man do with only one good arm? The other was nothing but a dead weight, he thought disgustedly. He'd be better off without it.

Eventually, he went to work as a cleaner on Lime Street station where he pushed a trolley containing the cleaning tools and managed the broom using his good arm. Although he hated it, the job wasn't as difficult as expected, and it gave him a sense of pride to come home on Friday nights with his wages and hand them to Martha, keeping just a few bob for himself; he still enjoyed a pint or two of an evening, though was trying to cut down.

Carlo sometimes wondered if he was being watched during that period, that someone on high was keeping an eye on him, and that, by taking the cleaning job, he'd shown what he could do when it came down to it. He felt he'd established to the world that at long last he was a man determined to look after his family. After a month working on the station, a letter arrived out of the blue, requesting he attend an interview at the munitions factory over the water where he'd been told the pay was sky-high.

'It's a miracle,' he told Martha when he got home from the interview. 'They're taking me on in the office as an invoice checker.'

'What's an invoice?' Martha asked. He'd grown ten years younger since leaving the house that morning. She couldn't remember when she'd last seen him so excited.

'A bill,' he informed her. 'If you sell something, or do something for someone, you send an invoice so the person can pay you. I write fine with my left hand. And Martha,' he continued in hushed tones, 'for this I am to be paid three pounds and ten shillings a week!'

'Bloody hell!' Martha yelled, and nearly fainted.

It meant that Martha's baby wasn't born in King's Court as she'd dreaded, but in a smart, three-bedroom terraced house in Globe Street, Bootle, with a proper midwife present. It was Clive who'd found the house, which had an incredibly low rent. In fact, Clive had secretly purchased it for twenty-five pounds with the Rossis in mind. His father had revealed a good side to his nature and was responsible for Carlo getting the job in the munitions factory.

Martha had really enjoyed buying the furniture, all second-hand. Lily had the smallest bedroom all to herself, and Frank and Georgie shared the middle one, though with his mother nicely settled in her new home, and his father working, Frank eventually resorted to his old, dissolute way of life and sometimes disappeared for days at a time. Martha didn't ask what he was up to. Any minute now and he'd be in the Army and all she could do then was pray.

'Oh, she's so *gorgeous!*' Kate gasped, staring ecstatically at the snow-white baby with creamy hair lying asleep in Martha's arms. 'Carlo said you're going to call her Josephine.'

'Her name's Josephine, but she's going to be called Jo.' Martha looked up at her friend. 'See, now I can say the name Jo with a smile on me face. I never thought I'd ever do that again.'

On behalf of the *Lancashire Post*, where he still worked, Clive arranged for a photographer to call at the house in Globe Street and take Martha's photograph with the baby. 'Take a few,' he advised the man. 'One with the husband and one with the kids. Oh, and they've got a cat now – well, a kitten. Include that, too, if you can.'

Edgar Henderson of the *Post* decided the photo of the entire family was the most attractive. It was published in the paper the following day and taken up by the national papers which had reported 'Martha's Journey'. It showed Martha seated with Jo in her arms, Carlo standing directly behind, with Joyce and Frank on either side. Lily and Georgie were kneeling at their mother's feet, and Tarzan, the fluffy black kitten, posed prettily in front of his new family.

On a gloriously sunny July day, the salt in the air giving the small town of Bootle a brilliant, crystalline sparkle, Clive bought copies of all the papers to show Martha. She was peeling potatoes in the kitchen, while Jo slept in a laundry basket on the table in the living room. Wiping her hands on her pinny, she poured water in the kettle to make tea. Clive had never seen her looking so supremely, rosily happy, but there was a glimmer of sadness in her eyes that not everyone might have noticed had they not known her history, a sadness he suspected would never go away.

'Look at this,' she said, waving her hand dramatically around the room.

'What, Martha?' he asked dutifully. She was showing off the wonders of the house again, something she did regularly.

'A sink, a proper sink, with a draining board each side.' She stood back and regarded the sink with the air of an art lover admiring a valuable painting. 'And a cupboard with shelves, a gas boiler for the clothes, and a clothes rack. I really missed having a clothes rack when we were in King's Court.'

'How do you get hot water?' Clive asked. He hadn't thought to ask when he'd bought the place.

'The water's heated up by the kitchen range. I boil water for tea on the fire. And that's where the oven is. Right now, there's a lamb stew in there for our tea.' She looked at him fondly. 'Trust a man not to know something like that.'

They went into the living room where she checked on Jo and put the kettle on the hob, showing him the way it swung over the fire.

'People have sent money after seeing your photograph,' Clive said when they were seated. 'And presents for the baby, as well as for Lily and Georgie.'

322

'Oh, aren't people lovely,' she cried tearfully. 'I'd love the pressies, but you can give the money to a charity like before.' More than a hundred pounds had been donated after she'd finished her walk, but she'd refused to touch a penny. 'It'd be like being paid for our Joe's death,' she maintained. 'There must be thousands of families who need it more than us.'

'And we've had more requests for interviews,' Clive reminded her.

'Just put in the paper that we're all fine,' she told him, 'and thank everyone for the pressies.' She stared into the fire. 'A letter came for us this morning,' she said. 'It was sent to King's Court, but someone brought it round here. Would you like to read it?'

Dear Mrs Rossi,

You won't have heard of me – I know because I found a half-written letter Joe had started to write to his mam telling about life in France, but he never got round to finishing. (The Army took the letter away otherwise I would have sent it to you.)

My name is Reggie Moules, Sergeant, and I met your Joe in Calais, where he was in a camp with the youngsters waiting to be sent back to Blighty. Being as he was such an intelligent lad with the ability to read as well as anyone, he was allocated to me to help set up a communications centre in St Omer. He insisted on bringing his mate, Albie, with him.

Just in case you were wondering how Joe was before he died, I assure you that both lads had a whale of a time. Albie turned out to be a good cook, and during the day your Joe would fly over the hills on his bike taking messages all over the place, while Albie was in the kitchen making the dinner. Sometimes, Joe took Albie with him, which is what happened the day Captain Whitley-Neville came across them. Two days later, Joe was dead and Albie had been badly injured.

I shouldn't say this, Mrs Rossi, but since that happened, a night hasn't passed when I haven't prayed that the captain would suffer a horrible death. He had no right to send two young lads to the front line.

I mustn't forget to mention Emily, the dog Joe rescued from certain death. These days, she's as healthy as a horse and my best mate in the world. If I'm not allowed to bring her back to Blighty, then I've a good mind to stay in France with Emily. Me and that dog are determined not to be separated.

Well, lass, I suppose it's time I finished. All I can say is it was a pleasure knowing that grand lad of yours. He deserves a medal for what he did for Albie.

Yours in sorrow and in hope that this cruel war will soon be over,

Reginald Moules

Afterwards, Clive walked down to the Dock Road, which was crammed nose to tail with traffic and seamen from all over the world. Languages he'd never heard before were being spoken by men whose skin colours ranged from white to the blackest of black. Strange smells assailed him, strange sights intrigued him, such as the three little Chinese girls being pulled in a cart by a woman on a bicycle. A white horse wearing a garland of paper flowers trotted past, a vehicle with a chimney puffing smoke followed. He had no idea what it was for or what it was called.

He did, however, know the fate of Captain

Whitley-Neville, mentioned by Sergeant Moules in his letter to Martha.

These days, he read the *Manchester Guardian*, so he could keep an eye on what his friend Alex Scott was up to. He'd noticed the announcement of the death of a serving officer in the war, not on the battlefield but at home on leave in Abingdon in Oxfordshire. What particularly sparked his attention was the name. Whitley-Neville. He remembered Albie's statement referring to an officer as 'the devil'.

Alex offered to investigate for him and eventually reported that the captain, who'd been present at the battle of Loos, had died by his own hand, but the papers had been instructed by the War Office not to reveal the truth.

Clive was still debating with himself whether Martha would feel better knowing the truth, or worse. Perhaps the captain had been driven mad by the decisions he'd had to take and the slaughter that was taking place around him. It could be that he felt personally responsible for the death of young Joe Rossi.

He sighed and wondered why, in the midst of this throbbing slice of Liverpool at its noisiest and liveliest, he should feel so depressed. He'd felt it ever since he'd returned from accompanying Martha on her trek to London. There was a lack of something in his life; it had no meaning, was devoid of purpose. While men younger than him were dying on his behalf in France in their thousands, he was doing nothing in return.

But he had to do *something*. He *had* to contribute. For once this bloody war was over and he'd made no move to take part, he would be ashamed of himself for ever. He had no wish to kill anyone, even if they were German, but there were ways of helping.

He resolved that as soon as he got back to the office, he would write to the War Office, as he had planned to do over Christmas before breaking his arm, and inform them he was a conscientious objector but wished to serve in some capacity on the Front. He doubted if he would pass the medical if called up, for his fractured arm had still not mended properly. At times, the pain was agonizing and he doubted if he could carry a rifle, let alone fire one.

What he wanted was to help the injured, not create more. Then, after he had served his time, he would marry Kate – if she would have him.

Kate had written an article about Martha's journey to London and it had been published in a Socialist magazine with a small circulation. She had been paid half a guinea. It would have been best had she not been published because it gave her the idea that she would walk right into a job with a newspaper, which hadn't happened despite her efforts.

She finished her year's course at commercial college, and her parents celebrated the event by going out to dinner and inviting Clive. They met in Southport at their favourite hotel, not quite as grand as the Adelphi, but considerably cheaper.

'Are there any women working for the *Lancashire Post*?' Kate asked Clive.

'Quite a few. Though there aren't any female reporters, apart from Margaret Humble, who contributes a handicraft column on Saturdays. I suppose she's more a columnist than a reporter.'

Kate snorted and made a frightful face. 'I don't want to write about *knitting*. I want to write about the war and murders and crimes of passion.'

'Kate!' her mother said, shocked at her daughter's face, her words, or both.

'Well,' Kate said mutinously. 'Why should I be treated any differently from Clive or Alex?'

'Because you *are* different, Kate,' her mother replied. 'You are a girl and they are men.'

'I'm a *woman*, not a girl,' Kate stressed, making an even more frightful face.

Even her mild father felt obliged to remonstrate. 'Kate, dear, girl or woman, what does it matter? Whatever you are, you're not being exactly *lady*like.'

Kate was always more inclined to listen to her father. 'Well, it's not fair,' she said sulkily. 'I bet if I wrote to every newspaper in the land, they wouldn't give me a job as a reporter. I know,' her face brightened, 'from now on, I could write and pretend I'm a man.'

'They might notice you're not when you turned up for interview.'

'Then I'd show them I'm as good as any man, Daddy.'

'Who's Alex?' Mrs Kellaway asked. 'You mentioned him before.'

'You could always get married,' said Clive.

'Get married!' Kate was enraged. 'Do you think getting married is better than being a reporter? Why don't *you* get married and let me have your job?'

Clive shrugged. 'I will if you like.'

'*What?*' She stared at him in astonishment.

'What do you mean by that, Clive?' Kate's mother asked in a gentler tone.

'It means that I'm off to France at the end of next week,' Clive explained. 'I've given in my notice at the *Lancashire Post*, and asked the editor if he would employ Kate in my place. He agreed to give her a month's trial.'

Kate managed to look subdued, pleased and worried all at the same time.

Mr Kellaway frowned. 'Don't tell me you've joined the Army, son?'

'No, I registered as a conscientious objector and I'm going as a stretcher-bearer.'

Mrs Kellaway laid her hand on Clive's arm. 'You're a lovely young man, Clive,' she said huskily. 'When you said you were willing to get married, did you have anyone in mind?'

'Kate, of course.'

Kate's mother turned to her daughter. 'What do you say, darling?'

'Well, yes, I suppose.'

'You could show a bit more enthusiasm,' her father remarked.

'But he didn't ask *me* to get married, he asked the whole table.'

'I only meant you, Kate,' Clive smiled, 'not your mother or your father. We could meet next week and choose an engagement ring. What d'you say?'

Kate shrugged. 'All right.'

Mr Kellaway signalled the waiter. 'I've no idea what's happening, whether our daughter is getting married or not, but I feel it is necessary to order a bottle of champagne. When it arrives, perhaps someone will advise me who or what to toast.'

★

'Aren't you pleased, darling?' Mrs Kellaway asked in the car on the way back to Ormskirk.

'Of course I am, Mother.'

'You don't exactly look it.'

'I might be more pleased tomorrow than today. Just now, I'm a bit stunned, if you must know.' Not pleased? She was massively, enormously, *hugely* pleased. On Monday, she was meeting Clive and he would buy her a ring and tell her that he loved her. Her mother was talking about the ring now.

'How many diamonds do you want, darling?' she asked. 'Three or five? Or would you prefer a solitaire?'

'I've no idea what I want.' Yes, she did. She wanted to be on her own and able to think about marrying Clive, where they would live, how many children they would have and what they would look like.

Not long afterwards, she was in bed and in the middle of designing her wedding dress when she fell asleep.

Clive wandered, dazed, through the carpet of bodies – British, French, German, mostly dead. They lay where they had fallen, curled like babies or spread like windmills in the mud, some missing a limb or perhaps two, occasionally a head. He could smell the blood. Now and then, there would be a moan to indicate a live one and he would kneel beside the man, clutch his hand, and whisper, 'Help is coming. Hang on, old chap.'

A voice called from the mist or the smoke or the darkness of the night, *'Dexter, where are you?'* But Clive took no notice.

There was a choking sound, a head moved, and he squelched through the thick mud towards the sound. It came from a white-faced boy, who was much too young to be there.

'Joe!' Clive whispered. 'I thought you were dead, son. Your mother thinks you're dead.' He gently laid his hand over the boy's eyes and they closed for ever. In his heart, he knew it wasn't Joe, just a trick of his tortured mind. It was a year since Joe Rossi had died.

Clive turned away and was sick. The temptation that he'd had before, to pick up a pistol and finish himself off, returned. He'd sooner end it than be a part of a world where it was normal for a day to finish with thousands of innocent dead bodies carpeting the ground. On only the first day of this particular battle, the Somme, almost 20,000 British men had been slaughtered, and many thousands more were missing or terribly wounded.

Oh, Christ, the monstrousness of it! Women he would never know had become widows, children had lost their fathers. The ripples of an anguished world spread, taking in brothers and sisters, grandparents, aunts and uncles, until one day there would be no one left who hadn't lost a relative, by which time the earth would be red with blood.

What a way to run the world, allowing Death to stalk the fields and the devil to rule.

'*Dexter, are you out there?*'

'*Clive, old chap.*'

Clive touched the boy's cheek and struggled to his feet – the mud was holding him back, wanting to keep him there. He stood over the corpse and tried to imagine he was this boy's father. It was only then he noticed the lad was wearing a German uniform.

A wave of rage swept over him until it formed a

lump in his throat and he could easily have choked. How dare they? How bloody fucking dare they, those jumped-up, arrogant, merciless individuals who conducted wars, who started wars with the stroke of a pen, who considered human life to be worthless?

If he married Kate and they had a child and if the child was a boy, then *this* might well be his fate:

'Christ,' he murmured. 'Christ Almighty.'

The bullet struck him in the chest, and Clive fell slowly and gracefully into the mud. He didn't have time to wonder whether he'd been mistaken by his own side for an enemy, or if it was a German soldier claiming his final victim.

Thoughts tumbled crazily, feverishly through his head in no particular sequence. He was playing cards with his brother, pushing his sister on her swing, arguing with his father, on his mother's knee while she read him a story, buying Kate her ring, kissing her lips.

But when it came to his last breath, his last thought, Clive saw a woman in a black shawl marching purposefully through the mud towards him. He stretched out an arm.

'Martha!' he called. 'I'm here.'

Epilogue

Christmas
1940

'Oh, but I expected you to marry Clive,' Betty cried. 'He sounded lovely.'

'He *was* lovely,' Kate assured her. 'And he was also very brave, which is why he went to France.' She looked at her watch. Almost exactly noon and there was still no sign of Martha.

'Were you sad when he was killed?'

'Heartbroken.' She'd actually begun to make her wedding dress when she'd heard that he was dead. She was only eighteen, had never experienced tragedy before, and felt as if her life had come to an end. The engagement ring he'd bought her she still wore on the third finger of her right hand.

'What happened to . . . oh, there were so many people.' The girl put her finger to her chin. 'What happened to Martha's other children?'

Kate shifted in the chair. She'd been sitting still for so long that her bottom had gone numb. The room was no warmer, but she'd grown used to it. She remembered her intention about an hour ago to set the fire for when Martha came home. She'd do it in a minute – which was what she'd promised herself earlier.

'Well, Joyce married Edward, who was injured

during the war.' Edward's lungs had been damaged by mustard gas and they'd gone to live in a place with a healthier climate, the Liverpool air being notoriously damp. 'They have three children,' she told Betty, 'and manage a little hotel on the Isle of Man. I've been there a few times on holiday.'

'Frank sounded lovely, too, but a bit of a divil, not like Joe.'

Kate laughed. 'You're right about that. Frank was – still is – a bit of a divil. He sailed through the war without a scratch on him, then went to work in a garage. Now he has a garage of his own.'

'Did he get married?'

'No.' She didn't explain that Frank preferred a succession of girlfriends to a wife, a different one every week. There were quite a few children around who referred to him as 'Uncle Frank'. 'Before you ask,' she went on, 'Lily didn't get married. She studied and studied, became a teacher, and lives in Maghull.' Though, last time they spoke, Lily was considering giving up teaching for war work.

Who was next? Georgie! 'Georgie,' she said, 'grew up to be a fine young man and is now a successful commercial artist. He's married with two children and lives in London.' With Georgie being only thirty-four, Martha was terrified the time would come when he'd be called up. 'And Jo, the baby, is also in London with my own daughter, Lucie. They're training to be nurses.'

'What interesting lives some people lead!' Betty rolled her eyes in frustration. 'Me own life is as dull as ditchwater. Nothing exciting ever happens.'

'I bet my life was as dull as ditchwater when I was

fourteen.' She couldn't remember what her life was like then, so mustn't have minded. 'There's one person you forgot to ask about,' she pointed out. 'You forgot Carlo, Martha's husband. He died of pneumonia in nineteen thirty. He was only in his fifties.' It had happened suddenly. Everyone was shocked, but Jo was the most shocked of all. She'd never known the father who hadn't worked for nearly ten years and had depended on his wife to keep him.

There was a rattling sound as the front door key was dragged through the letterbox and the door opened. Kate went into the hall, expecting Martha, but it was Ethel Daniels from next door. Having finished the cleaning, it seemed she wanted her granddaughter back.

'I reckon she's been getting on your nerves for long enough.'

Kate smiled. 'She hasn't been getting on my nerves at all. We've just had an interesting talk.'

'We really have, Gran,' Betty assured her. 'We discussed the First World War. When I go back to school, I'm going to look in the library for a book about it.'

Ethel shook her head. 'Always got her nose stuck in a book, has this young lady,' she complained, and at the same time looked incredibly proud. 'You should've lit the fire, Kate. Shall I do it for you now?'

'Of course not!' Kate was shocked at the idea. 'I'll do it myself. You go home, Ethel, sit down and have a rest. You deserve it. As for me, I'll make myself a cup of tea in a minute.'

'Are you sure?' Ethel bit her lip and looked doubtful.

I must give the impression of being absolutely useless, Kate thought. 'Sure I'm sure,' she said stoutly.

'Well, if you want anything, girl, don't hesitate to ask. I'll be in for the rest of the day.'

Kate promised not to hesitate and the visitors left, Betty far more reluctantly than her grandmother. She was probably hoping for more tales of days gone by – Martha's tales. Twenty-four years ago, Martha Rossi had briefly been a household name, but since then had remained completely anonymous.

Kate went into the yard and managed to fill half a bucket, a good proportion of it dust, out of Martha's now empty coal store. She collected a few pieces of firewood and an old newspaper from the same place, and took everything into the kitchen. A single fire-lighter was revealed in the cupboard beneath the sink. I won't light the fire until Martha's home, she said to herself, in case I make a mess of things and waste the firelighter. She was hopeless at lighting fires, at most household tasks.

Though I was a good reporter, she thought as she knelt in front of the empty grate. She'd taken over Clive's job, but throughout her short time at the *Lancashire Post* she hadn't dealt with a single murder or crime of passion as she'd hoped. Nowadays, she contributed little articles about the war from the civilian side of the conflict. She'd always promised herself she'd go back to reporting once the children had grown up, but then Harry had come along unexpectedly and her plans had to be postponed. Amazingly, she hadn't minded. She would sooner have had Harry any day.

She opened the newspaper, rolled the sheets into long tubes, wound each tube into a tight coil and laid it on the grate, carefully placing the firewood on top and, using the tongs, the coal on top of that – she hated touching coal with her fingers and making them all black. She tucked the firelighter somewhere in the centre. Before the war, her husband had lit the fires. She'd had to get used to a lot of things since he'd gone away. He, Peter and Lucie had left at about the same time – would she ever get used to an almost empty house?

Standing up, she rubbed her aching back. I'm getting old, she thought, and nearly shot through the ceiling when she felt something touch her legs.

'Tarzan!' she cried. 'Where have you been?'

Tarzan the third was an enormous, highly affection-ate tabby. He usually slept on Martha's bed during a raid. 'Have you been upstairs by yourself all this time?' She picked him up and could have sworn the cat deliberately put his paws around her neck and kissed her. 'They should have called you Romeo,' she said. She told him she was about to make herself some tea and carried him into the kitchen where she opened the larder door. The cat jumped out of her arms when he saw the milk on the bottom shelf.

Kate poured some on a saucer, put it in his place on the floor, and he began to lap it noisily up. He was probably hungry as well as thirsty. Well, she wasn't going to touch Martha's precious bacon that glistened on a plate, or the half-used tin of sardines. She gave him a slice of bread and told him his mother would feed him properly when she came home.

There was tea in the caddy, not much, and she wished she'd brought some with her, then remem-bered she had hardly any left herself. She poured water in the kettle, lit a ring on the gas stove, and put the kettle on to boil.

While she waited, someone began to play 'Chopsticks' on the front door knocker.

'Alex,' she cried, running to the door. 'Oh, Alex.'

He was outside, forty-seven years old and as handsome as ever. She pulled him into the hall where he picked her up and kissed her as he carried her into the living room.

'I got a lift,' he said when they'd stopped kissing, but were still in each other's arms. 'One of the chaps had something to deliver to Manchester and I hitched a lift from there.'

'How long are you home for?' How wonderful if he would answer, 'for ever'.

He made a face. 'Four days. But I suppose that's better than nothing.'

'It means you'll be here on Christmas Day and Boxing Day. Four days will do just fine.' 'For ever' would have been much better. She studied him. 'Have I ever told you, when we first met I thought you would make a perfect model? You know, the sort whose photograph is in posh magazines advertising evening clothes. You'd look the gear in a cloak and a top hat leaning on a gold-topped cane.'

'And smoking a cigarette in a silver holder! You must have told me that a dozen times.' He pulled her close again. 'When *I* first met *you*, I thought, "*That's* the young woman I want to marry." Then I realized Clive already had the same idea and took it for granted I didn't stand a chance.'

'Poor Clive,' Kate said soberly. She often wondered if she and Clive would have been happy together had they got married. And how strange it was, unnatural almost, that her love for him should pass so smoothly and effortlessly to Alex, who'd become his best friend.

'How did you know I was here?' she asked.

He sat in Martha's armchair and pulled her on to his knee. 'Harry left a note on the table saying you were at Martha's. Apparently, you'd told him I might be coming home. Just in case, he wanted me to know where you were. It also said he'd gone to lunch with his grandma. He spelt lunch, l-u-n-s-h, by the way.'

'Both spellings sound the same when you say the word.'

'I know. From now on, in honour of our Harry, I'm going to spell lunch with "s" instead of a "c".'

There was more activity in the region of the door. Once again, the key was being pulled through the letterbox and the door unlocked. This time, it was Martha. She stopped to hang her coat in the hall.

'Why is me kitchen full of steam?' she asked when she came into the living room.

'Damn!' Kate almost fell off her husband's knee. 'I was just in the middle of making tea when Alex turned up.'

'Well, I'd like the first cup, if you don't mind,' Martha said. She stood in the middle of the room and studied the fireplace. 'And Alex, luv, will you please put a match to that disgracefully set fire and give the firelighter a shove inside with the poker. It should be under everything, not floating round in the middle. That wife of yours has no idea how to make anything, not even a simple cake, let alone a fire.'

Alex did as he was told and Kate made the tea. 'Where on earth have you been?' she asked when, tea in hand, all three sat in front of the fire, waiting anxiously for it to take hold. Tarzan, stuffed with bread, was sitting purring on Martha's knee, clearly pleased to have her back.

She looked very smart today, Martha, in a simple brown frock with a row of amber beads around her neck. Perhaps it was because Kate had only recently told Betty about their first meeting that she found it hard to connect this woman with the one she'd met twenty-five years ago wearing an old woollen shawl over her shabby, ankle-length frock. Then, her hair had been long, brown and untidy; now she was sixty and it was short and neat, with most of the brown turned to grey.

'I've been to a Christmas party,' she explained. 'It was at Arthur Hanson's house in Sefton Park.' Ten years ago, when Norman Brown had died of liver poisoning, his assistant, Arthur Hanson, had been elected Member of Parliament for Liverpool Central in his place. 'The raid got so bad that hardly anyone went home; instead, we sheltered in the cellar and sang carols at the top of our voices to shut out the sound of the bombs. This morning, I helped Arthur clear up after everyone had gone.'

'You see a lot of Arthur Hanson,' Kate remarked.

'Well, I work for him, don't I?' Martha replied pugnaciously, as if she suspected Kate of hinting at something.

Kate merely smiled. After teaching herself to read, years later Martha had taught herself to type and became Arthur Hanson's part-time secretary. 'Anyway, Martha, now I know you're safely home, Alex and I will make ourselves scarce. We might get back before my mother and Harry, who'll be thrilled to bits to find his dad's home.'

Martha stood, kissed both of them affectionately, and pinched Kate's cheek. 'Thank you for worrying about me,' she said. 'It was nice to find someone in when I got home, even if they were about to burn the bottom out of me kettle.'

'You'll try and come to see us over Christmas, won't you?' Kate said. 'Either that, or we'll come and see you.'

'We'll do something,' Martha promised. She encouraged them out of the house with little pats of her hands. 'Go on home to Harry and your mother,' she urged.

The house seemed awfully quiet once Kate and Alex had gone, but then it felt quiet, much too quiet, after most people had left. There were only one or two folk she was pleased to see the back of.

Martha sighed and went into the kitchen, where she tried to squeeze another cup of tea out of the pot. She almost managed, but it was cold when she took a sip. She boiled a small amount of water and filled the cup.

'And how have you been today?' she asked when she returned to the living room. She picked up Joe's photograph from the sideboard and put it on the table beside the armchair where she was about to sit. She talked to Joe more than she did any other of her children. He had remained a boy, a lad of fourteen in her heart and in her head, while the others had grown older and older. Joyce was forty-one and Frank a year younger.

'You'll never guess what happened today, luv.' She

340

paused for effect. 'I got a proposal of marriage!' She looked at Joe's young face. 'Now, what d'you think o' that?'

Tarzan jumped on to her knee and she ruffled the fur around his neck. 'I'll give you something to eat in a minute,' she promised.

'Are you going to accept?' Joe asked.

'I dunno, luv. I dunno.'

She had five grandchildren that she hardly ever saw, Frank and Lily didn't live too far away, but they both led busy lives and she was lucky if she saw them once a week, and now Jo was down in London with Kate's Lucie, training to be a nurse. She was proud of all her kids – oh, but she didn't half miss them!

Perhaps I was only born to be a wife and mother, she thought. Perhaps I wouldn't feel so bad if Carlo was still here. We could go out together at the weekend to New Brighton and the like. It seemed unnatural to go to Mass on her own. It seemed unnatural to do most things without at least a couple of kids trailing after her.

'But what about this marriage proposal?' Joe asked.

What about it, eh?

Martha ached for more tea while she thought about it, but steeled herself to do without. Living without gallons of tea shouldn't be too much to ask of the civilian population, not when so many Merchant Navy lads were losing their lives bringing it from India or China or somewhere else far away.

'It was Arthur Hanson that asked me, luv.' He hadn't claimed to love her or ask if she loved him. They liked each other, they got on well, were good friends. He didn't try to kiss her – she wondered what she would have done if he had?

But was she, Martha Rossi, who couldn't read until she was thirty-seven, a suitable person to become the wife of a Member of Parliament who lived in Sefton Park, a dead posh part of Liverpool?

Well, why not? she asked of herself, rather than Joe.

Why ever not? She was a woman who'd walked all the way to London when she was no longer young as well as being six months pregnant.

Not exactly, she conceded. She'd been driven most of the way and limped the rest. But she'd tried. Her heart had been in it, though she wouldn't have done it without Clive.

Damn! Thinking about Clive always made her cry. Joe and Clive, two wonderful young men; martyrs in their way. What a terrible waste. Once the war was over, she and Carlo had gone to France to see Joe's grave, just a little patch of earth and a cross with his name and age; 'Giuseppi Antonio Rossi, aged 14'. Oh, lord if she didn't stand up, do something, she'd collapse into buckets of tears.

Now she was getting maudlin! She'd have a glass of sherry instead of tea, hardly a sacrifice. Anyroad, it was nearly Christmas. And it was time she did something extra towards the war; become an ARP warden, for instance, join the Women's Voluntary Service, marry Arthur and run his home as well as his office.

She'd sleep on it and make up her mind tomorrow.

NOTES

The following books were of assistance in the writing of this novel.

How We Lived Then by Norman Longmate, Arrow Books
Private 12768, Memoir of a Tommy, John Jackson. Tempus Publishing Ltd
The Guardian First World War Series
Boy Soldiers of the Great War, Richard Van Emden, Headline.

Sir Arthur Markham, MP mentioned in the book, actually existed and campaigned tirelessly to have the practice of allowing children to fight banned. With the advent of conscription in 1916, plus a rule that would-be soldiers be forced to produce a birth certificate, the incidence of young boys being sent to war came to an eventual end.

MAUREEN LEE

MAUREEN LEE IS ONE OF THE BEST-LOVED SAGA WRITERS AROUND. All her novels are set in Liverpool and the world she evokes is always peopled with characters you'll never forget. Her familiarity with Liverpool and its people brings the terraced streets and tight-knit communities vividly to life in her books. Maureen is a born story-teller and her many fans love her for her powerful tales of love and life, tragedy and joy in Liverpool.

The Girl from Bootle

Born into a working-class family in Bootle, Liverpool, Maureen Lee spent her early years in a terraced house near the docks – an area that was relentlessly bombed during the Second World War. As a child she was bombed out of the house in Bootle and the family were forced to move.

Maureen left her convent school at fifteen and wanted to become an actress. However, her shocked mother, who said that it was 'as bad as selling your body on the streets', put her foot down and Maureen had to give up her dreams and go to secretarial college instead.

As a child, Maureen was bombed out of her terraced house in Bootle

Family Life

A regular theme in her books is the fact that apparently happy homes often conceal pain and resentment and she sometimes draws on her own early life for inspiration. 'My mother always seemed to disapprove of me – she never said "well done" to me. My brother was the favourite,' Maureen says.

> 'I know she would never have approved of my books'

As she and her brother grew up they grew apart. 'We just see things differently in every way,' says Maureen. This, and a falling out during the difficult time when her mother was dying, led to an estrangement that has lasted 24 years. 'Despite the fact that I didn't see eye-to-eye with my mum, I loved her very much. I deserted my own family and lived in her flat in Liverpool after she went into hospital for the final time. My brother, who she thought the world of, never went near. Towards the end when she was fading, she kept asking where he was. To comfort her, I had to pretend that he'd been to see her the day before, which was awful. I found it hard to get past that.'

Freedom – Moving on to a Family of Her Own

Maureen is well known for writing with realism about subjects like motherhood: 'I had a painful time giving birth to my children – the middle one was born in the back of a two-door car. So I know things don't always go as planned.'

'My middle son was born in the back of a two-door car'

The twists and turns of Maureen's life have been as interesting as the plots of her books. When she met her husband, Richard, he was getting divorced, and despite falling instantly in love and getting engaged after only two weeks, the pair couldn't marry. Keen that Maureen should escape her strict family home, they moved to London and lived together before marrying. 'Had she known, my mother would never have forgiven me. She never knew that Richard had been married before.' The Lees had to pretend they were married even to their landlord. Of course, they did marry as soon as possible and have had a very happy family life.

Success at Last

Despite leaving school at fifteen, Maureen was determined to succeed as a writer. Like Kitty in *Kitty and Her Sisters* and Millie in *Dancing in the Dark*, she went to night school and ended up getting two A levels. 'I think it's good to "better yourself". It gives you confidence,' she says. After her sons grew up she had the time to pursue her dream, but it took several years and a lot of disappointment before she was successful. 'I was *determined* to succeed. My husband was one hundred per cent supportive. I wrote lots of

> 'I think it's good to "better yourself". It gives you confidence'

articles and short stories. I also started a saga which was eventually called *Stepping Stones*. Then Orion commissioned me to finish it, it was published – and you know the rest.'

What are your memories of your early years in Bootle?

Of being poor, but not poverty-stricken. Of women wearing shawls instead of coats. Of knowing everybody in the street. Of crowds gathering outside houses in the case of a funeral or a wedding, or if an ambulance came to collect a patient, who was carried out in a red blanket. I longed to be such a patient, but when I had diptheria and an ambulance came for me, I was too sick to be aware of the crowds. There were street parties, swings on lamp-posts, hardly any traffic, loads of children playing in the street, dogs without leads. Even though we didn't have much money, Christmas as a child was fun. I'm sure we appreciated our few presents more than children do now.

What was it like being young in Liverpool in the fifties?

The late fifties were a wonderful time for my friends and me. We had so many places to go: numerous dance halls, The Philharmonic Hall, The Cavern Club, theatres, including The Playhouse where you could buy tickets for ninepence. We were crushed together on benches at the very back. As a teenager I loved the theatre – I was in a dramatic society. I also used to make my own clothes, which meant I could have the latest fashions in just the right sizes, which I loved. Sometimes we'd go on boat trips across the water to New Brighton or on the train to Southport. We'd go for the day and visit the fairground and then go to the dance hall in the evening.

> 'We clicked instantly and got engaged two weeks later'

I met Richard at a dance when he asked my friend Margaret up. When she came back she said, 'Oh, he was nice.' And then somebody else asked her to dance – she was very glamorous, with blonde hair – still is, as it happens. So Richard asked me to dance because she had gone! We clicked instantly and got engaged two weeks later. I'm not impulsive generally, but I just knew that he was the one.

*Do you consider yourself independent
and adventurous like Annemarie in* The
Leaving of Liverpool *or Kitty in* Kitty
and her Sisters?

In some ways. In the late fifties, when I was
sixteen, Margaret and I hitchhiked to the
Continent. It was really, really exciting. We
got a lift from London to Dover on the back
of a lorry. We sat on top of stacks of beer
crates – we didn't half get cold! We ended up
sleeping on the side of the road in Calais
because we hadn't found a hotel. We travelled
on to Switzerland and got jobs in the United
Nations in Geneva as secretaries. It was a
great way to see the world. I've no idea what
inspired us to go. I think we just wanted some
adventure, like lots of my heroines.

*Your books often look at the difficult side
of family relationships. What experiences do
you draw on when you write about that?*

I didn't always find it easy to get on with my
mother because she held very rigid views.
She was terribly ashamed when I went to
Europe. She said, 'If you leave this house
you're not coming back!' But when we got to
Switzerland we got fantastic wages at the
United Nations – about four times as much as

we got at home. When I wrote and told her she suddenly forgave me and went around telling everybody, 'Our Maureen's working at the United Nations in Geneva.'

> 'If you leave this house you're not coming back!'

She was very much the kind of woman who worried what the neighbours would think. When we moved to Kirkby, our neighbours were a bit posher than us and at first she even hung our curtains round the wrong way, so it was the neighbours who would see the pattern and we just had the inside to look at. It seems unbelievable now, but it wasn't unusual then – my mother-in-law was even worse. When she bought a new three-piece she covered every bit of it with odd bits of curtaining so it wouldn't wear out – it looked horrible.

My mother-in-law was a strange woman. She hated the world and everyone in it. We had a wary sort of relationship. She gave Richard's brother an awful life – she was very controlling and he never left home. She died in the early nineties and for the next few years my kind, gentle brother-in-law had a relationship with a wonderful woman who ran an animal sanctuary. People tend to keep their family problems private but you don't have to look further than your immediate neighbours to see how things really are and I try to reflect that in my books.

'You don't have to look further than your immediate neighbours to see how things really are'

Is there anything you'd change about your life?

I don't feel nostalgic for my youth, but I do feel nostalgic for the years when I was a young mum. I didn't anticipate how I'd feel when the boys left home. I just couldn't believe they'd gone and I still miss them being around although I'm very happy that they're happy.

Are friendships important to you?

Vastly important. I always stay with Margaret when I visit Liverpool and we email each other two or three times a week. Old friends are the best sort as you have shared with them the ups and downs of your life. I have other friends in Liverpool that I have known all my adult life. I have also made many new ones who send me things that they think will be useful when I write my books.

Have you ever shared an experience with one of your characters?

Richard's son from his first marriage recently got in touch with us. It was quite a shock as he's been in Australia for most of his life and we've never known him. He turned out to be a charming person with a lovely family. I've written about long-lost family members returning in *Kitty and Her Sisters* and *The Leaving of Liverpool* so it was strange for me to find my life reflecting the plot of one of my books.

Describe an average writing day for you.

Wake up, Richard brings me tea in bed and I watch breakfast television for a bit. Go downstairs at around eight o'clock with the intention of doing housework. Sit and argue with Richard about politics until it's midday and time to go to my shed and start writing. Come in from time to time to make drinks and do the crossword. If I'm stuck, we might drive to Sainsbury's for a coffee and read all the newspapers we refuse to have in the house. Back in my shed, I stay till about half seven and return to the house in time to see *EastEnders*.

Don't miss Maureen's bestselling novels:

Stepping Stones
Lights Out Liverpool
Put Out the Fires
Through the Storm
Liverpool Annie
Dancing in the Dark
The Girl from Barefoot House
Laceys of Liverpool
The House by Princes Park
Lime Street Blues
Queen of the Mersey
The Old House on the Corner
The September Girls
Kitty and Her Sisters
The Leaving of Liverpool
Mother of Pearl